IN THE BLOOD

'This creeping disquieting story, complete with a bitter courtroom drama and strong female protagonist, had me guessing until the rollar coaster end. A thoroughly satisfying addition to the genre.' **LESLEY THOMSON**

'I tore through it once I'd started. A fantastic thriller that grips you from the first page and doesn't let go until the explosive finish. Brilliant.' **JENNY BLACKHURST**

'A fast-paced, compelling storyline full of clever twists and a rousing, dramatic courtroom finale.' **ABI SILVER**

'Full of unexpected twists and turns that keep you guessing. I couldn't put it down.' **JESSICA JARLVI**

'A cracking story which pulls you in and simply doesn't let go... The plotting is superb.' *THE BOOKBAG*

D1353152

RUTH MANCINI is a criminal defence lawyer, author and freelance writer. She is also the author of *The Lies You Tell* and *His Perfect Lies*. She lives in Oxfordshire with her husband and two children.

RUTH MANCINI

IN THE BLOOD

HEAD of ZEUS

First published in the UK by Head of Zeus Ltd in 2018
This paperback editon published in 2019 by Head of Zeus Ltd

9 7 5 3 1 2 4 6 8

A catalogue record for this book is available from the British Library

ISBN (PB): 9781788543323
ISBN (E): 9781788543293

Printed and bound in Great Britain by
CPI Group (UK) Ltd, Croydon CR0 4YY

Head of Zeus Ltd
First Floor East
5–8 Hardwick Street
London EC1R 4RG

WWW.HEADOFZEUS.COM

For Helen Bishop and Lisa Harris – and for all the staff who worked at the Roundabout Centre in Oxford in 2003–7. You rescued me when I was at rock bottom and I thank you with all my heart.

PROLOGUE

A buzz and a click; the door opens and closes. The ward is quiet and the lights are low. The children are sleeping, the night shift now doing their rounds, checking observations, peering at charts. It's warm and he's wearing just his nappy, the rising and falling of his little chest a bit too laboured still. Her fingers brush the side of the cot, where the IV tube protrudes between the bars, a single red line carrying his blood into the machine he still needs to stay alive.

She bends over the cot and watches him. His eyelids flutter as he dreams. His fingers curl and uncurl next to the blue bunny that he's still too weak to grip. He's a beautiful child; there's no doubt about that. She leans forward and strokes back the shock of blond hair that's damp against his forehead, then lifts him gently into her arms, careful not to dislodge the tube that's taped to his chest. She holds him for a moment, feeling the weight of his head against her forearm, breathing in his sweet baby scent, before laying him gently back down.

He hasn't stirred. He won't wake. His face is peaceful, his features relaxed. Her eyes flicker down to the clover-shaped sticking plaster that's holding the tube in place just underneath his left armpit. Her fingers reach over and feel for its rough edges where they meet the softness of his baby skin. Her fingernail picks at the tape and peels it back a little, then a little more, until it comes away. She tugs at the end of the tube and places it on the sheet beside him. A small crimson stain soon appears.

It's time to leave him now, to let him sleep.

She covers him with the blanket that's folded neatly on top of the cabinet next to his cot and walks silently away.

1

It's a Tuesday in mid-August when I get the call. Ben has kept me up half the night and I've come to the office with his lunchbag (pureed carrot and ricotta, Marmite soldiers, Peppa Pig yoghurt), while he's at nursery with mine (tuna bean salad and fizzy water). It's eleven thirty when the phone rings, and I'm playing the game I play where I divide the day into manageable quarters. I've already made it from breakfast to the mid-morning crime team diary meeting and, by lunchtime, I'll be halfway there. There will only be another two quarters of the day – I can't even begin to think of it as a fourteen-hour stretch; that's way too long – until I can crawl back under the duvet and close my eyes, even if just for a while.

I pick up the phone. Lucy, our receptionist, says, 'Annalise Finch for you,' and then she's gone.

'Sarah! How are you?' Annalise speaks earnestly into the receiver, with an emphasis on the 'you'. She waits for an answer (which not everybody does).

'Yeah, good. Good,' I tell her, and then I feel the bitter sting of tears. This is my latent, Pavlovian response to any gesture of kindness towards me, no matter how small. Annalise is an ex-work colleague, but I also think of her as a friend. Do I tell her that I haven't had a decent night's sleep in months? That my

3

head is throbbing and my eye sockets ache? Do I warn her that I'm scared to open my mouth and talk, on days like today, for fear of jumbling up my sentences or dropping nouns?

I know Annalise well enough to know that she's not the sort of person that judges you, and besides, she's a woman who has had small children, so she's halfway to knowing what this is like. Although her children are ordinary, regular children, of course. *Her children are normal.* I wonder, fleetingly, whether I will ever be able to think about another woman's ordinary, regular children without feeling overwhelmed with grief and pain.

'Sarah?' she asks. 'Are you still there?'

'Sorry. Yes,' I tell her. 'How are *you*? It's nice to hear from you.'

It is. I had forgotten how much I liked Annalise, or Anna as I've always known her at work. She's a family lawyer. She gets called a divorce lawyer but that's not really what she does. She deals with child custody, mostly, specifically public law cases, the ones where there are child protection issues and the local authority want to take the child away. We used to see each other at the local magistrates' court sometimes when we both worked at Cartwright & Taylor, and when we were both there late, as we often were, we would stop off for a drink on the way home.

Of course, that was before Ben. I don't get to do things like that very much these days, but I'm happy to hear a friendly voice on the phone, the voice of someone with whom – on a day like today, when I'm feeling at my very most mortal – I don't have to pretend to be the sort of professional superwoman that I'm always reading about in the *Law Society Gazette*.

4

'I'd love to chat,' Anna says, 'but, listen, I've got a case for you.' Her voice echoes a little down the receiver. I'm guessing I'm on speakerphone. 'It's serious. It's an attempted murder. Of a child.'

And then she's off, talking rapidly, and I'm missing what she's said. I reach for a pen, grabbing the notebook that's on the desk in front of me and finding a fresh page. As I do so I nudge my coffee cup and a stream of light brown liquid leaps over the rim and across the desk. I'm instantly overwhelmed with the urge to either punch somebody or throw myself out of the window, the small puddle of coffee in front of me magnified by lack of sleep into Atlantic proportions. Instead I tuck the phone under my chin, pull a pack of baby wipes out of my handbag, take out a handful and drop them, one by one, onto the desk.

'You're really the best person I can think of for this,' Anna is saying.

'I'm really sorry, Anna,' I interrupt her. 'I didn't catch all of that. Would you mind starting again?'

'Oh. No. Of course not.' She picks up the phone, and her voice comes into focus. 'It's one of my clients. She's accused of trying to kill her eleven-month-old baby. Her name's Ellie. She's a young mum – twenty years old. Cut a long story short, she's poisoned him. Then, while he's in hospital recovering, she's gone onto the ward and tried to kill him again.'

'Jesus. How?'

'He was on dialysis after his kidneys failed. She pulled out the tube – the line, they call it – that took the blood out of his body and into the machine, and of course the machine just kept pumping the blood out of him. She covered him with a blanket to hide it. He nearly bled to death.'

'Jesus,' I say again. 'What's the evidence that it was her?'

'Well, no one saw it happen. But she was there when they found him. She was asleep on a camp bed beside him – or pretending to be; that's what the police are saying. A nurse spotted a pool of blood under the cot. He'd lost around a quarter of it, gone into heart failure. They managed to resuscitate him, but he's still in a critical condition.'

'Which hospital is it?'

'Southwark St Martin's.'

I feel a sharp jolt of pain. St Martin's. The same hospital. I throw the bundle of soggy wipes into the bin under my desk and sit back in my chair. I can see the ward; I can feel the heat of it, smell the antiseptic air. I can see the cot and the blanket – white, crocheted with a blue and white Southwark St Martin's trim. I can see the baby, pale and still. I can picture it all, as if I'm there.

'Also, he was with her when he was poisoned,' adds Anna.

I pull a fresh notepad from my drawer. 'How was he poisoned?'

'Salt.'

'*Salt?*'

'Yep. It causes a potentially fatal electrolyte imbalance. It's called hypernatraemia.'

I think about this for a moment. I think about Ben. 'How do you force salt into a one-year-old?'

'I don't know. But somebody did. And he was with her. Ellie. She'd had him overnight, unsupervised, for the first time in months. He was in care at the time. He'd already been taken away from her.'

'Why?'

'They found injuries. Bruises – and burns – when he was around eight months old. That's how I got her case. Although

6

we managed to fight it that time. Our expert report was favourable; it said that no one could be certain that the injuries were non-accidental. She was well on the way to getting him back again, but then he's admitted to hospital with what they think is a virus, which turns out to be sodium poisoning.'

'And they left her alone with him, in hospital?'

'They knew he was seriously ill, but they didn't know he'd been poisoned at that stage, not until the tests came back.'

Anna pauses. My pen hovers above the page while I take this in.

'I've got to admit, it doesn't look great for her,' Anna says. 'The prosecution case is that the three separate incidences of harm combine to build an overall picture of deliberate abuse. They each support each other. It all kind of stacks up. And Ellie... well, unfortunately, she doesn't come across well.'

'Why? What does she say?'

'Oh, she denies it – all of it. Says she'd never hurt her baby. But she wasn't great in interview. She can't explain how it happened, any of it, other than to say it wasn't her. She doesn't... well, volunteer information. She just gets angry and then clams up. I know she's scared. She's a "looked after" kid herself – she grew up in a care home in Stockwell – and she's like many of our young people: naturally reticent and suspicious of the authorities. She has no faith that anyone is going to believe her side of things. But it comes across the wrong way. She appears... overly defensive. And secretive, as if she's hiding something.'

'What's her previous?'

'Thefts, cars and stuff as a youth. Peer pressure probably. Nothing like this, and nothing for a while.'

'So, when's the first hearing?' I look up as the door opens and Matt, my colleague, walks in. He takes off his coat and sits down at the desk next to me. I flash him a smile. He purses his lips and switches on his computer.

'That's the thing,' Anna says. 'It's been and gone. The case has been sent to Inner London Crown Court. She's been remanded to Bronzefield. There's a bail hearing tomorrow.'

'Tomorrow?!'

'I'm sorry, I know it's short notice. But I was on holiday when they arrested and charged her. We went to Sri Lanka, Tim and I and the girls, for a fortnight. I didn't find out until I got back into the office this morning.'

'Sri Lanka. Wow. Sounds wonderful.' I can't help feeling a stab of envy; I can't take those sorts of holidays any more.

'Look, are you OK with this?' Anna asks me. 'I mean, I did think about it, that it might drag stuff up for you. But that's why I also think you'd be the best person to take this on. You spent a lot of time in hospitals when Ben was small. You know what it's like to have a sick child.'

'Yes, I… it's fine. Really,' I say. 'I want to do it.'

'Oh, good,' Anna says, pleased. 'Ellie asked for the duty solicitor at the police station and again when the case was allocated to the Crown Court, but she wants to instruct you, on my recommendation. I know you'll need her at court, so I've asked for her to be produced. She'll sign an authority to transfer tomorrow, and she's happy for us to talk to each other about her case. I've some papers I can give you. I'm going to have to go now, I've got a client waiting, but we can meet for lunch, if you like?'

We arrange to meet at a quiet pub off the beaten track in Gray's Inn Gardens. I don't normally take a proper lunch break;

I don't normally have time. But this is about work, and it's good to have an excuse to see Anna. Besides, I don't have much appetite for whizzed up carrot and ricotta.

Oh my God. I grab my mobile. Ben's lunch. I still haven't called the nursery to explain the mix-up and to ask them very nicely to find Ben something from the kitchen, just for today. I meant to do it an hour ago. But I also have to book Counsel for tomorrow; it's short notice as it is and people are away on holidays. I force my brain into action. Which to do first?

I glance at the luminous white digits on my phone before scrolling through my favourites and finding the number for the nursery. It's eleven forty-five. They'll be OK about this. They're bound to have a spare yoghurt. What else? I rack my brain. Fruit. They always have fruit. He can eat soft fruit. Melon and banana and stuff. Oh, God – they won't try to give him my tuna bean salad, will they? But they know. They know, Sarah, I tell myself. Stop worrying. They won't let him choke.

The day manager, Lisa, answers. I *love* Lisa. Really. I actually love her. She's my hero and my saviour and the only person, apart from Helen, his keyworker, who has spent enough time with Ben to know him the way that I do. She reassures me with calm efficiency that they won't let Ben choke or starve, and that he's had a really good morning, most of which has been spent spinning the wheels of an upended dolls' pram.

I thank her profusely, tell her I'll see her at six, and then locate the number for 5 Temple Square Chambers. Kevin, the clerk, tells me that Dan Bradstock – who would have been perfect for this case – is booked out on a five-day trial at the Bailey but that Will Gaskin – do I know Will Gaskin? – is at ILCC tomorrow with other cases, if I want to give him the brief?

'Yes, I know Will,' I say, pleased. 'Thank you. I'll email you the papers this afternoon.'

When I put the phone down it immediately rings again. It's just one long ring, which means it's an internal call. It's my boss, Gareth. 'Can you pop in?' he asks.

'Sure.'

I walk down the corridor to his room and tap on the door. He stands up to greet me and pushes the door closed. I know immediately, instinctively, that something is wrong.

He waves me into a chair. 'Sit down, Sarah.'

I do as I'm told.

'I'm not going to beat about the bush,' says Gareth. He crosses and then uncrosses his legs, and then swings round in his chair to face me. He leans forward. 'The thing is, there have been complaints about you.'

My heart leaps. 'Complaints? From who?'

Gareth sits and looks at me for a moment. He takes his lower lip between his teeth and sucks it.

'Was it Robin Crowthorn?' I ask. 'You know he has schizophrenia? I spent ages trying to calm him down yesterday, but he's not well. He wants me to take a civil action against the police. He thinks they've got him under surveillance via a microchip in his brain.'

'It's not a client.'

'It's not?' I'm genuinely baffled now.

'Look, the fact is that your billing is twenty per cent lower than the others in your team. They feel they're carrying you, that you're not pulling your weight.'

'What?' I'm genuinely astonished to hear this. 'Matt?' I ask. 'Matt's complained about me?'

'Not just Matt.'

'Well, who?'

Gareth sighs and licks his lips. 'I'm told you're on the phone to your... your son's nursery a lot. And that you took a long personal call this morning.'

Lucy. I take a deep breath, in and out, before I answer. 'That was about work. It was Annalise Finch. She's just given me a new Crown Court case. It's an attempted murder. Of a baby.'

Gareth looks up at me. 'Really?'

'Yes. There's a bail hearing tomorrow. I need to be there. Sorry, but someone else will need to cover the magistrates' court.'

I watch his face as his eyes first express interest and then narrow slightly. 'Are you sure you're the best person to take on another Crown Court case?' he asks. 'I mean... well, it might be better if we sent Matt along instead.'

I feel my jaw drop. I look up at him. 'What? Why?'

'Because the case will be time-consuming and...' Gareth looks uncomfortable. 'And it's clear that you have other priorities.'

To my horror, I can feel myself starting to cry. I know that it's lack of sleep that's to blame, that I'd be more robust if I hadn't been up half the night. I turn my face towards the window and blink hard. I say, 'They bill twenty per cent more than me because they go to the police station at night. I can't do that.'

Gareth picks up a pen and taps it against his desk. 'I think that's part of the problem.'

I glance down at my lap and blink hard again. 'I'm sorry. But I have Ben. I can't...'

'Do you not have a family member? Someone who could...'

'No.' I shake my head. 'There's no one I can ask.'

'Then, a babysitter? And, before you say anything, I know it would cost you more than you'd earn. But if you could just show willing... If you were on call a few nights per month, plus one weekend, maybe, it would keep everyone happy, show you were doing your bit. What do you say?'

'It's not that simple,' I tell him. 'My son has special needs.'

Gareth's face is impassive. 'Sarah, I'm aware that you've got... personal difficulties. But, at the end of the day, we all have busy lives. Everyone's got their problems.'

I don't know what to say to that. I sit and look at him for a moment. 'It's hard to explain,' I say. 'But... but trying to get someone to look after him who... someone who can deal with him... I don't know anyone who... but that doesn't mean that I don't work hard. It doesn't mean I can't do my job.'

Gareth sighs. 'Well, if you can't go to the police station out of hours, you're going to have to manage your time better.'

I open my mouth and then close it again. Gareth surveys me in silence.

'She gave the case to me,' I say, finally. 'I'm aware that Matt wants a shot at something bigger, but this is about doing what's right for the client. For Ellie.'

Gareth looks me in the eye for a long moment. 'OK. I'll send Matt to the mags tomorrow. But you'll still have your other cases to run. So, do whatever you have to do to make up the time. You see your client, you take instructions, you say goodbye. The Robin Crowthorns – you bin them off. Send them away.'

'That's easier said than done,' I object. 'He's in a bad way. In his mind, he's being watched and followed. He's frightened.'

'We're not social workers, Sarah. We don't get paid to deal with that kind of stuff. Times are hard. It's the way things are.'

I stand up. 'Is that all?'

Gareth says, 'Yes. For now.' As I reach the doorway, he calls my name. I turn to face him. 'A baby, you say?'

'Yes. Eleventh months old.'

Gareth narrows his eyes again. His tone is far from friendly when he says, 'Just don't get too involved.'

*

When I arrive at the pub, Anna's sitting on a dark green leather sofa. She stands up to kiss me and I hug her tall, thin, somewhat bony frame. She's almost the polar opposite of me, with her olive skin and her slim hips; I'm shorter, fair-skinned, blonde and just a little too curvy. But she's naturally thin, it seems; she's not one of those waif-like model types that never eats. On the contrary, she loves food and loves to cook. I remember her being addicted to *Masterchef* and bringing me delicious soups and stews into the office, wrapped in tinfoil, several times a week. That was my evening meal sorted out, more than once. It helped more than she knew. Or maybe she did.

Today, she's wearing a grey trouser suit and – since I saw her last – she's had her curly jet-black hair straightened and cut into a pretty bob.

'It suits you,' I say, nodding at her hair. 'It's lovely.'

'Thanks.' Anna sits back down again, stretches out her long legs and crosses her ankles.

'Nice suntan,' I add, smiling. 'I'm extremely jealous. You look amazing.'

Anna looks up and smiles. She can't say the same back to me because I look like shit. Instead, she leans forward and pulls out the menu from a dark wooden cradle on the table.

She chooses coffee and a cheese and ham panini and I tell her I'll have the same. She goes up to the bar to place our order and I lean back into the soft leather folds of the sofa and close my eyes. I instantly feel the stress and tension melting out of me. The leather feels amazing under my legs and up against my back – it's cool and refreshing, a stark contrast to the heat of the August sun outside. I want to curl up into a ball and put my feet up and to never have to get up again.

I feel the sofa move slightly against the pressure of Anna's body as she sits back down beside me. I open my eyes and sit up slightly.

'You were asleep!' she accuses me, laughing.

'No. Just resting my eyes.' I smile. But I think I *was* asleep.

She leans over and lifts a wisp of hair from my face and tucks it behind my ear. 'Don't take this the wrong way, but you look completely exhausted.'

'It's Ben,' I sigh. 'He just doesn't sleep. He goes down OK, but then he's up again a couple of hours later. The minute he wakes, he thinks it's time to get up and then that's it until dawn.'

She pushes a cup of coffee across the table towards me. 'How old is he now?'

'He's nearly five. He'll be starting school in September.'

Anna reaches out and touches my hand. 'I wish I could tell you he'd grow out of it, but I know it's not that simple with Ben. Is there no one who can help? Give you a bit of a break for a night or two?' she asks.

I shake my head. 'Not really. I don't really have any family nearby.'

'I could have him one night if you like,' Anna offers. 'I don't mind.'

'That's sweet of you, Anna. I may just take you up on that.' I know that I won't. It's too much to ask of her. 'So, tell me about Ellie,' I say.

Anna opens her briefcase. She hands me a plastic wallet with a charge sheet, police summary and conviction history inside.

'This all you've got?' I ask.

'So far. Sorry, I can't disclose the papers from the family proceedings,' Anna says. 'Not without the judge's permission.'

'Of course.' I glance at the papers. 'So. Her name's Ellis. Ellis Stephens.'

'Yeah. Calls herself Ellie. She has no family. She was an only child; her parents were drug addicts and she was removed from them as a baby. She's spent most of her life in care and, despite her young age and the hand she's been dealt, she hasn't done badly. She seems to manage her life well enough. She works, she pays her rent, she stays away from the wrong people. Considering she's been through so much and has virtually no support network...' She pauses and glances up at me. 'She's doing far better than some that I know. And although history appears to be repeating itself, with the child being taken away... well, she's still here, fighting to clear her name, fighting for her son. It would be too much for a lot of people, going through all that alone.' She takes a pack of sugar from the table, tears it open and tips it into her cup. 'On the other hand, of course, it's the perfect storm.' She picks up a spoon and gives her coffee a vigorous stir. 'She has the textbook profile of a young woman who harms her child. That'll be the prosecution case, for sure.'

'So how's the baby doing?' I ask her. 'Will he live?'

'It's touch and go. He's in a critical condition. He's had a blood transfusion, but there are still problems with his kidneys.

15

The blood loss caused his heart to fail. There are other complications as a result.'

'So the charge could become one of murder?'

Anna bites her lip and nods slowly.

I glance back down at the papers in front of me. 'So the baby's name is Finn. And what about the father? Is he around?'

'Kind of. His name's Jay. He's older than her and from quite a well-to-do family: the Barrington-Browns. Old money. Father's a life peer and mother's from a family of doctors. Her father's an Old Etonian, a fellow of the Royal College of Surgeons. Their backgrounds couldn't be more different.'

Anna pauses as our food arrives. The waiter leaves and returns again, bringing napkins, ketchup and mustard.

'They met at a party, apparently, at a hotel in Chelsea. Ellie was working there as a waitress for a catering company and Jay was there – having a good time, it seems. He took a shine to her, she stayed the night, and the rest is history. They went out a few times, but it looks as though their relationship was fairly short-lived. I don't know whether he ever actually cared for her, but I don't think she stood a chance with him, to be honest. The Barrington-Browns own a ten-million-pound house in Richmond. Jay has a flat in Markham Square, Chelsea. Ellie, meanwhile, lives in a housing association flat in Camberwell. It was all pretty much stacked against her.

'But then she fell pregnant. When she told Jay, she says she had no expectations, other than that he'd help her financially. She thought he'd want her to get rid of the baby and she says she considered it, but after the initial shock had worn off he seemed keen to help her bring up the child, or at least to do his share. All seemed fine for the first few months. Finn appeared to be thriving, no one reports any concerns. Then, when he's around eight months old, Finn gets a chest infection and is admitted to hospital. The A&E nurses find a number of bruises and what appear to be cigarette burns. Social Services get an emergency protection order and Finn's taken away while they investigate. Ellie's got no family and Jay works long hours, so Finn's gone to the grandparents – Jay's parents. That's when Ellie came to me. We spent the next three months working hard towards getting Finn back. We had a bit of a fight on our hands for a while. Ellie didn't get on with her social worker.'

'Heather Grainger,' I say, referring to the papers in front of me. 'She's one of the key prosecution witnesses.'

Anna nods. 'Ellie will tell you that Heather had it in for her, right from the start.'

'And did she?'

Anna looks at me and wrinkles up her nose. 'No. I don't think so. She's a professional. She wouldn't let things get personal.' She leans back in her seat. 'But, to be fair to Ellie, Heather's not the most sympathetic of people. And she goes by the book. She can be a bit... prescriptive.'

'You mean, controlling?'

Anna laughs. 'A little.'

'So they clashed, basically.'

'Well, yeah. Heather was "on her case all the time" as Ellie saw it – which, of course, she was. Quite literally. Ellie, in the meantime, was highly defensive, said she'd done nothing wrong. There was a bit of a battle of wills.'

'Over what?'

'Oh, the usual stuff. Prop-feeding, co-sleeping – things that are probably normal to most of the mothers on the estate where

17

Ellie lives. Ellie was willing to be educated, but not by Heather; she came on too strong.'

'But she got Finn back, didn't she? She must have done something right?'

Anna nods. 'Like I said, Social Services couldn't prove definitively that the injuries had been deliberately inflicted. Ellie learned to toe the line. We were at the stage where she'd been given unsupervised contact a couple of times per week. And then she gets to have him overnight, for the first time.' She takes a sip of her coffee and looks up at me. 'But something happens during the night. When Heather turns up in the morning, Finn's seriously unwell. He's awake and conscious, just, but not moving. He's floppy and his eyes are glazed. She can see straight away that there's something really wrong. She calls an ambulance and he's rushed back to hospital. He's vomiting and having seizures on the way.'

I feel a familiar knot in my gut, a tightness forming in my chest as she talks. I breathe in deeply and hold it there for a second or two. Anna pauses for a moment and looks up at me, her face softening.

'Carry on,' I say.

'They didn't know what it was at first,' she continues. 'They knew that his blood sodium level was high, but presumed he was dehydrated. They suspected meningitis, or some kind of virus, until the tests came back. Meanwhile, Finn has been treated, he's turned a corner and seems to be on the mend. He's released from the ICU to the renal paediatric unit – Peregrine Ward – where he's having treatment for the damage the sodium has done to his kidneys. So, it's his first night on Peregrine Ward. Ellie arrives – she stays the night. Nurses on the evening shift all say that Finn was fine when they left. Then one of the night shift nurses spots a pool of blood on the floor under his cot and there's Finn lying there, unconscious and bleeding heavily, with Ellie asleep on a camp bed next to him, or so she says. She says she woke up to a commotion, the nurse calling for the doctor. She swears she knew nothing about what happened.'

'And no one saw anything?'

'No. Except one nurse, apparently, who says that as she was going off shift at around ten p.m., she saw Ellie leaning over the cot and picking up the baby. That's all they've got. But someone disconnected his tube not long afterwards, and as Ellie was the last one seen with him… and she was there, right next to where he was found… the doors to the ward are security protected, they've viewed the CCTV and say no one else came in or out. Then the tests come back showing these hugely elevated sodium levels in his body at the point he came into hospital… and well, with everything put together, they obviously believe they've got enough evidence to convict.'

I sweep up a few stray crumbs from the table and fold them into a napkin. 'Is there… any way the baby could have dislodged the tube himself?'

Anna shakes her head. 'The hospital say no. He was still sedated from the operation.'

'What about the nurses? Is it possible that the tube hadn't been taped in place properly?'

'Well, I suppose it's possible, but the nurses say they'd left him uncovered, in line with procedure, so that they could see the exit site of the line at all times. Someone had covered him with a blanket. The medical tape had been completely ripped off. That, combined with the position of the tube when they found him, has led the doctors to believe it was deliberate.'

I look up. 'Well, they'd be bound to say that, wouldn't they? If the hospital had allowed an accident to happen, they'd hardly admit it.'

Anna looks doubtful. 'St Martin's is a leading paediatric hospital,' she reminds me.

I nod. 'It's where Ben was. They're brilliant there. But it only takes one person to make a mistake.'

Anna presses her lips together. 'But then there's the poisoning too. How do you explain that?'

I think about this for a moment. 'Was he definitely poisoned?' I ask. 'Are there other reasons why a baby's sodium levels might be high?'

'Possibly. But he was really sick when he came into A&E. He was fitting. He nearly died.' Anna glances at me. She's still wondering if I'm OK with this.

I give her a wry smile, to reassure her. 'Well, there are a lot of things that can cause a seizure.'

Anna shrugs. 'Of course.'

'Look, I'm the last person who would want to criticise the nurses or point my finger at the hospital,' I tell her. 'Not after everything they did there for Ben. But I'd have to explore that as a potential defence. If Ellie says she didn't do it, any of it, then it's my job to find out who did.'

'Sure.' Anna looks at me and her nose twitches.

'Things aren't always as they seem,' I say. 'Especially when it comes to children.'

Anna takes a last bite of her panini, chews and swallows it and then picks up her coffee cup. 'That's why I wanted you on this case.'

I study her face as she takes a sip of her coffee. I notice that

Anna wears no make-up other than a thick line of navy eyeliner, which streaks across her eyelid and up at the corner. Dark lashes frame her almond-shaped eyes.

'But you don't believe her, right?' I ask, shaking my head. 'You think she did it?'

She sips at her coffee and peers at me over the rim of the cup. Her dark eyes meet mine. 'Persuade me otherwise,' she says.

2

When I pick up Ben, he's as exhausted as I am. I pray that this means he'll sleep tonight. Helen is clearing up, and one of the newer girls, Kayleigh, has him laid across her lap on a heavy blue crash mat on the floor. She's sitting stroking his thick hair away from his face, in soft regular movements, so that it's standing up in a big blond halo. When he lifts his head at the sound of my voice, he looks startled, as if he's been through a wind tunnel. I laugh and Ben starts laughing too, even though he doesn't know what he's laughing at. His giggle is infectious and Kayleigh and Helen both join in.

I bend down and stroke Ben's hair back, before lifting him into my arms. His glasses are smeared with food and it's obvious that he can't see properly. Well, it's obvious to me; I'm the only one who seems to have noticed. I take them off his nose and rub them on the hem of my blouse.

'Dirty specs.' I smile at Kayleigh, hoping she'll get the hint.

But they're so good with him here, so loving and caring, that I can't find it in myself to complain. Not after what happened at his first nursery. I still feel the hurt as if it was yesterday, when I think about the owner taking me aside and telling me that Ben was too much work for them. 'We have to allocate one full-time playworker to him,' she told me. 'We can't help him. He needs too much attention. It's not fair on the other children... I have to think of them.'

I'd cried on and off for days after that conversation, and though I knew it was wrong of them, that in law they ought to have made the appropriate arrangements to accommodate him, it had felt just about as personal as it could possibly get. I didn't want my son spending his day with them if they didn't want him; I'd find somewhere else.

I took a week off work and sat with my laptop in my little living room with Ben, looking at every nursery between Finsbury Park and Islington and asking questions on the phone. I walked the backstreets along Blackstock Road with Ben in his buggy and Google Maps open on my phone, poking my head through doorways or watching through railings, spying on the pre-schoolers – or more specifically the nursery staff – to see if the children were happy and the staff kind. It had only been a few weeks since I'd moved with Ben to the two-bedroomed ground-floor flat in a converted terraced house behind the Holloway Road from the flat in Southwark where we'd lived since he was born, and Little Angels, not far from Angel Tube station, had come to me on recommendation from one of the ushers at court. I didn't know any other nurseries in the area, so I'd given it a go, much to my regret.

But then the woman who ran the corner shop on the end of my street had told me about the Roundabout Centre. It was located in a run-down street off the Caledonian Road, and a little off the beaten track between home and the office at Highbury Corner where I worked, but from the minute I walked through the door I had known that it felt right. Ben, as usual, wasn't so sure, and had immediately started to cry. Lisa, the manager, had looked

24

up from her desk and walked over, bending down and smiling at him, unperturbed by the fact that his wailing was getting increasingly louder, to the point that neither of us could hear what the other was saying. She'd then stood up, and asked me if I'd like her to come and see me – and Ben – at home instead, so that he could get used to her in an environment he knew.

I couldn't believe my ears. I'd been certain that she was going to tell me that she'd made a mistake when I'd spoken to her on the phone, that the nursery was full, and that they couldn't have him after all. Instead, sitting in my living room later that evening, while Ben sat in his chair eating Marmite fingers and refusing to make eye contact with her, she told me that he could start on Monday and that she was going to assign him to Helen, who had over fourteen years' experience of working with children with special needs and would be exactly the right person for Ben. She said that her staff ratios were sufficient that Helen would be able to work with him virtually one on one, for as much time as was needed.

That was a year ago, and I still want to fling my arms around her every time I see her. The same goes for Helen, who appears to be completely unfazed by Ben's irregular behaviour, his regular wailing, and the daily repetitiveness of play – with so very little progress – that I know from experience can be utterly monotonous and infinitely unrewarding, no matter how much you love him, no matter how much you care.

'He's had a really good day,' Helen tells me, putting the last of the mats back onto a pile in the corner and walking over. 'He loved spinning the wheels of the pram this morning and so Lisa said we're going to get some spinning tops in for him, to try and encourage him to work on his fine motor skills.'

'Oh, Helen, that's lovely,' I say. 'Thank you.'

'Spinning seems to be his thing,' she continues. 'It's called a "schema"? Have you heard of that? It's a pattern of play that motivates him and builds connections in his brain. So we can work on introducing other activities that build on that.'

I want to cry again. I know it's tiredness as much as anything, but I am also overwhelmed with gratitude. Who else but Helen and Lisa could see the positive in a five-year-old who's obsessed with the wheels of a dolls' pram?

I wish Helen and Kayleigh a good evening, strap Ben into his buggy and set off up the Caledonian Road. As we turn the corner and cross the Holloway Road towards Waitrose, I contemplate going in. I mentally scour my fridge and cupboards; we need bread, milk and cheese. And cereal. Ben could do with some more bananas. I need coffee. I *really* need coffee; I had the last spoonful this morning. I glance down at my son. He's watching the cars as they whizz past us, flapping his arms and giving involuntary shudders of delight. A bus pulls up at the bus stop and his feet fly out and land back against the buggy, kicking it hard. I peer over his head to gauge his expression, but can see that he is smiling; he likes the bus! And then I remember: his spinning schema. Of course. It'll be the wheels. He likes the wheels on the bus. It's a different matter being on one. That doesn't always go down so well.

With that in mind, I decide that I won't risk the shops, not tonight. He's tired, but he's had a good day; it's not worth upsetting him, upsetting us both. Instead I crouch down next to him, put my head close to his, and sing, 'The wheels on the bus go round and round, round and round, round and round.' Ben turns and makes eye contact with me, gives me a big smile. Is that a smile of recognition, I wonder? Has he made the connection between the big red vehicle in front of him and the song? Does he know now that it's called a bus, and will that help the next time we have to travel on one? I know that it probably won't, that it's more likely he's just pleased that I've decided to sing to him, right here, right now, in the middle of this busy street. But I have to keep trying, repeating words like these in contexts that might make sense to him, in the hope that one day it'll sink in.

The bus has moved off. Ben stops smiling and lets out a short loud wail. 'All right, my love,' I sigh. 'We're going. We're going home.'

My spirits lift just a little as we round the corner to our street and I see our little house waiting for us, looking all Victorian and beautiful, just as we left it this morning. I've grown to love this house, and I still see it with new eyes each time I come home, even though we only own the ground floor, and even though the move from Southwark was hard and saying goodbye to that flat had been painful. It was the home I'd bought and shared for five years with Ben's father, Andy. But it wasn't big enough once we had Ben, and the last few years had been a squeeze – in more ways than one.

Fortunately, the flat had gone up in value during that time, and there was enough equity for a decent deposit on a bigger place. But then Andy had told me that he wasn't moving with us, that he was going back to Australia, for good. He was homesick, he said, he missed his family, and I knew in that moment that Ben and I had never really been his family, that he'd always been a tourist in our lives. He didn't want any of the money from the sale, he said, I could keep it, for me and Ben – his way of easing his conscience, no doubt, at having bailed out, leaving me to bring up our disabled child alone. He told me he'd come back whenever he could, and assured me that I would be welcome with Ben any time I wanted to visit Perth. But we both knew that this wasn't true. And besides, if I struggled to keep Ben calm on a ten-minute bus journey in London, I didn't even want to think about what he'd be like on a twenty-four-hour flight halfway round the world.

I pause outside the corner shop on the end of the street, and briefly contemplate popping in to get the few essentials that we need, but again dismiss the idea. You don't really 'pop' anywhere with Ben; it's always an ordeal. He is so heavy now, and his Maclaren Major buggy so big, that it's difficult to negotiate through the doorway and round the aisles of a shop that small, especially with Ben yelling his head off and waving his arms. I can't face being stared at, not tonight, even though I'm used to the disapproving looks, the looks that say, 'She's a bad mother who can't control her child.' But you can't 'control' a child like Ben. You can't negotiate with him. You can't tell him he's going to get a treat if he stops crying and behaves himself, because he doesn't understand; he doesn't understand what you're saying, he doesn't understand what a shop is or why you've brought him there, and he doesn't know whether he's going to be stuck there in his buggy – staring at rows of tins and people's legs – for five minutes, for half an hour or for the rest of his life.

So instead, I lean forward and kiss the top of Ben's tousled, wind-tunnel hair and we walk on past the shop and up the street, and open the gate to our house. Once inside, I give Ben his tea, then we snuggle up on the sofa and I flick on his favourite DVD.

Ben grunts appreciatively as the sun comes up on the TV screen and giggles at us. He has been watching the same *Teletubbies*

DVDs every day for the past four years and, while I long ago reached the stage where I wanted to wrestle Tinky Winky's stupid red bag from his arm and shove it up his big purple bottom, I'm instead going to listen patiently while he bleats on about it, about Dipsy's hat and about Laa-Laa's ball, while the horn on Po's scooter parps its way through my nerve endings, and the endless repetition of the same few bars of music makes me want to weep in despair. Because Ben, unlike me, finds comfort in that same familiarity, in the constant repetition of image, music and sound – and since Ben lives in a world that makes so little sense to him, this is what we do, day after day, year on year.

'Uh-oh!' I repeat when Tinky Winky drops his bag, and 'Where's Dipsy's hat?' I ask, patting my head, and wrinkling up my face in mock concern. I know that Ben doesn't care about Dipsy's hat any more than I do; he just likes the music, the dancing and the noise. But he joins in the game and smiles and reaches up and touches my face. I respond with a squeeze ('Big hug,' I tell him), along with a kiss on the nose.

After a while I get up and give him his medication. It always makes him sleepy and it's not long before his eyelids are drooping and I'm putting him to bed. Ironically, though, when I finally crawl into my own bed, I'm wide awake.

I lie in the dark and think about Ellie who, at this moment, is lying in a prison cell, and I wonder how low you'd have to feel to hurt your child. Pretty low, is the answer; and I should know. There have been times, there have been dark moments in the past five years, when I've been so utterly wrung-out and unhappy that I've allowed my mind to wander into a world that doesn't have Ben in it, where Ben ends up back in hospital and I lose him, where I no longer spend my days running in a sleep-deprived fog from work to nursery to home and back again, where I'm not constantly, endlessly, at someone else's beck and call. I guiltily imagine having the life I used to have, the life where I got to eat out with friends and go to the cinema, the life where I used to be able to go on a holiday abroad, to lie on a beach in the sun.

Right now, I'd settle for being able to read a book or watch a movie or eat a plate of food without interruption, without being needed for *something* – to change a DVD or a nappy, or to sing, or to soothe, without having to leap up to prevent an accident or to provide a change of scene with a car ride or a trip out to feed the ducks. It would be so good not to have to try and guess, guess, guess all the time what it is that Ben wants, why it is that he's wailing, so that I can calm him, stop him from screaming the house down, from hurting himself, from biting himself or me. I mash food, I watch for accidents, for hazards, for steps that could trip him, for small objects that could choke him. I try to anticipate the triggers that will upset him, the noises that will wake him. After five years of being permanently 'on call' I'm hardwired to report for duty, and it's got so that, even on the nights that Ben doesn't wake, I still do, the slightest movement from his room, or sound from the street, like an alarm going off in my brain, jerking me awake and calling me to action.

But I'd never harm my baby – I know that about myself. I love him deeply, desperately, more than I've loved anyone before or since the day that he was born. Just the thought of any harm coming to him causes me to get out of bed and creep into his room. I stand in the doorway for a moment, listening for the soft, regular snuffle that tells me he's asleep. When I hear it, I creep nearer. I can see in the soft light from the streetlight outside that he's kicked off his duvet and is on his back, his arms and legs flung out around him, his face tipped towards me, his beautiful features at peace beneath the shock of gorgeous thick strawberry blond hair that's still sticking up over his brow. Mild relief floods my veins. He's asleep; there's nothing wrong. There's been no thrashing or jerking, no banging of limbs against his cot, no rolling of his eyes. I know that this is what I've been half expecting. It's what I'm always expecting, with Ben: the worst.

I put his duvet back loosely over his body, and give him the lightest of kisses on his forehead. Back in bed, I pull my own duvet tightly round me. In spite of the heat, I'm chilled to the core and teardrops escape from the corners of my eyes as Ben and Finn blur into one in my mind. I force myself to imagine slapping and punching Ben, taking his little hands and crushing cigarettes out on them, feeding him salt, by the spoonful, while his eyes look trustingly up into mine. I then see myself on the hospital ward, calmly, calculatingly, removing a tube that's keeping him alive and then getting into bed beside him and closing my eyes, knowing that, beside me, he's bleeding to death.

I know she's little more than a child herself, but I just can't imagine how Ellie could do what they say she's done, and if she did, quite how bad she'd have to feel to do it. I know that everyone has their limit, their pain threshold, that there's only so much each person can take (look at Andy), and maybe I just haven't quite got there yet. But I know that I could *never* hurt my baby, no matter how bad things got. I still remember how it felt to be rigid with fear the first time his body started its jerking and twitching and then to hold him as he lay, lifeless, in my arms, the ambulance weaving its way through the early-evening traffic. I still remember how it felt to watch him being hooked up to tubes, his little chest caving inwards on every breath as his muscles, weak and immature, struggled to fight off yet another lung infection, to let in air. I remember how hard it was to take a proper breath myself as I looked on in terror, petrified that I was going to lose him, berating myself for every dark thought I'd ever had, making bargains with God and begging Him not to take my son from me.

No. I don't want to be without Ben. *Ever.*

I just don't want to be so alone.

I close my eyes and imagine a man's arms wrapped round me, his body warm next to mine, his breath on my shoulder. I imagine talking to him about the way I'm feeling, and I imagine him being completely OK with, and accepting of Ben. Soon he's kissing me, and then we're making love, and before I know it he's packed his bags and is moving in. But then reality kicks in. I can't allow myself to have a dream like that. Let's face it, who'd want to take on a woman with a son like mine? My experience of the people I meet during my daily life is that most of them will fall silent or recoil in embarrassment and change the subject if I talk about Ben openly, honestly; if I talk about things as they really are. I'd like to feel connected to the world, the way others feel connected: through shared experience and common ground. But there is none, not for me.

People say that when you have kids you lose touch with your single friends, that your best friends become other parents, the ones that won't get bored of talking and laughing with you about baby sick and spit-up, about crawling, talking, first steps, first day at nursery, first day at school, about each new achievement, about the latest funny thing that their son or daughter did or said. But I can't do that, because Ben can't talk. His first steps still haven't happened, and his new achievements are paltry by comparison. ('Oh, listen, this is so funny – Ben spent the morning spinning the wheels of a dolls' pram. Does your son like to do that?') My experience of raising a child is so vastly, immensely different from anyone else's, that all I can do is keep my mouth shut and listen and smile. I'm stuck on the outside of those conversations by a wall of glass; I can hear them, but I can't join in. I'm not included. I'm not in their club.

I'm in nobody's club any more. That is what I have lost.

I wish for the millionth time that my mum was here.

I screw my eyes up tight as I think of her and I ask her, as I always do, to help me get through this time, to let it get easier somehow, to let me come out the other side.

I wait patiently, as always, until I feel her hand in mine.

Now, at last, I will sleep.

The day starts badly at seven a.m., when I realise that we've overslept. I flick the kettle on before running to the bathroom, but then remember that I have no coffee. I wash and dress us both hastily, give Ben the last two slices of bread, cut up into fingers, and toast the crusts for myself while I pack our lunches. I then lock up and jog behind Ben in his buggy most of the way to the nursery. I run for the bus and again for the crowded Tube train, where I stand, upright, like a tin soldier, sandwiched so tightly between my fellow travellers that I don't even need a handrail for support.

I breathe a sigh of relief as I exit the station at Elephant and Castle and walk up the street and through the gate to the Inner London Crown Court. The stench of cigarette smoke soon wafts towards me from a disparate crowd of lawyers, court staff and defendants who are gathered outside, sneaking in a quick ciggy before the day's list gets under way. I spot Will near the steps, already robed and bewigged, deep in discussion with the prosecutor, both of them puffing away and flicking ash idly onto the pavement.

'Ms Kellerman!' Will exclaims, as he sees me walking towards him. He squashes his cigarette out against the railing and flicks it into a litter bin.

'Filthy habit,' I reprimand him.

'I know.' He makes a remorseful face and looks round at the court building behind us. 'I'm thinking of giving it up. I'm going to retrain as a bus driver. The pay's better.'

I laugh.

'But since we're both here,' he says, taking my arm, 'let's go and talk to our young lady. Serco prison van's just arrived.'

'You got the papers OK?'

'Yes. Interesting brief. Thank you.'

'How's Finn? The baby?' I ask. 'Did Carmel tell you anything?' Will shakes his head. 'No change. That's all she knows.'

'You know she denies it?' I tell him. 'It's going to be a "not guilty" by the looks of things.'

'Yes, well they won't expect a plea today. We're missing several key statements, including the father's. We have one from the social worker assigned to Finn's case and also one from the ICU nurse, the one who says she saw Ellie pick up the baby. Although Carmel' – he nods his head at the prosecutor, who's walking back up the steps ahead of us – 'says they're in some difficulty there. She was an agency nurse, it seems. African. She's left the hospital. They don't know where she's gone. Possibly back to Africa.'

'Really? So what will they do?'

'Well, they'll try to get her statement read at trial, I expect.'

I look at him and shake my head. 'You think they'll make a hearsay application?'

'We'll challenge it, of course,' he continues. 'But for today's purposes, it makes no odds. Today's about getting her bail.'

Will waits to one side while I go through security and then I follow him down the steps to the court cells. He speaks into the intercom and then there is a rattling of doors, a jangling of keys and the clunking and turning of the lock before the solid grey metal door swings open.

'Morning,' says Lorraine, the jailer. 'You're here for Ellis Stephens, right? She's not good this morning. She's on cell watch.'

'Why? What's happened?' I ask.

She shrugs. 'Other inmates at the prison, I'm told. You've got to expect that sort of thing. Women don't like that she tried to kill her own baby.'

'Allegedly,' I say.

Lorraine shoots me an apologetic look. 'Yeah. Right. Allegedly.'

'Room two!' shouts someone else, from behind a door.

Will and I are shown into conference room two, which is in fact just an empty cell with a table and two chairs. It's warm inside, and seasonably ripe with the all too familiar aroma of body sweat and unwashed feet, courtesy of the previous occupant and the August sun, which is already warming the morning air. I'd like to open a window, but of course there aren't any. Breathing in the stench of short-term human incarceration is an occupational hazard for the likes of Will and me. We're destined to enter the court or police cell just a little too long after the detained person's last shower, and just a little too soon before their next one on arrival at prison or back home. Hopefully home for Ellie.

Will waves me into one of the seats that are nailed to the floor and leans against the wall. Soon I can hear the sound of handcuffs being removed, and then the door opens and a tall, slim young woman walks in. Her movements are graceful, her back straight as she pauses in front of me for a moment, then glides effortlessly across the room. She's dressed in a simple grey sweatshirt and jeans, but I can see that she has the figure of a catwalk model, and the face to match: symmetrical features, big blue eyes, chiselled cheekbones, Keira Knightley eyebrows and narrow chin. Her long blonde hair is pulled back into a thick shiny ponytail that falls to her waist and swings as she walks. I'm unprepared for quite how beautiful she is and surprised Anna hadn't mentioned this. I glance at Will to gauge his reaction. To his credit, he's not looking at Ellie, but at his papers.

'Hello, Ellie. I'm Sarah, your solicitor.' I stand up and hold out my hand and she takes it. Her own is small, cold and clammy. She gives me a gentle but firm handgrip and slips into the seat in front of me.

I sit back down. 'The jailer mentioned that you're on cell watch.'

She nods and I look into her eyes, to try and read her. They're bright blue – almost turquoise – and naturally framed by long dark lashes. Her cheeks are flushed, even without make-up. When Anna had told me about her past, I'd somehow imagined her as the kind of young woman I'm used to seeing in the cells – someone who was once pretty but who is now too thin, her face ashen and lined, sores on her mouth and chin and heroin tracks on her arms. Now it's entirely obvious why Jay Barrington-Brown had been attracted to this young woman. There couldn't be a man in London who wouldn't be proud to be seen with Ellie on his arm, whatever her background, wherever she was from.

'So, what's going on?' I ask. 'Has someone hurt you?'

Ellie folds her arms across her chest and grips the sleeves of her sweatshirt, a decisive, defensive movement. 'I'm OK.'

'Right.'

She looks up at me. 'Is Finn... is he going to be all right? They won't tell me anything in... in there.' Her voice cracks as she speaks and then fades to a whisper. 'He's not... he's not going to die, is he?'

Will and I glance at each other. 'We don't know,' I admit. 'He's had a blood transfusion, but he's still very poorly. Everyone's hoping that he'll get better...'

Ellie watches my face as I speak, her mouth dropping open slightly in alarm. 'But he might not?'

I bite my lip and breathe in deeply. 'They just don't know yet, Ellie. I'm sorry.'

Tears glisten in the corners of her eyes. 'I need to see him,' she says. 'Am I going to get bail?'

I look at Will. He clears his throat and puts his papers down onto the table next to me, before straightening up again.

'The thing is, Ellie,' he tells her. 'As I'm sure you realise, this is just about as serious as it could possibly be. If Finn... if Finn doesn't make it, the charge will become one of murder.'

I glance at Will again. He's speaking kindly, gently, but his words are direct.

Ellie looks up at him. 'Do you think I don't know that?'

Will nods, slowly. 'Of course you do. But what I'm getting at is that it's unusual for bail to be granted in a murder case. It happens, don't get me wrong. But it's the exception, rather than the rule.'

Ellie stares at him, her brow furrowed. 'So why are you here, then?' she asks, her voice breaking up again. 'If that's it? A done deal?'

'It's not a done deal,' Will tells her. 'And you have certain things in your favour. You're young. You're vulnerable. You

39

have very little history of offending, certainly no previous history of violence. But we would need to offer a strict package of conditions. Ones that would satisfy the judge that you won't have any contact with Finn whatsoever. Not until this is all over.'

'But I didn't do it!' Ellie cries out. She flings her arms up into the air and brings them crashing down onto the table before sinking her head down on top of them. 'I didn't do it,' she says into her arms, obstinately, her voice muffled.

'Do you have somewhere to go?' I ask.

Ellie lifts her head up, slowly. 'My flat.'

'Is it…?'

'It's still mine.'

'Good.' Will nods. 'Address?'

'Thirty-six A Cedar Court, Eastfield Road, Camberwell.'

I check this against the charge sheet.

'And do you work at all?'

Ellie looks silently at Will for a moment. 'I'm a hairdresser,' she says.

'OK. Good. Do you work at a shop? Or are you… mobile?'

'Mobile.'

'And what do you take home?'

She looks up sharply. 'What?'

'What are your net earnings?' Will asks. 'After tax?'

'Does it matter?'

I stop writing and look up. 'Of course,' I tell her. 'The judge will care that you're financially independent. No one wants to lock up someone and take away their job if they don't absolutely have to. If you have a good job that pays well…'

Ellie picks at the cuticle of her left thumb. 'It pays well.'

'Can you prove it?'

She shakes her head. 'It's cash in hand.'

'OK, let's move on.' Will leans back against the wall and props himself up with one leg, his black gown falling back and his suit trouser leg riding up to reveal an incongruous bright royal blue and red superhero sock with a big fist and the word *Thwack* emblazoned across the ankle. I bite my lip to stop myself from laughing and look up at him as he speaks. He has a nice, honest face. His skin is olive, his eyes hazel behind black-rimmed reading glasses. He has angular cheekbones, a long straight nose and an engaging mouth, which is pleasantly visible above his clean-shaven chin, in defiance of the current trend towards hairy faces. I watch him as he pushes a lock of dark hair from his forehead and tilts his glasses up with one finger, scanning the pages in front of him as he does so.

'The evidence against you,' he says, glancing up as he speaks, 'is largely circumstantial, but it usually is in a case like this. I'm going to be honest with you, Ellie. In the absence of anything to rebut the suggestion that you did these things to your baby, the finger is going to point to you.'

Ellie looks up at Will, her big blue eyes locked on his.

'We don't have many statements as yet,' Will continues, 'and we'll go through everything in much more detail later on. But the summary of the evidence suggests – on your own account to the police – that you were the only person who had access to Finn during the period when he received his injuries – the burns and the bruises. And that you were the only person in your flat that night in July, the night you had your first unsupervised contact with Finn, following which he fell seriously ill. We *do* have a statement from Heather Grainger, the social worker who

41

arrived at your flat the following morning. She says that when you opened the door to her, she could see straight away that he was extremely unwell.'

I glance up at Ellie. Her eyelids flicker and she bites her bottom lip.

'She describes Finn as being a strange colour, droopy and lifeless,' Will continues. 'She says he was having trouble breathing. She called an ambulance. We're expecting a further statement from the doctor who treated him in A&E. But we do have a short-form toxicology report – which is essentially a signed summary of the findings – and this states that there were near-fatal levels of sodium in his body.'

Will pauses briefly and glances at Ellie.

'I don't know how it happened,' she whispers and shakes her head. 'I don't know. He just got ill. I swear. I didn't poison him – I'd never do that. I love Finn. I'd never hurt him.'

Will nods. 'Well, we'll come back to that. We'll need to get our own reports. But this last witness is crucial. We have a signed statement from a Mary Ngombe, one of the nurses who was looking after him on the paediatric intensive care ward during the week that Finn was there. She was responsible for transferring him across to Peregrine Ward – the renal unit – on the twenty-fifth of July. She says that once he'd been settled and the handover done, she went back to the ICU, but came back across to Peregrine again to say goodbye to him before she went off shift for the night. She says that as she entered the ward, she saw you pick up Finn from his cot and then put him back down again. A short while later he's found unconscious, with his dialysis line removed and lying next to him in his cot.'

Ellie shakes her head vigorously while Will is speaking. When he stops, she says, 'No. She's lying. That's not true. I never picked him up! I was asleep!'

Will looks up at her. 'Well, this nurse appears to have left the hospital and it's not clear at this stage whether she'll give evidence – or whether her evidence will be admissible if she doesn't – but if it does go in, I'd say it's key. You were the last person seen to touch Finn before his tube was tampered with – before the night-shift nurse found him and raised the alarm.'

'I didn't touch him,' Ellie repeats, slowly, enunciating each word angrily.

'You didn't pick him up?'

'No!'

'Why would the nurse say that if it didn't happen?' I ask.

Ellie shrugs. 'I don't know, do I? She's got the wrong person, obviously.'

'Ellie, she names you,' I say, gently. 'She knows you as the baby's mother. She says she saw you there on the ICU ward every day, visiting Finn.'

'Well, she's lying,' Ellie says. 'It wasn't me. I was asleep.'

'If you picked him up, you can tell us,' I say. 'It's understandable that you'd want to. He's your baby.'

Ellie looks me in the eye. 'But I didn't!' she protests. 'I told you. He was asleep when I got there. I didn't want to wake him up.'

'OK.' Will raises his hands.

'No, it's not OK!' Ellie pushes her chair back and leaps to her feet, angry tears springing to her eyes. 'Why won't anyone believe me?' She flings her fist towards the door and points a finger. 'The police should be out there catching the person who did this, not wasting their time trying to stitch me up. Why would I try to kill my own baby, for fuck's sake? Why would

I do that to the one person I actually love in this world and who loves me? It's his birthday today, did you know that? He's one year old today. I should be with him now, giving him his birthday cake and watching him open his presents, not stuck in prison with a bunch of murderers and thugs.' She sinks back down into her seat and puts her head in her hands.

Will and I glance at each other.

'OK,' says Will. 'Well, today is about getting you bail, so let's focus on that. The strength – or otherwise – of the evidence does have some bearing on our application, but only to the extent that you're likely to abscond – skip bail and not turn up for your trial – which is not the issue here. I think we can make a strong argument for bail...'

Ellie looks up at him, her mouth opening slightly, hopefully.

'... if we can offer the court a condition that you won't attempt to contact Finn. I'm sorry, Ellie, but that's the best outcome that you can possibly hope for at this stage.'

Ellie looks back down at the table. 'I can't go back to that place,' she says.

I nod. 'I know.'

Ellie takes a deep breath and chews at her thumbnail for a moment before looking up at me. 'How long before we get into court?'

Will looks at his watch. 'Hopefully soon. Almost certainly this morning.'

Ellie stands up. 'OK,' she says, and walks towards the door.

*

Will does a good job in court and it helps that Judge Collins is in a good mood. He even tells us, jovially, that he is going on holiday to Malta tomorrow, albeit within the context of the next hearing date and the directions he has just made. Ellie is released with stringent bail conditions and I go back down to the cells to say goodbye to her while Will finishes dealing with the other cases he's been instructed on this morning. I watch as Ellie takes a belt, earrings and handbag out of her property bag and then bends down to lace up her trainers, her tiny waist visible above her jeans, the back of her elegant, porcelain white neck protruding from her sweatshirt. Her long blonde ponytail jigs around in front of her as she focuses on the task in hand. Once dressed, she straightens up, flicks her hair back over her shoulder and switches on her phone.

Try as I might, I can't picture her as a mother. Even in the clothes she's worn all week in prison, she appears glamorous, unspoiled. She doesn't have the kind of spine that's been bent out of shape from carrying the weight of a baby, the kind of boobs that have been tucked in and out of a nursing bra. If I can't picture her as a mother, what will the jury think?

'I'll need you to come into the office,' I tell her. 'I need to take your full instructions. We should have most of the key statements by early next week, so it will probably be Tuesday or Wednesday. But I'll call you. Keep your phone switched on. OK?'

Ellie nods. I check that she still has the business card I gave her when we met earlier this morning, and although she pulls it out of her jeans pocket to show me, I can tell her mind is elsewhere. She's planning what she'll do next, when she gets out of here, how she's going to spend her first day of freedom, who she's going to call.

'So who was that woman at the back of the courtroom?' I ask her. 'I'm guessing it was Jay's mother? Lady Barrington-Brown?'

'Yeah. I knew she'd come.' She taps intently at her phone screen with one thumb, wisps of hair escaping from her ponytail and falling across one eye.

'So where's Jay?' I persist.

She shrugs. 'He works long hours.'

'All the same, Finn's his son. How does he feel about all of this? How does he feel about you?'

She shrugs again. 'How should I know?'

'Well,' I explain, 'I'm trying to establish what his evidence will be. Whether he'll say something that hurts your defence… or whether he might say something that helps you?'

'No! He won't!' Ellie looks up abruptly. She pushes her phone into her pocket as her eyes meet mine. 'I don't want you to talk to him. He doesn't know anything.'

'About what?'

'I don't want you to talk to him!' she exclaims again, her neck flushing pink.

I touch her arm. 'Calm down. I'm not going to talk to him.'

I feel her arm relax a little. 'You promise?'

'I promise,' I reassure her. 'I *can't* talk to him, even if I wanted to. Well, technically, I could…'

Ellie stiffens again. Her eyes are still locked on mine.

'But I won't,' I insist. 'It would be highly inappropriate of me to do so. He's named as a prosecution witness. I could be accused of interfering with a witness, trying to influence his evidence. Or even trying to persuade him not to come to court at all.'

Ellie's jaw first tightens then relaxes. 'Good. Well… maybe he won't anyway.' She picks up her bag. 'So, are we done?'

'For now,' I agree.

I watch her intently as she picks up her bag and heads out of the room. I follow her out into the corridor and Lorraine walks over to meet her. Although it's something of an afterthought, she turns back and thanks me for my help as Lorraine unlocks the door back up to the courtroom and lets me out.

Back on the concourse, I phone Annalise and give her the news about Ellie's bail. I then check in with the office to see if there have been any new arrests.

As I finish talking, Will exits the double doors that lead to the courtroom. I slip my phone back into my bag and stand up to greet him.

'Good job, Mr Gaskin.' I smile.

'Why, thank you, Ms Kellerman,' he replies. 'Do you have time for some lunch?'

I shake my head. 'I've got a sentence at Camberwell Magistrates' plus one in at the police station, so it looks as though I'm going to have to go. But you'll keep the brief, won't you?'

'I'd be delighted to. Although I don't think she likes me.'

'I don't think she likes anyone,' I say. 'But you got her bail. So that's a good start.'

Will looks at me and narrows his eyes. 'So, what do you think? Did she do it?'

'Honestly?' I ask him. 'I don't know. She's definitely hiding something. She virtually begged me not to talk to Jay Barrington-Brown...'

'Jay Barrington-Brown?' Will interrupts, frowning. 'He's a prosecution witness. The father of the victim. Why would you talk to him?'

I nod. 'Exactly. But she was very concerned about it for some reason. She told me he "didn't know anything".'

'About what?'

'That's what she wouldn't tell me. She got quite upset. She looked… scared. But, then again, why wouldn't she be? She's been charged with attempted murder.' I think about this for a moment. 'And she's young. She's had a rubbish upbringing. Righteous anger and mistrust of her lawyers are par for the course with your average teenager, guilty or not.'

'She's not a teenager,' Will points out. 'She's twenty.'

'Yeah. Of course she is. She seems younger somehow.'

'True.'

'I can see why she didn't come across well in the police interview,' I continue. 'She's way too defensive. Her arguments have no punch. But on the other hand, she really does seem to love her baby. I don't know if you noticed, but it wasn't just bail she was after; she wanted to be allowed to see Finn. She seemed genuinely upset about the "no contact" condition. She seemed genuinely upset about it all.'

'Hmm.' Will scratches his chin. 'Well, we'll see what the rest of the evidence is like. But the statement from the nurse is pretty damning. If it goes in, we're on the back foot, that's for sure. And I'm not sure what kind of a witness our young lady will make. She's emotional, without a doubt but, as you say, she hasn't told us anything that's terribly helpful so far.'

'So, we might have to think about not putting her on the stand?' I suggest. 'As you say, she doesn't really come across too well, and I can't see the female jurors empathising with her. She's too pretty. She's going to make them feel inadequate.'

Will smiles. 'I hope you're not feeling inadequate, Ms Kellerman.'

'I always feel inadequate.' I smile back.

Will frowns. 'Don't be silly. You're one of the most adequate solicitors I know.'

'Sometimes. When I'm being an adequate solicitor, I'm being an inadequate mother. That's how it works.'

Will's face softens. 'Sounds as though you need a drink. Are you sure you can't spare half an hour for a quick one at the Uxbridge Arms?'

'Sorry. Spare half-hours are not to be squandered lightly. They're for shopping for essentials. For things you can't do with a baby in tow.' I pick up my bag and wonder briefly if Will knows how old Ben is, whether he's wondering why I've called him a baby. The truth is, he's still a baby in every way that matters, and it doesn't seem likely that this is going to change very much in the years to come. I'm starting – slowly, painfully – to accept that now.

Will touches my arm. 'Well, let me know as soon as you get the papers.'

'I will. I'll be in touch.' I check my phone one last time before tucking it into the zip pocket of my handbag. 'Will,' I call after him as he walks off down the concourse. He turns to look at me. I nod at his ankles. 'What's with the socks?'

Will glances down at his feet and back up at me. He winks. 'They're my lucky socks.'

I smile. 'Well, they certainly worked today.'

I turn to go back to the advocates' room to collect my bag. As I do so, the double doors that lead to the courtroom open and Carmel walks out, followed by the middle-aged woman who was sitting at the back: Lady Barrington-Brown. Carmel walks off down the concourse, but the woman stops in her tracks and looks in my direction. She's tall, slim, and elegantly dressed in a fawn calf-length silk dress with bell sleeves. Her shoulder-length light brown hair is drawn back into a loose ponytail at the base of her neck. Our eyes connect and she gives me the briefest of smiles before pushing her handbag onto her shoulder and taking a step towards the door.

Before I can stop myself, I'm running after her down the concourse.

'Wait,' I call. 'Lady Barrington-Brown. Please wait.'

She stops and turns back to face me again.

'I'm Sarah Kellerman. Ellie's lawyer,' I say.

Her heavy-lidded brown eyes meet mine. Her eyelids are powder blue, her lips a creamy pink. 'I saw you in the court-room,' she says.

'Have you seen Finn?' I ask her.

She nods. 'Yesterday evening.'

'And how's he doing?' I breathe in sharply as I wait for her reply.

'As well as can be expected. He's hanging on in there.' She swallows and touches her throat, forcing a smile. 'His kidney function is improved. His heart's been under a lot of strain and he still needs the ventilator. But his condition certainly hasn't become any worse, so there's still hope. There's always hope, right?'

'Right,' I agree. 'Definitely. I… well, my son was very ill in hospital when he was Finn's age and we had a discussion about that – my partner and I – and we decided that we would hope for the best, rather than prepare ourselves for the worst, because… because you never really *do* prepare yourself for the worst, anyway. You can't actually imagine "the worst" properly until it's happened, and so there's no point in putting yourself through that. You may as well hang on to that hope…' I tail off and cringe inwardly at myself. 'I'm so sorry. I'm rambling. That probably doesn't make any sense at all.'

She reaches out and touches my hand. Her face softens, suddenly, and her forehead creases. Her eyes glisten with tears and her lashes flicker as she says, softly, 'It makes perfect sense. And I agree with you entirely. We will one hundred per cent hope for the best. Thank you, Ms Kellerman, for your very kind words.'

'I'm so sorry,' I say, quickly. 'I really didn't mean to upset you.'

She shakes her head. 'You didn't. Really. The truth is, I haven't been sleeping well.'

As I look at the pained expression on her face, my heart melts. I know what it's like to worry about a child. I know what it's like to wake up in a cold sweat in the early hours of the morning, to lie there in the dark, turning things over and over in your mind until you drive yourself crazy, knowing all the while that there's nothing you can do, except drag yourself out of bed and stumble through another day. 'I'm so sorry,' I tell her again. 'For what you're going through... I understand. I really do.'

She looks hard into my eyes for a moment. Then she says, 'But *do* you, Ms Kellerman?'

'What? What do you mean?' I ask, confused.

'I'm talking about Ellis,' she says, kindly. She looks down at her feet before looking back up again. She heaves a sigh. 'I'm really very worried that she's got bail.'

'Are you involved in the case?' I ask her quickly. 'Are you going to be a prosecution witness? Because if you are, I shouldn't be talking to you.'

'No.' She puts a hand on my arm. 'No, I'm not. I wouldn't do that. I'm very fond of Ellis. We all are. She's the mother of James's child, after all. We don't want her locked up for this. But on the other hand, we have to make sure that Finn is safe.'

'Well, the judge thought...'

'The judge doesn't know Ellis, not the way we do,' she interrupts, in a whisper. 'She's a troubled young woman. She loves Finn, I know she does. But she has problems. There's something about her... it's difficult to explain, but there's something about her that's not quite right...'

'I'm sorry,' I say, abruptly. 'But I really can't discuss this with you. I'm Ellie's lawyer. I have a duty towards her.'

'I know. And I'm sorry.' She smiles. 'It's just... well, you seem such a lovely person. So sensitive and kind. How are you going to feel if she gains access to him and... well, something happens?'

Mild anxiety grips my chest as I consider the possibility that this woman could be right, that Ellie could be lying to me – that she could ignore her bail conditions and get access to Finn.

'She's not allowed to go anywhere near him,' I point out. 'She's not allowed to go to the hospital.'

'And if she does?'

'Well, as soon as anyone sees her, they'll call the police and she'll be arrested.'

Her forehead creases, anxiously. 'But what if no one sees her?'

I open my mouth and close it again.

'Look,' I tell her. 'Ellie's innocent until proven guilty. I can see how worried you are, but the judge believed that it was safe to grant her bail.'

Lady Barrington-Brown presses her lips together and nods. 'And what do *you* think? Do *you* think it was safe for him to grant her bail?'

'It doesn't matter what I think,' I say, weakly. 'It's not my decision to make.'

She shakes her head, slowly, her face softening again. 'No. No, of course it's not. Please, take no notice of me… as I said, I haven't been sleeping well. I'm really not myself today.' She forces a smile and clutches at the strap of her handbag. With her other hand, she reaches out and takes mine. She shakes it firmly. 'It was so nice to have met you, Ms Kellerman. Have a good day.'

I watch as she walks down the concourse and then turn back towards the advocates' room. A vague sense of unease flutters in my chest and stays with me all day.

4

When I reach the magistrates' court, there's just enough time to speak to the probation service and collect their report before the case is called on. I deal with the sentence hearing and then hop on a bus to Walworth, where I spend the rest of the afternoon.

I'm just leaving custody when my phone rings. I glance at the screen. It's the office. I've got less than an hour to pick up Ben, but against my better judgement I answer it.

'Sarah.' It's Lucy. 'Are you still at the police station?'

'Well, yes,' I say, 'but I'm just leaving.'

'There's another one in. Matt wants to know if you can deal with it.'

'I can't,' I tell her. 'I have to pick up Ben, now. I'm late as it is.'

'Hang on,' says Lucy, and then she's gone and Matt is on the line.

'Sarah,' he says, 'can you deal with this job? The officers are ready to go. I tried to catch you in custody before you left.'

'Matt, I can't. I've got to pick up Ben. I'm running late as it is.'

Silence. 'Well, you're there already. It makes sense if you deal with it.'

'But I told you, I—'

'Can't someone else pick him up for you? One of his friends' parents or something? This won't take you long.'

'Not really. I don't really have anyone I can ask—'

'It's rush hour.' Matt's voice is exasperated. 'It's going to take me over an hour to get there. You'll have dealt with it before I even arrive.'

'I know, but… I have to pick up Ben.'

Silence. Then, 'Right. OK.'

'I'm sorry,' I say. 'If you want me to cover something for you tomorrow, I can. I could do—'

But he's gone.

I power-walk to Kennington and then take the Piccadilly line from Leicester Square, positioning myself next to the train doors, where I'm ready to leap off and sprint towards the exit as soon as they open at Caledonian Road. Although there are only five stops to go, there's a delay at Russell Square and the journey takes over half an hour. My stomach tightens with the familiar knot of mild panic that I experience daily from around three o'clock onwards, as I look repeatedly at the nearest clock and wonder if I'm going to finish and get to nursery on time. My worries are, in fact, well founded today; I'm fifteen minutes late. The building is locked and I arrive to find Helen and Lisa waiting outside for me, with Ben already strapped into his buggy. I've run all the way from the Tube station and I'm desperately out of breath, but that doesn't stop me noticing the look of mild agitation on Lisa's normally calm and smiling face.

Of all the people that are angry with me this evening, Ben is the angriest, and he expresses his dissatisfaction all the way to Waitrose. I bitterly regret my decision not to have gone yesterday, but I have no choice this evening, because there's nothing left in the fridge with which to make a meal. Ben's wailing turns to yelling as the double doors slide open and we enter the brightly lit store.

I grab a basket and hook it awkwardly over one handle of the Maclaren Major. It doesn't fit properly and digs into me as I walk, but it's the best I can do; Ben's too big for the baby trolleys, and the trolleys for the disabled are all designed to hook into a wheelchair. I once found a store that had a trolley with a seat designed for a disabled person to sit in and I was elated, resolving to do all my shopping at this store for ever more. But when I went back it had gone. A member of staff told me that it had been locked away and that I'd have to ask each time I wanted it. An assistant first went off to find the key, then to fetch the trolley. It all took what seemed like an age, and by the time she came back Ben had got himself into such a state that he'd thrown up all over the floor.

I glance down at Ben as I negotiate my way past the fruit and veg, grabbing a bag of potatoes and a bunch of bananas and moving on as quickly as I can. He's calmed a little, thrown out of kilter, it seems, by the high speed at which I'm moving. The aisles are busy and I have to weave quickly round other shoppers, which I know is not entirely considerate, but these are my choices: it's Ben or them. It's at times like this that I wish the Maclaren Major came with a bell, or a horn.

I manage to grab cheese, yoghurt and milk before the wailing starts up again.

'OK, OK,' I say. 'But bread. We've got to have bread, and eggs. And coffee, Ben. Mummy needs her coffee. It keeps her going.'

I locate the bread and, finally, the eggs, which are in a different place than they used to be. I don't know why they have to keep moving things around in supermarkets. Well, I do, but it doesn't help people like me.

As we round the corner to the tea and coffee aisle, Ben ramps it up a decibel.

'All right, honey. Nearly done,' I say, knowing that this means nothing to Ben. I can hear the whiny, high-pitched trill of desperation creeping into my voice as I try to reassure him. Ben's own voice, in contrast, just gets louder. Heads are turning in our direction. The all too familiar feeling of panic sets into my chest for the second time today. We've still got the checkout to negotiate and so we are not, in fact, nearly done. Why, oh why, did I attempt this? I should have just… what? I don't know what I should have done. I take a deep breath. I can do this. We've got almost everything we need and here we are now, in the coffee aisle. All I have to do is grab a jar and then get us out of here as quickly as I can.

I reach out for my favourite brand, which is on the top shelf. It's the last one and it's set back a little, so that I have to stand on tiptoes to get it. As I brush it with my fingertips, it topples and falls, bouncing against the handle of the Maclaren Major and narrowly missing Ben's head, before it crashes to the ground. The jar explodes, slivers of glass and coffee grounds spreading across the shiny floor.

'Oh, fuck!' I shriek, before I can stop myself. I bend down to pick it up.

'Don't touch it!' a male voice warns me. 'You'll hurt yourself.'

The man crouches down beside me, takes my elbow and guides me to my feet. He turns and calls out to someone and I then see a shop assistant heading towards us. He points to the mess on the floor. 'Can we get some help here please?'

The assistant nods and goes off towards the rear of the shop.

I wipe my brow with the back of my hand. 'I'm sorry I swore,' I say.

The man smiles. 'Not at all. It's good for you. Scientists say that it's actually advisable to swear at moments like this.'

'Really?'

'Yes. It relieves stress. Although, if you swear all the time, it doesn't work. You have to save it up for the times you really need it.'

'What if you really need it all the time?'

He raises his eyebrows. 'That bad?'

I sigh deeply and nod at Ben.

'Hey, buddy,' the man says, crouching down and facing Ben. 'What's up? Want to tell me what's wrong?'

Ben ignores him and carries on wailing.

'He doesn't understand you,' I say. 'He can't talk.'

'Oh. OK.'

But the man remains there, crouching down and smiling gently at my son, in spite of all the noise he's making. Through the fog of my inner turmoil, I notice that he has a nice face – his features are even, his eyes kind. He appears to be in his late thirties and is wearing a smart beige suit – like me, he's probably just finished work. He has well-cut fair hair which is receding only very slightly and still leaves a fringe which flops about his forehead as he waggles his head at Ben, trying to make him laugh.

Ben, predictably, continues to ignore him, and after a few moments the man stands up. 'Must be hard for you,' he says. 'Well, for him, of course,' he adds. 'But for you, too.'

I look at him, my mouth falling open. 'Yes,' I admit. 'It is.' Tears prick my eyes. I can't help it. He's being so kind, and this is so unexpected.

'Hey,' he says, soothingly. After a moment's hesitation he reaches out and pats my shoulder. It's an awkward, schoolboyish gesture, but his eyes are full of concern.

An assistant arrives and begins to sweep up the glass.

'I'm sorry,' I tell her.

'Oh, don't worry,' she says. 'That's OK. You two carry on with your shopping. I'll see to this.'

She thinks we're a couple. I shoot an embarrassed glance at the man in the suit, but he simply grins back at me and nods at the broken jar. 'Do you want another one?'

I shake my head. 'It was the last one.'

'Do you have another one of those?' he asks the shop assistant.

'I'm not sure,' she says. 'I'll check.'

'Great. Thanks,' says the man. 'We'll wait here.'

I glance at him again in disbelief. Will we? Doesn't he care about the racket Ben's making? It's loud. It's impossible to ignore. I can't understand why he's still here.

But Ben is not going to wait for my jar of coffee to arrive, that much is clear. He's roaring now, like an angry lion, his thick mane of hair framing his face, his mouth shaped into a furious 'O'.

'It's OK. I need to get him home,' I say, nodding at Ben. 'But thank you anyway.'

'Not at all.' He watches as I grab hold of the Maclaren Major and wheel Ben towards the checkouts.

Ben stops crying for a few glorious moments, as he sees that we are on the move again and senses the exit looming near. I glance around at each checkout in turn, but there are queues at every one. I join what appears to be the shortest queue, with the sales assistant – a young girl in her twenties – who looks to be bleeping everything through the fastest, but there are still three people ahead of us and it's not long before Ben's off again, his sobs getting louder and louder by the minute, his voice resonating round the store.

The woman in the queue ahead of me glances round at him, her face impassive. 'His nose is running,' she says, accusingly.

'Yes. Yes. I know.' I root around in my bag for a tissue and hold it against Ben's nose. As I do so, Ben flings his arm out and bats my hand away. He then shoves his fist into his mouth and starts to bite down on it as hard as he can. I can feel my own tears pricking at the backs of my eyes again as I bend down to stop him. I gently pull his hand away from his mouth.

'No, Ben,' I plead. 'Don't do that. Don't hurt yourself like that.'

Ben bats my hand away for a second time and shoves his own back into his mouth, clamping down again with his sharp little teeth.

I crouch down beside him and start to sing, softly, in a wobbly, tearful voice, 'Twinkle twinkle, little star, how I wonder what you are,' but I already know that we're way beyond the sing-soothing stage. I've just made the decision to abandon my basket and leave the store by the nearest exit, when I feel a tap on my shoulder.

'Here,' says the man in the suit, as I stand back up. He hands me a jar of coffee, the brand that I'd wanted.

I take a deep breath and fight back the tears; I can't cry in front of him again. 'Thank you. You're so kind. But he's getting too upset now, so I think I'm just going to—'

'Excuse me!' the man calls loudly to the girl at the checkout, who's finished serving one customer and is about to start on the next. 'Can you serve this lady next, please?'

He frowns, subtly, but discernibly, at the woman in front of me and then says loudly, so that everyone in the queue can hear, 'Can't you see that this lady is struggling, here?'

The checkout girl nods. 'Bring your basket up here,' she says.

The lady at the front of the queue turns and looks back at me. 'Oh. Yes. Of course,' she says, and moves back to let me past.

I grab Ben's hand away from his mouth for a third time and shove his buggy forward at the same time. 'Ben, we're moving,' I say brightly. 'Look! Look!' But, what with Ben's flailing arms and the Maclaren Major's size and the basket sticking out at an angle, there's not actually enough room to get by.

'Here,' says the man in the suit, taking my hand gently but firmly, removing it from the handle of the buggy and unhooking my basket for me. He passes it to the woman at the front of the queue, who then hands it to the checkout girl.

'Go,' he says. 'I'll get this. Wait for me outside.'

'But—'

'No buts,' he nods his head towards the door, 'just get yourself outside and sort your little man out. I'll see you in a minute.'

I don't need to be told a third time. I put the Maclaren Major into rapid reverse, and we speed like lightning towards the exit. There must be at least one store detective who thinks I've stolen something and am making a run for it, but I'll take my chances. Getting gripped up by security staff couldn't raise my cortisol levels any higher than they already are. Getting Ben out of the store is the only thing I care about right now; nothing else matters.

The relief I feel when I reach the doors is overwhelming. As if by magic, when they slide open and I wheel Ben onto the pavement, his yelling stops. I crouch down in front of him, unstrap him and take him in my arms, kissing the red bite marks on his hand and wiping his nose, before wrapping his legs round my waist and holding him tight against my chest. I can feel his little heart beating against mine, rapidly at first, but slowing down as the tension eases from his body, and as it does so, from my own.

'There, there,' I soothe him. 'My poor boy. My poor boy. It's OK.'

Ben lays his head against my shoulder for a moment, then looks up, takes one last, heaving sob and rewards me with a smile, his eyes still glistening with the tears he no longer needs.

'Bah bah,' he says.

'I know,' I say. 'You don't like shopping. I know.'

Ben watches me speak and then puts his fingers inside my mouth.

'Teeth,' I say. 'Sharp.' I close my teeth very gently onto his fingers. 'See?' I say. 'We mustn't do that. It hurts.' But I know that's why he does it. I know that he'll do it again, next time. There's always a next time.

But for now, me and my boy, we're OK.

We stand on the pavement outside and rock gently back and forth together as the early-evening traffic whizzes by. The road empties for a few moments as the cars stop for the lights behind us and we watch a flock of birds take off from the branches of one of the trees across the road. I feel the stillness of the air, the stillness of my son who, exhausted by our ordeal, lies motionless in my arms, his head resting on my shoulder. The lights change and the traffic breaks through again. A motorbike whizzes past and Ben lifts up his head to follow it.

The doors to the store slide open and the man in the suit wanders out with my shopping. He glances round briefly, then spots me and Ben. I give a little wave and he walks over.

'How much do I owe you?' I ask immediately. I'm already heavily indebted to this man. I don't want to owe him actual money a minute longer than is necessary.

'The receipt's in the bag,' he says. 'But there's no hurry. We can sort it out later.'

He hooks the two bags of shopping onto the Maclaren Major and it immediately falls over backwards.

'Don't...' I say at the same time, but it's too late. The shopping hits the pavement and the buggy falls on top.

'Oops. There goes another jar of coffee,' he says, and we both laugh. He leans over to pick up the bags while I seat Ben back into the buggy and strap him in, his weight now stabilising the shopping that's hanging over the back.

'Do you live nearby?' he asks. 'Can I walk you home?'

I hesitate. I've only just met him, after all. He *seems* nice, but what if he's a stalker? Or worse? A rapist? Or a paedophile? How would I know?

He takes a step away from me. 'Oh God, I didn't mean...' He shakes his head and looks distraught. 'I just meant... I could carry your shopping for you, that's all, to your door. It's all been a bit stressful for you. I just wanted to make sure you got home OK. But I can see how it might look... so, honestly, forget I said that.'

He smiles apologetically as he clutches the handle of his own shopping bag with one hand and brushes his hair back from his face again with the other. He's actually blushing – and stuttering – and his diffidence makes me smile too. He reminds me of Hugh Grant in *Four Weddings and a Funeral*. He's far too awkward to be a rapist.

'I live just round the corner,' I say. I lift the two bags of shopping from the handles of the Maclaren Major and hand them back to him. 'And, actually, it would be a real help if you could take these. Shopping weighs the buggy down. Well, you know that.' I grin. 'It'll make it much easier to push.'

'Of course.'

I swivel Ben round and we walk up past Wetherspoons and the Coronet, before turning the corner into the side road which leads down to the street where I live.

'I'm Sarah, by the way,' I tell him. 'And this is Ben.'

He looks at me for a moment, as if he's forgotten what his name is. I laugh.

'Alex,' he says, and attempts to hold out his hand, but it has a bag of shopping in it, and I laugh again.

'So, do you live on your own?' he asks, and then says, immediately, 'No! Don't answer that! God, every time I open my mouth, I sound more and more like some crazy stalker.'

I smile. He's actually reassuring me. Stalkers don't usually give you a heads up that they're stalkers.

'Yes, I live alone,' I tell him. 'Ben's dad is Australian. He went back to Perth. He found it really hard, with Ben... he couldn't cope with the situation. That's the bottom line.'

'How long ago was that?'

'Just over a year. So, it's been just me and Ben ever since.'

'Do you mind me asking what's wrong?'

'With Ben?'

'I'm sorry. If you don't want to talk about it...'

'It's fine,' I say. 'I'm glad you asked. When people just ignore it, it feels as though they're ignoring him, and me. It can make you feel very cut off.'

He nods. 'I'll bet it does.'

'Global developmental delay is the diagnosis he was given,'

I say. 'Which isn't actually a diagnosis, in fact. It just means that he's – well, to use the term that most people understand – retarded. They don't know why. All they know is that his brain doesn't work properly. He just didn't develop the way he should.'

'Did you notice it straight away?'

I shake my head. 'No. Everything seemed fine at first. The pregnancy was normal. His birth was a bit traumatic: an emergency caesarean. But everything seemed fine afterwards. It was a few months before we found out that anything was wrong.'

'It must have been a shock.'

'It was. Although, there were a few signs there, if I'm honest, and we did have some concerns. He was slow to bat toys with his hands and pick them up, for instance, and he wasn't able to sit up, even at around seven or eight months old. We mentioned it to the health visitor but she didn't seem too concerned. She just said that he was lazy, a typical boy.'

'Oh, really?'

'Her words, not mine,' I add, smiling.

'It's all true.' Alex smiles back.

'Do you have children?' I ask.

He glances at me and pushes his hair back from his eyes with his upper arm. 'No. I'm… I'm not with anyone.' He pulls a face. 'There I go, sounding like a stalker again.'

I laugh. 'I've met quite a few stalkers. You're nothing like any of them.'

He raises his eyebrows.

'Through my work,' I add, quickly. 'Not through my personal life.'

He nods. 'That's good. To have one stalker would be unfortunate. To have more than one would be…'

'Careless?' I suggest.

'I was going to say "very bad luck". Although perhaps, then, you could encourage them to stalk each other instead of you.'

I laugh. As we reach the end of the street, I slow down. 'This is where I live.' I point towards the house and Ben kicks the buggy in anticipation.

Alex and I turn to face each other. He nods towards Ben. 'He seems to have settled now.'

'Thanks for everything,' I say, at the same time.

Our eyes meet and we laugh again, and I tell myself that even if he hadn't just come to my rescue, stuck up for me, acknowledged Ben and the reality of my existence and exposed it to the world (well, four people in a shopping queue), and even if he hadn't then paid for and helped me home with my shopping – I would still really, *really* like this man. 'Look, would you like to come in?' I find myself saying. 'For a cup of tea?'

Alex frowns and shakes his head. 'No. Honestly. Don't feel you have to... I really only wanted to see that you were OK. And you are. So there.'

I look him in the eye again. 'Please. I'd like you to. And besides, I need to give you some money.'

He nods, decisively. 'Thank you. A cup of tea would be very nice.'

Ben's feet land heavily against the buggy again and he lets out a wail. I push him down the path and Alex follows. I turn the key in the lock and bend down to unstrap Ben and lift him out. Alex puts the shopping down in the doorway. 'Want me to fold this up?' he asks.

'Yes please.' I nod. 'The hallway's pretty narrow. There's not enough room to leave it up.' I indicate the levers on the sides.

'You have to pull those up and then fold it in at the same time. There's a bit of a knack to it.'

But Alex releases the levers, squeezes the handles together and snaps the back down in one swift movement. He places the folded buggy behind the door and follows me into the kitchen with the shopping. 'Why don't I make the tea?' he suggests. 'I expect you need to see to your little man.'

I nod. 'That would be a help. Cups are up there.' I point to a cupboard above the microwave. 'And tea is in the tin just there. Unless you want coffee. You know where the coffee is.'

We both laugh.

Alex fills the kettle and finds the mugs, milk and teabags, while I seat Ben in his chair, locate his sippy cup (on the floor) and give him a piece of bread, which he shoves into his mouth and gobbles down, his cheeks bulging.

Alex smiles. 'You liked that, didn't you, buddy?' He picks up the pack of bread. 'Shall I give him some more?'

'Yes please.'

I watch him for a moment as he opens the plastic bag, takes out a slice of bread and hands it to Ben. He then turns and taps the teaspoon against the mugs, making a tinkling sound. He looks at Ben, who laughs. 'Huh?' he says to Ben. 'Nice noise, huh?'

I finish unpacking the shopping and put a pan of eggs on the stove to boil. Behind me, Alex places two mugs of tea onto the table and sits down. He loosens his tie and removes his suit jacket to reveal a white shirt, which is now open at the neck. I realise, suddenly, how handsome he is. His eyes are deep-set, navy blue and are smiling at me, creasing up attractively at the corners.

'Thank you,' I say, picking up my tea.

'Bah bah,' says Ben from his chair.

I look from Ben to Alex in shock. 'Did you hear that?' I ask.

Alex smiles. 'He was copying you.'

I go over to Ben and crouch down to his eye level. 'Good talking, Ben!' I tell him. 'Clever boy!' I turn to Alex. 'He's never done that before,' I say. 'He's always babbled. But never meaningfully. I know it doesn't seem much, but...'

'Of course it is,' Alex says. 'It's huge. He's talking to you. Maybe not in *our* language. But he's communicating with you, all the same.'

'You're right.' I feel uplifted as I stand back up and wash my hands at the sink. Ben's progress has been so slow, that any new thing he does, no matter how small, can make me feel as though I've won the lottery. Well, maybe not the lottery, but a scratch card. This is definitely a scratch card.

I chop up chunks of cheese and banana, which I place onto Ben's tray. I sit down opposite Alex at the table and we watch as Ben swipes up the food into his fist and shovels it into his mouth.

Alex takes a sip of his tea. 'So how did you find out that there was a problem? With Ben, I mean.'

'Well, we started to notice that he was drifting off a bit when he was awake. It was hard to tell at first, whether he was just getting sleepy, needing a nap. But it was happening more and more. His eyes would go blank and we'd wave at him, but it was as though he was looking straight through us. Then he'd jump, suddenly, as if we'd startled him.'

'He was having absence seizures, right?'

I look up at him. 'Yes. How did you know? You know about seizures?'

He nods and opens his mouth as if he's about to say something, but then says, 'Go on.'

'Well, then, when he was nine months old, he had a proper fit. I mean, a full-blown seizure. It went on for a long time, for a good ten minutes, and afterwards he was really still. His eyes had rolled right back in his head and he wasn't moving at all. Andy called an ambulance and he was rushed into hospital. I really thought he was going to die.'

'You must have been very scared.'

'It was the most frightening experience of my life.'

Alex puts his cup down and we look at each other in silence for a moment across the table.

'They did all the tests,' I continue. 'They ruled out all the usual things. But then, the neurologist called us into his room and told us that there was something seriously wrong with Ben, that he wasn't developing normally, that he should be sitting up, crawling, into everything by now. They said that he had a significant, global – as in, across the board, all areas, speech, language, everything – developmental delay. When we asked if he'd ever walk or talk, the doctors couldn't say. We didn't know at that stage if he would develop at all, whether he would catch up at some stage – or whether he would spend the rest of his life in a wheelchair needing round-the-clock care. They just didn't know. No one could tell us. As time's gone on, of course, I've learned that it's likely to be something in between. But it's not just that. He's also autistic. He's just been diagnosed. The fear of crowds and busy places, the comfort he finds in repetition, his intolerance of change or new situations. Things like that – they all make life a bit of a challenge.'

'It must be unbelievably tough. And you're doing this alone?'

I get up and take the pan from the stove. I fetch two egg cups from the cupboard, sit the eggs inside them and slice the tops off with a knife. 'I don't know if it was any easier when Andy was still here, to be honest.'

I sit down next to Ben and feed him the soft-boiled eggs with a spoon. Ben opens his mouth obligingly, like a little bird.

'He was great at first,' I continue. 'When the doctors first told us, Andy seemed to take it better than I did. But then after a few weeks, I realised he was drinking too much and hiding the bottles in the bin outside. He'd stay up late, long after Ben and I had gone to bed, and I'd wake to hear him crying through the bedroom wall.'

'Understandable,' says Alex.

I look up in surprise. I'm glad that he doesn't attack Andy, judge him, or suggest that he'd have been any different. Because it's actually quite hard to imagine how any other man would have dealt differently with this sudden, devastating blow. Ben wasn't an accident; he was planned. This was Andy's first-born son, the boy he'd wanted to play football and rugby with, the son he'd wanted to take on fishing trips and to cricket matches, the son who would one day graduate with honours and become an astronaut or a doctor, his pride and joy. He'd taken it hard; anyone would. And, in the end, he couldn't take it any more. I could understand that. I'd felt that way myself. And after he'd gone, there was an element of relief that I no longer had to take care of his feelings as well as my own.

'On a practical level, of course, it was easier to have another adult around. I can't deny that,' I tell him. 'And Andy did his share. But on an emotional level, it was hard work for me. I tried, of course, to help him, to reassure him, to promise we'd get through it together. But in the end, it wasn't enough. He needed to go back to his family in Perth, and I needed to focus on Ben.'

'But you must be tired. You need a break.'

'I manage.'

'Do you get much help? From family?'

I shake my head. 'My mum died a few years ago and my dad's in Devon. We don't get on too well. I have a brother, but he lives in Maidenhead and has his own family. I don't think he actually realises the extent of Ben's problems and I'm not that sure that he cares enough to find out. So that's it.'

'What about friends?'

'They offer, sometimes. But it never quite works out. Everyone has busy lives, don't they? The ones who have kids of their own have got their hands full, and the ones who haven't are working way too hard. Plus, I don't like to ask them to... well, you've seen what Ben can be like. It's tough to deal with. And, besides... Ben's not toilet trained.'

Alex shrugs. 'That's what friends are for.'

'No,' I correct him. 'You borrow clothes and money from friends. You phone them up and moan about your problems. You don't ask them to clean up a five-year-old's... well, you know.'

'I don't see why not.'

I smile. 'So if I asked you to change his nappy?'

'Yeah, I'd do it.'

Oh my God, I think to myself. Is this guy for real?

He stands up. 'But, not right now, if you don't mind, because I need to make a move.'

He pulls his jacket from the chair. Here we go, I tell myself.

He's done the right thing. He's helped out a damsel in distress. Now, here's the great escape.

But then Alex looks me in the eye and says, 'Could I take you both out on Saturday, for lunch maybe?'

My heart leaps. Did he really just say that? I don't get it. He's had all these chances to walk away and he hasn't taken a single one. For a moment, I'm too stunned to speak. Then, 'That would be really nice,' I say. 'But it's a bit limiting, with Ben. He isn't really very good with bright lights and crowded places, hence the supermarket fiasco today... I've never been able to eat out in a restaurant with him.'

I'm aware that this might sound as though I'm making excuses not to see him, but Alex is unshaken. 'Well, what does he like to do?'

I consider this for a moment. 'He likes the park. He loves to feed the ducks.'

Alex nods, slowly. 'Sounds good. Isn't Finsbury Park just round the corner? We could have a picnic.'

'Really?' I look him in the eye, dubiously. This is the kind of date that most men would cancel as soon as they'd got away and had a chance to cool off. But I can't think of anything else to offer him, nothing that comes with such good odds that there won't be a repetition of the meltdown that Alex witnessed today.

'Why not?' He shrugs. 'It'll be fun.'

'OK,' I say. 'The duck pond it is.'

'Great!' Alex shoves his hands into his pockets and grins at me. He pulls out his phone. I give him my number and watch as he taps it in.

Then he picks up his shopping bag, leans over and ruffles Ben's hair. 'See you Saturday, buddy.'

'Bah bah,' says Ben.

'Quite,' says Alex, and I clap my hands together. Ben's talking! He's really talking! Well, he's not, obviously. But, then again, he is.

5

When I arrive at the office on Friday morning, there's a message from Ellie.

'It's urgent.' Lucy hands me a telephone attendance note. 'She needs you to call her back straight away. I tried you on your mobile.'

'I've only just left court,' I tell her. 'I haven't had a chance to listen to my messages yet.'

I head up the stairs to my room and dial Ellie's number.

She picks up immediately. 'Sarah?'

'Hi, Ellie. Everything OK?'

'Yes, but I need to get my bail conditions changed. I need to go away this weekend.'

'Has something happened?'

A pause. 'Yes. My gran's ill. I think she's dying. I need to go and see her before she... before she...'

'OK. Leave it with me. I'll contact the court. When do you need to leave?'

'This afternoon.'

'Where does she live?'

'Kent.'

'And when will you be back?'

'I'm not sure. Can't you just get the condition removed?'

I hesitate for a moment. 'It's not that simple, Ellie. The court normally asks for two days' notice.'

'Two days? No way. My gran could be dead by then. I need the condition removed today.'

I glance at the clock on my phone. I've got to get to Camberwell for two. But there should be enough time. 'I'll see what I can do. But it's tricky. You were lucky to get bail in the first place. We might need to offer something in return.'

'Like what?'

I think about this for a moment. 'Do you have a passport?'

'Yes.'

'Well, if you could get me your passport this afternoon, I might be able to sort something out.'

'Why do you need my passport?' Ellie sounds unhappy.

'It will be an assurance to the court that you're not going to leave the country, that you'll answer your bail a week on Tuesday.'

Ellie sighs. 'OK. Tell them whatever you have to tell them. But please get it sorted today. I don't want the police to come knocking on my door again tonight, 'cause I'm not going to be there.'

'Ellie... wait...'

But she's gone.

After several phone calls and emails to the court, my application is placed before a judge, who agrees that if Ellie's passport can be handed in to her nearest police station this afternoon, the condition to live and sleep at her home address will be removed.

'Good news,' I tell Ellie when she picks up the phone.

'It's sorted? Great. Thanks a lot, Sarah.'

'Hold your horses,' I tell her. 'They need your passport first. Can you drop it in to me? Or to your nearest police station?'

'Seriously? I have to do that today?'

'Ellie,' I reprimand her. 'I did tell you this!'

'Thing is,' she says, 'I'm not at home right now.'

'Well, where are you?'

'I'm… I'm on the King's Road. I'm nowhere near my place.'

I sigh. 'Look, Ellie, this isn't going to happen unless you surrender your passport. That's the deal. How long will you be?'

She is silent for a moment. 'Thing is, I was hoping to go this afternoon, straight from here.'

'To Kent?'

'Yes.'

'Where's your passport? At home?'

She hesitates. 'Yes.'

I'm trying to figure out which train she'd need to take, from which station – London Bridge? No, probably Victoria – when she says, 'I've got to go. I'll call you back.'

'Ellie. Wait,' I say quickly.

'What?'

'I've got a hearing at Camberwell Magistrates' this afternoon. Is there anyone who can pick up the passport for you?' I ask. 'Get it to me at court?'

She says, 'My neighbour might.'

'Who's your neighbour?'

'Marie. Marie Thacker. She's got a key.'

'Get it to me there, OK? I'll hand it in for you.'

'Yeah, OK.'

'So, what time can I expect your neighbour?' I ask her.

'I don't know. I'll… I'll call you.'

'When?'

'As soon as I can.' And then she's gone.

I'm finished at court by three o'clock, but there's still no word from Ellie. I call her number and leave two messages before leaving a further message with the ushers and walking up Camberwell New Road to the shops. I stand at the bus stop, trying to decide what to do. If she doesn't hand her passport in today, then the bail condition to go home tonight stands. If she does neither and the police knock on her door tonight, she'll be circulated as wanted. If that happens, she'll be arrested and her chances of getting bail again will be virtually zero. She hated it in prison; they had her on suicide watch. She might not see the light of day again for months. Years, if she's convicted. I can't understand why she isn't taking this more seriously.

I pull my phone out of my pocket and select Ellie's number again. It rings out, yet again, and goes to voicemail, where a husky-voiced but typically laconic Ellie says, 'It's Ellie. Leave me a message.'

I end the call, open Google Maps and tap in Ellie's address.

I'm directed across the road and down a narrow street that's tucked in between a nail bar and an Indian takeaway. The delicious scent of spices emanates from the back door of the restaurant, making me feel hungry in spite of the run-down appearance of the street. As I turn the corner, I'm faced with the grubby backyard to the restaurant, which is full of tatty, dirty-looking cardboard boxes and potato peelings. A skinny cat snakes its way in and out of the boxes, looking for food.

I'm conscious that I'm going out of my way to help Ellie, doing exactly what Gareth told me not to do: getting involved. But I somehow can't bring myself to get on a bus and head back to Holloway, not just yet. She's a young girl without a mother or father, a child, still, in so many ways, alone in the world. Underneath her abrasive veneer, I know that she's suffering. I can't bring myself to abandon her to her fate.

Cedar Court is an ugly mottled brown concrete block with white PVC frontages on the edge of a small estate at the bottom of Eastfield Road. I can hear the distant shrieks of children, coming from the local primary school, and as I walk up the steps and along the first-floor balcony, I can hear more shrieking coming from inside one of the flats. It's the noise of a man and a woman shouting, I realise, as it gets louder and I get closer, but it's not until I'm right outside that I realise it's coming from the flat next door to Ellie's. Could this be Marie Thacker? I wonder. The neighbour with the key?

I hesitate a moment, before knocking, but the argument is in full flow and doesn't appear likely to stop in the very near future. There's no door knocker or bell, so I tap on the glass of the front-door window as hard as I can. The man's voice bellows something out in the background. I hear the woman respond and I wonder for a moment if they are just going to ignore me and carry on their argument. I am about to knock for a second time, when I hear the woman's voice, still shouting, but getting closer.

'Just shut the fuck up, will you, there's someone at the door!' she screeches, from the other side. I hear the rattle of a chain and then the door opens and a woman appears. She is significantly overweight, a disadvantage that isn't assisted by her hairstyle, scraped back against her head in a tight greasy bun to reveal a larger than average neck and the broadest of shoulders. A gigantic cleavage protrudes from underneath a grubby white vest-top. The woman has a lit cigarette in her hand, which she's waving unsteadily in the air. She reeks of alcohol.

'Marie?' I ask.

A spiral of cigarette smoke snakes its way from her hand to my face, making me cough.

She looks at me suspiciously. 'Who are you?'

'My name's Sarah. Sarah Kellerman. I've come to pick up something for Ellie Stephens, your neighbour. She said she was going to call you about it. She says you have a key to her flat?'

Marie wobbles a little and appears to look straight through me.

'Give… me… the fucking… money!' bellows the male voice from inside.

'No!' Marie yells back at him. 'Not if you're going straight back down the Camby Arms to spend it on that tart.'

She disappears out of sight, leaving the door ajar. Everything goes quiet for a moment, but then I hear a thump and can see through the gap left by the open door that there is a shaven head and a bare shoulder moving around in the hallway, followed by a huge tattooed forearm. The door bangs shut and then bounces open again, and I realise with alarm that this is because Marie is behind it, trying to get it open, while the man pins her up against the wall, one arm twisted up behind her back. I can see she's in too much pain to speak.

'That's it. Let it go,' he tells her, as if talking to a small child.

'Get the fuck off me,' she screeches, finally, but her voice is muffled.

'Marie?' I call her name, tentatively.

The door flies open and the shaven head and full set of tattooed shoulders appears. 'Who the fuck are you?'

Marie appears behind him. I can see that she's crying.

'I'm here to collect something for Ellie, next door,' I say. 'Do you know where she is?'

Marie wipes her nose with the back of her hand and looks me up and down. 'Are you her solicitor?' she asks me.

I nod. 'Yes.'

'Hmm. She's probably at work.'

'Work?' the tattooed man sneers at Marie. 'Is that what she's calling it these days?'

Marie flashes back, 'Yeah, well I didn't hear you dissing her when you were taking her money.'

The tattooed man glares first at her, then at me. His face then breaks into a smile. He turns back towards Marie and cups her chin in his hand, leaning his face in towards hers and pushing his mouth up close to hers. For one awkward moment, I think he's going to start kissing her, that they're going to make up, with me just standing there in the doorway. But then I hear him hiss, softly, into her face, 'Shut... your... fucking... trap.'

The door opens fully. The man briefly inspects a bundle of notes that he's holding in one hand and then shoves them into his jeans pocket before stepping brusquely past me and heading off down the balcony towards the stairs.

'Wait!' Marie screams after him. 'I'm coming with you!'

The man ignores her and carries on walking.

'Are you OK?' I ask.

Marie nods and wipes her eyes with the backs of her hands. 'Oh shit,' she says, glancing down at the floor. She crouches down to retrieve the still smouldering cigarette end she's dropped. She winces as she stands back up.

'Are you hurt?' I ask. 'Do you want me to call someone?'

Marie ignores me. She lifts her right arm high in the air and launches the lit cigarette over the edge of the balcony behind me. She winces again with the movement, which clearly causes her pain, and then lurches past me in the direction she's just thrown the cigarette end and hoists herself up, so that she's hanging over the wall.

'Marie, stop!' I shout, thinking she's about to either jump or fall right over the edge.

'Darren, fucking wait, will you?' she yells, and then, 'Fuck you!' at the top of her voice. 'Bastard!'

She drops back down again onto the balcony and rubs her shoulder. She turns and looks at me, as if seeing me for the first time. 'You're the one who got her bail,' she observes.

'Yes,' I agree.

She nods slowly, moving her head up and down in an exaggerated manner. 'You did good,' she says, approvingly. 'You looked after El. Got her out of that fucking hole. Well done.'

'Well… thanks,' I say. 'But the thing is, she's disappeared on me. I need her passport. She needs to hand it in to the police this afternoon. If she doesn't, she's heading right back to prison.'

Marie frowns. Her eyes meet mine. Hers are glazed, red and tired, her face pink, blotchy and lined. She's probably only in her early twenties, not much older than Ellie, but there's a world of difference between them. 'No.' She shakes her head vigorously. 'That ain't gonna happen. Wait there,' she says, and steps past me, back into her flat.

A moment later she reappears. She steps out and slams her front door behind her, walks next door to Ellie's and pokes a key into the lock, wiggling it around a little before it finally goes in and the door swings open.

'Come on,' she says, moving her arm in a wide arc and pointing it at the door.

'Marie, I...'

But before I can say any more, she disappears inside. I tentatively step in after her. I know this is wrong. I shouldn't be here – who knows what I might find? Drugs? Guns? But I also know that, whatever happens, Ellie's not coming back here tonight and I really don't want to be explaining my involvement to the judge, or to Ellie, when she gets picked up and produced in the cells for breaching her bail. I haven't got time to mess around. I'm with Marie, after all, and Ellie's given her a key.

I follow Marie down the hallway to the living room. It's a nice little flat, small but homely, and surprisingly neat and tidy. Marie goes into the kitchen and starts to rummage through the cabinets and drawers.

'Check the bedroom,' she calls out to me. 'If it's not here, it's gonna be in one of the drawers in there.'

I find the door to the bedroom, which is pretty and feminine. Lilac drapes hang from the small window and there are matching lilac cushions with patchwork hearts scattered over the bed, along with a fluffy pink throw. Finn's cot is wedged tight between the bed and the wardrobe, a lone stuffed sheep sitting on top of the baby blue summer duvet.

I open the top drawer of the chest of drawers and feel around inside, the soft sensation of silk underwear cool against my hand.

Marie appears in the room behind me.

'I can't do this,' I tell her. 'I shouldn't be here. I should go.'

'Do you want El to go back to the slammer?' she asks me, taking over and rummaging through the drawers below.

'No, but—'

'So come on then.' She checks the bedside cabinet and then slides back the mirrored door to the wardrobe. It's full to bursting with expensive-looking dresses and handbags and a shoe rack that's crammed with an impressive selection of patent leather heels. Is Ellie shoplifting? I wonder, suddenly. Is that what she's up to? Or are Marie and Darren stealing for her? Is that why she's giving them money? How else could she afford clothes like these?

'I'll wait out there,' I tell Marie, nodding towards the hallway.

A moment later Marie finishes looking through the bedroom and pushes past me to the living room. I follow her and watch as she lifts sofa cushions and rifles through more drawers and shelves.

Eventually she stops and puts her hands on her hips. 'It's not here. I've looked everywhere,' she says. 'There ain't nowhere else to look.'

I nod. 'OK.'

'Did she definitely say it was here?' she asks me.

I think about this for a moment. 'Not exactly.'

We stand in the living room for a moment looking at each other. Suddenly, there's a loud bleeping noise, which makes me jump out of my skin. Marie wrestles her phone out of her jeans pocket. She glares at it for a moment, utters the word, 'Bastard!' and then makes a bolt for the door.

'Marie, wait!' I run after her into the hallway, but she doesn't stop. I follow her outside and slam the door behind me, watching as she wobbles unsteadily along the balcony and, seconds later, disappears into the stairwell.

I follow her down the steps and then walk along the road in the direction of the Oval, back to the bus stop.

My phone rings. It's Anna.

'How are you getting on?' she asks.

'If you mean with Ellie, I'm not sure, to be honest. What do you know about a grandmother who lives in Kent?'

Anna hesitates a moment before saying, 'What grandmother?'

'She asked me to get her bail varied so that she could go and visit her this weekend. She's sick, apparently. Dying.'

'She's never mentioned her to me,' Anna says. 'She told me she had no family at all. I've asked her the question, outright, and she told me "no". It would have made all the difference with the child protection proceedings if she'd had a family member who could have supported her in keeping Finn with her.'

'Hmm. That's what I thought.' I contemplate this for a moment. 'She's supposed to have handed her passport into the police this afternoon. I went to her flat. She's not there and neither, it seems, is her passport.'

'What? So what are you saying?' asks Anna.

'I don't know for sure,' I tell her. 'It's just a hunch – and I hope I'm wrong. But I think she may have jumped bail.'

6

When I get home on Friday evening, I make pasta and cheese and run a bath for Ben. I've heard nothing from Alex since Wednesday and have just decided that I'm not going to – and that it's probably for the best – when my phone bleeps and then his name is there, sitting on my phone screen, in my hand, just as if it belongs there, as if he's someone that I know: *Alex*. I realise then that I don't even know his surname, that I didn't ask, or tell him mine. There is so much that I don't know about him, so much to be anxious about. There are innumerable ways in which this could all go horribly wrong.

But then I open the message and read: *Fancy a coffee?* and I laugh out loud as I realise that he *is* someone that I know, a little bit at least, and who knows me a little too – and that's how it starts, isn't it? Andy, after all, was once just a Christian name tapped into my mobile phone. And in spite of the way things turned out, I've never once regretted meeting, knowing… loving him.

I lift Ben into the bath and sit down on the toilet seat to watch him. As I do so I catch a glimpse of myself in the bathroom mirror, seeing my face as Alex might see it, lit up and twinkling, alive with the possibility of something more than Friday-night bathtime with a five-year-old. I may not have Anna's long legs or Ellis Stephens' striking looks, but I'm aware that I have a pretty face and nice eyes, and that my thick fair hair – when it's freshly washed and hanging in loose, shaggy waves around my shoulders – is worthy of a second glance.

I click inside the box below Alex's message and type in: *Sorry, not tonight. Am washing Ben's hair!* I tap the send button and glance back at Ben, who is leaning forward and putting his face into the bathwater, trying out the sensation against his nose and mouth. When he lifts his face up, he has beard-like bubbles stuck to his chin and the tip of his fringe is drenched with water, which is now running down his nose. I see him first glance at the green and yellow plastic jug on the side of the bath and then at me, as he tries to figure out where the water is coming from. His eyes narrow and squint as they focus in on his nose, as if it might hold a clue. He looks so funny that I start to giggle, and Ben looks up at me and giggles too.

A second later my phone bleeps and a new message appears. *Tomorrow then? As planned? I will wash my hair too.*

I chuckle again. Ben is delighted with this new game of cause and effect: the phone bleeps and then Mummy laughs – this is a good game!

'AAAAY.' He applauds our interaction, loudly. His voice is deep and echoes round the bathroom. He brings his hands up into the air and crashes them, palms down, against the water.

'Careful, Ben,' I warn him, still laughing. 'Big splash. Too wet.'

Sure, I text Alex back. *What time?*

A thrill of anticipation runs through me as I shampoo and rinse Ben's hair, lift him out of the bath and wrap him in a towel. I take him into the bedroom to get him into his nappy and pyjamas, and then put him on the floor and follow him as he, predictably, crawls out of the door and into the living room towards the telly. He pulls himself up and presses his nose to the screen.

'Bah bah,' he says.

'All right, Ben.' I smile. 'Bah bah it is.'

I slip the *Teletubbies* DVD into the Panasonic and flick on the telly. I can hear my phone bleeping from the kitchen table, and I savour the moment of not knowing what it says, but knowing all the same that I have a… A what? What do I have? I have a text exchange with a man going on, a man who likes me, is interested in me, a man who wants to see me tomorrow. It's more than I've had for a very long time. It feels as though he's… well, my boyfriend. The thought is intoxicating, after so long without this, after so many nights of getting Ben and myself ready for bed with nothing more to look forward to the following day than the prospect of having to keep Ben entertained all weekend on my own.

I pick up my phone. There are two messages. I read them in the correct order. The first one says: *Shall I pick you up at 10.00? I'm making a picnic. I've got hard-boiled eggs and bananas for Ben.* The second one says: *And coffee for you.*

I laugh again and Ben looks up at me with a smile.

'Ben, look,' I tell him, excitedly, and show him my phone. 'We have a date!'

Ben reaches out his hand and taps the screen of my phone, which of course fails to bleep on cue as he's expecting.

'Bah bah,' he says, unimpressed, and turns back to Tinky Winky, who at this moment in time has far more to offer than I.

I type back: :) *See you tomorrow.*

*

Amazingly, for once, Ben sleeps right through the night, and this time doesn't wake until eight thirty the following morning. When I look at the clock on my phone I realise with alarm that we're left with only an hour and a half to get up, dressed and ready before Alex arrives. But when I check myself in the bathroom mirror and see my even, bag-free eyes and rested face looking back, I know it's going to be worth it. Instead of the foggy-headed woman who drags herself through the day and divides it up into quarters, it's my fresh-faced, clear-headed former self that is meeting Alex today. Plucked eyebrows and painted nails are definitely of secondary importance when compared to a fully functioning brain, and it's only once I've given Ben his breakfast and got him dressed, our teeth and hair brushed and a picnic packed, that I turn my mind to my own wardrobe.

I've spent most of the warmer months of the year in three-quarter-length leggings, tunic tops and trainers, but I settle instead for a simple navy gypsy skirt, a white vest-top and a matching bolero-style chiffon cardie. I've no idea what the top and cardie will end up looking like after a day out with Ben, but it's the newest-looking outfit I've got and I do at least want to look as though I've made an effort.

Alex pulls up outside a few minutes before ten. He's driving a silver BMW, which is really smart, but not too flashy. I make a mental note that he's one of those people that's actually on time for things, unlike me; I'll have to mend my ways. Nonetheless, Ben and I are all but ready, Ben's bag is packed, as is our contribution to the picnic – tuna sandwiches and a Ben-friendly onion- and dressing-free Greek salad of chopped up cucumber, tomatoes and feta cheese.

I walk outside to meet Alex with Ben in my arms. He waves as he gets out of his car. 'Is it all right here?' he asks, from a distance.

'It'll be fine for a moment,' I tell him. 'We won't be long.'

'Can't we walk there?'

I shake my head. 'We'd probably need the car nearby, just in case.'

Alex nods and I'm struck once again by the knowledge that he isn't exactly a stranger to me. I know already that I don't need to explain the 'just in case' to Alex: he gets it. He's standing next to the car looking at his phone when I leave the house with Ben's car seat in one arm and Ben in the other. He immediately looks up, pushes his phone into his pocket and walks over to help me, taking the car seat and putting it in the back of the car. He then takes Ben from me and puts him into his seat. He stands back and watches as I strap him in.

'You look nice,' he says, from behind me.

I feel myself blush and swing round to face him.

'Thanks. So do you.' I smile. For an awkward moment we stand in the road, looking at each other. He's quite a bit taller than me and I have to look up. In the bright morning light, with his face just inches away from mine, he appears a little older than I remembered, but he's every bit as handsome. His navy-blue eyes crinkle up at the corners with mirth as we both try to think of something to say, the easy conversation we had just a few days ago lost in the realisation that we've now progressed from a man helping out a stressed woman with her shopping to a couple on a first date.

Alex resolves the situation by gently touching my arm and saying, 'It's good to see you. I wasn't sure if you'd change your mind.'

I look into his eyes to see if he's teasing me, but he's not. 'Why would I do that?' I ask.

He smiles and shrugs by way of reply and then opens the passenger door for me before walking round and getting into the car. I glance across at him as he revs up the engine, baffled by his diffidence. As far as I'm concerned, he's the one in the driving seat – in more ways than one.

I glance back over my shoulder at Ben, then duck my head down behind the seat and pop up again, making a funny face. A smile breaks across Ben's face. He seems remarkably relaxed and although I've brought his nursery rhyme CD for a bit of reassurance and familiarity on the journey, I don't want to inflict it on Alex unless I have to.

I direct him straight across Seven Sisters Road, which is tailed back with traffic. Alex glances round at the run-down shops and B&Bs that line the street.

'Hmm. Exotic, indeed,' he comments as we pass a hair salon of the same name.

'You're not from round here, right?' I tease.

Alex looks momentarily embarrassed. 'No. I live with a friend. Lewisham,' he adds.

'Lewisham's nice.'

'It's a bit of a bachelor pad, I'm afraid.'

'So, what were you doing on the Holloway Road on Wednesday?' I ask.

'Wednesday? Oh, I'd been up north. For work,' he says. 'I thought I'd head down the A1. Just stopped off at the shops to get a couple of bits on my way home.'

Alex slows down outside the entrance to the park.

'Go on in,' I tell him. 'You can park inside.'

We follow the road round to the right and park up next to the basketball courts, which are covered in a pretty sky-blue concrete that makes them look from a distance like a swimming pool.

Alex cuts the engine. Ben spots the boating lake on the other side of the road, where a large mêlée of gulls, geese, ducks and swans is gathered, both on the water and spilling onto the path beside it. A flock of pigeons alights from its midst and settles in an orderly row along the railings.

'AAAAY!' Ben applauds loudly.

Alex laughs. 'AAAAAY,' he cheers back at Ben.

I look up at him. 'That's really great,' I comment. 'The way you copy him. I've heard you do it before. It's what the speech therapist told me to do. When you mirror his noises back to him, it's reinforcement for him.'

Alex says, 'OK. I'll remember to do it some more.'

From the back of the car, Ben suddenly lets out an enormous raspberry. I'm not quite sure which end it's come from, to tell the truth, but the look on Alex's face is priceless as he turns to me and says, 'You want me to do that too?'

Ben erupts in peals of laughter the minute we do, and we are all three still giggling as we get out of the car. Any enduring first-date tension is now easing right out of me and we continue to joke easily as we unfold the buggy and unpack the picnic and walk across the road in the direction of the lake. As we reach the water, I take Ben out of his buggy and let him stand, holding onto the railings, where he reaches up to the intrepid pigeons – who are sitting there within arm's length of us – and launches them one by one into the air with a tap on each plump chest. He continues down the line, moving with the aid of the railings, tapping each pigeon in quick succession.

'It's real-life Angry Birds,' I laugh, as each pigeon takes off, only to land again a little further up the railing. 'He really does think it's some sort of game. They have touch-screen computers at nursery. When we go to the aquarium, he taps the glass as each fish swims past. I have to stop him, because it frightens them. He doesn't realise that, of course. It's just cause and effect to him...'

Ben moves himself along, hand over hand, towards the newly formed pigeon line-up. Suddenly, without warning, Alex leaps forwards and pulls Ben back with one arm. The pigeons swoop up and take off over the lake.

'What's wrong?' I ask.

'I don't think he should get so close to the water,' Alex says.

'But there's a railing...'

'Not further up, there's not.'

Alex takes Ben's hands and walks him away from the lake and onto the grass, towards the playground. 'One... two... three,' he counts Ben's steps.

I stand there for a moment, wondering what just happened. Did Alex just overreact? Or am I a careless parent? I'd have caught up with Ben easily before he reached the end of the railings. Maybe Alex doesn't realise that Ben can't move that fast.

But Ben seems satisfied with this change of direction and Alex seems to be genuinely enjoying himself. I watch them for a moment, my confusion turning to delight as I notice how at ease they are with each other – or, more to the point, how uncharacteristically at ease Ben is in the company of someone new. His face breaks into a smile as Alex continues to count,

'Seven, eight, nine...' so I call out to Alex and ask him to watch Ben for a moment while I go into the café for some birdseed, which they sell behind the counter with the teas and coffees.

When I come out of the shop, Alex is walking Ben over the grass towards me, holding just one of his hands. I watch him as he leans over Ben, his back bent. Ben is stretching his arm up and holding on tight to Alex's hand, his face racked with concentration. At the same time, he looks pleased with himself and I hear him say, 'Bah bah,' when he sees me coming into view. While Ben is distracted by my reappearance, Alex takes the opportunity to let go of his hand. Ben wobbles a little and Alex bends and quickly catches him.

'He's nearly there, isn't he?' he says as I approach them. 'I'd bet he could let go of my hand and keep going.'

'He has the balance,' I agree, 'but he panics. Of course, it's much further to the ground for him than it is for a baby that's learning to walk.'

'OK. Well we should try it again on the grass. I have a plan.'

I smile at him, gratefully. 'Thank you. I'd like that.'

I give Ben a handful of birdseed which he tries to eat and then drops. He then takes my hand and pushes it in the direction of the water, indicating that he wants me to feed the ducks myself. Alex picks Ben up and straps him into his buggy as we move closer to the lake. I throw a few handfuls of seed into the water and there is an immediate flurry of activity as the gulls and pigeons swoop down over the ducks and geese and try to get in on the action.

'AAAAY!' cheers Ben, appreciatively, and flaps his hands.

When all the birdseed is gone we head up past the café. We stop at the playground, but it's too busy for Ben, who wails when

I try to unstrap him. Instead, we follow the path until we find a patch of grass in the shade between a beautiful russet maple tree and a lush green hornbeam. I spread out the blanket I've brought while Alex reaches down and picks up a small piece of branch that has fallen from the tree.

'Here,' he says. 'This is perfect. We just need to get him to hold onto this instead of your hand. That's step one. Then, once he's got used to it, we move onto step two: we let go. Want me to try?'

'OK.' I sit down on the blanket as Alex unstraps Ben and stands him on the grass. Ben looks at me anxiously when Alex offers him the stick, but Alex lifts his hand to indicate that I should stay where I am and coaxes Ben gently until he clutches it and walks towards me with Alex holding the other end. When he reaches the blanket Ben lets go and drops down onto his bottom.

'Good walking, Ben!' I encourage him, before rewarding him with a banana and a Marmite finger.

Ben sits happily on the rug with a plastic plate full of food and I sit back against the tree trunk, relaxed in the knowledge that there is someone else there to take turns in leaping up and running after him if he crawls away or picks up and tries to eat one of the helicopter seeds that are twirling down from the tree.

'You're so good with him,' I tell Alex. 'It's so nice for me to watch.'

He smiles. 'It's nice for me too. I want to help Ben. And you.'

I look up at him. 'It's a lot to ask,' I say.

He reaches out and touches my arm. 'I wanted to see you; and you have Ben. I don't mind, anyway. It's fun. I like kids.'

'It's different with Ben, though. It's hard work.'

'Well, for you, it must be relentless.' He glances at me. 'And you have a job as well, don't you? You were wearing a suit when I met you.'

'I'm a solicitor. A criminal defence advocate.'

'You go to court?'

'Yes, most days.'

'Wow. You do a job like that and then come home and take care of Ben?'

I shrug. 'It's what I did before I had him. Life goes on. We have to live. I have to keep a roof over our heads and pay the bills.'

'Of course.'

'To be honest,' I admit, 'although it's hard juggling both, it's work that keeps me sane. When Ben was first diagnosed, work was a real escape for me, a chance to immerse myself in something else, a chance to feel normal again. I had to get away... not from Ben, but just... well, just from this permanent feeling of loss I had whenever I was with him.'

'It must have been like losing a child. A bereavement. I imagine it feels the same. You lost the child you thought you were going to have, the future that you were expecting.'

'Yes. That's exactly how it was.'

Alex looks up. He can see I'm upset, but I'm glad that he doesn't try to change the subject. I know that the only way I'm ever going to get over the pain and begin the process of truly accepting the life that's been handed to me is to talk about this, and for some reason that entirely escapes me, Alex seems to want to listen. So I talk about the times I really did think I'd lost him, how Ben ended up in hospital so many times, with seizures or chest infections. Pneumonia, bronchitis, he'd had the lot. 'I think some people expected me to give up work and stay home with Ben,' I tell him. 'Dedicate myself to him, night and day. I don't mind admitting that it would have driven me crazy. Really, I wouldn't have made it this far.'

'I'm not surprised. Not many people would. And anyway, what do you do then? Live off the state for the rest of your life? End up with no savings or pension, living in poverty?'

'Some of my work colleagues resent it though,' I tell him. 'They think I'm not pulling my weight.'

'I think that's what most working women experience, even those with children who don't need extra help, even in this day of supposed equality in the workplace.' Alex unscrews the thermos he's brought with him and pours us both a second beaker of coffee. 'I once overheard a male colleague complaining when another female colleague left work to collect a sick child,' he tells me. 'He said it was her choice to have children and his choice not to, and that he didn't see why he – as a taxpayer – should have to pay her child benefit *and* pick up her work for her after she'd left for the day.'

I gasp. 'What did you say?'

'I told him that one day her children will be the taxpayers who are paying his pension, the GPs that are treating him, or the carers that are looking after him in his nursing home and emptying his bedpan when he's too old to look after himself. I told him he should be thanking her, not criticising her.'

I laugh. 'Good point. What did he say to that?'

'Nothing.' He smiles. 'What could he say?'

I look over at Ben, who has finished his food and is starting to moan. I wipe his mouth with a paper towel, and tip some crisps onto his plate: his favourite snack. Ben instantly gobbles them up and holds out his hands for more. 'Ben's not going to be looking after anyone, though,' I say.

'All the more reason why *we* need to look after *him*.'

We. I look at him gratefully. I'm not sure whether he means *we* as in society, or *we* as in he and I, but I feel an unexpected tug at my heartstrings as I realise just how much I like this man. 'So what do you do?' I ask him. 'For work?'

Alex looks at me for a moment. 'Oh, nothing as interesting as your job. Seriously. Brokerage. Corporate finance. Stocks and shares and hedge funds. It's boring. Don't make me go there on a Saturday.'

I laugh. 'OK, I won't.'

'Your job sounds far more glamorous,' he says.

'Well, I do enjoy it,' I admit. 'I love being there for people who are in trouble, people who are scared and need my help. And of course, it's interesting. No two days are the same.'

'So what's your most interesting case?'

'What, ever?'

'Or… right now. What are you dealing with at the moment?'

I hesitate. 'Well, I'm not allowed to talk about individual cases, not in any way that makes them identifiable. But I have one at the moment, involving a child who's been hurt.'

'Hurt?'

'Badly hurt,' I tell him. 'They say the mother tried to kill him.'

'And did she?'

'I don't know.'

'But what if she's guilty?'

'That's for the court to decide. My job is to test the evidence. Make sure it stands up to scrutiny.'

'And does it?' he asks.

'I don't know yet.'

'So what does she say about it?' he asks. 'Has she admitted it to you?'

'Alex!' I smack him playfully on the arm. 'You must know I can't tell you that.'

'Go on,' he says.

'No,' I laugh. 'But if you can get some time off work and come along to the Old Bailey a week on Tuesday, you'll hear it all first-hand, for yourself.'

'The Old Bailey,' Alex repeats. 'Wow.'

'It's been transferred there from another court,' I tell him. 'The next hearing is where we enter a plea. Only...'

'Only what?'

'Nothing.'

'What?' he persists.

Only I don't know if Ellie will be there. I'm worried she's jumped bail. I'm expecting a call from the Defence Solicitor Call Centre at any moment to say she's been arrested. Or worse, she's snatched Finn from hospital and is nowhere to be found. But I can't tell him that. 'Enough,' I smile. 'I'm not telling you any more!'

Alex smiles back. 'OK. But, seriously, though. It sounds so illustrious – and exciting.'

'Well, it can be hard work. The people we represent often have mental health problems or addictions and can be highly stressed and difficult to deal with – or otherwise uncooperative.'

'Hmm. Yes,' Alex muses, knowingly. 'I can imagine.'

I glance up at him, but he's now watching Ben, who has finished his crisps and has thrown his plastic plate onto the grass and is crawling off the blanket away from us. Alex gets up, creeps up behind Ben and gives him a quick tickle under the armpits, which has the desired effect of stopping him in his tracks while Ben tries to work out what just happened. Alex picks up the plate and Ben starts to crawl away again, then seems to change his mind and starts wailing instead. I get up to pick him up while Alex packs the picnic things away.

As we cross the grass, Alex spots another stick that's just the right size for Ben to hold. 'Let's have another go,' he says. I put Ben back down on his feet and, holding him up by the arms, I offer him the stick. Ben takes it with one hand and clutches at the buggy with the other, but is soon walking steadily across the grass with just the stick connecting us.

Alex comes up behind me. 'Here, let me take the stick,' he says. 'You can be the carrot. Run ahead and then crouch down and face him, and let's see if he'll walk to you. Here, take these,' he says, grabbing a pack of crisps from the picnic bag and giving them to me.

Alex takes the stick from me and after an initial wobble and wail of protest, Ben continues to trot steadily over the grass after me, as I run ahead with the crisps. I stop and hold the pack out to Ben. 'Crisps, Ben,' I call. 'Come and get them.'

'Bah bah,' says Ben, smiling as he trots towards me.

'Come on,' I call to him. 'Come to Mummy. Come and get the crisps, Ben.'

When Ben is just a few feet away from me, Alex lets go of the stick. Ben is so intent on reaching me, or more importantly, the crisps I'm holding, that he doesn't notice at first that there is no one supporting him and he carries on, taking his very first steps on his own, his gait wide and unsteady, his hand still clutching his end of the stick.

I take a deep breath and clap my hand to my chest; my heart surges with joy. I can't believe it. 'Ben, you're walking!' I screech at him.

Alex quickly whips out his phone and points the camera at Ben, who instinctively glances over his left shoulder, realising suddenly that Alex is no longer beside him and that he is going it alone. His smile disappears and his face drops in a combination of fear and concentration, but instead of collapsing onto his bottom as I'd thought he might, he carries on walking steadily towards me for at least ten paces, before tumbling into my arms.

'Ben, you did it!' I wrap him in my arms and kiss him repeatedly. I'm so happy, I could cry. 'Good walking, Ben. Good walking,' I tell him over and over again.

*

When we get home, Alex helps me in with Ben's things and comes in for tea. He turns on my laptop and uploads the footage of Ben's first steps. We play it back to Ben, showing him what he has achieved and cheering along with our own voices on the screen. Later, while I get Ben ready for bed, Alex goes out for pizza and a bottle of wine and we watch *Strictly Come Dancing* on the telly.

'That looks like a lot of fun,' Alex says, nodding at the TV screen.

'You like dancing?'

'Hmm. I'd have a go at that,' he says.

'Really?'

'Yes. If you were my partner.'

'How do you know I can dance?'

'Something tells me you can.'

I look up at him. His eyes are smiling.

We both sit there facing each other for a moment and I wonder if something is about to happen between us. But then, 'Whoa, careful,' Alex suddenly glances over towards Ben, who is standing up, holding onto the TV with just one hand. Right on cue, as we watch him, he lets go and walks steadily across the room. I take a sharp inward breath. Ben just keeps going, across the carpet, until he reaches us on the sofa. I reach out to catch him but as the music on the TV starts up, he pushes himself off my knee and wobbles back in the direction of the telly.

He is definitely walking. It wasn't a one-off. He knows he can do this now, and there's no stopping him. It's like a light switch has turned on in his brain.

I feel elated. I can't believe what an amazing day it's been, and it's all down to Alex. It's as though he's brought us luck. This is no scratch card: this is the lottery.

Later, as I show him out of the front door and watch as he walks down the path, I know that I have to see him again.

'Alex,' I call. He turns and comes back down the path.

'What have I forgotten?' he asks.

He steps back through the doorway, and I touch his face.

'This,' I say, leaning forward. I feel the stubble of his chin graze my cheek ever so slightly, and then his hand is circling my waist and his mouth is on mine.

'I'll find a babysitter,' I tell him. 'Let's go dancing.'

Alex kisses me again. 'I'll look forward to that.'

After he's gone and after Ben's gone to bed, I lie awake for a long time and allow myself the luxury of imagining that this might be for real, that this might be the way my future is heading: a world with Alex in it – Alex, me and Ben. This is the point where my daydreams usually end; this is where reality always kicks in. But is it different this time?

Hope rises inside me like a balloon. This man – this lovely man who has seen my son at his very, *very* worst – wants to go out with me again. I've only met him twice, but I know already that he is a kind, caring, gentle person who has brought a ray of sunshine into my world and who genuinely seems to want to help Ben. For some reason that's beyond my comprehension, he seems to think that the package that is me and Ben – and he can be in no doubt that we are indeed a package – is one that's worth having. But why? What's in it for him? What if he changes his mind about me? What if he doesn't? What do I really know about him, after all?

My father's voice creeps into my head: 'If something seems too good to be true, it usually is.' I contemplate this long after the streetlights have dimmed and the traffic noise that normally reaches me from the Holloway Road has dulled into an occasional distant swish and hum. I try to summon up my mother's voice instead of my father's, to hear her talking to me, to imagine what she'd tell me, what advice she'd give, but it's been so long since I've heard her speak that I can't quite reconstruct the intonation, the pitch, the cadence of her voice.

But as tiredness finally sweeps over me and my body stills and my mind opens itself up to the funny, random, abstract thoughts that pop into your head when you're on the cusp of sleep, I feel her hand in mine. I suddenly remember something muddled about strangers being angels, and never being afraid.

7

The prosecution papers arrive on Tuesday as directed by the court. I phone and leave yet another message for Ellie – yet another call that she doesn't return. By Friday afternoon, I wonder if I should notify the court that I've lost touch with her. On the one hand, I have a duty to let them know if I'm unable to prepare her case for a fully effective hearing. On the other hand, there's still time. She may yet appear. I wonder if the police have discovered she's missing yet. Has she been arrested? Am I about to get a call?

I send an email to Will: *Still no sign of her. Not looking good.*

Will emails back, *Give her until Monday. Call me if you've heard nothing by then.*

Alex texts on Friday evening to tell me that he's been working late all week and will be spending the weekend at a conference, but will call round early the following week – that he has something for me, or more specifically, for Ben. I spend both days of the weekend in the park, walking Ben round and round the duck pond. He intermittently grabs at the railings or the leg of my jeans, but quickly lets go again and pushes my hand away if I try to help him, keen to prove to himself and to me that he can go it alone. This is the first time I've experienced this aspect of his character, this will to be independent, and although I'm under no illusion that he'll ever, in fact, be truly independent of me, this new development still fills me with hope and joy.

On Monday I drop Ben off at nursery and head to court for a morning trial. I'm halfway through when I get a message from Lucy to say that there's a client waiting for me at the office. I call her while the magistrates are out making their decision.

'It's Ellis Stephens,' she tells me.

'Tell her to wait for me,' I insist. 'Don't let her go anywhere. Lock her in if you have to.'

'Isn't that illegal?' asks Lucy.

I sigh. 'I'll be back as soon as I can.'

When I arrive back at the office an hour later, Ellie has gone.

'She said she was going to the shops,' Lucy tells me. 'She's left her number though. She said to call her when you get back.'

Lucy hands me a pink post-it with a mobile number scrawled on it in her big bubbly handwriting. I note with irony that it's the same number I have stored for Ellie, the number I've been calling for the past week. I take out my phone and ring it.

'Hi,' says Ellie, picking up.

'Ellie, where on earth have you been?' I reprimand her. 'I've left you a billion messages.'

'Oh. Yeah. Sorry about that. I… I lost my phone.'

'But you found it again?'

'Yes.'

'So how's your gran?' I ask her.

A pause. 'OK,' she says.

'And what about your passport? Where is it?'

'I've just been and handed it in.'

'And they didn't arrest you?'

'No. They just took it. I don't think they've been round.'

'Jeez, Ellie. You've been sailing close to the wind,' I say. 'Are you OK? I've been worried.'

'Really?' Ellie sounds surprised.

'Really. The court hearing's tomorrow. I thought you'd done a runner.'

'I'm sorry,' she says. 'Thanks for trying to help. Marie told me you came round.'

Did she tell you that I was inside your flat with her, poking around? I wonder. 'Yes, well, I'm sorry if I intruded,' I tell her. 'I was worried that you'd get arrested and banged up again. Neither of us wants that.'

'No,' she agrees.

'Well, hurry up and get back here. We've a lot to get through.'

'OK,' she says. 'I'm on my way.'

*

Ellie slides her phone across the desk towards me. It's an iPhone 7: top of the range. I note that her hands are perfectly manicured, her nails painted a pretty baby pink.

'That's Finn,' she says.

Both Finn and Ellie are in the picture. Finn is beautiful, like his mother; I wouldn't have expected anything else. His eyes are a startling blue and his face is creased up into a gigantic smile as he looks adoringly up into Ellie's eyes.

'He's gorgeous. He looks like you,' I say. I hand her back the phone. 'So, how did you meet him?'

'Who?'

'Jay Barrington-Brown.'

Ellie looks down at her hands and picks at the cuticle surrounding her pink thumbnail. 'At a party.'

'A party... where?'

'The Royal Cadogan. Knightsbridge.'

'So what were you doing there?'

'Working.'

'Doing what?'

Ellie sighs. 'Didn't Anna tell you all of this? Do I really need to go over it again?'

'All right. We'll come back to that later. Let's go through the statements. The initial case papers came in last week.' I open the file of papers in front of me and hand a set to Ellie.

I look up. Ellie looks back at me in silence.

'So, first we have the witness statement from your social worker Heather Grainger. She was assigned to your case in April after Finn was admitted to hospital for the first time.'

'He had a chest infection, that's all. A virus.'

'I know,' I agree. 'No one is suggesting that it was anything else on that occasion. But we also have statements from the two nurses that treated him, who say that when they removed his clothing, he had a number of injuries which varied in age and ranged from smaller ones on his arms, finger-sized bruises that looked as though he'd been grabbed or held too tightly, to larger ones on his legs and trunk, which had the appearance of knuckle marks.'

Ellie shakes her head. 'Anna said they couldn't prove that. The expert in the other case – he said they were accidental.'

'He didn't say that. He said that he couldn't say definitively that they *weren't* accidental. There's a difference. The prosecution in the criminal proceedings can still use their own findings as part of their case. This evidence is important, Ellie.' I look up at her. 'The number of injuries and the period of time over which they occurred help to build an overall picture of harm to Finn whilst he was in your care, which they'll use as a backdrop to what happens next.'

I pull out the colour copies of the medical exhibit photographs of Finn's arms, trunk and legs and spread them across my desk, so that she can see them. 'There are quite a few bruises, there's no getting away from it.' I peer at a close-up shot of what I imagine, after cross-referencing with the nurse's statements, is Finn's abdomen. 'This one on his tummy is big. Then there are these,' I continue, pointing to some healed scabs of varying ages which are scattered on his legs and on the backs of his hands. 'The prosecution expert says these are cigarette burns. And, whatever the expert said in the family proceedings, a jury might well conclude that all of these injuries were deliberately inflicted.'

Ellie says, stubbornly, 'Well, they weren't.'

'Then, how did they get there?'

Ellie colours a little. 'Finn was accident-prone. He was always climbing onto things, falling off…' She tails off.

I put the exhibits down on the desk and look Ellie in the eye. She glances up and meets my gaze. 'Did anyone else look after Finn for you?' I ask her. 'During that period, did anyone else babysit?'

She shakes her head.

'What… never?' I persist. 'Not even once? A neighbour, perhaps? While you popped to the shop?'

Ellie's eyelashes flicker for a second. 'No,' she says, firmly. 'No one.'

'And when you went to work? Hairdressing,' I add, looking her squarely in the eye.

'I took him with me.'

'Really? Every time?'

She shrugs. 'Yeah.'

I let out a sigh and turn back to the papers in front of me. 'OK. Well, Heather Grainger's now made a second statement. She cites a number of instances, when Finn was first taken into care, when you had supervised contact, when your care of him was lacking. She says that she had a number of concerns about your parenting.'

Ellie heaves a sigh and rolls her eyes.

'Why would she say that?'

'Because she hates me, that's why.' She folds her arms and sits back in her chair.

'She does agree that her relationship with you was a difficult one,' I agree. 'She mentions several arguments you'd had, about you prop-feeding Finn, sleeping in the same bed with him, things like that. She was concerned that you thought you knew best, that you wouldn't be told anything, that you were unwilling to acknowledge any problems.'

'She was in my face all the time,' Ellie says, sulkily. 'I did what she said, but it was never good enough for her.'

I nod. 'OK. Well that's open to interpretation, I suppose. But she also says that, on one occasion, she asked you about the bruises and you told her that you may have grabbed Finn, or held him too hard.'

'I don't remember saying that. But if I did, it's not true.'

I look up. 'Then, why—'

'Look,' Ellie protests. 'I was trying to get Finn back, OK? Anna told me that I had to cooperate. I was supposed to tell her what she wanted to hear.'

'Not if it wasn't true.'

'Of course it wasn't true. I would never hurt Finn. I told you, I don't know how he got those bruises,' Ellie insists, then shakes her head, dismissively. She folds her arms and swings back on her chair leg. 'But why does any of this matter? I told you, they were going to give Finn back to me. They gave me overnight contact, unsupervised!'

I nod. 'Which was when Finn fell seriously ill.'

Ellie glares at me, her cheeks flushed. 'Aren't you supposed to be on my side?'

'Ellie, I *am* on your side,' I sigh. 'But I'm putting the case to you – the case against you – and I need to know your answers before anyone else in that courtroom does. Trust me, when you're standing in the witness box and the prosecutor is asking you the same questions I'm asking you, she's *not* going to be on your side and you're going to know about it. She's going to rip you to shreds.'

'She can try,' Ellie mutters. She takes her phone back out of her bag and starts to scroll through her messages.

I look at her in silence until she looks up to face me and meets my gaze. Her face is like stone, her eyes angry.

'I know the prosecutor,' I tell her. 'Carmel Oliver. She's the Crown's instructed advocate in this case and she's good. She does all their children cases. You want to know what she's going to do?'

Ellie doesn't answer, but she's looking at me.

'Here's what she's going to do. First of all she's going to do everything she can to show you up in the worst possible light as a mother. She's going to get you to admit that you were inadequate, that you didn't look after Finn properly, that you didn't always respond when he cried, or dress him appropriately

111

for the weather. That you didn't get him the medical attention that he needed when he needed it.'

'But Will said there's no direct evidence—'

'There's evidence.' I cut Ellie off, sharply, the exasperation I'm feeling now creeping into my voice. 'And what Heather Grainger witnessed is supported by the circumstantial evidence that is your background, your upbringing. As Will has already told you, in the absence of any other credible explanation, the finger is going to point firmly and squarely at you.'

I pause, as I watch Ellie take this in. I now have her full attention. I can see that taking the hard line with her is the right thing to do.

'The prosecutor is going to do everything she can to show the jury that you did a lot more than neglect Finn,' I continue, 'but she's not going to do it straight away. First, she's going to show them why. First, she's going to get you to talk about your parents.' I look at Ellie with sympathy for a moment, as I imagine the prosecutor might, and then I say, 'They were drug addicts, weren't they, Ellie? Junkies. Their instinct, their motivation, was not to protect and nurture the child they'd made together; it was to secure their next fix – and that was all. They were so bound up in their own needs, their own desires, that they were unable to see you. They didn't love you, Ellie. They didn't want you. Your *own parents* didn't want you. God, that must hurt. How does that make you feel?'

Ellie's face turns pink.

'You were in the way,' I persist. 'You were a nuisance. You were abandoned, used, misused by them. You were left to crawl around the flat and pick up the sharps that they and their druggy friends had dropped. You were left in a stinking nappy for

112

hours until your bottom was sore. When you were hungry and crying and found your parents slumped on the sofa, when you tried to crawl up beside them to get their attention, you were met with their spaced-out faces, their eyeballs rolling back in their heads. You must have been so scared, Ellie. These were your parents – the ones who were supposed to take care of you, protect you, feed you, love you… who was going to look after you? Who was in charge?'

Ellie says. 'So what? What does that prove? I don't remember any of that, anyway.'

'Just because you don't remember it consciously, it doesn't mean it isn't all stored away in here.' I tap my head. 'You were twelve months old, the same age as Finn is now, when you went into care. But Finn knows you're his mother, right? You carried him in your womb for nine months, it's your voice he heard every day. You're the person who he snuggled up to in the first few months of his life, who gave him his first experience of security. He was a helpless baby. He needed you, just like you needed *your* mother. But she wasn't there for you. No one was.'

Ellie bites her lip.

'There is no granny in Kent, is there Ellie?' I continue. 'You had no mother, no father, no grandparents – no one; no one who had any emotional connection with you whatsoever. All you had was a series of staff members in a care home who had twenty other kids to look after. There was no one who was there just for *you*, to pick you up when you fell over, to stroke your hair and tell you funny stories when you were sad, to wipe away your tears and… and to *love* you, Ellie, to love you, in the way that you so desperately needed, in the way that you deserved.'

Ellie looks away at the window. Her lips are pursed and angry tears are forming in the corners of her eyes. I wait a moment, but she refuses to look at me.

'If there was no one to do that,' I say, allowing the emotion to creep into my voice, 'if there was no one to care for you and be there for you when you needed them most, if no one has ever touched you or held you, or brushed your tears away when you cried… then how could you have ever learned to love your own baby?'

'But I do love him,' Ellie protests. 'I do! I can.'

'No, you don't! You can't. You don't know how! When Finn cries, it's just noise to you. You try. You try to be patient, but he's so demanding. He needs so much from you. You never get any time to yourself. You get so angry with him, so mad, when he needs you that way. After all, no one was ever there for you, so why should he be special, huh?'

'He *is* special,' Ellie says. 'He's beautiful.'

'So were *you*, Ellie. But it wasn't enough, was it? Babies are hard work. They don't stop needing you just because you're tired and at the end of your rope. Finn needed you too much, didn't he? He just wanted everything. He sucked every little drop of energy out of you, he took over your life. You weren't prepared for it. And after a few weeks of this, of trying to do the right thing, you couldn't cope any more. You snapped.'

Ellie shakes her head vigorously, her face contorting in rage and pain, her eyes glistening. 'No!'

'Oh, you didn't mean to,' I say. 'The first time you picked him up a bit too roughly and saw the fingermarks on his arms, you were mortified. You thought to yourself, did I do that? Can I cause a bruise like that, just by holding his arms? But the next time he cried, the only way you could stop him was to slap him – which worked at first, but… but then it didn't any more, and before you knew it you were smacking him regularly. Then one day you punched him in the stomach until you'd winded him. That shut him up, didn't it?'

'No, because I didn't do it!' Ellie sobs.

'Then who did?!' I yell.

'I don't know!' Ellie yells back, tears now streaming down her face. She pulls the sleeves of her top down over her hands and wipes her eyes with them.

I pick up my pen and start tapping it on the desk. 'You don't know?' I repeat, my voice loaded with sarcasm. 'You're his mother! How could you not know? You say no one else looked after him for you, that you were with him all the time. And yet, you don't know how he got these injuries. Your story doesn't add up. It makes no sense. And that's because there *is* no other explanation, is there, Ellie?' I push the photo exhibits across the desk towards her. 'It was *you* who did this to Finn!'

'All right!' Ellie cries angrily. She inhales deeply and licks her lips. 'You can stop now,' she says. 'I get the picture.'

I shake my head. 'But I don't think you do. That's just for starters. After that, once she's made you cry and got you to admit you had a crappy childhood and are unable to empathise with your baby, she's going to go beyond that. She's going to suggest that you've got a bit of a sadistic streak, that you've started to enjoy this power you had over Finn. After all, you had so little control over anything when you were growing up, and here it is at last, the power to finally make another human being shut up and listen to you, to behave the way you want him to. You've beaten Finn, you've burned him with cigarettes and you've fed him salt until he's so sick that he's practically unconscious. If Heather Grainger hadn't arrived when she did, Finn would have died.'

'That's not true!' Ellie protests. 'I was just about to call someone!'

'But you didn't, Ellie. You didn't call anyone and the jury will only have your word that you were going to do so. Heather Grainger says that Finn was barely conscious when she arrived. The jury will want to know why in God's name you hadn't dialled nine-nine-nine already.'

Ellie puts her head in her hands. After a moment, she flicks her hair back and looks up again. 'Because I was scared, OK? I... I knew how it would look, and I was scared.'

'Of what? What is it that you're hiding from me?'

A tiny flicker of fear crosses her face. 'I... I didn't know what was wrong with him, OK? I knew they'd ask me loads of questions, about how he'd got like that, but I didn't know the answers. I was worried they'd take him away from me again if they knew...'

'Knew what?'

'That I'd left him with Marie and gone to work! OK?' she splutters, her eyes wide and frightened.

I look at her in silence for a moment. 'He was with Marie?'

She nods.

'When he became ill?'

She hesitates. I can see she's thinking hard about what she's about to say. 'Well, I can't remember exactly if he became ill then, or... maybe, was it after he got back? It's hard to...'

'Why are you protecting her, Ellie?'

'I'm not. Marie hasn't done anything wrong.'

116

'Are they threatening you?' I ask her. 'Her and her boyfriend? Are they blackmailing you?'

She looks up at me and sneers, unconvincingly. 'No.'

I put down my pen and look her in the eye. 'Ellie, I know. OK? I know why Marie was babysitting for you. I want to help you, but if I'm to have any chance of properly preparing your case you need to start telling me the truth.'

She looks at me silently for a moment. 'What?' she whispers. 'How…'

'Look at you.' I wave my hand at her. 'You're beautiful. You're immaculately dressed. Your handbag's… what? Louis Vuitton? Or is it Miu Miu? Your perfume… I don't know what that is, but I can tell it's expensive. When you were collecting your property in the cells… then when I went to collect your passport with Marie and I saw what was inside your wardrobe…'

I wait for her to speak. She scrutinises my face, but says nothing.

'Ellie, I saw your underwear,' I confess.

She bites her lip and her neck flushes pink.

'You do realise, don't you, that if this comes out in court and you haven't fully discussed it with Will and me, we're going to be at a disadvantage. We won't be able to defend you properly.'

Ellie looks startled. 'Do they know? The prosecution?'

'Not that I'm aware of. It's not mentioned in any of the statements we've received so far. But we haven't yet seen what Jay has to say.'

She shakes her head. 'He won't give a statement,' she says. 'He won't give evidence against me. He doesn't want anyone to know about… about that.'

I nod, slowly. 'So that's how you met. And why you didn't want me to talk to him.'

Ellie looks down at her lap. She says nothing for a moment. 'If I tell you... if I tell you everything, do you have to tell the court?'

'No. But I think it might be helpful if *you* did.'

'What!' Her mouth drops open. 'How's that going to help? They already think I'm a bad mother. What are they going to say when they find out I'm a whore?'

'I thought the job title was "escort"?'

She gives me a wry smile. 'I thought you wanted me to be straight with you?'

'Look, Ellie, there might not be much difference between an escort and a whore,' I say. 'But there's a big difference between making mistakes as a parent and deliberately hurting your child. Most of us do the former. The latter is what you're being prosecuted for.'

Ellie sighs, heavily. 'It would be in the papers. Everyone would know.'

'That's probably true. But it's not illegal, and it hasn't necessarily harmed Finn. So long as you've been careful...'

'I'm always careful.'

'... and you haven't got involved with drugs.'

'I wouldn't touch that muck.'

'Then, you haven't done anything wrong, not in the eyes of the law, anyway. Whereas if you're locked up for... for *this*... well, it's unlikely you'll ever see Finn again.'

Ellie squeezes her eyes shut. A teardrop escapes. She moves her head sharply down and her forehead furrows. After a moment she opens her eyes and looks up at me. 'But I might not ever see him again,' she says, her voice barely more than a whisper. 'I don't know if I'm ever going to see him again, do I?'

I take a deep breath. I lean forward and touch her hand.

'It's been over two weeks and he's still alive, Ellie. There's still hope.'

She shakes her head, her eyes brimming with tears again. 'Have you any idea what this is like?' she asks. 'Waking up every day, without him. Every day, it's like I'm there in the hospital again, seeing my baby's blood all over the floor... seeing him lying there unconscious and watching the doctors trying to save his life. I didn't even have a chance to kiss him goodbye. The cops dragged me away. That was the last time I saw him. I spend a week in prison, not knowing if he was going to live or die, and now this... It's killing me,' she sobs. 'Not seeing him, not being able to hold him and be with him. It's tearing me apart!' She waves her hands at the photo exhibits. 'Do you think I don't want to know who did all this stuff, who pulled that fucking tube out? Do you think I don't worry, every minute of every day, that it's going to happen again?'

I nod. I know the kind of fear that she's describing – the icy kind of fear that clutches at your stomach, that lives with you, hour after hour, day after day.

'We can't stop time while we wait for Finn to get better,' I tell her. 'We have to prepare your case. What happened in the hospital... well, the evidence against you is largely circumstantial. We'll explore that further once we get the CCTV. But who caused the injuries, how and what he swallowed on the day he was admitted to hospital... this is crucial to the case as a whole. Finn was in your care. At this moment in time, the finger is pointing at you, fairly and squarely. If you didn't hurt Finn – and I believe you that you didn't – you are going to need to tell the court who did. You need to tell the truth.'

Ellie turns her tear-streaked face towards the window again for a minute, and then says, 'I don't want to get Marie into trouble.'

'Ellie!' I shake my head, my voice rising in disbelief. 'Don't you care that he's been poisoned while she was looking after him? If it was me, I'd have been banging her front door down, demanding to know what she's done to my child.'

'But I don't think she hurt Finn. She'd never hurt Finn.'

'So you've never even confronted her about any of this?'

'Of course I have. I asked her about it, all of it,' Ellie protests. 'She said she didn't know.'

'And that was good enough for you? You just accepted that and handed Finn back over to her?'

'No! It wasn't like that!'

'Well, what was it like, then?' I demand.

She looks up, plaintively. 'I thought the bruises were accidental. I really did. That's what the expert said.' She catches my eye and corrects herself. 'That's kind of what he said. But I didn't know then what I know now...' She tails off.

I pull my computer keyboard towards me and open a new document. 'Go on.'

Ellie pulls her sleeves down over her hands again and wipes at her eyes. 'I did notice some bruises a few times,' she says. 'But they were small, and there weren't that many, nothing like that.' She waves her hand at the exhibits, which are now stacked into a pile on the corner of my desk. 'I bruise easily,' she adds. 'I just thought Finn did too. He learned to sit up and then he was crawling and then he was pulling himself up onto furniture and falling down again all the time, and... But those pictures... I honestly didn't realise he had so many bruises. I'd been away.'

'Away?'

'The week before he got that virus and went into hospital. I'd been away with a client. An overseas booking. He was a… a politician. Quite a well-known one.' She glances up at me and I think for a moment that she's going to tell me who it is. 'When I got back and picked Finn up from Marie and got him changed for bed, I was really shocked, and worried, when I saw how many bruises he had, and that big one… the one on his tummy. I'd never seen that before, I swear. But I still thought they must have been an accident. Once he was on the move, there was no stopping him. He could climb onto anything, the sofa, the coffee table… he was always falling off.'

'And the cigarette burns?'

'I thought he had impetigo.'

I look up from the computer screen. 'Impetigo?'

'I had it when I was a kid,' she explains. 'That's kind of what it looks like. I never… I never thought for even a moment that someone had burned him.'

'So, did you take him to the doctor?'

'It wasn't that bad.' She looks up. 'I mean, obviously it was if it was what they're saying it was. But I thought it was just a few… scabs. I always used to have to just keep them clean. You're not supposed to do anything about impetigo unless it gets infected.'

I tap at my keyboard and she waits for me to catch up with what she's said, before adding, 'I can't believe Marie would do that. She wouldn't do anything to hurt him. Not on purpose.'

'Maybe not on purpose. But she drinks and she smokes and she's clumsy, Ellie. She nearly set fire to her carpet when I was there. And then there's her boyfriend. Darren.'

'You met Darren?'

'Yes. Tell me about him.'

Ellie pushes a strand of hair behind her ear, sighs and looks away at the window again. 'His name's Darren Webb. They've been together ages. I thought he was OK. I even kind of liked him. I mean, I knew he was a bit... I knew he liked a drink and that. I knew they argued, him and Marie. But it didn't seem anything to worry about. But now I know other things about him. I've heard stuff. And when I got arrested the first time, he threatened me. He was waiting outside the police station when they released me on bail.'

I look up. 'What did he say?'

'He said that if I dragged him into any of this, he'd tell Social Services that I was a hooker and I'd never see Finn again.'

I stop typing and look at her. 'He threatened you?'

'Yes. And I believed him. Especially later, when I found out...'

'What?'

'That he's a drug dealer. I've seen people coming and going from Marie's flat. I've seen people getting into his car on the back of the estate. And I've heard he carries a knife.'

'So is it possible that he did these things to Finn?'

'Well, yes. Of course it's possible.' She glances at me. 'And I feel terrible. I would never have left Finn anywhere near him if I'd known.'

I think about this for a moment. 'Is it possible that Darren left drugs lying around? That Finn could have swallowed something, the day he fell ill?'

She shrugs. 'Well, yeah. Of course it is. Like I said, Finn was into everything... every cupboard, every drawer. But if you say anything... he'll just deny it. How are you going to prove it was him?'

'I don't know yet. But in the meantime, you need to tell me the truth about their involvement with Finn, his and Marie's.'

'OK,' she agrees.

'So, when did Marie start looking after him?'

'From day one,' she says. 'Pretty much. Well, not day one, obviously, but she had him a few times for me, here and there from when he was around three months old. And then when he was a bit bigger, I just took on more and more work.'

'So when did you first start to leave him for any length of time?'

'I don't know. When he was around five or six months old, I suppose. Marie started having him overnight.'

I flick through my bundle of papers and pull out the statement of the A&E nurses. 'So would that coincide with when the bruises first began to appear?'

'Yes. Probably.'

'Do you have any dates? Dates that you worked?'

'I didn't keep a diary. I would just get a call asking me to work, and I'd go. I kept it all in here.' She taps her head.

'Who was in charge of your bookings?'

'The agency. It's called Charms of Chelsea. It's just off Sloane Square.'

I tap Ellie's words into the computer. 'So, can you speak to them? They must have a record.'

'OK.'

'Get the dates, and then we'll go through the statements in detail. So... if Darren knew what you were doing, presumably Marie knew too?'

'Yes. It was a friend of hers who introduced me to the agency. She got me into it in the first place.'

'Really?'

'Her friend, not Marie. Marie isn't really cut out for the escort business.'

'No. I can… I can see that wouldn't be an obvious choice for her.'

Ellie says, 'She hasn't always looked how she does now. She used to be quite slim. But it wasn't for her anyway. She said she'd rather have a pint than a shag.'

'She likes a drink, does she?'

Ellie frowns. 'She's not an alcoholic, if that's what you're saying.'

'She was drunk when I was there.'

'Maybe, but she's not like that all the time.' She looks up. 'Marie's a good friend,' she insists. 'And she was willing to have Finn whenever I wanted, and keep him overnight. She's just next door. It was easy. I thought I was doing the right thing, for me and for Finn; I was just trying to earn enough money to get a better life for us both, to get us off the estate.'

'So, how much did you earn?'

'Anything between a hundred and fifteen hundred pounds per client. It would depend.'

I nod, quickly. I know what it depends on; I don't need the detail.

'And how much did you pay Marie?'

'I paid her well. It depends on what I earned but if I was out all night she'd get a hundred plus.'

'OK. So how often would she have Finn?'

'Whenever I got work. It could be one night per week or three or four clients in one day.'

I try my hardest not to picture this. 'So, is it fair to say that there were weeks when you weren't at home very much?'

'Yes.'

'And Marie would have Finn every time?'

'Yes. She was really good. I could just get a call, pick Finn up with his things and take him next door five minutes later. She'd have him overnight for as long as I needed her to.'

'Well, I'm not surprised. I expect she was more than happy to have him; she must have been making pretty good money herself. But what about Jay? Why didn't you ask him? Or his parents?'

Ellie shakes her head. 'Jay's mum offered to babysit, but I just told her I was breastfeeding Finn and couldn't express much milk. I think Jay knew that that wasn't true, but he didn't want her to get wind of what I did for a living any more than I did.'

'So was there ever a genuine relationship between the two of you?'

Ellie hesitates for a moment. 'No. Although... he was a regular client. I saw him for at least six months before I fell pregnant.'

'So, how did that happen? If you're always careful?'

Ellie shrugs. 'I was sick, messed up with my pills that month. I always make them use a rubber anyway. But he liked to do it without. He was always asking and just the one time I let him. I never did that for anyone else.'

I look at her. 'Do you think you were falling for him?'

Ellie doesn't answer.

'Did he have feelings for you?'

Ellie shakes her head. 'I don't think so. I don't know. But I'm not stupid. He was never going to marry me, a hooker from

125

a housing estate. He would never have done anything about it if he had.'

*

By the time we've been through the toxicology report and I've taken details of what Ellie's given Finn to eat, I can see that she's had enough. We still don't know if the evidence from the agency nurse will be admissible and there's nothing yet from the doctors, so I tell her that we will call it a day.

I follow her down the stairs into the reception area. 'Ellie, tell me something,' I ask. 'About the escorting.'

'I've stopped,' she says, quickly. 'I'm not doing it any more, I promise. That last one… the one last week. That was a one-off. I owed him. He'd bought me a lot of nice clothes and stuff. But I can't risk it any more. They'll hold it against me. I can't risk losing Finn.'

'That wasn't what I was going to ask, actually.'

She turns to face me. 'Oh. So, what? You want an introduction?' she asks.

I laugh and glance over at Lucy who, fortunately, has her headphones on and is busy typing.

'You've got a good figure. You're pretty,' Ellie adds. 'You could make some good money.'

'Thanks,' I smile. 'I'll bear that in mind when the next round of legal aid cuts comes in. But what I want to know is, what do you talk about? I mean, isn't the idea behind escorting that you provide great company and witty, sparkling conversation and generally make the man feel as though he's on a first date, albeit one that comes with a guarantee of sex at the end?'

'Pretty much,' she agrees.

'So, don't take this the wrong way, but conversation doesn't exactly seem to be your thing. What do you talk about?'

Ellie looks at me for a moment. 'Cars,' she says.

'Cars?'

'I watch *Top Gear* and I read the *Telegraph*. That pretty much covers it. After that you just have to listen.'

I smile. 'I'd bet you could teach us women a thing or two about men.'

Ellie shrugs. 'There's only one thing you need to know about men.'

'What's that?'

'They're not women,' she says, before pushing the door open and walking out into the street.

8

The public entrance to the Old Bailey is tailed back with visitors, all queuing for a seat at the high-profile murder trial that is going on in Court Two. I walk round the corner past the swarms of journalists and video crews to the lawyers' entrance, where I show my ID and am directed through the glass doors inside. My bag is checked and I am patted down by security before I'm allowed to walk through the entrance and up the staircase into the imposing stone hallway of the Central Criminal Court. Above the marbled grey walls and lemon vaulted ceiling, sunlight is spilling through the glass of three magnificent muralled domes onto the polished mosaic floor below. As always, I am awed by the intricate collision of arches and slopes, by the sombre stillness that surrounds me.

Will is outside Court One in his wig and gown. He glances up from his brief when he sees me. 'Good morning, Ms Kellerman. Is your client here?'

I shake my head. 'Not yet. But we need to talk. I got you a coffee.' I hand him a paper cup, take his arm, and steer him into one of the nearby alcoves. I pull a handful of sugar sachets and a wooden stirrer out of the zip-up pocket of my handbag and slide them across the table towards him. 'So.' I lower my voice. 'Do you want the good news or the bad news?'

Will screws up his face and picks up his coffee cup. 'Don't tell me – she's not coming?'

'No, no – it's not that. She's on her way.' I hold up my phone to show him the text I've just received from Ellie. 'And not only that, but she has a defence. A credible one.'

'Really? What is it?'

'She's a hooker, not a hairdresser.' I smile.

Will splutters a little and puts down his cup. 'That's her defence?'

'Yes. And so... she was at work when Finn was injured, and again when he was poisoned. Her neighbour was babysitting.'

Will cocks his head to one side. 'So is that the good news or the bad news?'

'It's both. I know. It's a tricky one.'

Will scratches his head. 'It won't sit well with a jury, that's for sure. But I suppose it explains why she didn't mention anything to the police.'

I nod. 'She knew how it would look. She didn't want anyone to know.'

'But we're going to tell them, is that right?'

I put down my coffee and look him in the eye. 'The thing is, Will, I think we have to. It's the only angle we've got: Ellie didn't do it because she wasn't there. She's going to get me a list of her bookings from the agency that she worked for, which will prove that she was out with clients on numerous occasions between the dates that the injuries first started to appear and Finn's first hospitalisation in April. Most notably, she was away on an overseas trip with a client – a well-known politician, apparently – the week before Finn went into hospital and the medical exhibits were taken. She says she had no idea the injuries were that bad until she got home. And then she was arrested and Finn was taken away from her.'

Will nods, slowly, as he takes this in. 'So who's the babysitter?'

'Her next-door neighbour, Marie.'

'So Marie caused the injuries, is that what we're saying?'

'Her… or her boyfriend, Darren Webb. They both drink. He knocks her about. He threatened Ellie. He might have caused the injuries to Finn.'

'Can we prove it?'

'Not exactly. Marie won't talk to us; Ellie's tried. But we can prove that Ellie was at work, that someone else was looking after Finn. Enough to raise sufficient doubt, surely, especially if Ellie was abroad when the most serious injuries occurred?'

Will narrows his eyes playfully. 'So, come on. Who's the politician?'

'I don't know. To her credit, she didn't tell me.'

Will smiles. 'Ah, yes. Because that would be a breach of the Call Girl Codes of Conduct. But,' he holds up one hand as I snigger into my coffee. 'No, no – don't laugh. It's very admirable that she wishes to abide by the ethical standards of the…' He taps his head. 'No, sorry, I just can't recall the name of her professional body. But you're right. It would be career suicide. She doesn't want to get struck off the… the Roll of Escorts *and* get found guilty of attempted murder.'

'You want me to ask her?' I say, still laughing.

Will grins. 'Yeah. Go on. Let's expose him.'

'Well, the agency won't tell. It *would* be career suicide for them. And anyway, whoever he is, he'll deny it.'

Will smiles and folds his arms. 'Then we'll run the "Mandy Rice-Davies defence".'

131

'Which is?'

'"He would say that, wouldn't he?"'

When I don't answer, Will peers at me. 'You're too young to remember that, aren't you? It's what Mandy-Rice Davies said, in the witness box, during the Profumo affair. She gives evidence that Lord Astor has been having an affair with her. He denies it. When the prosecutor puts it to her – his denial, that is – she says, "He would say that, wouldn't he?" It made her famous.'

'Really? Why?'

'It was irreverent, for the times. The upper crust were still above scrutiny, protected by the class system, and here she was, an ordinary young woman – a call girl, according to the press – telling it like it was, in public. "Dissing him", I think you'd say, these days.'

'Good for her.' I smile. 'But Ellie's not Mandy Rice-Davies, and she doesn't want to be famous. So maybe we could just exhibit her passport instead? With the stamps to show she went in and out of the country at the relevant time.'

'You are absolutely no fun whatsoever,' Will reprimands me. 'OK. Well, at least we've got something to work with now.'

'Exactly,' I agree. 'It also gives us the opportunity to refute any suggestion that Ellie was holed up in a tiny flat with Finn all day, going stir crazy, unable to cope. Far from it. She was getting glammed up and dining out in swanky hotel restaurants, drinking expensive wine and taking compliments from rich men.'

Will raises his eyebrows. 'Taking compliments? Is that a euphemism?'

'I don't know,' I say. 'I've never been in that line of work.'

'Well, I'm sure you'd be very popular,' Will replies, puckering his mouth to stifle a smile. 'If you ever wanted a change of career, that is.'

I laugh. 'Funny. That's what Ellie said.'

Will's face breaks into a grin. 'Seriously? Well, she's right. I'd be your number-one customer.'

'You're a legal aid lawyer,' I say, thumping him on the arm. 'You couldn't afford me.'

'No,' he says, pensively, and sighs. 'Ain't that the truth.' He glances at his watch. 'OK, so, assuming we can show that Ellie left the baby with Marie, who was under the coercive control of her boyfriend… what about the sodium poisoning? Accusing Darren of getting drunk and thumping the child is one thing, but why would he want to poison him?'

'Well, maybe he wouldn't; not deliberately, anyway. There are lots of things that can cause hypernatraemia. Salty food, mistaking salt for sugar in feeds. Dehydration. It was hot in July. Maybe they didn't give him enough to drink. And then there's drugs.'

Will looks up. 'Drugs?'

I nod. 'Word is that Darren Webb is a drug dealer. Finn might have swallowed something.' I reach into my bag and pull out my iPad. I locate the web page that I've bookmarked. 'This is the most up-to-date medical report I can find on drug-induced hypernatraemia. It's written by a committee commissioned by the LCP – the London College of Paediatrics – and I've compared it to the findings in the toxicology report. It says that there have been several reports of drug-induced electrolyte abnormalities and that they can eventually cause congestive heart, liver and renal failure. Failure to drink enough water can also elevate the sodium levels in the blood plasma. The combination can be lethal.' I put down my iPad and look up at Will. 'The whole poisoning thing... it may have been an accident.'

Will hesitates a moment before saying, 'OK, that's helpful.'

I frown. 'Well it is, isn't it? Or at least it will be if we can instruct an expert to say the same. Reasonable doubt is all we need, surely?'

'A confession from your man Darren would be better.' Will smiles. 'And if you can get him to admit to pulling the dialysis line at the hospital while you're at it, we're home and dry.'

I look him in the eye. 'You don't think much of this as a defence?'

Will shrugs. 'We'll ask for the full prosecution toxicology report and run our own tests. But even if they show the presence of drugs, it doesn't prove that it was anyone but Ellie who gave them to him. We're going to need more evidence of Marie and Darren and their involvement if we want to run with it.'

'Well, it's all we've got at the moment,' I tell him. 'So it will have to do for now.'

'All right.' He stands up. 'I'd better get into court. Let me know when she's here.'

Ellie arrives ten minutes later. I collect her from security and show her to a seat in the alcove before slipping into the courtroom and passing a message to the usher for Will. When I get back Ellie is scrolling through her phone. 'Look,' she says. 'I just got this from Marie.'

She reads the message out loud: *Split up with Darren last night. Feel like shit. Call me?*

'Good,' I tell her. 'So, do you think she'll talk to me now? About Darren?'

'I don't know. I'll meet up with her later. I'll find out.'

Will enters the alcove and pulls out a seat.

'OK,' he says, leaning forward and shaking Ellie's hand. 'We've got a bit more time.' To me, he says, 'Judge wants to hear the prosecution's hearsay application today.'

'Really?'

'What does that mean?' Ellie asks.

'The police can't find the nurse,' he tells her. 'Mary Ngombe, the one who says she saw you holding Finn shortly before his dialysis line was removed. She's left the hospital and they've no idea where she's gone. The prosecution are going to ask the judge if they can have the nurse's statement read out at trial.'

Ellie's face falls. 'Can they do that?'

'They can if the judge agrees.'

'So the judge has waived notice?' I ask him.

'Yes. He's put the application back to this afternoon to give us a bit of time. I couldn't reasonably object and it's probably in our interests to get this dealt with sooner rather than later, so that we know where we stand as regards Count Three.'

Ellie frowns. 'What do you mean, where we stand?'

Will turns to her. 'If the judge kicks the prosecution application into touch, then it might be hard for them to prove that you were the last person to have contact with Finn before his dialysis line was tampered with.'

'And if he doesn't?'

'Then the case against you is a lot stronger.'

Ellie's eyes flicker between us. 'So everything is riding on this?'

'Not everything,' I say, quickly, sensing her panic. 'But if the nurse's evidence goes in, we'll have to work much harder to try and convince the jury that it wasn't you.'

135

'We need it out, ideally,' says Will.

'So what's the basis of their application?' I ask him.

'They're relying on subsection d,' says Will, 'that she can't be found and they've taken all reasonable steps to find her.'

'And have they?'

'She's left the nursing agency she worked for. It seems her UK sponsorship and working visa may have expired. They've concluded that she's gone back to Africa. I expect that'll be enough for the judge.'

'So you think they'll win?' asks Ellie, aghast.

'No, not necessarily. But I think the judge will have sympathy with their application, within the context of the case as a whole. Mary Ngombe names you as the person who picked up the baby. It's a material piece of evidence in the prosecution case.'

'The description is all wrong, though,' Ellie protests. 'She says I'm fifteen or sixteen and that I'm wearing a blue scarf. I don't own a blue scarf. And I'm twenty. What, she thinks I had Finn when I was fifteen?'

'It happens. And people aren't always very good with ages,' I tell her.

Will looks at her kindly. 'The problem is that she names you. She says your name is "Ellie" and that she knows you as the baby's mother.'

'But she's lying,' Ellie insists. Her eyes widen and her mouth falls open. 'I don't remember her. I've never even spoken to her, and I never picked up Finn. Why would she say that I did?'

'Well, that's the million-dollar question,' says Will. 'And we aren't going to be able to ask her that if she's not here. But, we have a reasonable chance of kicking her statement out, OK?'

I ask him, 'Is there anything I can do?'

Will chews on his bottom lip. 'You could make enquiries with the agency and find out about the work visa and when it expired. And check her immigration status. If we can show that she's overstayed or worked illegally then it may call into question the reliability of her evidence, her credibility as a witness.' Will pushes his chair back and stands up. 'Let's reconvene at one o'clock. That will also give us time to complete the pre-trial forms and discuss your pleas.'

'There's nothing to discuss,' Ellie says. 'I'm pleading not guilty, all the way.'

Will smiles. 'Fine,' he says. 'We'll talk at one. Don't be late.'

*

I say goodbye to Ellie outside near the main entrance and walk down Ludgate Hill and onto Fleet Street, where the nursing agency is located. It's a tall, modern building constructed of seamless black glass with uninviting privacy windows. Given its popular location, I'm expecting to enter a bustling office where no one really has the time or inclination to speak to me, but when I push open the glass door to the entrance, the office is small and virtually empty, apart from a woman with silver-grey hair, cut into a neat bob, who is wearing a yellow cashmere sweater. She is sitting at a desk in the corner of the room, peering at her computer screen, and doesn't look up.

'Bear with,' she says, as she finishes tapping her keyboard. A small smile plays on her lips when I let out a snicker of laughter at her parody of upper-class Tilly, one of my favourite *Miranda* TV characters. She finishes typing and looks up. 'Done. Fabulasmic.' She removes her half-rim spectacles and beams at me. 'I'm Allison. How can I help?'

'Ah. Allison Davies?' I ask hopefully.

She blinks. 'Yes?'

'Just the person.'

I had been expecting a whole bundle of data protection red tape, but when I show her my identity card and my copy of the statement she's made to the police on behalf of the agency, Allison simply nods, gives me a brisk handshake, and offers me a seat. She tugs at a gold eyeglass-chain around her neck and props her spectacles back onto her nose before tapping at the keyboard again and bringing up Mary Ngombe's file on her computer screen.

'Miss Ngombe,' she says. 'I remember her well.'

'You do?'

Allison contorts her mouth in an exaggerated manner and bites her lip. 'I'm not saying it's right – because it's not,' she explains, 'but there just aren't many experienced black specialist nurses, working in paediatric intensive care. When she came onto our books, she stood out. But she was good. A hard worker. Reliable. The reports back from the hospitals were generally excellent.'

My heart sinks. *Hard-working. Reliable.* This isn't looking promising. We needed Mary Ngombe to be unreliable and untrustworthy, her evidence dubious at the very least.

Allison peers at the computer screen. 'She has a tier-two general visa – three years, term unexpired, but drawing close to the deadline for extension.'

'So, is that maybe why she's disappeared?'

'Well, possibly, although she can apply to extend it for a further two years – more in some circumstances. Her sponsorship has ended, but she's registered with the NMC, and PIC nursing qualifies her to work independently for up to twenty hours per week.' She takes her spectacles off her nose and looks up at me. 'It's a shortage occupation.'

'I see. So... she's in demand.'

'Quite.'

'And, as far as you're aware, she's not overstayed or worked illegally at any time?'

Allison shakes her head. 'No. We vet our nurses very carefully. That wouldn't be allowed to happen.'

'So I wonder why she hasn't come back to you for work?' I ask.

Allison raises her eyes and squints, pensively. 'It was all quite odd, really. Her contract at Southwark St Martin's was due to finish on the Friday, but they wanted to renew, and she'd indicated her intention to do so. Then, out of the blue, she phoned and said that she was leaving us.'

'And she didn't say why?'

'Nope.' Allison shakes her head. 'She just said that her plans had changed. Of course, it's possible that she got a better offer via another agency, but she may have just decided to return home to Ghana. That would be my guess. Possibly she couldn't afford the visa renewal fee.'

'You'd have thought she could have been sponsored again.'

'You'd have thought,' Allison repeats, but it's clear she knows no more than this.

'Who was her first sponsor?' I ask.

'St Bartholomew's. The PICU there. Do you want a name?'

I consider this for a moment. 'Yes. Yes please.'

Allison nods, then turns back to her computer screen, clicks on a link and scrolls down a little, before scribbling a name on a piece of paper and handing it to me. I fold the paper and put it into the zip pocket of my handbag, then reach out and shake her hand.

'Thanks, Allison. You've been extremely helpful.'

'No problemo,' she replies. 'Ciao for now.'

Outside on the street, I look at the clock on my phone. It's half past eleven. There's still an hour and a half before I have to be back at court and I'd noticed signs to St Bart's on the corner next to the Old Bailey, which would mean that it was probably only a short walk away and a matter of minutes back to court again afterwards. It might be cutting it fine, but I have nothing else to do between now and one o'clock, and if I can get any sort of lead on Mary Ngombe's whereabouts, that will at least give Will an argument to present to the judge this afternoon.

As I walk back past the court building, I spot Will on the corner of the street, smoking a cigarette. He has his wig on and his back to me, but I can tell it's him. One of his legs is propped up against the wall outside the building, and I can see a bright green sock protruding, which makes me smile. He turns as I approach him.

'You're not wearing your lucky socks,' I accuse him.

He looks down at his feet and smiles. 'Not today,' he says. 'I don't want to wear them out.' He takes a last puff of his cigarette and squashes it against the railing. 'So where have you been?'

'To the agency.'

'And?'

'No go.' I shake my head. 'Mary Ngombe is a reliable, hard-working paediatric specialist nurse, with a full working visa and a UK sponsor, who I'm just on my way to talk to.'

'Crap. Who's the sponsor?'

'St Bart's ICU. I have a name.' I fumble for the zip of my bag and pull out the piece of paper. 'Mark Greenhalgh,' I say. 'Head of Paediatrics.'

Will nods. 'Good work, Ms Kellerman. Worth talking to him, if you've time.'

'Do you want to come with me?' I venture.

Will shakes his head. 'I've got another mention in Court Eight before lunch. Judge is just out reading the papers. I'd better get back.'

*

My trip to St Bart's paediatrics department is unfruitful. Mark Greenhalgh, it seems, has left the department and moved on to the John Radcliffe Hospital at Oxford to combine his clinical work with a teaching post at the university's Department of Medicine. I'm given a number to call, but it rings out for several moments before eventually diverting to the voicemail of a secretary that I can't be sure is his. Attempts to get through to him via the main switchboard are equally futile and I spend a good forty-five minutes on the phone being passed from department to department and having to start all over again with my explanation as to why I need to find Dr Greenhalgh today, rather than tomorrow. Eventually I extract a promise from a helpful assistant to a consultant in the outpatients department that she will track down Dr Greenhalgh and have him call me back as soon as she can.

It seems that Will should have worn his lucky socks after all because on my return to court, and after a twenty-minute hearing – during which Ellie becomes increasingly agitated at the prosecutor's assertions against her – the judge finds that

Mary Ngombe's statement should be admitted in evidence as 'a reliable account from an independent medical professional' which, if excluded, would result in considerable unfairness to the prosecution.

'Jesus Christ,' Ellie proclaims loudly as he delivers his judgment.

'My Lord,' Will leaps up. 'The probative value of this statement, as weighed up against the prejudice to the defendant—'

'Any prejudice to the defendant,' interrupts Judge Collins, who is suntanned and irritable, no doubt wishing himself still on his holiday in Malta, 'can be dealt with by way of a direction to the jury. They'll be made fully aware of the circumstances behind the statement's admission and the weight that should attached.'

'But, My Lord—'

Judge Collins simultaneously lifts one hand and takes off his glasses with the other. He rubs hard at each eye in turn, before putting his glasses back on. 'I'm satisfied that it's in the interests of justice to admit this statement, Mr Gaskin. I'm persuaded as to its importance in the context of the case as a whole and by the fact that it's a statement made immediately after the event by an independent professional witness. I've given my judgment.'

'Yes, My Lord.' Will sits down.

The judge continues. 'Ms Stephens has entered her pleas and directions have been made. The trial will begin on the fifth of February next year. It will be listed for five days. Any issues that are likely to affect trial readiness are to be notified to the Court a fortnight before the opening of the prosecution case. Court rise.'

'It wasn't me!' Ellie yells as the judge exits the courtroom. 'It wasn't me,' she yells again at the prosecutor as the usher lets her out of the dock. Carmel simply blinks at Ellie and continues to gather her papers and pack them into a flight case at her feet. She turns to talk to Will as he approaches her.

I take Ellie's elbow and steer her out of the courtroom. 'It's a setback,' I tell her. 'But it's not fatal to your case. As the judge said, the jury will be warned that her evidence has not been tested. Challenged, you know? And they'll be told to bear that in mind.'

'No,' Ellie says, flinging her handbag over her shoulder and flicking back her hair angrily. Her voice echoes around the hallway, breaking the silent stillness of the air. 'No, what he said is that she's a nurse, an upstanding member of society, and I'm just a scumbag whore. He's made his mind up already who to believe.'

'When it comes to the making up of minds about you, it's not his decision, Ellie, it's the jury's,' I tell her. 'And no one knows about that yet…'

'Yeah, great,' says Ellie, her lip curling up. 'So, if this is how things are playing out now, what with a piece of paper – written by a copper and supposedly signed by a nurse that nobody can find – being more important than a real person, whose life is in the balance, then what are they going to say when they find *that* out about me?'

I glance at Will, who has appeared behind us. 'I'm sorry, Ellie,' he says. 'I know you're disappointed. I am too.'

Ellie looks at him for a moment. 'It's not your fault,' she says, calming down a little. 'You did a good job. Thank you.'

Will says, 'Let's meet again in a week or two and, in the meantime, see if you can get Marie on board.'

'OK.' Ellie nods. She heaves a sigh and taps my arm. 'I'll see you, Sarah.'

Will and I watch as she strides off across the hallway and disappears down the staircase.

I heave a sigh. 'You can't blame her for being upset.'

'At least she's talking to us now,' Will says. 'I don't know what you've done to get through to her, but the angry, involved Ellie is a damned sight more useful to us than the sullen, silent one.'

'Hmm. Well my next job is to try and take a statement from Marie before she goes and makes up with the indomitable Darren.'

Will puts his hand on my arm. 'OK. But first, let me buy you a drink.'

I shake my head. 'I should get back to the office.'

Will frowns.

'They're on my case a bit,' I add.

'Really?'

'Don't ask.'

Will looks disappointed. 'I was just going to suggest we finish up our conference over a nice bottle of Sauvignon at Ye Olde Cheshire Cheese off Shoe Lane. It's where I do all my best thinking.'

'I'm sorry,' I say. 'Another time. So what happened in there...' I nod my head towards the courtroom. 'Is it appealable?'

Will shakes his head. 'Probably not. I think we're just going to have to suck this one up.'

'Unless...'

Will rolls his eyes. 'No. Whatever it is, I don't want to hear it.'

I bite my lip and try to stop myself from smirking.

Will gives in and smiles.

'OK,' I tell him. 'What would you say if I could find the nurse?'

'You want to find the nurse?'

'Sure I do. If I find the nurse, then subsection d doesn't apply. She's no longer missing. They'd have to rescind their application...'

'And call her to give evidence, during which she might make a positive identification of Ellie!'

'She might not. What if she doesn't?'

'What if she does?'

'What if she doesn't?'

Will sighs. 'So you're going to go looking for her? How are you going to do that?'

I shrug. 'Dunno yet. So what do you think?'

Will narrows his eyes. 'I think she's a prosecution witness.'

'An independent one, as Judge Collins kept reminding us.'

'I think you'll be playing with fire.'

'What's the alternative? Let Ellie get convicted on the basis of hearsay and circumstance? Because, you and I both know that that will be the outcome unless we find out what really happened.'

Will looks me in the eye. 'Unless what really happened is that Ellie tried to kill her baby.'

'But what if she didn't?'

'Then who did?'

'I don't know. But if Ellie's telling the truth, then it points to one of two things: either the police have missed someone going on or off the ward – or it was one of the nurses. Someone who was already working on the ward that night.'

'An angel of mercy? Of death? Is that what you're suggesting?' Will frowns. 'Some kind of crazy nurse?'

I shrug. 'Possibly. Or maybe it was an accident. Look, we need the CCTV. We need to view it for ourselves. We need to ask around at the hospital, find out who else was working on the ward that night, if anyone saw anything that could help us. We need to find Mary Ngombe, ask her some questions, scrutinise her account. Don't you think it's even a tiny bit weird that she disappeared so suddenly, so soon after what happened to Finn?'

Will regards me in silence for a moment, his face inscrutable. 'So, will the legal aid fund pay for you to hunt down the nurse?' he says finally.

'I'll do it on my own time.'

Will shakes his head. 'Don't you have enough going on in your life, Ms Kellerman?'

'Yeah, well...' I smile. 'You know what they say: if you want something done, ask a busy person.' I look up at him. 'So you're in?'

'OK.' Will nods. He takes off his glasses and studies my face. 'But only because I don't think you'll find her.'

I look him in the eye and bite my lip. 'Care to make this interesting?'

Will's eyes widen. 'You want to place a bet with me?'

I hold out my hand. 'A bottle of Sauvignon at Ye Olde Cheshire Cheese says I can find the nurse.'

Will looks at me for a moment, poker-faced, before taking my hand. 'A bottle of Sauvignon it is.'

'May the best man – or woman – win,' I add.

The corners of Will's mouth twitch. 'I certainly hope so,' he says.

9

Anna and Tim arrive just before seven on Saturday evening. Alex knocks at the door a few minutes later. Ben is momentarily alarmed by the number of people who have suddenly appeared in his living room, but the lure of the computer screen in front of him is enough to allay the usual wails of protest and the fight to get away. Instead, he clutches the mouse firmly in his right hand and clicks on the 'play' button on the YouTube video that I've opened for him on the screen, the noise and music softening the sound of our voices and taking him away into Teletubby world.

'He's doing really well with that,' Alex comments, nodding at Ben. 'Has he been using it a lot?'

'All the time,' I say. 'He's completely motivated. He's even worked out how to drag the cursor back on the video clip to rewind it. I can't get him out of the chair – unless it's to get the DVD player going in sync,' I add, with a smile.

'He's dual screening.' Alex gives a pretend roll of the eyes. 'They're all the same, the kids of today.'

I smile back at him. I love it when he talks like this, as if Ben's just like other kids, even though we both know that he's not. Other five-year-olds actually watch the video, they don't keep rewinding it and watching the same bit, over and over again.

But it makes me feel good when Alex talks this way. 'Thank you so much for the computer,' I say, gratefully. 'I just can't believe how he's picked it up, using a mouse like that.'

'I honestly only had to show him a couple of times,' Alex said. 'He just seemed to get it.'

'He's still bringing all his fingers down together, you know, left and right clicking at the same time. He can't isolate his index finger yet, so he keeps on bringing up a pop-up box every time he clicks,' I say, 'but it doesn't seem to bother him.'

'He'll get there.' Alex walks over and ruffles Ben's hair. 'We can work on that, can't we, buddy?'

I laugh as Ben lets out a loud 'Aargh!' which I know from experience means, 'What use is a pat on the head? Either do something to help me, or step away.'

Anna is watching us both keenly as we talk, looking from one to the other. She says to Alex, 'I hear you were responsible for Ben's first steps.'

Alex looks pleased but says, modestly, 'He was nearly there anyway. The groundwork was all laid by his mother.' With that, he gives me an admiring smile.

'She's pretty amazing,' Anna tells him.

Alex sits down, leans back into the sofa and says, 'I'm not going to argue with that.'

'OK,' I say to Anna, hastily steering the conversation away from my virtues and on to the practicalities. 'Ben's had a bath and some dinner, so he should be getting tired and ready for bed in half an hour or so. He likes his music played when he goes down. And then there's his medication. Let me show you.'

I glance at Ben.

'Leave him,' says Alex. 'He's happy. He's fine with us.'

I nod and beckon to Anna and she follows me down the hall and into Ben's room.

'He bought Ben a computer?' Anna whispers, shutting the door and nodding her head towards the living room. Her eyes widen.

I shrug. 'It's just an old recycled one of his that he doesn't use any more.'

'Even so... he's so lovely. He's so sweet with Ben. And so handsome,' she gushes.

'I know,' I agree. 'He *is* just a bit perfect, isn't he? That's the thing. I just don't quite get why he likes me.'

'Sarah! Why wouldn't he?' Anna objects. 'You're smart, you're pretty, you're funny... and, well, you've got the boobs, haven't you?'

I slap her playfully on the arm. 'You think that's it?'

'No, of course not. It's everything. The whole package.'

'Yeah, exactly. The whole package, which includes Ben. That's what worries me. Why would a good-looking man, who's got a good job, a nice car, his own hair and teeth...'

'How do you know they're his own teeth?'

I slap her on the arm again. 'He's the real deal, isn't he? He's what women want. And if he's what women want, then he could have any woman he wanted. Why go for one with a child like Ben?'

Anna contemplates this for a moment and I'm glad she doesn't say something crass about Ben being a lovely boy. He *is* a lovely boy, of course – to me. But there's no denying that he's hard work.

'Maybe he genuinely likes Ben. Maybe he sees how difficult life is for you and wants to help you both.'

'Well, that's what he says.'

'So maybe it's true?'

I look her in the eye. 'Ben's vulnerable. He can't talk. My biggest fear is that someone might hurt him and he wouldn't be able to tell me.'

Anna considers this for a moment. 'But that could be true of anyone, couldn't it? Are you telling me you're never going to have a boyfriend again, just in case?'

She walks over to the window and I join her. We look out at the overgrown tumble of bindweed and morning glory that borders the patio, at the wild buckwheat that's invaded my pot plants over the summer.

'Thing is, Sarah, you're vulnerable too. Isn't it more likely that Alex is just a nice bloke who's turned into a knight in shining armour after meeting a damsel in distress?'

'Probably,' I agree.

'What do your instincts tell you?'

'What you just said.'

'Well there you go. Listen to your instincts and give him the benefit of the doubt. If he says or does anything that sets off alarm bells, you'll know what to do to protect Ben.' She smiles. 'You know, since us women got the vote, and the right to own land and property and go out to work and bring home our own bacon, there are a lot of displaced men out there whose instincts are still to be the provider, the protector, and a lot of women just don't want or need that role any more. Maybe you just tick all the boxes for him. Maybe you're exactly what he wants.'

'Well, I hope he doesn't want a doormat,' I tell her. 'I'm not that person, either.'

'Hardly. Anyone can see that you have remarkable inner strength; that's almost certainly one of the things he likes about you. But maybe he's been hurt in the past; and maybe he's aware that you're not in a position to run off with someone else and hurt him quite so easily as the next person. Maybe you make him feel safe in that way, and good about himself at the same time for helping you.'

I look up. 'Maybe you're right.'

'And you know, he's attracted to you, you're attracted to him. That sort of thing doesn't come along every day, no matter how good-looking and eligible you are. Maybe he could have any woman he wanted, but you still have to click with someone, and maybe he just didn't find anyone he clicked with until he met you.'

I put up my hand. 'OK. Sold,' I smile, 'to the lady in the red dress.'

'Who looks lovely, by the way. Radiant.' Anna smiles and tucks a strand of my hair behind my ear.

I take her hand. 'Thanks so much for this, Anna. I hope he's OK for you. He might wake up. He can be a bit difficult. He sometimes gets upset and it's hard to know what's wrong.'

'We'll cope, don't worry.' She smiles, reassuringly.

'I'm going to be a bag of nerves.'

'No, you're not, you're going to have an amazing night out.'

'But if anything happens... if he has a seizure... There are things that you need to watch out for, certain signs...'

'Sarah, I'm married to a nurse,' she says, nodding towards the door. 'Tim will know what to do.'

'Of course he will. That's reassuring.' I put my arms round her. 'Thanks so much, Anna. I mean it.'

'Any time,' she says, pulling me to her and hugging me back. 'And I mean *that*.'

I smile, wryly. 'So, can I tell Gareth that I'll go on the police station rota?'

'No, you can't,' Anna reprimands me. 'I'm not doing this for your work colleagues. I'm doing this for *you*.'

When we get back to the living room, Ben is still playing the same section of the same Teletubby clip. Alex and Tim are standing near the window, looking out at Alex's BMW and talking about cars. I think of Ellie's comments to me, about men, and smile to myself.

Alex turns as we enter the room. 'Ready?'

'In a minute. Tim, before we go, can I ask you a question?' I say. 'How would I go about tracking down a nurse who worked in the paediatric intensive care unit at St Martin's earlier this year?'

'Hmm. Do you have a name?' Tim asks.

'Yes. Mary Ngombe. She's African, worked there as an agency nurse apparently. She was originally seconded to the paediatric department at St Bart's, but then moved to St Martin's when her sponsorship ended. Now she's left the hospital and no one knows where she's gone.'

'Back to Africa?' Anna suggests. 'Isn't that what you said?'

'Possibly,' I say. 'But they don't know that for sure.'

'Well, she'd have to be a registered children's nurse,' Tim says. 'Which involves a lot of extra training, so you don't normally go through that unless you're making it a career choice. So if she's still in the country, it means she would probably be in a neonatal or paediatric ward somewhere else now. It's actually a fairly small world, especially somewhere like PICU.'

'Do you know her? Have you ever worked as a children's nurse?'

Tim shakes his head. 'No, but my friend Shelley has, and she's worked at St Bart's PICU too. I could speak to her.'

'Why do you want to find this nurse?' asks Alex.

'She's given a statement to the police, and it's going to be read in court under the hearsay provisions. It's fairly damning, and yet there are gaps in her account, which we can no longer test because she won't be there to give live evidence. If I can find her, then she'll have to come to court. It's the only way to stop her statement going in as it is.'

'Can you do that?' Alex asks. 'Are you allowed to talk to a prosecution witness?'

'We don't usually, for very good reasons. But there's no property in a witness,' I explain. 'Which means that no one can "own" her. So technically there's nothing to stop me talking to her and taking my own statement. And in these circumstances I think it's worth the risk.'

'I'll speak to Shelley,' Tim says. 'See if she knows her, or anyone else who might. I'll get you the names of the main nursing agencies, too. If she hasn't left the country, she might be on someone's books somewhere. They might tell you something.'

'Thanks, Tim,' I tell him. 'I appreciate that.'

*

Alex drives into the West End and finds a parking space in a backstreet somewhere behind the British Museum. We stroll through Bloomsbury Square Gardens and down to Covent Garden, where we eat dinner at a lovely fish restaurant. I also drink two glasses of prosecco while Alex sips at a Beck's Blue. It's been so long since I've been out anywhere really nice for dinner that I can't help but feel a little like an impostor as the waiter pulls back my chair and tucks me under the table, the starched white tablecloth brushing my bare knees. For some reason, Ellie slips into my mind as I unfold the thick, soft linen napkin in front of me and pick up the heavy cutlery. I wonder what it's like to eat dinner with someone, knowing that in an hour or two you'll be the dessert. Did she go to the same hotel restaurant each time, I wonder? Did the waiters know her by sight? Was it a ritual for them, to greet her and run down the specials board for her? And is there a particular meal choice that's lighter on the stomach, one that's less likely to tug at her suspender belt or produce acid reflux when bouncing around or bending over? You wouldn't want to eat beans, that's for sure.

'Something funny?' Alex smiles. He puts down his fork.

'Oh,' I laugh. 'No. No, not at all. I was just… just wondering what it would be like to eat out like this all the time.'

'You'd like to?'

'Who wouldn't?' I smile. 'That wasn't a hint,' I add, hastily.

Alex wipes his mouth and folds his napkin, placing it on the table in front of him. 'If I'm honest,' he says, 'it was just as nice eating hard-boiled eggs and olives out of Tupperware pots with you last Saturday, lying on a blanket in the shade of a sycamore tree.'

I'm secretly touched that he might feel this way, and hope suddenly that he doesn't think that being wined and dined is what I expect from him. 'I agree. Who needs fancy meals?' I ask, and then jokingly grab the edges of my plate. 'Although, I'll fight the person who tries to take this sea bass away from me.'

Alex looks at me seriously for a moment, his eyes flicking up to meet mine and watching my face. I was only making a throwaway comment – a joke – but it appears as though I've somehow said something that matters, that's caused him pain. I think back to my jokes with Will about his earnings and hope that I haven't touched a nerve this time. Maybe that's why Alex doesn't want to talk about his job? Maybe, like Will, he doesn't earn as much money as people might think. Maybe his work is tough, commission-based, insecure; after all, the economic outlook is pretty uncertain at the moment. Maybe he's worried about his financial future and is checking me out to see how much all of this matters to me? I hope he doesn't think that I'm one of those women who is looking for a rich husband, someone who's ready to dump him as soon as his true prospects are revealed.

'I mean, it doesn't matter, does it?' I add, hastily. 'You're right. This is very nice, but… I agree. A picnic in the park is just as special. Money can't buy you happiness, after all.'

Alex smiles back at me, suddenly, as if he's only just become aware that he's frowning. 'Money *can* buy happiness,' he says. 'At least, to the extent that you have a roof over your head and enough to eat, and that you don't have to work for someone you dislike or lie awake at night worrying about how to pay the bills. But once you have a certain level of financial security, I don't think that having any extra after that is… well, it's not going to make you any happier.'

'So, you don't long to drive a Ferrari and retire at fifty?' I smile. My experience is that most men want exactly that: wealth and status in some form or another. Andy was always talking about how much he was going to earn and what he was going to own one day.

Alex gives me a long hard look. 'No, not really. Those things

155

don't matter, at least, not for long. We always want more. It's human nature. As soon as we get something, it's no longer enough, or at least that's how it can be if we don't pay attention to where happiness really comes from.'

'Within?' I smile.

'Actually, no. Research has shown that it's our social connections and the experiences we have together that are most important. Friendship, basically, is what makes us happy.'

I consider this. 'OK. So... what about hearing an amazing piece of music, reading an inspiring book, or... or fulfilling your creative aspirations?'

'Well, yes. But again, they're all free,' says Alex. 'More or less. You don't need to buy a lottery ticket to do any of that.'

'Except that you need the time,' I say. 'To study, create something or pursue your dreams. And time is money, after all. Or, at least, money buys you time.'

'Maybe. But then again, the harder time you have achieving what you want, the better it feels when you get it, isn't that right? You fly to the top of a mountain in a helicopter and the view is amazing, but you won't get that same feeling that you'll get when you've spent a month of sweat, blood and tears climbing up there from the ground. The greater the well of your misfortune, the deeper your capacity for happiness – I think that's how it goes. Look at what you've been through with Ben. You must have experienced some real lows.'

I smile. 'Just a few. Are you going to tell me that my reward will be in heaven?'

'Lord no.' Alex grins and takes my hand across the table. 'A little sooner than that, I'd say.'

*

We walk to a nightclub on Great Queen Street, just off Drury Lane. I feel alive, as though I'm walking on air – as though I'm twenty again – as we stroll along the pavement, hand in hand, past the bars and restaurants and the people who are spilling out onto the streets, chatting and laughing and blowing clouds of cigarette smoke into the summer evening air. When we reach the club, Alex nods to the doorman and guides me in, past the cloakroom and down a flight of steps into a basement where music is blasting from the speakers. While Alex goes to the bar, I stand in the darkness, mesmerised by the silhouettes of the dancers and the coloured lights that are flickering across the ceiling. Alex comes back a moment later with a bottle of beer in one hand and a glass of white wine in the other, which he hands to me before circling my waist with his arm and pulling me to him and pressing his cheek against mine. I can smell his aftershave, and it's delicious.

'It's not *Strictly Ballroom*,' he says, his mouth pressed up against my ear. 'But I think you'll like it.'

As if on cue, there is a burst of piano and bass-heavy Motown with a rhythm that makes it impossible not to swing my hips to the beat. Alex smiles and takes my hand and leads me onto the dance floor.

We spend the next two hours dancing; we just can't stop. The music is amazing and bounces back and forth through the decades from the sixties through to the present day. Every time I think that I'll sit the next one out and have a rest, another song comes on that makes me want to get right back onto the dance floor again. Alex leaves me only to fetch us bottles of water from the bar, and we fall into each new rock, funk or disco rhythm with a delighted smile, Alex periodically leaning forward to grab my hand, twist me round or mouth something to me over the music.

'I knew you'd be a great dancer,' he says, pressing his mouth up against my ear.

Occasionally I pull my phone out of my bag and peer at the latest text message from Anna, but there's never any cause for concern. Her periodic updates say simply, *Ben's still watching the Teletubbies. Tim's asleep X*; *Tim now watching the Teletubbies, Ben's asleep X*; *All good, both boys fast asleep*; and *Hope you're having a fantastic time, all good here, don't rush back X*.

We tiptoe in at half past two in the morning. Tim is on his back on the sofa, snoring softly, and Anna's curled up on my bed, clutching a pillow, Ben's monitor next to her head and her long legs tucked up neatly underneath her.

'Don't wake them,' Alex whispers. 'It's fine. Forget the cup of tea. I'll just head home.'

'I'm sorry,' I say. 'I should have thought this through… now you have to drive all the way back.'

'It's fine.' Alex puts his finger to his lips as Tim turns over in his sleep, his arm now hanging off the sofa and trailing the floor. He lifts it up and scratches his nose, but he doesn't wake.

Alex leads me gently back out into the hallway and puts his arms round me.

'I've had such a great time,' I tell him.

'Me too,' he says. 'The best time. I'll call you tomorrow, OK? We can make a plan for next week?'

'OK.' I stand on my toes and put my hands behind his neck.

Alex kisses me, gently at first, but then his whole body weight is pressing up against me and we fall back against the wall.

'I want you to stay,' I whisper.

'I want to stay,' he says, and laughs. 'But there's someone in your bed.'

'Next time,' I say.

'Next time,' he repeats and kisses me again. 'Definitely next time.'

When he's gone, I climb into bed next to Anna, pull the duvet over me and lie in the dark awhile, too wired for sleep. Instead, I close my eyes and replay the evening, like a movie soundtrack in the darkness. I recall the easy, interesting conversation over dinner, the flashing lights and music in the club. I feel Alex take my hand, our bodies connecting, and then intertwining, the heat of the club making us hot and sticky as we move against each other.

And then I picture him as he locks his car and walks up the path to my house, his shirt open at the neck and his hair tousled from dancing. I remember the feeling of electric anticipation (would he stay or would he go?) and my heart flutters in my chest as I recall the way he'd held me, and the passion with which he'd kissed me in the hallway and pushed me up against the wall.

And because I don't want the evening to end, I then rewind right back to the restaurant, when Alex had taken my hand across the table top and looked into my eyes. *The greater the well of your misfortune, the deeper your capacity for happiness – I think that's how it goes.* I think about the very deep 'well' of my unhappiness before I met him, the endless nights I'd lain here feeling desperately tired and lonely, as compared with the overflowing elation and overwhelming joy I'm feeling right now. I think about this until I'm ready to fall asleep. I think that it might be the truest thing I've ever known.

10

As Ben's first day at the Samuel Watson School approaches, I'm so anxious that I book the day off work. I'm fully expecting a call from the headteacher before lunchtime to say that he's using up too much in the way of staff resources, that he'll have to come home, that we'll have to explore other options for him; I daren't risk being in court when that happens. I sit in the kitchen with my laptop, drinking coffee and searching on the internet for nursing agencies, glancing intermittently at my phone to check if I've lost my signal or missed a call.

When I've heard nothing by mid-morning – and ensuring that I've got the 'call interrupt' box ticked in my phone settings – I telephone the numbers for the agencies that Tim has given me, followed by a few more that I've found for myself. As I expected, no one can tell me if there's a Mary Ngombe on their books, nor does anyone particularly care why it is that I want to know. One of the agency employees suggests, rather condescendingly, that I need to go through the police and ask them to carry out these enquiries instead. I thank her, but I know from experience that the police won't take the search for the nurse any further than they already have.

By twelve o'clock, I'm convinced I've written my phone number down wrong on the school registration form. The image in my head of Ben, crying loudly and biting his hand as a small crowd of teaching staff looks on helplessly, is too powerful for me to bear. The school receptionist is kind when I call and immediately puts me through to the classroom, where, to my relief, Ben's teacher, Jennie, answers.

I apologise for being a neurotic parent.

'It's fine,' Jennie tells me, in a reassuring voice. 'I'm glad you phoned. Ben's doing just fine.'

I breathe a sigh of relief and sit back down at the kitchen table. 'Really? He is?'

'Really. He loves the whiteboard we use and he's got a bit of an aptitude for the computer, it seems. He's on there right now with Tracey, one of the teaching assistants. He's using ChooseIt! Maker.'

'Really? What's ChooseIt! Maker?'

'It's an inclusive technology programme. There's a lot you can do with it, but right now Ben's finding the odd one out from three pictures. And he's getting a lot of the answers right!'

The relief I feel is immense. As always, this simple act of kindness, the trouble this stranger has taken out of her busy day to try and help me feel better, makes my eyes well with tears. But to hear that the teachers have already discovered my little boy's strengths and are working on them, that Ben is actually learning something, as opposed to screaming the place down, is like another winning scratch card in my hand.

'I've taken the day off work,' I say, laughing through my tears. 'I thought you'd have excluded him by lunchtime.'

'Good lord. We wouldn't do anything of the sort,' Jennie says. 'We deal with all sorts of behaviour here and we're well staffed. Ben is going to be just fine with us. So go and enjoy your day off and, really, there's no need to worry.'

*

Just over an hour later, I'm standing in Ellie's kitchen while she makes me a cup of tea. She picks up her phone from the worktop as it bleeps. 'She'll be here in a minute.' She hands me a mug and nods towards the living room.

'You can't stay,' I tell her. 'I'll need to talk to her in private. Can you go out for a bit? Do some shopping?'

Ellie looks doubtful. 'I don't know if she'll talk to you without me here,' she says. 'She doesn't really trust people in authority.'

'I understand,' I say. 'But I'm not allowed to talk to her while you're present, sorry.'

'Who would know?' she asks.

'Me.'

'So I'm not allowed to know what she says?'

'Of course you are, after she's said it. But if you're both in the same room when she's talking, you could influence each other. You could be accused of helping each other to get your stories straight. I'll handle Marie, don't worry.'

'Famous last words,' Ellie mutters, as the doorbell rings and she walks out to answer it. I hear the front door open and then Marie's voice drifts into the hallway.

'I haven't got long,' I hear her say. 'Darren's on his way round. He says he's sorry. He wants to talk. I told him if he's gonna start chattin' shit again, he's gonna be... what?'

I hear Ellie say something and Marie's head appears from behind the living-room door and stares at me.

'Oh. You. I remember you.'

'Hi, Marie,' I say, and give her a little wave.

163

Marie steps into the room and Ellie appears behind her. She mouths something at me from behind Marie, but I can't make out what she's saying.

'I was wondering if I could talk to you,' I say. 'About Ellie's case.'

'Oh, no.' Marie puts her hands up. 'I'm not getting involved in no court case.' She turns to Ellie and says, 'Sorry, babe. I told you, I'll help you out in any way I can, but I ain't touching nothing that involves the law. I've got enough of my own shit going down.'

'Come and sit down, Marie,' I say. 'Let's just have an off-record chat. I'm not going to write down anything you say or ask you to sign anything.'

Marie remains standing in the doorway. Her phone bleeps suddenly and, while she wriggles her hips abundantly in an attempt to fish it out of her jeans pocket, I mouth, 'Go,' to Ellie, and give her a quick wave of the hand. Ellie looks back and forth at me and then at Marie uncertainly for a moment, but Marie is too busy yelling into her phone to notice, and so after a moment's hesitation she nods, and backs out down the hallway. I hear the front door close.

'If you ain't even going to say you're sorry for what you done, you can forget it,' Marie is saying, emphatically. 'I don't wanna know. In fact, why don't you do us both a favour and go down Denmark Hill instead and get yourself an STI test? Because if you think you're the only one that bitch has fucked in the past seven days, you're more stupid than I thought.'

With that she ends the call. In spite of her bravado and strong language, I can see that she's shaking. She looks at me for a moment, and then says, 'Don't suppose you've got a fag?'

164

I shake my head. 'Sorry. I don't smoke.'

'Fuck. I'm gagging for one, and I've got no money. Bloody bank machine's swallowed up my card.' She looks round. 'Where's El gone?'

'She had to pop out. Come on.' I stand up. 'I've got some money. Where's the nearest newsagent?'

Marie looks at me and narrows her eyes. 'You'll buy me some fags?'

I shrug and pick up my bag. 'I used to smoke, once. When you need a fag, you need a fag. And, believe me, I can still remember how much I needed one when I found out that my boyfriend of three years had been cheating on me.'

Marie stares at me for a moment. 'Come on, then,' she says.

She follows me down the hallway and out onto the balcony. I pull Ellie's front door shut behind us and hope that she has her key. We walk down the steps, which smell of urine, and out into the heat of the afternoon. The sun beats down on us relentlessly as we zigzag through the concrete alleys of the estate and out onto a playing field.

'So, why did your boyfriend cheat on you?' Marie asks, as we cross the expanse of grass towards a small, wire-fenced play area. 'I mean, in your case, obviously it's not because you're fat and ugly.'

I glance up at her. 'That's not why Darren cheated on you.'

'You don't think?' Marie's voice is loaded with sarcasm, but I don't let that put me off.

'No,' I say. 'He did it because of him.' Marie gives me a look which tells me that she is curious as to what I mean by that, but doesn't trust me. 'Do you think you're the only woman he's ever cheated on?' I persist.

Marie thinks about this for a moment. 'He cheated on his last girlfriend. He told me. That's why she kicked him out.'

'So there you go. And, of course, this woman…'

'Tanya.'

'Tanya was there. He liked the idea of sex with someone new, and she was willing to have it with him.'

Marie sneers, 'Him and half of the London Borough of bloody Southwark.'

'Exactly. So, he cheated because he's Darren. She slept with him because she's Tanya. And my boyfriend did it because he could. Life goes on. I got a better one.'

'Did you?'

'I'm not with him any more. But he was much, much nicer.'

'So why did you break up with him?'

'Long story,' I say. 'But nothing to do with anyone else coming along.' I think about this for a moment. I think about Ben, who of course did come along and blow our world apart. 'Well, at least, not another woman,' I add.

'He was gay?' Marie's eyes widen.

'He was Australian…'

'Ah,' Marie says. 'I get it: *Priscilla, Queen of the Desert.*'

I smile. This conversation has somehow turned Andy into a drag queen, but I decide it's simpler to leave it at that, rather than trying to explain about Ben.

We skirt round the edge of the play area, which is set back from the road in front of us. A group of kids on bikes are riding around on the grass outside the perimeter.

'Well, at least he didn't hit you,' says Marie.

'No,' I agree. 'That's true. Darren hit you though, right? I saw what he did to you, when I came round last time.'

Marie shrugs. 'He's got a temper. Don't get me wrong, I give as good as I get. I'm mouthy, I know that. But he's a bloke at the end of the day. Men shouldn't hit women, should they?'

I glance at her. 'No one should hit anyone,' I say.

We cross the road and turn the corner into a side street, with a newsagent on the corner. I stop, open my purse and hand Marie a ten-pound note. 'Keep the change,' I tell her.

'Thanks.' Marie goes into the shop.

I stand outside, shading my eyes from the bright glare of the sun, and watch the group of kids on bikes, who are now circling the play area and shouting at some smaller kids inside. I strain my ears to listen to what's being said, worried for a moment that the smaller kids are being bullied.

'Go fuck your mother,' shouts a seven-year-old, who is sitting on top of the slide.

The kids on the bikes laugh and ride off.

Marie comes out of the shop, unwrapping the cellophane from a silver-papered pack of Royals. She wrestles a lighter from her jeans pocket and lights up a cigarette, inhaling deeply and looking over the road at the kids, who are trying to climb the wrong way up the slide to reach their friend at the top.

'So,' she says, her tone of voice less friendly now that she's got her cigarettes. 'What do you want?'

'I just want to ask you about Finn. I understand you were a bit like a second mum to him?'

Marie gives me a sideways glance. 'I know what they're accusing El of. It weren't me, if that's what you want to know.'

'I know,' I agree, although I don't really know this at all.

Marie gives me another sideways glance and says nothing. She walks forward and crosses the road over to the park, so I follow her. When the kid on the slide sees her coming, he shouts, 'Marie! I just seen Darren down the Camby Arms with Tanya Small. They were k-i-s-s-i-n-g!' The kid wraps his arms round himself and makes a smooching action.

Marie flicks her cigarette into the road, launches forward suddenly and runs towards the park, her muffin-top waistline wobbling around through her T-shirt and spilling over the edges of her jeans. The kids all scream and jump from the slide, exiting the park and running back in the direction of the estate. 'Yeah, and you know what, you little bastard?' Marie screams after him. 'I saw your dad with her on Sunday in the Camby Arms car park, on the back seat of his car. They were f-u-c-k-i-n-g!'

The kid just laughs and follows his friends, their attention now diverted towards a car near the entrance to the estate. I watch for a moment as they circle it, kicking its tyres. The boys on the bikes reappear and they all run off again.

Marie sits down on a big tyre swing and lights another cigarette. I sit down on the swing next to her.

'Sounds as though you're better off without him,' I venture.

'You reckon?'

I hesitate a moment before asking, 'So, did he hit you often?'

'When he'd been drinking,' she says.

'How often was that?'

'Most days, as it happens.'

'So, what did he think about having a baby around? I mean, you looked after Finn a lot, right?'

'He liked the money,' she says.

'Did he ever get angry with him?'

Marie purses her lips and blows out a smoke ring. She pulls a face. 'Why would he get angry with a baby?'

'Well, they cry, don't they? They need things. He doesn't seem to me as though he's a very patient kind of man.'

Marie's lip curls slightly and the look in her eyes tells me quite plainly that I'm barking up the wrong tree. She takes a long puff of her cigarette and flicks the end towards the roundabout. 'He didn't have anything to do with the baby,' she says. 'He left him to me. He went down the pub and didn't come back till closing. The baby was mostly asleep by then.'

'And yet, he liked the money, you said? You still gave him some of the money you got for babysitting?'

Marie gives me another one of her sideways looks. 'He took it.'

I nod. 'As in... what he did to get the money from you that time I came round?'

'Yep.' Marie's voice is terse and indignant. 'If I didn't give it to him.'

'So, what if he came home from the pub, drunk, and started a fight with you over the money...?'

'He never touched the baby.'

'Ever?'

'No. Only me. Like I said, the baby was usually asleep.'

'And if he woke in the night?'

'Who?'

'Finn?'

'Then I got him up and fed him.'

'And Darren?'

'He never woke, not once he was asleep.'

'OK. Fine.' I can see that this line of questioning will take me no further, so I try a different angle. 'Where did the baby sleep?' I ask.

'In my room. He had a basket.'

169

'Always?'

'Mostly. Until he was around six or seven months. Then he had like a pram thing, one you could carry around.'

'Could he have fallen out, ever?'

Marie looks at me as if I'm stupid. 'Of course not.'

'And Darren never picked him up? He never held him?'

'Now and again, when it suited him to play with him. But I looked after him, the nappies, the feeding...'

'He never fed him?'

'He might have given him a bottle now and again.'

'Did he ever make up his feed?'

Marie lets out a snort of hollow laughter. 'You've got to be joking. If it don't come with a ring pull or a bottle top, or from the pizza place or the Akash Tandoori up the road, he doesn't want to know.'

'So he never fed him solid food then?'

Marie shakes her head. 'No.'

'Did you?'

'Well, yeah, obviously. Once he was old enough, he had the odd thing.'

'Like what?'

'Whatever she brought round.' As Marie says this, she glances up at me.

'Ellie?'

'Yeah. Of course. Ellie.'

'And what sort of thing did she bring round?'

'I don't know. It was in jars. Containers,' she adds, impatiently. 'I just used to give it to him.'

'So you didn't ever give him anything you made yourself? Like a ready meal or... packet mash?'

Marie looks at me. 'I don't know. I can't remember now. Jesus, it's not an offence to feed a baby, is it?'

'No,' I say. 'It's not. But, as you know, Finn is in hospital. He's been seriously ill. He's still in a critical condition; and he was barely conscious when they took him in.'

'What's that got to do with me?'

'Ellie says he was with you when he became ill. Is that true?'

Marie turns and looks at me for a moment as if she doesn't understand the question, but I can see that her face is flushed and she is breathing rapidly, her ample bosom rising and falling steadily against her chest. 'He was ill. Yes,' she says, finally, her voice clipped and condescending in tone. 'That's why I rang El as soon as I got home. He had a virus, didn't he?' She says this aggressively, not as a question, but as a fact that I should know.

'Possibly. Possibly not. The prosecution are saying someone had poisoned him. With salt.'

'Well it weren't me,' Marie says, defiantly.

'No. No, of course not.' I nod my agreement, aware that I'm about to blow this.

She takes a deep breath and looks away across the playing field.

'You said, "when you got home". What did you mean?'

'What?' Marie turns round and faces me. Her face is flushed and her neck is pink.

'You just said, "That's why I rang El as soon as I got home." What did you mean? How did he fall ill, Marie? What happened? Where were you?'

Marie hesitates a moment. 'I told you. He had a virus. He was hot. I called El as soon as I... as soon as I realised. That's what I meant.'

She begins to wriggle and heave herself out of the tyre seat. The swing begins to creak and rattle noisily; I reach across and grab the chain. 'Marie, did you go out and leave Finn with anyone else? With Darren?'

She pushes herself up and off the swing. 'No. I told you.'

'Never?'

'No.' She starts to walk off out of the park.

I get up and run after her, but she stops at the gate and holds up her hand. 'That's it. I've had enough,' she says. 'No more questions. I've told you what I know and I ain't done nothing wrong.'

'Sure,' I agree. 'I'm sorry. No more questions.'

She turns and semi-trots across the grass away from me in the direction of the estate. In spite of her weight, I have to run a little to keep up. I trail a few steps behind her through the alleys. When we get near to the flats, she strides off ahead of me and up the steps.

'Marie. Wait,' I call. 'Just one more thing. Please.'

She turns on the steps and looks at me. 'What?'

I run to catch her up. 'Why did Darren take your money?'

'I told you.'

'I know, but... why would he think he had a right to your babysitting money, if he did nothing to help with the baby?'

Marie doesn't answer. She turns and walks on up the steps.

'Marie, wait,' I call after her.

'What for? I ain't got nothing more to say.'

'But...'

She continues walking, holding her palm up behind her as she goes. 'Talk to the hand,' she yells over her shoulder, and disappears into the stairwell.

My phone rings. It's Ellie. 'Where are you?' she asks.

'Outside your flat.'

'Did she talk to you?'

'Yes, a little.'

'OK, wait there. I'm coming back.'

I walk up the steps and along the balcony. As I pass the flat next to Marie's, the other side to Ellie's, the net curtain in the kitchen is pulled back and an elderly woman's face appears. She watches me for a moment, impassively, and then drops the curtain back down.

I peer over the edge of the balcony, looking out for Ellie. As I do so, a red Mondeo pulls up sharply at the edge of the estate and two men jump out. The passenger leans up against the car and lights a cigarette, while the driver slams his door shut and marches purposefully towards the flats. As he approaches I can see that it's Darren. I jump back and turn around, looking for somewhere to hide, but there isn't anywhere, just a long row of flats. I race to the stairwell and up the steps to the floor above. In less than a minute I can hear loud footsteps clattering up the steps beneath me and then Darren's head appears. I quickly duck back and tiptoe along the balcony until I'm level with Marie's flat on the floor below. A second later, I can hear a loud banging followed by Darren's voice shouting, 'Marie! Open this fucking door.'

The door opens and I hear Marie say something and Darren yell back, 'What the fuck have you said, you stupid cow? I thought I told you to keep your trap shut.'

I hear Marie cry out, 'I didn't tell her anything. Get off me!' and then it all goes quiet and I hear the door slam shut. I run back down the steps and along the balcony to Marie's flat. I can hear loud voices inside and the sound of Marie crying out. I hammer on the door with my fists, but the shouting continues. I bend down and shout through the letter box, 'You've got two seconds to open this door and then I'm calling the police!'

A moment later, the front door opens and Marie comes stumbling out. Her cheek is red and swollen and her lip is bleeding. Darren steps out behind her. He glares hard at me for a moment, then pushes past Marie and walks off along the balcony.

'Are you OK?' I ask Marie. I pull a tissue from my handbag and hold it out towards her.

She bats my hand away and wipes her mouth on the back of her sleeve. 'Just leave me alone,' she snarls. 'This is all *your* fault.' She stares after Darren as he strides along the balcony and disappears into the stairwell. When he's gone, she turns and goes back inside her flat.

'Marie, wait—' I take a step towards her.

'Stay the fuck away from me,' she hisses, lifting a finger and pointing it into my face as she speaks. 'I mean it. Come near me again and you're dead.'

She pushes the door shut in my face.

11

As I walk through the entrance of Southwark St Martin's, a strange sensation creeps over me. Nothing has changed; there's the same multicoloured seating and soft play area off to my right, the League of Friends' coffee shop to my left. It's as though time has stood still since I was last here, walking these corridors, fear and tension eating me up inside. First Ben, and now Finn. He's not my child, of course; it's not the same. But there's a familiar knot in my stomach, regardless, the relic of an emotion that has lain dormant within me, waiting for the next emergency to strike.

I turn the corner to the ICU and press the buzzer. A voice sounds over the intercom.

'I'm here about Finn Stephens,' I say.

There's a palpable silence before the voice asks, 'Are you a relative?'

'No,' I admit. 'I'm a solicitor. I'd like to talk to someone about him.'

There's a muffled sound and the intercom goes dead. A moment later the voice says, 'I'm sorry, but he's no longer with us.'

My heart stops. 'What? What do you mean?'

'I... I can't tell you anything,' the voice says. 'Unless you're a relative, I'm afraid I really can't talk to you.'

The knot in my gut tightens as I walk back down the corridor to the main foyer and follow the signs to the hospital administration department. A receptionist tells me that someone will be out to speak to me shortly and asks me to take a seat. I sit in the waiting area for the best part of an hour, turning everything over in my mind. Has the worst happened? Has Finn finally lost his battle for life – has the damage to his little heart and kidneys proved too much, were they no longer able to keep him alive?

A door opens and a plump, green-eyed woman in her late fifties walks over to sit down beside me. 'I'm Marion Southgate, head of administration,' she says. Her voice is cool and officious. She's been told there's a solicitor waiting to see her and is on the defensive already, I can tell. A solicitor in a hospital; someone's looking to sue. That's what she's thinking, no doubt.

I pull out my identity card and hand it to her. She glances at it briefly, turning it over in her hand.

'My secretary has explained why you're here,' she says. 'But I don't know if I'm going to be able to help you. Data protection, you see. We can't reveal information about minors.'

I look up at her and frown. 'Not even to tell me if they're dead or alive?'

'Unfortunately, no, not unless you're a relative of the patient.'

I sigh, feeling my shoulders sag.

'Is there anything else?' she asks. She shifts in her seat, looking as though she's about to get up.

'Yes.' I nod, quickly. 'I'm investigating the events that led to Finn being taken back to the ICU on the twenty-fifth of July. I need to talk to any members of staff who were working on Peregrine Ward that night, the night that his dialysis line was

176

tampered with. One of the key witnesses for the prosecution – a nurse named Mary Ngombe – has disappeared. I'm hoping someone might be able to tell me how I can track her down.'

The woman hands my ID card back to me and shakes her head.

'She's not a staff member. We wouldn't keep a record. I've already told the police that.'

'OK. But one of your staff members might know where she is. Your website says that you have at least six to seven nurses plus a number of doctors working each shift. There was a change of shift from "lates" to "nights" at the time it happened, which means that there are potentially some twelve or more witnesses who might have seen something. The police have taken statements from four of them, but that's all. I need to speak to the rest. I'd like to go onto the ward.'

She shakes her head. 'I can't allow you to do that, I'm afraid. We can't have random strangers walking round our hospital wards.'

I frown and look up at her. 'I'm not a stranger. I've just told you who I am. You've seen my ID.'

'Sorry. It's against hospital policy.'

'Then can you get me a list?' I say. 'Of all the staff members who were working on Peregrine Ward that night, on the twenty-fifth of July.'

'Again, data protection,' she says.

'What?' I peer into her face. 'What data are you protecting?'

'I can't give out confidential information about staff.'

'How is it confidential?' I say, annoyed. 'I just want you to tell me who was working that night.'

She stands up. 'I'm afraid I can't do that. It's against hospital policy. You'll have to go through the police.'

I jump to my feet. 'But that's my point,' I snap. 'That's why I'm here. The police haven't talked to everyone who was working that night. They haven't taken all the statements that they could have done.'

She gives me a pointed look. 'Well then, maybe no one else saw anything, maybe they couldn't help. And I'm sorry, but neither can I. There's nothing more that I can do.'

She starts to walk away.

'Wait. What about the CCTV?' I call after her. 'Can you show me that at least? I'm entitled to see it.'

She shakes her head. 'Like I said already, you'll have to go through the police.'

'I've tried. But it hasn't been forthcoming. The police are dragging their heels.'

'I'm sorry,' she says. 'But there's nothing else I can do.'

I stare after her for a moment as she walks away, enters her office and shuts the door. I feel like running after her, banging on the door with my fists, demanding to know why she's being so obstructive. Is it because she takes pleasure in being so ridiculously high-handed? Or is it because someone at the hospital has something to hide?

Instead, I push my hands into my pockets and head back towards the main doors. I'll speak to Will. We'll make an application to the judge, I tell myself – force disclosure of the CCTV. It's not fair on Ellie that we've waited this long. It's only a matter of weeks until the trial and we still haven't had a chance to view it for ourselves, to see who entered the ward that night, to properly prepare her defence. As I approach the exit and see the sliding doors into the car park up ahead of me, I resolve to put this plan into action first thing tomorrow, as soon as I get into the office.

But then, before I've realised what I'm doing, I'm walking back down the corridor in the opposite direction, following the signs to the wards, or more specifically, to Peregrine Ward.

I stop outside and look up. There's a sign across the top of the door that bears the name of the ward with a child-like picture of a falcon. On the upper wall, either side of the sign, is a camera, which is pointing down at the double doors. Like the doors to the ICU, they're solid, without windows. I scratch my head. It's unlikely that there would be cameras inside the ward, but it would be useful to know.

I step aside as a nurse approaches the door. She bows her head slightly, tugging at the lanyard round her neck and flashing it at a keypad to the right of the door. The door clicks and buzzes open and the nurse steps inside. I watch for a moment as the door swings shut again, an idea forming in my mind.

I back away down a corridor to my right, looking up at the ceiling for cameras. There are none. I continue to walk, slowly backwards, my eye on the entrance to the ward. After a few minutes I see what I'm looking for: a young couple approaches the doors from the corridor to my left. The woman is carrying a polystyrene coffee cup in each hand, the man carrying a baby's car seat. Go, I tell myself. Now.

I stride forwards, watching as the man leans down and presses a buzzer. 'We're Jake Quinn's parents,' I hear him say into the intercom. A second later there's a click and a buzz. I move quickly, catching up with the couple just as the door opens. The man holds it open for the woman with his elbow as he manoeuvres the car seat through. I grab and hold it for him and we exchange smiles as I tailgate him through and onto the ward.

Inside, it's brightly lit. A colourful mural of an underwater scene with painted fish, shells and mermaids snakes the curved wall from the doors up to the nurses' station. A nurse looks up, briefly, from a distance. I smile and nod at her, then move purposefully into the room to my left, trying to appear as though I know where I'm going, as if I've been here before.

I glance up briefly as I enter the room. I can't see any cameras, but the sign above the door tells me that this is Room One. I realise suddenly that this is the room that Finn was in on the twenty-fifth of July; I remember this from the statement of Brooke Allen, the nurse who first found him lying bleeding in his cot and raised the alarm. I recognise the layout of the room from the description in her statement – there's the washbasin on the wall to my right; there's a cot next to it and there's the one that Finn was in, over by the window. My own blood chills as I visualise the scene: the pool of blood on the white vinyl floor beneath the cot, the panic-stricken faces of the nurses, the noise and commotion as the doctors come running in, dressed in scrubs, one of them turning over the bleeding baby, pressing the defibrillator pads to his chest and barking orders, whilst another tries to stem the flow of blood.

I glance around the room for a moment, taking in the size of it, the distance from the cot to the window, the space around the bed. I recall that the nurse described the camp bed as being between the cot and the window; I walk over and measure the distance in my head. It's only a couple of feet. It would have been a squeeze to get past the camp bed to the baby. The dialysis machine must have been round the other side and whoever removed the tube must have been standing on the opposite side of the cot. I don't know if any of this information will be of use to me, but I take a mental snapshot. I've won more than one trial on the basis of a site visit, on the basis of information that

I've gleaned from my presence at the scene – information that I wouldn't have otherwise known.

A woman looks up from the side of the cot next to me, where her baby is sleeping. 'Are you looking for someone?' she asks.

I shake my head. 'No,' I say. 'It's OK, I've just realised... I'm in the wrong room.'

I turn left outside and walk up past the nurses' station. The ward is busy with parents pushing children in wheelchairs or walking with them up and down the corridors, holding their hands. Nobody notices me as I walk past the desk and enter the next room to my left, although as I do so, four little heads turn and look my way. I give the children a wave. A nurse walks in and goes over to one of the beds and draws a curtain. She turns as she sees me.

'Can I help you?' she asks.

I think quickly. 'I'm here to visit my nephew,' I say. 'He's...' I nod my head out towards the door. 'In the other room.'

'Who's your nephew?' she asks.

I take a deep breath. 'Jake Quinn,' I say.

She nods and smiles. 'He's going home today, isn't he?'

I nod. 'Yes.' Quick; change the subject. 'Can I ask you something?'

'Fire away.'

'Have you been working here long? On this ward?'

She looks up at me. 'A month. Why?'

'I'm looking for someone – a nurse who used to work here. She was here in July.'

The nurse shakes her head. 'I wouldn't know. I'm agency. Have you asked at the desk?'

'No. I'll try that. Thank you.'

I walk out of the room and up the corridor, away from the nurses' station. There's no way I'm going to just go up to the desk and start asking questions; it would be far too obvious that I've sneaked onto the ward. On the other hand, I'm not having too much luck so far. But I only need to find one nurse who's willing to talk to me, I remind myself; just one. I'd then have a lead – someone who could give me names of other staff members, someone with whom I could leave my phone number and ask them to contact me.

I turn left again into the next room. There are two beds this time, the children both lying down, hooked up to dialysis machines, red lines of blood running out of their arms and into the equipment. The mother of one of the children, sitting beside her, looks up as I enter. I smile, 'Sorry. Wrong room,' before backing out again.

The next room I enter has four cots. Three of them are empty and an auxiliary nurse is changing the sheets. In one of the cots, near the window, I can see a young child, lying on his back. The nurse looks up. I smile and she smiles back. She's young, petite, with long black hair tied back into a ponytail. She has a South-East Asian appearance, Indonesian or Malaysian maybe.

'You come see Finn?' she asks, in broken English, still smiling.

I look back at her, my heart rate quickening. 'Finn?' I repeat. 'Did you say Finn?'

'Yes.' She nods over to the cot. 'You come see him?'

I quickly mask my surprise. 'Finn. Yes, that's right.'

'That good,' she says, moving out of my way. She pulls a sad face. 'He have no one here today. He too little to be all alone so long.'

I nod and walk over to the cot, glancing at the notes hanging on the end of his bed. I can see his name there, in black and white: Finn Stephens. It's definitely him.

He's still alive.

I feel elated. Of course, 'he's no longer with us' didn't have to mean that he was dead! On the contrary – it was good news. All they'd meant is that he was well enough to be moved out of the ICU.

As I bend over the cot, Finn opens his eyes. He's sucking a dummy, the top of it tapping against the tube that's sitting under his nose. I recognise his face from the photo on Ellie's phone. He's beautiful. His fair hair is almost white and his eyes are like Ellie's: huge, a deep blue, framed by long lashes. He's wearing a blue hospital gown with brown teddy bears dotted all over it, a standard issue white hospital blanket draped loosely over his legs. He turns his head and looks up at me solemnly as I lean over his cot and smile at him.

'Hello, Finn,' I say.

He continues to look up at me silently, sucking away at his dummy while his eyes move back and forth, studying my face. I reach over and pick up the blue bunny rabbit that's near his head, noticing, as I do so, the faded brown mark that's spread across its blue cotton tail. An uncomfortable image of how it got there springs into my mind: I suddenly see Finn lying there, dying, his mouth gaping open, his dummy falling, the colour draining from his cheeks as a crimson stain creeps its way slowly across the sheet.

I close my eyes tight to rid my mind of the image. I take a deep breath and open them again. Finn is still looking up at me, expectantly. His eyes shift and lock onto the rabbit. I waggle it around, make it dance a little and Finn's mouth breaks into a smile.

He lifts his hand and takes his dummy out. With his other hand he points. 'Wabbit,' he says, the tube that's sitting underneath his nostrils moving as he speaks. 'Mine.'

I nod. 'Your rabbit's dancing.'

'So who are you? Auntie?' The nurse calls across the room as she watches us play.

'That's right,' I lie. I suddenly remember why I'm here and seize my opportunity. 'I haven't seen you before,' I ask her. 'Have you worked here long?'

'No. I just start this week.'

I nod, disappointed, and look back down at Finn. He smiles again as I waggle the rabbit about, then raises his arm and reaches for it. I put the bunny into his hand and he pulls it to his chest.

'I leave you play,' says the nurse and leaves the room.

I look back down at Finn. He reaches out his arm to me, handing me the rabbit back. 'Again,' he commands.

'Sure. Your rabbit wants to dance again.' I take the bunny from him. For a few moments I continue to waggle it around, making it play peek-a-boo from behind the blanket and sing 'Head, Shoulders, Knees and Toes', while Finn's mild amusement turns to giggles. A myriad of emotions is rising up inside me. I'm at once overwhelmed with joy that Finn is still alive, but at the same time acutely pained, as always, to hear a child so much smaller than Ben talking, understanding, playing in a meaningful way. I can't help but watch him, assess him, compare him to Ben. It's what I do with every child I meet. I can't help myself. I don't want to do it, but I do.

A voice interrupts my thoughts. 'What on earth do you think you're doing?'

I look up and freeze, my hand in mid-air, a rabbit caught in the headlights. Standing in the doorway is the hospital administrator, Marion Southgate, and I can see that she's not on her own. I cast my mind around, searching for something to tell her, something to legitimise my visit, but then she moves into the room and I can see that the person behind her is Lady Barrington-Brown.

Marion Southgate walks over and takes the rabbit out of my hand. 'How did you get in here?' she demands. 'Who let you in?'

'No one,' I admit. My legs are rooted to the ground and I can't move. I'm scared. I know that I'm in big trouble. I have no excuse for being here. I look at Lady Barrington-Brown, apologetically. 'I just wanted to... I wanted to talk to some of the staff members who were here the night that Finn nearly died,' I explain.

'And I told you that you couldn't.' Marion Southgate's mouth is pinched. 'I told you that it wasn't allowed.' She turns to Lady Barrington-Brown. 'I'm really very sorry about this. This is highly irregular. It won't happen again.'

'I wanted to try and find out what happened, that's all.' I turn to Lady Barrington-Brown, pleading with her. 'I want the same as you. I want to know what happened...' I wave my hand at the cot. 'To your beautiful little grandson.'

Marion Southgate folds her arms and makes a huffing noise.

Lady Barrington-Brown looks confused. She says, 'But we already know what happened, don't we?'

'Maybe. Maybe not,' I reply, watching Marion's face as I speak. 'What if it was an accident? What if it was a member of staff, here at the hospital who accidentally—'

'Right, that's enough,' says Marion. 'I want you out of here.'

'Where's Mary Ngombe?' I ask her.

'I've told you already. I don't know her. She's not staff.'

'Then why won't you let me see the records, or talk to anyone? What have you got to hide?'

Marion doesn't answer. She glares at me in silence.

Beside me, Finn says, 'Wabbit dancing. More dancing.' He holds out his hand.

I say, 'Sorry, Finn. No more dancing. I have to go.'

Marion Southgate says, 'Stay where you are. I'm calling security.'

'Please. There's no need.' I put my hands up. 'I'll go. You don't have to throw me out.'

'No. I want you escorted off the premises,' she says.

'But there's no need. Please,' I beg her. 'I'm sorry, OK? I'm just trying to do my job. That's all. If you'd helped me, like I asked... you could have come onto the ward with me, escorted me round...'

'I'm afraid that's not good enough, Ms Kellerman,' she replies. 'It's not your place to decide whether you like my rules or not. You've trespassed onto a hospital children's ward. This is serious. I want you escorted out of here and then I'm going to have to consider reporting you to your regulatory body.'

She moves towards the door.

Lady Barrington-Brown looks from her to me and back again for a moment, then holds up her hand. 'Wait,' she says. 'There's really no need for that.'

Marion Southgate turns in the doorway. 'Thank you, madam, but this hospital has rules. She's broken them. It's my duty to—'

'No.' Lady Barrington-Brown turns to her. 'Please. I... Miss Kellerman and I know one another,' she says, quickly. 'We're friends.'

'What?' Marion frowns, incredulously. 'You can't be.'

'Oh, but we are,' Lady Barrington-Brown insists. She smiles and glances from Marion to me and back again. 'So everything's all right.'

'But…' Marion stares at her. 'That can't be right. She'd have said.'

Lady Barrington-Brown turns to her, her face reddening, her neck flushed. 'It *is* a little worrying, of course, that someone can gain access to the ward so easily. I mean, we should be grateful, I suppose, that it was Miss Kellerman that alerted us to the problem, and not someone else.'

Marion Southgate looks upset at the implied accusation. Her mouth drops open and she shakes her head. 'You don't need to worry, madam,' she says, energetically. 'We monitor everyone who comes on and off the ward. There are cameras everywhere. The security and surveillance systems in this hospital are state-of-the-art.'

'So I understand.' Lady Barrington-Brown nods. 'And yet… here we are.' She looks at me and raises her eyebrows.

I bite my lip as I sneak a glance at Marion Southgate's face; she's livid, I can tell. She says, 'Please let me reassure you, madam. This is an isolated incident, and one that won't be repeated.'

She closes her mouth tightly and leaves the ward without saying another word.

Lady Barrington-Brown walks over to Finn's cot and touches his cheek. She beckons to the auxiliary nurse who's now reappeared and is standing in the doorway. 'He needs changing. Could you attend to that, please?' she asks.

'Yes, madam.' The auxiliary nurse hurries over to the cot.

I turn to Lady Barrington-Brown. 'I don't know how to thank you,' I tell her. 'You really got me out of a hole there.'

She smiles. 'Come. I'll walk you to your car. Finn's turned a corner, but he's still very fragile. He's far from well. He mustn't get excited.'

'Of course.' I glance over at Finn, whose eyes are now closed. His dummy is back in his mouth and is moving gently up and down in rhythm with the rising and falling of his chest. She's right – he's tired. I feel ashamed, suddenly. He may not need to be in intensive care any longer, but I have no idea what his health is like. I shouldn't have just assumed that it was OK to walk in and play with him like that. 'I'm sorry,' I say, as I follow her out into the corridor and walk with her out towards the exit doors to the ward. 'You must still be very worried about him.'

She nods. 'We are.'

'But relieved,' I add. 'That he's out of the woods.'

'Yes. That's something. We'll just have to wait and see.' She gives me a sideways glance. 'But you know how it is. You never really relax. When something like this happens, it triggers something inside you. You sleep with one hand on your gun for ever more.'

'That's true,' I agree. 'That's exactly how it is.'

As we walk across the foyer and approach the sliding doors into the car park up ahead, Lady Barrington-Brown stops and touches my arm. 'I'll leave you here,' she says.

'Of course. And thanks again,' I say. 'I really appreciate what you did. It was very kind, given the circumstances.'

But Lady Barrington-Brown's eyes have clouded over. She looks tired, suddenly, absent, as if she can't hear me. She nods, says goodbye and heads back in the direction of the ward. I know that she's worrying about Ellie, or whoever hurt Finn, that they could get access to the ward, do the same thing over again. The ward is meant to be secure, but I've just proved it, haven't I? I've just proved that anyone could have gained access. Anyone at all.

12

The full prosecution case is served two weeks later.

'We have most of the statements you'd expect,' I tell Will, over the phone. 'And the toxicology report – which doesn't really tell us anything we don't already know. They've not tested for drugs. We'll seek secondary disclosure of the samples and run our own tests. But the main thing is that there's no CCTV from the hospital.'

'When are we going to get it?'

'That's the problem. We're not. The police say their copy is in an unplayable format. And they've served a statement from a Kathy Fosdyke, Senior Operations Manager and Head of IT at the hospital, who says that the disc has corrupted. Something to do with the compression and functionality of the time-lapse system. Basically, the relevant period of time is missing.'

'So that's that.'

'Sadly, yes. Can we make an "abuse of process" argument?' I ask.

Will is silent for a moment. He says, 'There's no other evidence of bad faith by anyone at the hospital or of any failing by the police to investigate or preserve the evidence. I don't think it will be enough to sustain it. It's a matter to raise at trial, but no more.'

'A nurse – a key prosecution witness – goes missing, and now there's no CCTV of who went in and out of the ward. Their systems are "state-of-the-art", according to the hospital administrator. It may not be bad faith, but it doesn't mean that someone, somewhere, hasn't made a big mistake.'

'So, where do we go from here?'

'Well… Anna's husband, Tim, has tracked down a nurse for me: Liberty Jones. She was working on the PICU ward at St Martin's in July, on the same shift as Mary. She's agreed to talk to me. I'm meeting her today. And we have two more names: in the unused material there's a statement from a nurse called Stacey Bennett, who also mentions a Dr Kent being on the ward that night. It seems Stacey is another agency nurse and Dr Kent's a locum. If I can find them, and speak to them, they might have seen something. As agency staff, they might be more willing to blow the whistle, to speak out about any improprieties. And if they saw anything irregular, we would be entitled to full disclosure of the hospital records.'

'Well, it's a long shot – and far from certain that that's where it's going to take you, but sure, it's worth speaking to them if you can. In the meantime, we need to take Ellie through the rest of the statements.'

'OK. I'm meeting Liberty at twelve thirty at Borough Market down on the South Bank. We could have our con after that, if you like?'

'That works well, actually. I'm down at Southwark Crown this afternoon for a two o'clock hearing. I shouldn't be more than half an hour, an hour tops. Why don't you and Ellie wait for me in the Côte Brasserie by the Thames at two thirty?'

'Great. I'll call Ellie and let her know.'

I can hear Matt's phone ringing and his voice answering. Out of the corner of my eye, I can see that he's looking across at me from his desk near the window. I look up and he points to the phone receiver in his hand and mouths something to me.

'Will, I'd better go,' I tell him. 'I think I have another call coming through. I'll see you this afternoon.'

'OK. See you then.'

As I hang up, Matt says, 'It's Lucy,' and transfers the call.

'Hi, Lucy, what's up?' I ask.

'We've got one in at the police station,' she says. 'Charing Cross. It's ready to go.'

I look at the clock on my phone. 'I can't do this one,' I tell her. 'I've got an appointment at twelve thirty on the South Bank. I've got to go.'

'Oh. I just asked Matt and he said you could do it.'

I look across at Matt who is tapping away at his keyboard and staring straight ahead at his computer screen. 'Matt, I have an appointment,' I tell him. 'I can't cover Charing Cross.'

Matt stops typing and looks at me. 'What? You're joking? What appointment?'

'A potential witness on the Ellis Stephens case. I have to meet her in less than an hour.'

'Ellis Stephens. Of course you do.' Matt starts typing again. I watch him for a moment, unsure if he is finishing up what he's doing or has decided that this is my problem and that he's leaving it with me.

'Lucy, I'll call you back,' I tell her. I put the phone receiver down and look across at Matt, but he carries on typing. 'I was just on the phone to Counsel about it,' I tell him. 'Maybe you didn't hear?'

'Can't you move it?' he asks.

'It's already arranged,' I tell him. 'She'll be on her way there by now. And besides, I need to talk to her – and I have a con with Counsel straight after.'

'Are we getting paid for this?' Matt asks, still typing.

'For what?'

'All this extra work you're doing on that case.'

I bite my lip. 'I believe that taking a witness statement from a potential defence witness is chargeable.'

Matt stops typing. 'It's a fixed fee,' he says, sharply. 'I've checked the page count and worked it out. We're going to get paid less than three thousand pounds for the whole case. You're never going to recover all your costs.'

'I can't let that influence me,' I reply. 'I have to defend her properly.'

Matt ignores me. He clicks and saves his document and switches off his monitor, before pulling his jacket off the back of his chair in an overly dramatic movement and picking up his bag. He heads out of the door and down the stairs.

I shut down my computer monitor and pick up my own bag. He's right that I'm spending more time on this case than we'll be paid for. But this is Ellie's life we're talking about. I'm not going to give up now.

I head down the stairs in the direction Matt has just gone. Lucy glances up as I pass her. 'So which one of you is covering Charing Cross?' she asks.

'Matt,' I tell her, although instinct tells me she knows that already.

As I head out of the door I hear Lucy say, 'Again,' but when I look back at her, she's busy typing and doesn't look up.

Liberty Jones is already seated at a table in the Borough Central café, eating a messy crêpe with one hand and emptying a sachet of sugar into a large latte with the other. She brushes some chocolate crumbs from her mouth with a paper napkin and waves when I walk in. She has striking curly red hair, which is tied up in a messy bun, stray ringlets escaping and tumbling around her ears. She's just as I imagined her from her description of herself: petite and attractive with an open, friendly face and a smattering of freckles across her nose.

'Sorry.' She grins apologetically, through a mouthful of pancake. 'I was starving. I couldn't wait.'

'Am I late?' I ask.

'No. I'm early. I just wanted to leave enough time to talk to you before my shift starts.'

'Thanks, I appreciate that.'

I pull out the chair opposite her. The waitress appears behind me and I order a crêpe and a latte too. Through the window beyond I can see the wholesale fruit and vegetable section of the market. Giant watermelons are stacked in a barrow just beyond the windows of the pub, and tray upon tray of apples, pears and bananas are piled high upon a bed of plastic grass.

'So,' I say, taking out my iPad. 'Do you mind if I make notes as we talk?'

Liberty shakes her head. 'Of course not. But you know I was in PICU, right? Finn had just been moved off PICU and onto Peregrine Ward. I wasn't there when it happened.'

'That's OK. Anything you can tell me might help. You remember the incident?' I ask her. 'You heard about it?'

'How could I forget? We all knew Finn. He was a gorgeous little boy. So lush with his big blue eyes and his cheeky smile. He'd only been with us for… well, it must have been less than a week when it happened.'

'So, do you remember much about that evening? Who was working – and where they were?'

Liberty picks up what's left of her crêpe and folds the last bit into her mouth. I wait for her to finish. 'I was on the late shift with Mary that day,' she says, swallowing and wiping her mouth with the napkin again. 'Mary was really attached to Finn. I remember when he was ready to go, she wanted to be the one to go with him over to Peregrine Ward for the handover. It was early evening and I remember she went over a couple more times to take his meds and check on him before we went off shift.'

The waitress appears again with my food.

Liberty continues, 'I was gobsmacked – we both were – when we came back on again the next afternoon and found him back there in PICU, intubated and sedated all over again, and fighting for his little life. It was unbelievable… shocking. He nearly died. The thought that someone could do that to an innocent little boy. A baby.' She shakes her head, then looks up at me. 'Sorry. I know you're her lawyer and everything, and I've never met her, so I don't know what she's like—'

I interrupt her. 'You've never met Ellie? Finn's mother?'

'No. I don't think so. It was the other lady that was there all the time.'

'The other lady?'

'The posh lady. Lady Bla Bla Bobbington-Plum or whatever her name was…'

I laugh. 'Barrington-Brown?' I suggest.

She grins. 'Yeah. That's the one.'

'So, was there anyone else who visited regularly?'

'There was that other woman from Social Services.' She rolls her eyes. 'Now, *she* was a piece of work.'

'How do you mean?'

She looks me in the eye. 'I probably shouldn't say this, but she was a bit of a bossy cow. I felt really sorry for Mary. She was totally on her back.'

'In what way?'

'Telling her what to do and when to do it,' Liberty confides. 'Always telling her she was doing stuff wrong.'

'Really? Like what?'

'Oh, I don't know. I can't remember now. There were various things that Mary was supposed to have done or not done. Mary was a good nurse, don't get me wrong. But she didn't always do everything by the book.'

I look her in the eye. 'Can you give me any examples?'

'Well, she didn't always remember to…' She tails off suddenly, and her friendly smile fades. 'Wait a minute, is this going to be used in Court?'

'Well, possibly,' I say. 'If you agree.'

She shakes her head. 'Well, then, no, I don't… I don't really want to say. It really wasn't anything much. I don't want to get Mary into trouble.'

I nod, calmly, reassuringly. Inside, my mind is racing. Mary didn't always get it right; Mary might have made a mistake. This is the first time that I've been told that Mary is anything other than hard-working and reliable. This evidence is crucial to Ellie's defence. But Liberty clearly isn't going to be the one to deliver it.

On the other hand, one person who *is* going to be giving

195

evidence in court is Heather Grainger. So, we can ask her, can't we? Cross-examine her – under oath – about Mary, about how she wasn't as careful as she should have been. This is definitely something to work with, even if Liberty doesn't want to get involved.

'OK. Not to worry,' I tell her. 'So did anyone else visit Finn?'

'There was the baby's dad, of course.'

'That's it? No one else?'

'Not that I remember. Why?'

'No reason,' I tell her. 'I'm just really surprised that you didn't bump into Ellie, that's all.'

She shrugs. 'Well, we were on lates. Came on at two and left at ten. So she might have been there in the morning. Or at night.'

'OK. So what else can you remember about what happened?' I ask her.

'Nothing. I just remember the police talking to everyone the following day.'

'Can you remember who they talked to?'

'Well, there was Brooke Allen, Susie Johnson... me and Mary. I can't remember who else. I couldn't really help them, though, I told them that. I was busy when it happened. I remember when Mary went over to Peregrine to say goodbye to Finn, the last time, we'd already finished our shift. I got collared at the same time by the parents of a little girl that I was looking after. I didn't see or talk to anyone about Finn until we came in and found him on PICU again the next day.'

'And what did Mary tell you about what happened?'

'Not much, as it goes. She told me she'd given a statement to the police and that she would be called to give evidence, but she didn't say any more. We were really busy that day. That would have been the Saturday. She did an early shift on the following

Monday. I was on lates and I did the handover. But, again, we didn't really have time to talk and I never saw her again after that. I think it was Wednesday or something when they told me she'd gone.'

'Gone? She left the PICU? Just like that?'

'She left the hospital. She came in on the Monday, and then never came back.'

'Were you surprised?'

Liberty pokes with a wooden stirrer at the froth that's clinging to the sides of her empty coffee mug. 'Well, not really, no. She was agency, at the end of the day. They come and go.'

'But… she left so suddenly after Finn's tube was tampered with. Didn't people wonder why? Did the managers tell you what had happened?'

'They said they didn't know.'

'Wasn't anyone suspicious?'

Liberty frowns. 'Of Mary? No. Why would they be?'

I shrug. 'No reason. Maybe it was just a coincidence…'

'What was?'

I push my iPad aside and lean towards her, my elbows on the table. 'Look, could it have been an accident?' I ask. 'What happened to Finn?'

'What do you mean? Could his mother have pulled the line out by accident?'

'No. I mean, could a member of hospital staff have done it? A nurse?'

Liberty stares blankly at me for a moment. 'Well, yes,' she says, finally. 'Technically. If the catheter was knocked out of the exit site, or if it hadn't been taped up properly. But that's never happened, not in all the time I've been nursing.'

'Would you know about it if it had?'

Liberty shrugs. 'I don't know. But it would be a huge mistake to make. The nurse would be suspended immediately... and she'd be disciplined. We'd know if another nurse was being disciplined. Word gets around...' Liberty tails off.

'But they couldn't discipline her if she wasn't there, could they?'

Liberty chews the end of the wooden stirrer and looks thoughtfully at her empty coffee mug.

'Would you like another?' I ask her.

She shakes her head and checks her watch. 'I'm going to have to go in a minute. Shift starts at two.'

'OK. I don't want to make you late... but can I just ask you a couple more questions?'

She hesitates. 'Go on then.'

'There's a statement here in the unused material...'

Liberty frowns.

'That's basically statements – and other evidence – that the prosecution have given to us because they are of no use to them but might help us.'

'That's nice of them,' she says.

'It's the rules. Equality of arms,' I tell her. 'The prosecution have a whole police force at their disposal to gather their evidence but we only have... well, me. So, this is a statement from a nurse called Stacey Bennett. It seems she's no longer at St Martin's. Do you know her?'

'I remember the name. She was agency. She was a ward nurse on Peregrine. She was also on the General Medical Ward for a while. I knew her, but not well.'

'Do you know where she is now?'

'No, sorry.'

'OK, well she mentions that she was – as you say – on Peregrine Ward on the twenty-fifth of July. She mentions a consultant looking after Finn that evening, a locum named Dr Kent. Do you know the name?'

Liberty frowns and purses her lips. 'No. Doesn't ring a bell. He's never worked on PICU. You should speak to someone on the ward, or the hospital admin department.'

I pull a face. 'Yeah, I tried that. I didn't get anywhere.'

'Sorry.' Liberty looks at her watch. 'Last question?' she smiles.

'OK,' I agree. 'Last question – the big question, now. There are three Mary Ngombes on Facebook. None of them would appear to be *our* Mary. Is there anyone who might know where she is?'

Liberty shakes her head. 'She wasn't... well, good friends with anyone, really. Don't get me wrong, I liked her and we got on. But it doesn't surprise me that she's not on Facebook, or that she hasn't kept in touch. She was the sort of person who kept herself to herself.'

'So there's no one who could tell me where she's gone?'

Liberty shakes her head. 'I'm sorry. Not that I know of, no.'

*

I head out of the wholesale section of the market, past the gigantic cheeses and huge tubs of olives. I wish I had time to stop and investigate the incredible aromas of fried chicken and Catalan stew, the rows of Turkish sweets and slabs of chocolate all mingling enticingly with the bitter scent of coffee. I circuit the cathedral and pass under London Bridge before heading along beside the choppy grey waters of the Thames towards Battle Bridge Lane. The wind whips my hair around my face so that I struggle to see where I'm going. I pull a hairband from my wrist and tie it back into a messy knot.

Before I get to the Crown Court building I can see the black metal and glass dome of the Hay's Galleria which houses the Côte Brasserie. Ellie is waiting for me outside, under the black-and-white striped awning of the restaurant. She's wearing a baby pink leather jacket and ripped skinny jeans with stylish brown riding boots. Her blonde hair hangs loose around her shoulders and falls across a pair of wide blue sunglasses as she stands with her hand on one hip, her thumb tapping away busily at the keyboard of her phone. I can see at least three waiters standing just inside the window with their tongues practically hanging out, but Ellie is oblivious to the looks she's getting from both the people inside the restaurant and the passers-by.

As I approach the restaurant, my own phone rings and Alex's name lights up the screen. My heart, as usual, gives a little lurch and I wonder briefly if his might do the same. We've been seeing each other several times a week since the evening in early September when we went dancing and he's made it plain that he likes me as much as I like him. But I'm still half expecting something to be wrong each time he calls. I can't quite believe he's still here.

I glance up to see that Ellie is still absorbed in her own conversation, and Will is clearly nowhere in sight, so I walk back towards the exit and take the call.

'Hi.'

'Hi, babe.'

I laugh out loud. This is the first time I've heard this. 'Hi, babe' is not an expression that sits comfortably within Alex's usual repertoire.

'What?' Alex's voice sounds mock-offended.

'It's just… "Babe"!' I giggle.

'Hi, babe,' Alex says again. 'What's wrong with that?'

'Nothing,' I smile. 'It's nice. It's better than "Sugar-tits".'

'"Sugar-tits"?'

'Ah. You obviously haven't seen *Gavin and Stacey*? I have the box-set. You are in for a treat!'

'I can't wait. Is it porn?'

I laugh. 'No. It's a comedy series. It's brilliant. You'll love it.'

'OK. Excellent. I'll look forward to it. And, as it happens, I've taken the afternoon off. I've already been shopping and I've got all the ingredients for an excellent Thai stir-fry which I intend to have ready for you when you get home tonight. Coriander, chilli, lemongrass, ginger, galangal and prawns. How does that sound? If you don't mind me letting myself in, that is?'

'It sounds amazing. You spoil me.'

'Good. I want to spoil you. You deserve to be spoiled. You are the most obvious candidate for a spoiling that I ever came across. I'm going to give you a good spoiling when I see you.'

I giggle again. 'Thank you. Do you still have my spare key?'

'Yep. So, I'll see you and Ben just after six, then?'

'OK.'

'Where are you, by the way? You're echoing.'

'I'm on the South Bank. I'm just entering Hay's Galleria.'

'What are you doing there?'

'I'm about to meet Will for a conference.'

Alex hesitates for a moment. 'So, would that be Will, the good-looking, intelligent barrister who never stops phoning you?'

'Alex! Are you jealous?'

'Of course I am. Why wouldn't I be?'

I can't think of an honest answer to this. Will *does* phone me a lot. As my instructing-solicitor-to-instructed-counsel relationships have gone, the one with Will has been by far the most intense.

'Because... because you're gorgeous,' I tell him. 'And... because I...'

'Because you what?'

My heart starts to race. 'Because I love you,' I tell him.

Alex is silent for a moment and I can actually feel my heart hammering against my chest. I had no idea I was going to say that. What have I done? What if I've scared him? Is he going to pack his chilli and his galangal and his lemongrass right back into his shopping bag and run back to Lewisham?

'Sarah.' That's all Alex says.

'Yes?' I reply, meekly. Out of the corner of my eye, I can see Ellie flicking her hair back and sliding her phone into her handbag. She spots me standing at the entrance to the shopping centre and waves.

'Sorry, Alex, I've got to go,' I tell him.

'OK,' he says. 'I'll see you tonight.'

*

Will orders a coffee each for him and Ellie and a lime and soda for me. We run through Stacey Bennett's statement.

'She was on lates that day,' I tell Ellie, 'which means she finished at ten. She says she remembers clearly that you got to the ward late, at around nine fifteen p.m. – and that it was quiet. There were no other parents on the ward; they'd all gone to the parents' quarters for the night, which is what they generally do if they want to stay.'

Ellie listens in silence and then nods when I pause to look at her.

I continue, 'She says that she remembers you, because you were a bit stressed when you arrived... that you buzzed repeatedly to be let in.'

'They wouldn't open the doors,' Ellie protests. 'My baby had been in intensive care all week. They'd moved him, and I wanted to see him. What does she expect?'

I look up. 'I don't think she was criticising you, Ellie. In fact, she says she felt sorry for you. She says you looked exhausted. She says that she asked you if you wanted to sleep next to Finn, since it was his first night off the ICU.'

Will sits down and the waiter brings the drinks over a moment later.

'Did you always go to the hospital at night?' I ask her.

Ellie nods. 'Every night. Often not until around nine or even later. I waited until I knew *she* would be gone.'

'Who? Finn's grandmother?'

'Well, there was her, yes. And Heather Grainger. Between the two of them, I knew they weren't going to let me anywhere near Finn.'

'But no one had stopped you seeing him at that point, or imposed any conditions on you?'

Ellie shakes her head. 'No. No one had said I couldn't see him. They didn't know how he'd got ill. No one at the hospital was blaming me, not then... So, basically, I just kept out of their way.'

'How did you work it out, then? The visits?'

'I just waited outside until I saw everyone leave. Heather was never there after six, but Jay's mum was sometimes there later. I worked out that night times were the only time I could be on my own with him, without being watched all the time.'

'So, on the night in question, who did you see?'

'No one. I got there late. Everyone had gone.'

I nod. 'Stacey says she came back with a camp bed for you. She came back again to check on Finn before she left at around five to ten, and she says you were already asleep.'

Ellie nods. 'Exactly. That's what I told you. I was asleep.'

I look back down at my iPad. I swipe up from Stacey's statement to Mary's and back again. 'So, Stacey left at ten, or just before. She confirms that Finn's observations were all fine and that both you and Finn were asleep. But, then we have Mary Ngombe. She says she also checked on Finn at around ten o'clock, when she went off shift. She doesn't mention seeing Stacey, and Stacey doesn't mention her, so we don't know for certain which one of them came along first. It seems likely, though, that Mary came shortly after Stacey had left. Stacey says she left on time that evening, while Mary says she'd finished her shift on the PICU and went to check on Finn on her way out. It's one of the things that the CCTV might have told us, if we'd had it.'

Will takes over. 'Crucially, as we know,' he says, 'Mary says that she saw you leaning over the cot with your back to her, and lifting Finn out. She says that you held him in your arms for a moment or two and then you laid him back down again. She describes you: five feet seven or eight, blonde hair, wearing jeans, a light-coloured top and a blue scarf.'

Ellie shrugs. 'I told you,' she says. 'It wasn't me.'

'What were you wearing?' I ask her. 'In bed?'

'Jeans,' mutters Ellie. 'A light blue T-shirt. The police have them.'

'Mary doesn't mention the camp bed next to the cot,' I say. 'Which is curious. And I think I've found another angle that might show the jury that Mary doesn't always get things right.'

'But she names you,' says Will. 'She's clear about that. She says your name is Ellie and she knows you as the baby's mother. I know that she gets your age slightly wrong, but she *is* clear that it's you she saw holding Finn – the last person to be seen with him before his dialysis line was pulled out. This is our biggest problem.'

Ellie shrugs again. 'Well she's wrong. It wasn't me. I don't know what else I can say.'

'You said last time that you don't even remember Mary?' I ask her.

'No.'

'So, who do you remember, then? Who did you see?'

Ellie shakes her head. 'I don't know. That nurse... Stacey, was it? I'm not sure.'

'Anyone else? Any doctors? Did you talk to anyone about Finn and how he was doing?'

Ellie shakes her head. 'They just said he was OK. Doing well.'

'Who did?'

'I'm not sure. That nurse, I think.'

'Mary or Stacey?'

'Stacey, I think.'

I ask, 'Do you remember a doctor called Dr Kent?'

Ellie shakes her head. 'No.'

I glance up at Will, who narrows his eyes behind his glasses and purses his lips. I know that he's thinking the same as me: if this is going to be the quality of Ellie's evidence, we're going to have to consider carefully whether we want to put her on the stand.

I pick up my phone to check the time and realise with alarm that I've missed a call from the school. I apologise to Ellie and Will and quickly dial the number and weave my way through the tables to the exit.

There's no answer from the school office, which has in all likelihood now closed. The after-school club staff aren't answering. I check my voicemail and am told that I have one new message. I dial to listen.

'Hello, Sarah,' says Amy from the after-school club, cheerfully. 'Nothing wrong, Ben's fine. But we've had two staff members go home sick. It seems there's a bit of a tummy bug going round and one of the children has gone home with it too. Could you collect Ben by four thirty please? We can't stay open any later, unfortunately, as we don't have enough staff. I'm so sorry for the inconvenience.'

I end the call and check the clock on my phone. I know instinctively that there's insufficient time for me to get back to the school by four thirty, even if I called a cab. I'd need a helicopter, not a taxi.

'Shit. Shit, shit, shit,' I say, mild panic rising inside me.

Will pokes his head round the door. 'What's happened? Are you OK?'

'It's Ben,' I tell him. 'I've got to pick him up.'

'When?'

I look at my phone again. 'I needed to have left about half an hour ago.'

'Oh, crap. What are you going to do?'

There's only one thing I can do, I already know that. I don't like it, but it's all I've got. I silently vow that I'll somehow change my life so that I am never south of the river in the afternoon again.

'Do me a favour, Will? Can you just go inside and explain to Ellie? I'm really sorry, but I just need to sort this out.'

'Of course.' Will narrows his eyes in sympathy and pats my arm, before heading back inside.

I call Alex and he answers straight away. 'Sarah.'

There's no 'Hi, babe' this time, but I can ask him this, can't I? Will he mind? Will Ben? Will I?

'Alex, I'm in a bit of a pickle.'

'Why, what's up?'

'I'm still at Hay's Galleria, having my con… my meeting. But Ben needs picking up. I just got a call. They're having to shut the after-school club early. I'm so sorry to ask you this, but I'll never get there on time…'

'OK, calm down. Remind me where the entrance is?'

'You'll go and get him?'

'Of course I'll go and get him. Stop panicking.'

'Oh, Alex, thank you so much. I don't know what I would have done without you…'

'Sarah, just tell me where to go,' Alex laughs.

'Right. Yes.' I give him directions to the entrance to the after-school club and tell him which buzzer he has to ring.

'Give them a call and tell them I'm on my way now,' Alex instructs me.

'OK. They'll ask you for my secret password. It's… "Tallulah".'

'Tallulah?' Alex laughs. 'Sounds like a porn name.'

I giggle. 'It's the name of my rabbit.'

'You have a rabbit?'

'Not any more,' I laugh. 'She was my first pet. Tallulah Louisiana. Will you remember that?'

'How could I forget?'

'And, Alex... I hope he's all right for you.'

'He'll be just fine.'

'Just give him... well, you know. Bread, or bananas or whatever. Nothing too difficult to swallow. No fruit with stones, or pips...'

'I know, Sarah, stop worrying. I'll take good care of him.'

'OK. I'll be back as soon as I can.'

'Take your time. Finish your meeting. We'll be fine.'

'OK.'

'And, Sarah,' he adds.

'Yes?'

'I love you too.'

I end the call and allow myself a moment to breathe a sigh of happiness and relief. But my joy is short-lived; almost as soon as I end the call to Alex, my phone bleeps again. It's the office, another missed call. I press and hold '1' for voicemail and listen. It's not Lucy, it's Gareth. 'Sarah, I need to talk to you. It's important. Come back to the office please.'

I quickly dial the office number. Lucy puts me through and Gareth answers on the first ring. 'Are you on your way back?' he asks.

'Well, no,' I say. 'I only just got your message. But I have to go home. Ben's after-school club's closed early. I have to get back for him.'

There's a silence on the other end. I can hear Gareth sighing. He says, 'I'll see you tomorrow morning then. First thing.'

'I'm in court tomorrow—'

'I'm taking you out.'

My stomach flips. 'What's this about?'

'There's been a complaint about you, Sarah.'

I sigh. 'Not Matt again? Seriously? Is this because I didn't go to Charing Cross this morning? I told him, I had an interview with a witness booked, a con with Counsel.'

Gareth says, 'That's part of it. But it's a little more serious than that. I'll see you tomorrow morning, first thing. Don't be late. In the meantime, say goodbye to your client and tell Counsel that Matt will be in touch. I want you off this case.'

13

Before I even reach the door to the flat, I can hear loud music playing and I instantly recognise it as *Toy Story*'s 'You've Got a Friend in Me'. Inside, Alex and Ben are seated at the computer, eating crisps and watching a video clip. The combination of the music and the words to the song, the anxiety I've been left with following my conversation with Gareth and the sight of them both, the two boys that I love, sitting there side by side, is overwhelming. Alex's head is bobbing around in time with the music, even though it keeps stopping and starting up again. Ben has the mouse and is making Woody fly down the banister repeatedly, sliding the cursor back and clicking at precisely the same point in the video each time, the same few bars of music playing over and over again. Alex freezes like a statue every time the music stops and then starts to jig around as it starts up again. He's singing in a lovely deep baritone voice and I realise in an instant that this is what I'd wanted and desperately waited for from Andy, but never got: total, unconditional, absolute acceptance of Ben.

'Oh, hello, Mummy.' Alex turns his head and beams at me. 'Look, Ben, it's… Sarah, what on earth's wrong?' He lowers the volume on the speakers, jumps up and puts his hands on my arms. Ben flashes me a smile and turns back to the video.

'Nothing.' I wipe my eyes. 'Ignore me. It's just… you looked so sweet together. And that song…'

'I know. It's a bit cheesy, isn't it?' Alex grins. 'But he loves it. He's been playing it repeatedly for close to an hour.'

'Oh God, poor neighbours,' I say, smiling. 'And poor you. You must be about ready to shoot yourself.'

'Not at all.' Alex grins. 'I love that movie. And that particular bit… well, it's my favourite bit, as it happens.' He raises his eyebrows and laughs.

I reach up and touch his cheek. 'Thank you,' I say. I turn towards Ben as the music stops, ready to go and select another video for him. Alex grabs my arm and pulls me back.

'Watch,' he says. 'Just watch.'

So I watch, with growing astonishment, as Ben, having finally finished with *Toy Story*, deftly clicks on the 'Exit Full Screen' cross at the bottom and scrolls his way through a list of suggestions on the right-hand side. He deliberates the pros and cons of the *Teletubbies Tubby Toast Accident* and *Frozen*'s 'Let It Go' before finally settling for a song that I recognise from *The Lion King*. 'The Lion Sleeps Tonight' opens in full screen and a hippo begins to sing.

'Oh my God!' I exclaim. 'That's… incredible.'

Because it is. Here's my son, the one with no speech and very little understanding, who doesn't even know what 'Sit down', 'Come here', or 'Wait a minute' means, who barely responds to his own name. And yet he can somehow use a computer mouse to click and navigate and find his way round a music website. He recognises the images and can meaningfully select and play the videos that he wants. I don't have to do a thing to help him. I know in an instant that the world has opened up, not just for Ben but for me too. For the first time ever, I can see a future in which I might get to eat a meal or read a book, while Ben occupies himself happily on his own.

'Oh my God, Alex,' I breathe. 'You've taught him to... to surf the Internet! Look! He's happy! He's doing it all by himself!'

Alex says, 'There's more to that lad than meets the eye.'

I nod, fighting back tears for the second time.

Alex frowns. 'What's wrong?' he asks. 'There's something. I can tell.'

I wipe my eyes and sigh. 'I'm in trouble at work,' I say.

'What kind of trouble?'

I bite my lower lip. 'This case I'm working on. Something I did.'

'Do you want to talk about it?'

I take off my shoes and hang my jacket on the back of a chair. I walk over to the sofa and Alex comes and sits down beside me. 'I was supposed to go back to the office this afternoon,' I tell him. 'Gareth – my boss – wanted a meeting. I called and told him about Ben, that I had to get home, so we're meeting tomorrow morning. But he told me there's been a complaint. A real one, this time.'

'From who?'

I lean back into the sofa cushions. 'I went to the hospital. I had a bit of a run-in with a senior administrator there. I thought everything was OK, but now I suspect she's taken it to her director and they've decided to report me to the Solicitors' Regulation Authority.'

Alex frowns. 'Why? What happened?'

I look up at him. 'I sneaked onto a children's ward after

they'd told me I couldn't go there. I lied to members of staff. I told them I was visiting somebody, when I wasn't.'

'But why?'

I look up at him and sigh. 'I wanted to try and find some witnesses. Nurses. Staff members who might have been on the ward in July, the evening that the baby nearly died.'

'And did you?'

'No.' I shake my head. 'But that's not the point. I shouldn't have been there, and I lied my way in. They might say that it's conduct unbefitting a solicitor. I could... I could get struck off.'

Alex takes my hand. 'I'm sure it won't come to that. You'll probably just get a telling-off.'

'I hope you're right.'

'You must have had good reason,' Alex adds.

I shrug. 'Well, I think I did. The administrator wouldn't let me onto the ward. She wouldn't tell me anything, she wouldn't give me names.' I look up at him. 'I was trying to find witnesses to an attempted murder. It makes me so angry. If I were a police officer, I wouldn't have needed to lie.'

Alex nods. 'Well, then you need to tell them that. You were trying to do your job. Surely your boss will support you?'

I shake my head. 'On the contrary. He thinks I've overstepped the mark. He thinks I've got too involved. He wants to take me off the case.'

Alex's eyes widen. 'Can he do that?'

I shrug. 'Well, of course he can. He's my boss. He can do what he wants.'

'But who will take over?'

I roll my eyes. 'Golden boy. Matt. Matt, who never puts a foot wrong.'

'But what about your client? Won't she mind?'

I stop and think about that for a moment. 'Maybe. I hope so.' I smile.

Alex smiles back. 'I know I would,' he says. 'If I was in trouble, I'd definitely want you.'

*

As soon as dinner is over and Ben is in bed, Alex takes my hand.

'Come on,' he says. 'Let me take your mind off things. We'll play a game. You be Tallulah Louisiana and I'll be Peter Rabbit.'

I laugh as he pulls me up and steers me towards the bedroom. We both undress and then I feel the soft warmth of the bed against my back as he pushes me gently down, the weight of his body on mine. He gazes intently at me for a moment, his fingers trailing over my eyes, my hair, my cheek. 'I don't want to lose you,' he whispers suddenly, urgently, shaking his head.

I reach up and cup his face in my hands. 'Alex! Why on earth would you say that? That's not going to happen.'

He gazes silently back into my eyes for a moment. A second later, his mouth, his hands, his hips are on mine and I've lost all sense of time.

Afterwards, as we lie in the darkness, I turn to face him. 'I want to know more about you,' I say.

'What do you want to know?'

'Well, about your family. Your parents. You never talk about them.'

Alex hesitates a moment before saying, 'My parents are dead.'

'Alex! I'm so sorry. How come you never told me?'

'Didn't I?'

'No.'

'Oh. Well. It's not really something that you just come out and say.'

I know what he means. I feel that way about my mother. You don't want to embarrass people, because they won't know what to say next.

'So, how did they die?'

'Car crash.' Alex squeezes my hand, to let me know that it's OK.

'Do you have brothers and sisters?'

'No.'

'So you have no one? You were an only child?

'I was a twin,' he says, after a moment. 'My brother died when we were kids.'

'Oh, Alex. Oh God. How awful. I'm so sorry. How did he die?'

'He drowned. He fell into a lake. I was there. I wasn't able to save him.'

I squeeze his hand back. 'How old was he... were you? When he died?'

'Five.'

I glance at him in the darkness, examining the outline of his features. I stroke his hair back from his brow. 'You were only five. What an awful thing to have witnessed.'

Alex hesitates. 'Well, the strange thing is, I don't actually remember it. I must have blocked out the memory. And my parents wouldn't tell me anything, either. It was just like... one day he wasn't there any more. When I asked where he was, they fobbed me off, changed the subject. I remember being really upset, feeling isolated. But then, eventually, when I confronted them, demanded to know where he was, they told me I was imagining things, that I'd never had a brother.'

I turn over and lean onto one elbow, facing him. 'Are you serious? They really told you that?'

He nods. 'Crazy, I know.'

'So what happened?'

'Well at first, I believed them. Sort of. I had no choice other than to believe them, although, deep down, I knew he was real. And then, one day, when I was around fifteen, I was searching through the attic for an old pair of rugby boots, and I found a photo of the two of us, together, me and my brother, aged around three or four, my father holding us both on his knee. And so I confronted them.'

'What did they say?'

'Well, my mother continued trying to deny it at first. She started making up some ridiculous story about him being a playmate. But he looked just like me – and just like my father, too. We weren't identical twins, but you could see we were all related. My father stepped in and told her to be quiet. He said that they hadn't wanted me to suffer, so they'd tried to shield me.'

'By pretending that he'd never existed?' I say, aghast.

'They knew I'd blame myself.'

'But how could you...'

Alex's chest stops moving underneath my head. I can tell that he's holding his breath. He says, 'I was there, wasn't I? He died, I survived.'

Suddenly, Alex's interest in helping Ben makes perfect sense. Now, I can see what's happening. No matter how ridiculous or unwarranted, he blames himself for his brother's death; and he has some deep-rooted need to find redemption for being the twin who didn't drown.

I lay my head against his shoulder and we lie still, saying nothing for several minutes as I feel his chest rise and fall beneath me. I hope that Alex isn't expecting too much from Ben. What he's learned to do on the computer feels like some kind of miracle, but I'm under no illusion that tomorrow is going to herald another leap forward in his development. Ben's problems are significant. They will always be significant. He's never going to develop into a normal child.

I roll over and kiss him. His arm circles my waist and he pulls me towards him.

'I'm sorry about your family,' I whisper into his ear. 'But you've got me. Me and Ben. If you want us, that is.'

Alex runs his hand down the length of my spine. I feel his chest rise and fall underneath me as he lets out an unmistakable, deep sigh. After a moment he cups my face in his hands and looks into my eyes. He opens his mouth as if he's about to say something, but then changes his mind and draws my head onto his shoulder.

'Of course I want you,' he says into my hair. 'I want you very much.'

*

In the morning, we wake late. Alex makes coffee and gives Ben his breakfast while I hurriedly take a shower and get dressed.

'Alex, have you seen my papers?' I call out to him, as I open and shut the doors to my wardrobe. I could have sworn I'd brought home the paper copies of the statements in Ellie's case after I'd scanned them the day before yesterday. I thought I'd left the file in a bag on the wardrobe floor.

'What papers?' Alex calls from the bathroom, where he's now shaving.

'You know,' I call back. 'The attempted murder case. Those papers you helped me scan to my iPad.'

'Oh. Those.' Alex walks out of the bathroom. He's bare-chested and he has shaving foam round his chin and a razor in his hand. 'Do you still need them? You've got it all on your iPad, haven't you?'

'Yes. But my boss has asked for them. I'm guessing he wants to give them to Matt.' I pull a face.

Alex frowns for a moment and then looks up. 'Ah. Hang on a minute, I remember now.' He strides off into the kitchen, opens a cabinet above the cooker, removes the lever-arch folder of papers I'd been looking for and hands them to me. 'I moved them into this cupboard. I'd completely forgotten.' He grins. 'Ben got hold of them.'

'Oh God. Thank you,' I say, taking the file from him and kissing him. 'I'm sorry. He's a nightmare.'

Alex ruffles the top of Ben's head. 'He's just keeping us on our toes,' he says. 'Give him a few years and he'll be running rings around us.'

I smile, and raise my eyebrows, inwardly elated that Alex is talking as if we have a future together. I'm not stupid; I know that this is how it is at the start of a relationship, how easy it is when you're all loved-up and optimistic to drop idle hints about the next steps together, to make promises and plans. I also know how it is once the bubble bursts and reality seeps in; I know about the competing demands of work, love and children, about the degree of compromise a relationship requires, especially when you have a child like Ben. But today, more than ever before, I understand what's in it for Alex. I believe, at last, that he might actually need me and Ben as much as we need him.

I walk over, stand on tiptoes and put my arms round his shoulders, pulling him to me and kissing him slowly. Alex wraps his arms round me and draws me close. His mouth is warm and tastes of coffee. His newly shaved skin is smooth, his aftershave delicious.

'I've got to go,' I tell him, reluctantly. 'I'm going to be late. Bloody Gareth.'

Alex lifts Ben out of his chair. 'Come on. Let me give you a lift down to the office and then I can drop Ben off afterwards.'

'You don't mind?'

He shakes his head. 'No. I've got a late-morning meeting. It's fine. You don't want to give Gareth anything else to be upset about.'

I give him a grateful smile. 'Thank you, Alex. I really appreciate this.'

As we sit in traffic on the Holloway Road, heading towards Highbury, I flick through the papers on my lap. I can't bear the thought of giving the case to Matt, of stepping aside and watching from the sidelines while he takes the case through to trial. But it looks as though I'm going to have no choice.

'So what's your meeting about?' I ask Alex.

Alex indicates and switches lanes. 'It's with one of my fund managers,' he says. 'See how the old stocks are doing.'

'It's been a turbulent year,' I say.

Alex gives me a sideways look and starts laughing.

'OK,' I confess. 'I have absolutely nothing else I can add to that conversation.'

'That's OK,' he smiles. 'As it happens, neither do I.'

'Alex,' I venture, after a moment. 'You know what we were talking about last night. About your family. Can I ask you a question?'

He hesitates for a moment. 'Sure.'

'How long ago did the car crash happen, the one that killed your parents?'

Alex looks over his shoulder and switches lanes again. He furrows his brow in concentration and then slows right down. 'I can't stop here. It's a red route. Can I turn here?' He points to the road on the right.

'Yes. You can go down this one. The office is just over there.'

He turns right into the road just ahead of the court building. As he slows down, shifts out of gear and pulls on the handbrake, I place my hand on his.

He turns to me and smiles. 'Sarah, actually, do you mind if we don't talk about that any more?'

'Of course,' I agree. 'I'm so sorry, I didn't mean to pry.'

He leans over and gives me a peck on the cheek, but he doesn't say, 'You weren't prying.' Instead, he says, 'Good luck. Really. I'll be thinking of you. I hope it goes OK.'

'Thank you.' I get out of the car and open the back door. I give Ben a kiss on the nose. I wave as Alex drives away then walk round the corner and cross the road to the office.

*

Matt is behind the reception desk talking to Lucy when I walk in. They both immediately stop talking as I enter; neither says 'hello'. I walk on past them up to Gareth's room and knock on the door.

He waves me into a seat. 'I've forwarded you the response form,' he says. 'From the SRA. It's your opportunity to put your side of things.'

'So, you do acknowledge that there's another side to all this?' I ask him.

Gareth sighs and leans back in his chair. 'I'm struggling to see one, Sarah, I have to say. But you're the advocate. So, you tell me. How do you justify breaching the hospital's rules, their security, in the way that you did? A children's hospital, of all places. A children's ward. Christ, you know all about child protection, the issues involved...'

'I was trying to find witnesses,' I say. 'That's all. The hospital administration manager was being obstructive. Someone at the hospital may well be hiding something. That might be what this is all about.'

Gareth sighs again and shakes his head, quickly, impatiently. 'Or it may just be a conspiracy theory on your part.'

I shrug. 'Maybe. I may be wrong. But that doesn't alter the fact that I have a duty to Ellie to try and find out.'

Gareth shakes his head. 'I disagree. You take your client's instructions and you prepare her defence based on those instructions. Poking around for witnesses that may not even exist is not what we're being paid for.'

'But that's the problem. Her instructions don't amount to anything.'

'Then maybe she's guilty.'

'But maybe she's not. She's told me she didn't do it, and it's my job to follow that through, test the evidence. If it's all going to come down to money every time, then we may as well give up now, bring back the death penalty, let them all hang.'

Gareth taps his pen on the table and looks at me for a moment. I can see that he's fuming. 'I'm told that you were found at the bedside of the baby, the victim in the case. That you were playing with the baby.'

I nod. I have no defence to this one. 'Yes. I… I came across him by accident. I was really only… sometimes it helps at trial, to set the scene.'

Gareth looks me in the eye. 'Not by breaking someone else's rules, it doesn't.'

I stare at the floor and bite my lip. 'Please don't give the case to Matt. It's not fair on Ellie, asking her to change solicitors a matter of weeks before her trial.'

Gareth sniffs. 'She's not changing law firms,' he says. 'You'll be on hand to help him if anything is unclear.'

I nod. I suppose I should be grateful that he's not sacking me.

'So, other than being on hand to help Matt if he needs it, what do you want me to do?'

'Trial preparation,' he says. 'In the office. At least until you've filed your response and we've heard back from the SRA.'

When I walk out of Gareth's room, Matt is in the hallway. I can tell that he's been hovering near the door, listening in. 'All right?' He smiles at me. 'Ready for the handover?'

I push the case file into his arms and follow him into our room. I pull my chair over to his desk and sit down next to him.

My phone rings. I pull it out of my handbag; it's the school. I glance up at Matt. 'I need to get this,' I say. Matt rolls his eyes towards the ceiling and purses his lips.

'Hi, Sarah,' says Ben's teacher, Jennie. 'I was just wondering… is Ben ill?'

My heart leaps. 'Why do you say that? What's happened?'

Jennie hesitates. 'Well, that's why I'm phoning you,' she says, sounding confused. 'I wondered whether he was coming in today.'

'What? You mean he's not there yet?'

'No. Should he have been?'

I move the phone away from my ear and peer at the time. It's gone ten o'clock. Alex left with Ben over an hour ago. What on earth can have happened to them? 'My partner was bringing him,' I say, weakly. 'I'll have to call him, find out where they are. I'll… I'll call you back as soon as I know.'

'Of course. Don't worry. I'm sure there's a logical explanation,' Jennie says. 'But let me know if there's anything I can do.'

'Thanks, Jennie.'

I end the call and quickly scroll to Alex's number. It goes straight to voicemail. My phone beeps as I hang up.

'Ready?' says Matt.

I glance up at him, my heart hammering against my chest. Have they had a car accident? Have they crashed? What other explanation could there be? 'No. You'll have to… read the papers and…' I tail off. 'My son's missing. I have to find him.'

Without waiting for his reply, I grab my coat and bag and run down the stairs and out of the office into the street. I run across the road to the side road where I last left Ben and Alex and then jog up the Holloway Road. Calm down, Sarah, I tell myself, reminding myself of Jennie's words. There's bound to be a logical explanation. But if they'd had an accident it would be along this stretch of the road, between here and the school, so if I just keep walking… and phoning… and walking some more…

I mentally tick off the side roads as I pass them. Liverpool Road, George's Road, Eden Grove. I'm nearly halfway there now. I tap on Alex's number again. It goes straight to voicemail for a second time. Is that a good sign? I wonder. Doesn't that mean he has no signal or is on another call? If he'd been hurt, if he couldn't answer, surely it would ring out? And come to think of it, if there'd been a serious accident between here and the school there'd be a tailback of traffic still, emergency vehicles… wouldn't there? I slow back down to a walking pace and catch my breath. But where can they be? And why hasn't Alex called me?

I cross the road just before Biddestone Park and head down Jackson Road in the direction of the school. Then I wonder if Alex has perhaps driven the other way, down Hornsey Road or maybe even further back at Drayton Park. I stop in my tracks and heave out a sigh. Maybe I should just head home. Perhaps they're there? Maybe there's a really simple explanation for this – one that I just haven't thought of yet.

My heart sinks as I turn the corner into my street and see that there's no sign of Alex's car outside my house. I let myself in and call out for him, but there's clearly nobody there. I ring the school again and am told that they still haven't arrived. I call Alex, twice. It's now approaching eleven o'clock. It's two hours since I left them.

I walk into the kitchen and put the kettle on. I pull a clean cup out of the dishwasher and drop a chamomile teabag into it. I need to calm down, I keep telling myself. Everything is going to be OK. While I wait for the kettle to boil, I stand at the window in the living room, looking out, trying to work out what to do next. Is it too early to call the police?

Suddenly, I hear the noise of a car engine outside and Alex's car pulls up. I almost faint with relief when I see him get out, go to the back door and open it. I race to the front door and run down the path. Alex is lifting Ben out of his car seat and holding him against his shoulder. I can see instantly that Ben is floppy, asleep or… worse?

'Alex?' I scream out. I run over and tug at his arm, trying to get a look at Ben's face. 'What's happened? What's happened to Ben?'

Alex looks up, clearly – from the look on his face – completely surprised to see me. 'Sarah. What are you doing here?'

'Me? Never mind what I'm doing. What's happened to Ben?'

Alex heaves Ben up onto his shoulder. He touches my arm. 'It's OK,' he says. 'Ben's fine. He's just a bit sleepy...'

'What the hell's happened? Where on earth have you been? I've been going out of my mind!' I shout at him. 'Why didn't you call me?'

Alex presses his key fob to lock the car. 'Shall we...' He nods towards my front door. I shake my head, infuriated that he's concerned with what the neighbours think when he still hasn't told me what's wrong with Ben. He carries Ben inside. I follow him up the path. 'Give him to me,' I insist, as soon as we're inside the hallway. Alex pushes the front door shut. I pull Ben out of his arms and kiss his face. He opens his eyes, sleepily, and gives me a faint smile.

Alex runs his hand through his hair, pushing his fringe back. He looks mortified. 'I'm so sorry, Sarah. Ben was sick, he threw up in the car right after you left. I took him straight to A&E. I knew you had your meeting. I didn't want to worry you. I didn't realise you'd be... that you'd know... how did you...?'

'The school phoned me,' I say stiffly. 'Wanting to know where he was.' I walk into the front room and lay Ben down on the sofa. 'Didn't you realise they'd be worried?'

'I'm really sorry,' Alex says again. 'I had no idea I'd worried them... you... anyone. I was trying to do the opposite. You had your meeting and... I was just thinking of Ben. I just thought, straight away… "Get him checked out. That's the best thing to do." Knowing his history, you know? I didn't want to take any chances.'

I take a deep breath. 'So what did they say at A&E? It's just a tummy bug, surely? It's been all round the nursery.'

Alex breathes out heavily and bites his lip. 'Of course. That's all it will be. They said he'd be fine. They just checked him over. Lots of fluid and rest. You know.'

I nod and let out a long sigh as I feel my pulse rate return to normal. I lean forward and stroke Ben's hair back from his head. 'He seems very sleepy,' I say.

Alex nods. 'Yes. He was very sick. He just needs some rest, to sleep it off.'

'You should have called me,' I reprimand him. '*Always* call me. I don't care what I'm doing, where I am. You need to always let me know.'

Alex scratches his head and looks at his feet. 'Of course. I'm sorry.'

I take another long breath. 'I'm sorry he threw up in your car,' I say. 'Is it a mess? Do you want me to clean it up?'

'It's fine.' Alex shakes his head. 'I'll sort it, don't worry. You stay with Ben.' He stands up. 'Do you want me to get a blanket from his room?'

'No. I'll put him to bed.'

'Let me.' Alex leans over and tucks his hands under Ben's body and lifts him gently off the sofa. I watch, my anger melting as he holds Ben's head against his arm with his spare hand, his long fingers gently stroking my son's beautiful hair. He loves Ben. He was thinking of Ben, that's all. And me. He was thinking of me, too. I should be grateful that he cares enough about both of us, enough to risk missing his morning meeting, to make sure I didn't miss mine, while he got Ben checked out, made sure he was definitely OK. I suddenly remember the way that Alex had reacted when Ben was at the lake in the park, how he'd sprung at Ben and pulled him away from the water. He may have overreacted a little, but isn't it better to have someone who's too cautious around Ben than someone who doesn't care?

I can hear my phone ringing from the coffee table where I've left it.

Alex nods at me. 'Get it. I'll go and put him down.'

'It's probably the office,' I sigh. 'Wondering where I am.'

I reach over and grab my phone from the table while Alex takes Ben in the direction of the bedroom. The ringing stops as I pick it up. Before I can even check the number and call it back, it rings again. I look at the screen, but it's a number I don't recognise. I'll let it go to voicemail, I decide. But then… 0-1-8-6-5. Where's that?

I swipe the slider to the right. A male voice that I don't recognise says, 'Hello. Is that Sarah Kellerman?'

'Yes. Who's calling?' I ask, a tiny flicker of impatience escaping into my voice. I should have let it go to voicemail. I need to see to Ben.

'My name's Mark Greenhalgh,' says the man. 'You left a message for me.'

'Mark…?' I stutter in surprise. 'Mark Greenhalgh? Really?'

'Yes, I know it's taken me a while to get back to you, and I'm sorry about that,' his voice continues. 'I did get your message, but I've hardly been in clinic at all since you called.'

'That's OK,' I say. 'Thank you for calling. I'm really glad you did.'

'So how can I help?'

'I'm a solicitor... did the message say?'

'Yes.'

'OK. Well, I'm... I've been working on a case. It's an important case. And there's an important witness for the prosecution – a nurse. The police took a statement from her, but after that they couldn't find her. She seems to have gone missing. You sponsored her for a while, I'm told. I wondered if you might know where she's gone.'

'What's her name?'

'Mary Ngombe. She's African. From Ghana.'

Mark Greenhalgh laughs. It's a deep, throaty laugh.

'What's so funny?' I ask.

'She's not missing,' he says. 'I don't know why the police couldn't find her.'

'Really? You know where she is?'

'I do indeed,' says Mark Greenhalgh. 'She's here at the John Radcliffe, with me.'

14

Rain lashes against the windscreen as we head up the M40 to Oxford. Alex is driving and Ben is strapped into his seat in the back. He loves the rain, and as I glance back over my shoulder I can see that he is being lulled into a meditative state by the rhythm of the windscreen wipers and the swishing of the tyres against the wet surface of the road. Alex, on the other hand, is locked in concentration, as the stretch of motorway ahead becomes less visible, the traffic slows and brake lights start to appear.

The satnav tells Alex to keep right.

'I am not keeping right, lady,' he says. 'I'm staying right where I am.'

'Junction seven,' I tell him, as we pass. 'The A329 to Thame. Next junction. Not far now.'

Half a mile later, Alex indicates left. Junction eight looms up ahead and we turn off onto the A40.

'I really appreciate this,' I say. 'It's not much of a way to spend a Saturday, is it?'

'It will be.' Alex glances at me. 'This rain won't last. And once we've been to the hospital, we can do something nice. It's ages since I've been to Oxford.'

'Thank you.' I put my hand on his thigh. He takes his left hand off the wheel and covers mine. 'I didn't want to leave this to Matt,' I add. 'He might not even bother. I really want to talk to this nurse today.' I give him a wry smile. 'Before she gets away again.'

Alex gives my hand a squeeze. 'That's OK. I understand.'

The rain does, in fact, ease and it's now only pattering gently against the roof as we pass the sign that welcomes us to Oxford. We sail through the traffic lights next to the Park & Ride and slow down as we enter a residential area that fringes the outskirts of the city. The satnav tells us that, at the roundabout, we should go straight on.

'I believe this is Headington,' says Alex, as we pause at the next set of traffic lights. 'This is where the hospital is.'

We drive through a busy built-up area full of shops and traffic and then turn right into a residential street. The hospital grounds are behind a wall at the bottom of the road on the left. Alex swings the car through an opening into a car park.

'I don't think you can drive any further,' I tell him. I point across a grassed area in the direction of the hospital building. 'It looks as though the main car park is over there.'

'That's OK. You jump out here if you like and walk across. You're going to be a while and it might work best for my buddy here if I drive round the block a few times and meet you round the other side.'

I look at him gratefully, before glancing round at Ben in the back. He seems happy enough. I'm leaving Alex a case full of nursery rhyme CDs and two portable DVD players, the second for when the first one runs out of charge. But Ben looks really dreamy and settled right now and Alex is right that driving him around for a while before he stops is likely to prove a good initial distraction. A bit of driving, a bit of *Teletubbies*, a CD.

He should be OK for the hour, or more, that this might take. I don't know what I'd have done without Alex today.

We say goodbye and I zip up my waterproof coat and step out of the warm car into the cold wetness of the light rain. I pull my hood up and cross the grassed area towards the hospital and cut through the women's centre and maternity unit. I'm able to find a way through to the main hospital and then on through corridor after corridor to the children's centre, where the PICU is to be found.

I look at the clock on my phone. It's ten past one. I desperately hope Mary's there. I've checked her shifts with the ward matron, as per Mark Greenhalgh's suggestion, and I've been told that she's on an 'early long' – from eight this morning until eight o'clock this evening – and that she usually takes a break around now. I hope that I've timed it right. I've actually no idea whether I'm going to have to wait around to see her, but I figure that if she's too busy I can try and pin her down on a time when I could come back. I think of Alex and Ben, waiting for me in the car, and silently pledge that I won't do this to them again.

As I approach the PICU ward, the door opens and a senior-looking staff nurse comes out. I seize my opportunity.

'Excuse me,' I ask her. 'I'm here to see Mary Ngombe. Is she on the ward?'

'Mary?' The nurse shakes her head. 'Mary's at lunch. Can I help?'

'Maybe. Would you happen to know where she's gone?'

'To the canteen, I imagine. It's through there.' She points in the direction I've just come. 'It's on the third floor in the main building. Just follow the signs.'

'Thank you. Thank you very much.'

I hurry back through the corridors to the main building and run up the stairs, rather than taking the lift. As I open the door to the third floor, I can smell food and I find the canteen immediately on my right.

It's full of people: nurses, doctors, patients and visitors. I scan the room for an African face, but there are several. One by one, I approach them, asking, 'Are you Mary, by any chance?' but none of them are.

I stand near to the tills and scan the room once more, before going up to the tea and coffee aisle and ordering a drink. I figure I might as well wait here for a minute, just in case she's stopped off somewhere on the way.

As I'm paying for my coffee, I feel a tap on my shoulder. I spin round to see a plump, black nurse, who appears to be in her late twenties. Her hair is pulled back against her scalp into tight, coiled braids which frame her wide, dimpled face.

'I hear you are looking for me,' says Mary Ngombe.

'Yes. Yes, I am,' I stutter, in relief.

'You are the solicitor?'

'That's right. Can I get you a drink?'

She shakes her head and holds up a bottle of something lime green. 'I have my Mountain Dew.'

'OK. Great. Do you mind if we have a chat, then?'

Mary waves at a table nearby, then turns on her heel. I pick up my coffee and follow her. She pulls out a chair and sits down. I take a seat opposite her and watch as she unwraps a cheese sandwich from its triangle-shaped plastic carton and takes a bite.

'So what is it that you want to talk about?' she asks.

'I want to ask you about the incident that happened back on

the twenty-fifth of July this year, when you were at Southwark St Martin's. The little boy who you were looking after – Finn Stephens – the one who had his dialysis line removed…'

'It was a very bad thing,' she says, shaking her head. 'Very bad indeed.'

'Yes,' I agree.

'I was very sad to leave him.' She lowers her head for a moment and then looks up again. 'Do you know how he is?'

'He's on the mend.' I smile. 'He's turned a corner. I don't expect he'll be leaving hospital any time soon, but… he's much better than he was.'

Mary beams. 'I am very pleased to hear that.'

'Me too,' I say. 'But his mother is on trial for trying to harm him. You gave a statement to the police…'

Mary frowns. 'I can't tell those policemen anything more, you know? I have already said what happened, and that' – she gives a decisive nod of the head – 'is what happened.'

I nod. Her voice is deep and throaty, her intonation heavily Ghanaian. I'm finding that I have to listen intently as she speaks.

'All the same, if I could just clarify one or two things… would that be OK?' I ask her.

She shrugs. 'I don't mind if you want to do that.'

'Thank you, Mary.' I pull my iPad out of my bag. 'Do you mind if I take notes while we talk?'

Mary takes another bite of her sandwich and shakes her head.

I scroll up on my iPad to her statement. 'OK,' I say. 'So you said you were doing late shifts that week. So that would have been two o'clock until ten. Is that right?'

'It's nine thirty really. But we would never leave until ten. Sometimes long after that.'

'OK. You say you looked after the baby, Finn, quite closely that week?'

'I was his nurse. That is right.'

'And it was you who took him over to Peregrine Ward for the treatment to his kidneys.'

'Yes. I was the one who did the handover. I checked his fluids, his cannula, to make sure that everything was still in place, and I talked to the ward nurse about his medications.'

'And which nurse was that?'

'You know, I am not very good with names. I think this nurse was called Tracey.'

'Could it have been Stacey? Stacey Bennett?'

'It might have been.'

'OK. So that was around six fifteen?'

'Uh-huh.'

'And then?'

'I went back to take his medications.'

'What time was that?'

'I don't know.'

'Well, in your statement, you said that it was around nine o'clock.'

'OK, so I would say that it must have been around nine o'clock.' Mary looks hard at me across the table, as though she thinks I might be a little bit dim.

'And which nurses did you see, at that time?'

'I am afraid I cannot remember that now.'

'OK. So did anyone else come to visit Finn while you were there?'

'Such as who?'

'Doctors?'

'I do not think so. Just Tracey.'

'Stacey?'

'Stacey. And then the baby's mother.'

'Ellie?' I say. 'You saw Ellie?'

'Yes. I came onto the ward and saw her. She had picked the baby up from the cot. She was holding him.'

'And what time was this exactly?'

'I can't recall, exactly. It would have been around nine or ten o'clock.'

I look up, sharply. 'Nine or ten? So was that... the last time you went to check on Finn, before you went off shift? Or the time before?'

'I think it was the last time.'

'But you're not sure?'

Mary is non-committal. 'It was whatever time I told the police.'

I swallow down my instinct to grasp at her previous concession to uncertainty and pin her down on it. I'm not here to cross-examine her; I don't want to alienate her. I decide to move on.

'So, you went off shift at ten?'

Mary unscrews the cap of her bottle of pop and takes a sip. 'I believe it was then.'

'So, at some point between nine and... let's say ten fifteen, when you returned to Peregrine Ward, you saw Ellie – the baby's mother – standing at Finn's bedside. And she was holding the baby.'

'Yes.'

'How close to her were you?'

'I was just a few feet away, just outside the door. I saw her clearly.'

'Did she see you?'

'No. I decided not to go onto the ward.'

'Why not?'

'Because she was there, with the baby. She was not someone I wanted to talk to.'

'Why not?'

Mary shrugs but doesn't reply.

'And are you one hundred per cent sure that it was the baby's mother?' I ask her.

'Of course I am. I knew who she was. I saw her every day.'

I look up. 'Every day? You saw her every day?'

'Every day. She was there all day, every day. She was always getting under my feet.'

'You mean on the PICU ward?'

'Ye-e-e-s.'

'You saw here there on the PICU ward. Every day? When you were on the late shift?'

'Ye-e-e-s.' Mary's eyes tell me that she thinks I really might be a little bit slow.

I think carefully for a moment. How can this be, when Liberty worked the same shift as Mary all week and had no idea who Ellie was?

'Are you sure we've got the same person here?' I ask. 'Are you sure you're talking about Ellie, the baby's mother?'

'You think I don't know who the baby's mother is?' Mary looks exasperated. 'She's the only mother I know who is too posh to change her own baby's nappy.'

I stare at her for a moment. 'Mary! That's not Ellie,' I exclaim. 'That's not the baby's mother. That's his grandmother, Lady Barrington-Brown.'

'She told me her name was Ellie,' Mary insists, sulkily.

I glance back down at her statement. 'But you describe her as a teenager, aged fifteen or sixteen?'

Mary throws her head back and explodes with laughter. I wait patiently for her to stop laughing. 'I said that she was fif-*tee* or six-*tee*,' she enunciates. 'She was a lady, not a girl.' She explodes into laughter again.

'But, Mary, you said she was the baby's mother!'

'No, *she* told me she was the baby's mother,' Mary insists.

'But, Mary!' I exclaim again. 'How can a woman in her fifties or sixties be the mother of a one-year-old child?'

Mary shrugs. 'It happens.'

'Not very often!' I protest.

'In Ghana – no,' Mary says, sagely. 'The women in Ghana have their babies when they are young and healthy. Women here – they wait until they are old. It is not good for the baby.' She shakes her head sorrowfully.

'But you signed a statement to say that the woman was "fifteen or sixteen",' I challenge her.

Mary looks at me for a moment. 'The policeman, he read it back to me,' she says, simply. 'Then he asked me to sign it. I just did as I was asked.'

I stare at her with my mouth open for a long moment, unable to comprehend that such a monumental mistake could have happened, but knowing at the same time that it so easily could. Some of my clients don't read and write so well, and it's embarrassing for them to admit it; and besides, my handwriting's not the best. I almost always just read their statements back to them, before asking them to sign on the dotted line.

'But the CCTV operators and the night-shift staff on Peregrine ward all say that no members of the public other than Ellie went in or out.' I'm thinking out loud. I know that this is not a question for Mary to answer.

'I don't know about that,' says Mary. 'But I know what I saw.'

I suddenly remember something. I scroll down through my emails until I find what I'm looking for: a photograph attached to Ellie's résumé, sent to me by the escort agency along with a letter covering some of the dates she'd worked towards the end of last year.

I open up the résumé and scroll up so that the name of the agency is hidden and only Ellie's head and shoulders appear. I turn my iPad around so that Mary can see it. 'Do you know her? Have you ever seen her?' I ask.

Mary shakes her head. 'No. I have never seen this lady before. I would have remembered. She is a very pretty girl.'

'She is,' I agree, trying to contain my desire to jump up and fling my arms around Mary's neck. Instead I look at her intently. 'Mary, *this* is Finn's mother. Not the other lady. This is the young woman who is accused of trying to kill her baby. Her name is Ellie.'

Mary looks surprised. 'Her name is Ellie, too?'

I nod, slowly, suddenly conscious that I have no idea what Lady Barrington-Brown's Christian name is. I close Ellie's résumé and quickly tap on the electronic file that contains the statements in Ellie's case and scroll through them. I find the family tree prepared by the social worker, and as soon as I see it on the page, I remember having read it previously. I want to kick myself. 'Eleanor,' I say out loud. 'Her name is Eleanor.'

'She said it was Ellie.' Mary sticks to her guns.

'Sure. Sure she did.' I want to laugh out loud. Why on earth didn't I notice this before? 'So, Mary.' I lean forward. 'If I were to let you get on with your work right now and go away and put what you've told me into a handwritten statement, would you sign it?'

'I would have to read it first,' says Mary, wisely.

'Of course. And then, would you come to court to give evidence?'

Mary looks doubtful. 'I don't know. When would that be?'

'February,' I tell her. 'The beginning of February.'

Mary shakes her head. 'I am sorry. I am going back to Ghana for Christmas.'

My heart sinks. 'You're not coming back?'

'Not this time. I have a fiancé back home. We are getting married on Christmas Day.'

I try my best to hide my disappointment as I observe Mary's evident joy. She smiles broadly, pretty dimples appearing in her cheeks.

'Congratulations,' I tell her. 'Well, you know what, Mary? I hope your wedding day is wonderful. At least, if you're willing to sign a statement about all of this, it will really help Ellie's defence.'

'OK,' Mary agrees. 'So, is that it? Can I go now? I need to get back to work.'

'One more thing. When you went onto Peregrine Ward, did you notice a camp bed on the floor? With anyone sleeping in it?'

Mary looks thoughtful for a moment. 'No,' she says. 'I do not recall seeing that at all.'

I start to pack up my things. 'Thank you. Thank you very much for your help, Mary. I really appreciate your time.'

Mary pushes her chair back and gets up. I follow her out of the canteen. My mind is racing. What does this mean for Ellie's defence? Lady Barrington-Brown... *Eleanor* Barrington-Brown – not Ellie – was, in fact, the last person to be seen holding the baby.

In itself, it doesn't mean a whole lot, I know. It doesn't mean that they'll drop the case against Ellie. They've still got the injuries and the sodium poisoning. And Ellie, not Eleanor, was there when Finn was found bleeding to death. The prosecution will no doubt argue that it's immaterial. The police have never spoken to Eleanor; I don't suppose anyone has directly asked her the question: did she go onto Peregrine Ward after Finn was moved from the PICU, and did she pick him up? Eleanor might, in fact, openly accept that she'd been onto the renal unit to see Finn before she left the hospital that evening, possibly before Ellie even arrived. If Mary didn't see the camp bed, then it probably wasn't there and neither was Ellie. Mary was, after all, somewhat unsure of her times.

But what this does mean is that the case against Ellie is weakened significantly. This is going to be a new piece of evidence that will be impossible for the judge to ignore: nobody can testify to the fact that Ellie herself picked up the baby shortly before his tube was pulled out. Also, if the CCTV operators and ward staff missed Eleanor going onto the ward, then who else did they miss? Reasonable doubt, that's all we need. In the meantime, we'll make our own application to the judge to have Mary's latest statement read in court. He can hardly refuse it, can he? With this new evidence before them, I seriously wonder if a jury would convict.

I say goodbye to Mary outside the canteen as she stops to wait for the lift. There are a number of other people waiting:

doctors, patients, porters, and I decide to take the stairs. I plan to run down, check on Alex and Ben, write up Mary's statement and get right back up to see her again as quickly as I can.

The lift pings and the doors to the lift open at the same time as my phone whistles repeatedly and a flurry of text messages arrives. Inside the canteen, I must have been out of range for a phone signal. I curse myself; I never realise when I'm out of range until it's too late.

Mary steps away from me towards the lift.

'Thank you so much,' I tell her. 'I'll come back and find you on the ward before eight. Is that OK?'

She replies, obligingly, 'That will be OK.'

I hurry down the stairs, checking my messages and trying not to trip as I go.

The messages are all from Alex. *Oh no*, I tell myself. *This is going to be a disaster, I know it. Ben's bored, or unhappy and he's having a meltdown. Ben's thrown up again. Alex can't cope.* Immediately, I visualise the scene: Alex crouching down and leaning through the back door of the car, coaxing Ben as he wails and bites himself, and kicks his feet against the seat. Or worse: Alex, sitting in the front seat of the car with his hands over his ears, stressed to the hilt and at a loss as to what to do, while Ben screams alone in the back.

This is all my fault. I've been too long. I have got some serious apologising to do.

But then I read the texts from Alex, and I realise that it's far, far worse than that.

15

When I enter the Accident and Emergency department, Alex is nowhere to be seen. I follow the signs to the reception desk and wait for what seems like for ever. Eventually, it's my turn and I give both mine and Ben's details to the nurse at the desk, before being calmly directed to a side room, where Alex is talking to a doctor. He looks up as I enter and holds out one arm to beckon me inside.

'Sarah, where were you?' he says. 'I've been texting you.'

'I know. I'm sorry, I… What's happened? Where's Ben?'

'Ms Kellerman?' says the doctor. He offers me his hand and I take it. 'I'm Kevin Cresswell. I'm the neurology registrar on duty this afternoon. Ben's epilepsy seems to have worsened and we need your permission to run some tests.'

'What do you mean, it's worsened?' My heart is pounding in my chest and my legs feel weak. I feel sick, sick to the stomach. I can't believe this is happening, all over again.

'Ben had a seizure,' Alex explains. 'When we were in the car.'

'No! No, no, no, no… Not again. Please, tell me, not again.' I know I sound hysterical, but I can't seem to stop myself.

Alex puts an arm round my shoulder.

'What happened? Was it a proper fit? How long did it last?

Where is he? Is he OK? I need to see him.' My words tumble out, one after the other.

'It lasted around ten minutes,' Alex says.

'Ten minutes? That's ages!' I shriek. 'Are you sure? Did you notice it straight away?'

Alex shakes his head. 'I was driving, unfortunately. I could see him in my mirror. I drove straight back to the hospital and ran in with him as quick as I could.'

'He's had ten milligrams of diazepam,' the registrar tells me. 'Along with twenty mils of sodium valproate. He's sedated and he's stable. We're now running some blood tests.'

'What for?'

'Well, meningitis, encephalitis...'

'Oh, God.'

'It's routine,' the registrar reassures me. 'We need to check that the seizure wasn't brought on by an underlying condition. But we need to run some further tests: an EEG and an MRI. We need your consent.'

I take a deep breath. 'OK.'

Once the forms are signed, I'm shown into a room where a nurse is taking Ben's bloods. He is sleeping peacefully and doesn't move or wake when I lean over and kiss his forehead. As soon as the blood is taken, a second nurse and a porter arrive and push his bed out of the room.

'It's best to do the EEG whilst he's lying still,' says the registrar, arriving in the doorway. 'We'll get a better reading.'

'I just don't understand,' I tell him. 'He hasn't had a seizure for over a year.'

'That's why we need to have a look and see what's going on,' he says. 'It's difficult to say what's happened at this stage, but sometimes seizures evolve and become unresponsive to medications. They can also be a result of side effects of those medications, or sometimes they are caused by infections in the brain – or head injuries.'

'Head injuries?' I say, with alarm. I look at Alex. 'He hasn't fallen, has he? He hasn't banged his head?'

Alex frowns. 'No. No, of course he hasn't.'

The registrar says, 'We'll know more when we've done the brain scans and once the blood tests come back.'

I am allowed to lift Ben off the bed and hold him in my arms while the nurse attaches the electrodes to his head. The tests take over forty minutes to do and the weight of Ben's head is heavy against my arm, but I am comforted by the rising and falling of his chest, by his heaving, shuddering sighs and the warmth of his body against mine. I lean over and kiss his little forehead and stroke his hand, while the nurse presses buttons and switches at a desk in the corner of the room.

After the EEG is done, Ben is sedated once again and taken for the MRI. I sit with Alex in the corridor while the doctors take pictures of Ben's brain.

'So, how did it happen?' I ask Alex. 'Tell me, from the start.'

He takes my hand. 'After you left, we drove up the road. I thought I might find the University Parks. Something to do, somewhere to drive with Ben, you know? And then, when we were at the traffic lights, I looked in the mirror and tried to make eye contact with him, but he didn't respond. I could see him looking to one side in a dreamy kind of way.'

'Oh no. He was having absence seizures?' I put my head in my hands. I cast my mind back to Ben's demeanour when Alex had stopped the car earlier to let me out. I recall the characteristic dreaminess that is often present before a seizure. I mentally check Ben over for the signs that might have told me – should have told me – he was unwell.

'Yes,' Alex continues. 'I pulled over and got out and opened the door and I could see straight away that he wasn't with me. He was looking straight at me, but I knew he couldn't see me. So I turned the car round and took him back to the hospital. About halfway back, I could see in the mirror that he'd gone from partial seizures into a generalised… into a full seizure. It was a medical emergency, Sarah. I had to bring him here.'

'Oh, God.' I clap my hand to my mouth. 'Of course. Of course you did. Thank you, Alex. I'm so glad he was with you, someone who would know what to do…' I stop suddenly in mid-sentence, casting my mind back to a much earlier conversation with Alex, a conversation we'd had the day that I met him. 'You know about seizures, don't you? When I first told you about Ben's absences, you knew what I was talking about.'

Alex nods and looks at the floor.

'How?' I ask. 'How do you know?'

'My brother,' he says. 'He had epilepsy. After I found out the truth about him, about how he died, I… I learned a bit about it. Head in medical books, you know.'

'Did he have a seizure the day he died? Is that how he fell into the water?'

'Yes, but…' He tails off.

I need him to finish his sentence. I need to know if it could happen to Ben. 'But what?' I persist.

Alex blinks and looks at me sympathetically. He has that awkward look on his face, the look that people give you when they don't want to tell you that everything is going to be OK, because they really don't know that it is. He says, 'Let's just wait and see what the tests reveal.'

I swallow deeply and nod.

We sit in silence for a few minutes.

'You were the one to give Ben his medication this morning,' I accuse him, suddenly. 'You did give it to him, didn't you?'

'Yes. Of course I did.'

My heart sinks. I was hoping, perversely, that he'd forgotten, that this might be the possible cause – a random mistake, a missed dose of Ben's medication. Nothing too serious – nothing that can't now be put right.

'OK. I'm sorry,' I say. 'I just… I just had to check.'

'I know.' Alex puts his arm round my shoulder and draws me close. I feel him sigh, heavily, as I lay my head against his shoulder.

I turn over the events of the past few days in my mind, searching for clues. What did we do? Where did we go? What was Ben like?

I pull abruptly away from Alex and look into his face. 'When you picked him up from nursery the other day… or the day after that, when he was sick… Did anything happen? Did he fall, or…?'

Alex colours a little, then shakes his head and frowns. 'No, Sarah. Nothing happened. I swear…'

I look into my lap. 'I'm sorry,' I mumble again. 'I don't mean to… I just don't understand. He's been fine for a year. And now this.'

Alex takes my hand. 'That's OK. I understand. But seizures can start up again. It can happen any time. You heard what the doctor said.'

By the time the tests come back, Ben has been admitted to the children's ward. He's still woozy from the sedation they've had to put him under to keep him still for the MRI and he's had another dose of his medication, which has made him sleepier still. Alex has gone to feed the car park meter when the registrar comes onto the ward, spots me sitting next to Ben's bed and gives me a smile. He asks me to follow him and waves me into a consultation room. He points to a sofa next to his desk and I quickly sit down.

I take a deep breath and brace myself for the worst.

'Well, I've good news for you, Ms Kellerman,' the registrar says, to my surprise. 'Ben's blood test results have all come back normal. There's no infection showing. So we can rule out any viral cause for the onset of the seizure today.'

'Seizures,' I say. 'Alex – my boyfriend – says there was more than one.'

The registrar shrugs. 'Well, possibly. But there doesn't appear to have been any lasting effect. Ben was fully conscious, if sleepy, when he came into triage, and the EEG doesn't show any unusual activity, at least nothing that you wouldn't expect for a child with his difficulties. Looking at his recent history, his medication appears to be working well. I think we'll keep him on the same dosage and we'll continue to monitor it. But I'd say that this was in all likelihood just one of those things. Seizures can happen at any time, unfortunately, but they don't usually cause any long-term problems.'

'What about the MRI?' I ask.

'Well, we won't have the results for a few days, but I can tell you that there didn't appear to be anything obviously wrong. The blood tests and the EEG support that. We'd like to keep Ben in for observation overnight, but he should be able to go home in the morning.'

I take a deep breath in and out and smile at him in relief.

He stands up. 'So, the nurses will monitor Ben this evening. He should have a comfortable night's sleep. We'll have a look at him in the morning and then hopefully you can all be on your way home.'

I pick up my bag and push myself to my feet with the aid of one hand. My legs feel as though they're made of jelly. 'Thank you,' I say. 'Thank you so much for all you've done.'

'My pleasure,' he replies, and shows me out of the door.

Alex is waiting for me at Ben's bedside. He looks up as he sees me walking back through the ward.

'What did he say?' His face contorts, anxiously, as he rises to greet me.

'It's OK.' I smile. I put my hand on his arm. 'He's fine. Ben's going to be just fine. They think it was a one-off.'

Alex looks surprised. 'Really? That's what he said? A one-off?'

I nod. 'That's what he said. He said there's nothing wrong.'

Alex looks from me to Ben, who is sleeping soundly in his bed, and then wipes his arm across his brow. 'Phew!' he says, finally, and his mouth breaks into a smile.

'Phew!' I repeat. 'I really thought... well, never mind.'

Alex takes me in his arms and holds me tight. His shirt's slightly damp, as if he's been running. I expect I could do with a shower, too.

'Did you get to the parking meter on time?' I ask.

'Yes. Although, it looks as though we now need to go and find something to eat and somewhere to stay,' he says. He nods at the window. 'It's getting late.'

I follow his eyes to the blackness of the window outside and then pull away from him, sharply.

'Oh my God, what time is it?' I reach into my bag for my phone. Alex points to a clock on the wall. 'It's half past eight,' he says. 'I don't know about you, but I'm starving.'

'Oh, no!'

'What's wrong?'

I glance up at the clock again, run over to Ben and kiss his head gently, throw my bag over my shoulder and run towards the door. 'Stay here,' I call to Alex. 'Please. Don't go anywhere. I'll be back as soon as I can.'

'What? Where are you going?' Alex calls after me.

'Please, just stay with Ben. I won't be long.'

I move through the children's ward as quickly as I can without drawing huge amounts of attention to myself and raising alarm bells. What did Mary tell me? That she often ends up working beyond the end of her shift. Let this be one of those days for her, I pray. Let her be running behind.

But a gut feeling tells me when I get to the PICU ward – and am buzzed in by the matron to a still, silent atmosphere – that Mary has left the building. And I am right; she is gone.

16

We eat warm pitta bread, hummus and chicken at a lovely Turkish restaurant on Oxford's Cowley Road, before driving back up to Headington and booking into a guest house nearer to the hospital for the night. I'd given serious consideration to the idea of sending Alex off alone, and the irony of the situation was not lost on me when I asked the nurses for a camp bed so that I could spend the night on the floor next to Ben. But he was out for the count, the nurses had told me; he would be unlikely to wake tonight after the sedation and the additional medication he'd been given. It was true that he hadn't stirred before or since I'd come back from the PICU ward. With a promise that they would phone me instantly if Ben took a turn for the worse, I had followed the nurses' suggestion that I take a break, get a decent meal inside me and then try to enjoy a good, child-free night's sleep.

The guest house is basic, but clean and comfortable. I drift in and out of sleep all night and am awake before dawn. I pull my phone out from under my pillow, shower and dress hurriedly and then whisper to Alex that I need to get back to the hospital before Ben wakes up. He nods sleepily, and pushes back the covers. Moments later, he too is dressed and we arrive back at the hospital just before seven. It flashes into my mind how strange it feels to be so unencumbered, to move around so quickly and easily, just me and Alex, without bags of belongings, without nappies and car seats, without Ben.

Ben is still sleeping soundly when we arrive back at the children's ward. We're told he's had a good night and after sitting with me for a bit, Alex heads off in search of coffee and pastries. I pull out my iPad and my notepaper and write up Mary's statement as the sun rises up over Oxford. I then kiss Ben and head up to the PICU ward to find Mary, the handwritten statement ready in my bag.

The same matron greets me as I enter the ward and gives me the bad news that, whilst she was supposed to be on shift today, Mary has phoned in sick. My heart sinks. What am I going to do? We've got to get back to London today. Alex has work in the morning and, although I've already decided to ask for a couple of days' unpaid leave so that I can keep an eye on Ben, it's not going to be practical to stay here in Oxford with him on my own. Even if I could, I don't know how long it will take before Mary's back at work again – or how I would get to see her in any event, with Ben in tow.

I consider my options – which are few. It's Matt's case now – I'm not even supposed to be here. Gareth will be furious if he knows I've got myself involved again. I can already imagine the fallout of my dumping of my next two days' workload onto Matt and others in the office while Ben recuperates, while I watch him like a hawk for the next forty-eight hours, which I know is what I'll be doing, whatever the doctors have said. Two days' leave will be, reluctantly, granted, I'm sure. But anything more than that will be pushing my luck. Eventually, I leave the statement with the ward matron, in an envelope, for Mary, with a note asking her to sign it and send it back as soon as possible.

Ben is discharged by lunchtime and we head out of the hospital into the crisp, cool sunshine. We drive back down the M40 in a companionable silence; Alex appears to know instinctively that I don't feel much like talking, and maybe he doesn't either. We've been told that Ben will be sleepy for the next twenty-four hours following his ordeal, but it doesn't stop me glancing over my shoulder every five minutes to examine his face for the characteristic dreaminess, the blank stares, the rolling of his eyes to one side that I'd checked for constantly for the first four years of his life – and that I'd so carelessly missed yesterday.

It's true that, in the past year or so, I've gradually become accustomed to Ben's new seizure-free status. Occasionally, if I hear a sudden thump or a bang – if he drops his sippy cup on the kitchen floor or turns over heavily in his sleep – my heart will skip a beat. But gradually, I've allowed myself to relax a little in the belief that his seizures are a thing of the past. Now, here I am again, back in that all too familiar place, that living, breathing state of hyper-vigilance that I know so well. I know that this is what my life is always going to be like and I know I will have to try my best to be pragmatic. I just have to learn to expect the unexpected, always. I have to come to terms with that, and in many ways I have. But, it's such a huge responsibility. Even with Alex now sitting beside me, and with the hint of a possibility that I might not be facing the future with Ben alone, Ben will always be my day, my evening and my night job. It will always be me who is watching vigil over him, me who looks out for him, not just while he's a child, but for the rest of my life.

Monday and Tuesday pass peacefully at home. Ben is subdued and happy to spend the first day lying on the sofa in my arms, watching *Teletubbies* DVDs. By Tuesday morning, though, he's up and ready for his next session on YouTube. I smile in pleasure as I watch him surf the website, finding clips of his beloved Tubbies in a multitude of languages that are not English, which he watches and listens to intently. I entertain myself by learning how to say 'tubby-toast' in German and 'naughty noo-noo' in Spanish. I can also count to four (sadly, there are only four Teletubbies) in at least five different languages by the end of the day. I even learn a whole sentence in Polish, when Ben finds one particular clip that's worthy of a half-hour rewind session. And, to Ben's delight, I can hum the tune and dance along with a cheery Romanian folk tune, one which the Teletubbies and the noo-noo appear to have adopted as their own.

I phone the John Radcliffe PICU every day, first from home and then from the office when I return on Wednesday. Mary is still off sick; Mary hasn't come in this morning; they don't know when Mary's next shift is; they can't say when she'll be back. On Thursday I phone Mark Greenhalgh and leave a message. By the following Friday, when I haven't heard from him, I ring again.

It's two days before Christmas when he returns my call. The signed statement from Mary still hasn't materialised. I already know that it's too late; Mary will be back in Ghana by now, picking out her jewellery and trying on her wedding dress. My heart sinks in despair as I think how close I just got to a major breakthrough, but that we're now back to where we were: square one.

That's not strictly true, of course. I may be able to give evidence myself of what Mary has told me, if the judge allows it. But it doesn't alter the fact that it will be hearsay; it won't have come directly from the horse's mouth. I'm not sure how persuasive I'll be when I tell the court, second-hand, that Mary had said, 'fifty or sixty', not 'fifteen or sixteen'. I can just picture the prosecutor, Carmel Oliver, leaping to her feet to cross-examine me, suggesting that it's me, not the police officer, who has got it wrong. It's me who has misunderstood Mary, who has struggled with her accent, she'll tell me. My evidence is no more than wishful thinking on my part.

The fact is that nothing is certain, and that's what I thought I'd achieved for Ellie: certainty. Even though I know that it was simply the unfortunate hand of fate that caused Ben to fall ill at the precise moment he did, it feels as though I've let an opportunity slip through my fingertips, and that I've let Ellie down.

*

Christmas is a low-key affair. Alex is unavoidably called away overseas on a last-minute business trip, an investment opportunity that can't wait until the New Year. Ben and I are invited to have Christmas lunch with my brother, who invites my father too. My brother lets Ben use his computer to play on YouTube while the presents are being unwrapped, but the internet connection is slower than Ben is used to, and before long, he is wailing and wobbling around on his unsteady legs, looking for the exit to the house. He gets more and more upset as he tries doors and cupboards, looking for the way out, while I try to steer him back into the front room again. It's a house which he doesn't know and which is full of people that he doesn't know either, at least not well enough for them to be of any comfort to him when he's this upset. I watch, hopelessly, as my father and my brother attempt to entertain him with various toys and gadgets in which I know instinctively he will have no interest, while my sister-in-law does her best to get the dinner onto the table as quickly as she can. The stress of the situation is too much for me and for everyone, not to mention Ben. After half an hour of this, I apologise, gather my crying son up in my arms and put him back in the car.

Back at home, I let Ben spend his Christmas in the way that he now loves best: on YouTube, surfing for video clips of nursery rhymes. I sit next to him and sing along, making the Makaton signs for 'Twinkle Twinkle, Little Star' and 'Five Green and Speckled Frogs' with one hand, a glass of wine in the other.

In early January, Ben's MRI results come back. My GP tells me that everything is normal and I breathe a sigh of relief. A week later, a letter comes through from the SRA to tell me that, while my conduct is regrettable, they won't be taking the matter any further. Gareth calls me into his room to tell me the news.

'So I can go back to court?' I ask.

'Yes.'

I stand up. 'Thank you. That's great.'

'One more thing...' he adds. 'Ellis Stephens wants you back.' I sit down again. Gareth turns to face me and presses his lips together. I can tell that he's finding this hard. 'She and Matt don't... they don't see eye to eye. She says that if we don't allow you to run her trial, she's leaving and going to another firm.'

I bite my lip, trying to hide my delight. 'So I'm back on the case? As from now?'

'It seems that way.'

I immediately phone Ellie, then Will for a conference. He suggests we meet at Ye Olde Cheshire Cheese the following day.

He's sitting at a table next to the fire when I enter. He looks up when I walk in and takes off his glasses. 'So. What happened to you?' He smiles. 'I've been waiting for you to call in your winnings.'

I smile. 'I found the nurse; I lost the nurse. I guess that makes us quits.'

I sit down at the table opposite him. He pushes a glass across the table towards me. 'Well, I got you this. Lime and soda, right?'

I nod. 'Thanks for remembering.' I shrug off my coat and turn to warm my hands against the amber flames that are flickering in the grate.

'So how did you find her?'

'Her sponsor called me eventually and told me where she was. But without her signed evidence, we're back where we started, aren't we? Even if the judge allows me to give evidence of what she told me, it's all hearsay. Carmel's just going to say that it's me who's misunderstood her, that it's me who's got it wrong.'

Will looks at me kindly. 'I suspect so. I don't think he'll allow it. Especially not now you're her defence lawyer.' He looks up. 'But well done, Sarah. Really. Ellie was made up when I told her what you'd done.'

I shrug. 'It's not quite the news that I was hoping to give her.'

'You're on her side. That's what matters to her. She'll be very pleased to have you back on board. I know I am.' He grins at me and narrows his eyes. 'Matt's OK, but he's not my type.'

I smile. 'He's not Ellie's, either, by the sound of things.'

Will shakes his head. 'He wanted her to plead guilty. He said she didn't have a defence.'

I frown. 'Seriously?'

Will puts his glasses back on and looks me in the eye. 'I am concerned, though. It's less than three weeks until the trial and we don't have much to work with.'

'We have enough,' I say.

Will leans forward and opens a fresh page on his notebook. 'So, what *have* we got?'

'OK.' I pull out my iPad. 'As regards the injuries, we have the schedules from the escort agency that confirm that Ellie was away for several dates between September and December last year, crucially for a whole week, on business with that politician, before Finn was hospitalised in December with the biggest and most pronounced of the bruises – the ones on his tummy, arms and legs.'

'But we don't have a name of the politician,' Will says, ruefully.

'No name. No politician, I'm afraid.'

'I bet it's Boris Johnson,' says Will.

'Maybe it's Theresa May?'

Will raises his eyebrows and we both burst out laughing.

'So, anyway,' I continue. 'Maria Shapiro, the owner of the escort agency, is happy to give evidence if needed, which is great.' I scroll through the notes on my iPad. 'We have some concessions from Paula Moore, Ellie's heath visitor, who says in her statement that she observed Finn and Ellie together, that they had bonded well and that Finn appeared to be thriving – which rebuts some of the things that Heather Grainger says. We have the expert report from the family proceedings, which Anna faxed across to me this morning. This is the expert that can't be sure that the injuries were deliberate. And we have our own toxicology report regarding the sodium levels, which is inconclusive and not very helpful, to be honest.'

'Let me have a look at the expert report.'

'Which one?'

'From the family proceedings. The one you got this morning.'

I hand it to him. Will puts on his glasses and inspects it.

'Oh, and Anna sent this, too. She got permission from the family judge last week.'

I hand the statement to Will. 'Ah-ha. Jay Barrington-Brown. Let's see what he has to say.'

'Not a lot,' I concede. 'I don't think you'll want to witness-summons him.'

Will scans the page and turns it over. 'Liss?' he queries, as he reads on. 'Who's Liss?'

'That's his name for Ellie. It's her escort name.'

Will glances up at me and then continues to read. 'Well,' he says, finally. 'He may regret the relationship with "Liss", but this guy clearly loves his child.'

'Yes. It's quite touching,' I agree. 'He seems completely distraught that Finn has been harmed. But in terms of hard evidence against Ellie, there's nothing there, nothing that he's witnessed or can corroborate for himself.'

Will wrinkles his nose. 'Forget him,' he says. 'He's not on the list of prosecution witnesses. Let's move on.'

We spend another hour running through the expert reports and create a schedule of both Finn's and Ellie's medical records. There are one or two helpful references to Ellie's impetigo back in 2008 and a note of the advice given: just keep the area clean and come back for antibiotic cream if it doesn't improve. When we've finished, we run through the prosecution response to our disclosure request. Will gives me some final pointers as to the remaining items of disclosure I need to chase up from the prosecution, and then we are done. We part company at the bus stop on Fetter Lane and agree to meet again with Ellie in a week's time.

*

On the Friday before the trial begins, Lucy calls up to tell me that Ellie is downstairs in reception to see me. I've just got back from Highbury Magistrates' Court across the road. It's freezing outside and I've grabbed a hot soup from the deli opposite the Tube station. Matt's gone to the pub with some of the others and the office is empty.

Ellie is tucked up warmly in a stylish, figure-hugging navy-blue parka and custard-coloured corduroys. Her face is framed by a plush fur ruff.

'So what are you wearing, then?' I smile. 'And who made the handbag?'

'Canada-goose down,' she says, pushing her hood down and flicking her hair out with one hand. She takes a seat. 'The handbag's Michael Kors.'

'Never heard of him,' I say, dismissively.

Ellie smiles. 'It's not what you're thinking. They're presents from a grateful ex-client, that's all.'

'So, how are you feeling?' I ask her.

'Nervous,' she says. 'In a way. But in another way... well, the sooner this is over, the sooner I get Finn back.'

I push my soup to one side. 'Look, Ellie. Don't get your hopes up too much, OK? I mean, it's always good to be optimistic, but... the case against you is strong.'

'But I've got you back now and Will's a brilliant lawyer,' Ellie says. 'If anyone can get me off, it's him.'

'I agree with that statement, Ellie. I agree with it entirely,' I tell her. 'But it's still a big "if". As Will told you the very first time he met you, in the absence of anything to rebut it, the presumption is going to be that it was you; you that injured Finn, you who poisoned him... and, therefore, you that pulled out his dialysis line.'

Ellie heaves a big sigh. 'But what about the escort agency? Maria says she will attend court if I need her to.'

'I know. But she can only tell the jury that you were away from Finn some of the time. She can't tell them that you didn't hurt him.'

Ellie looks away towards the window.

'And the same with the salt poisoning,' I tell her. 'We will imply that it was Marie, that she'd been careless when she fed Finn. Or that it was Darren. That he'd come home from the pub and given Chinese food to Finn, or something equally salty. We just have to hope that the jury can't be sure.'

'That won't exactly clear my name, though, will it?' Ellie says. 'If they're not sure?'

'They'd have to find you not guilty of attempted murder. You would walk free.'

'But I still might not get Finn back?'

'Ellie, I don't know,' I tell her. 'I'm sorry. I just don't know. Anna told me that he's going to be released from hospital next week. He'll go to the Barrington-Browns, to the house in Richmond. And as soon as the trial is over they'll apply for a care order. He's got his dad, his grandmother and his grandfather and a huge house. I don't want to alarm you, but I don't want to raise your expectations too high either. The fact is, you've got strong competition.'

Ellie heaves a sigh. She looks down and picks at the cuticle around her thumb.

'You've talked to Marie again?' I ask her, tentatively.

She lifts her chin up. 'I've tried. She's broken up with Darren, for good this time. But she doesn't want to know. She's worried that the finger is going to point at her. She's doing a childcare qualification. She wants to do childminding, properly, for a living.'

The door bursts open and Matt appears. 'Sarah, there are two in at the cop shop. Holborn. Can you cover?'

'What time is it?'

'Just gone two,' he says.

It's going to be pushing it, to get to Holborn, deal with two cases and then get back for Ben at six. But I can't say no, not this time. Matt's already upset about losing Ellie's case back to me, and I'm going to be out of the office all next week, shadowing Will on her trial.

'OK,' I agree, knowing that I've just created an afternoon of utter stress for myself.

Matt's face lights up. 'Good one,' he says.

'I'll just finish up with Ellie here, and then—'

'No worries. I'll get Lucy to let them know you're on your way.' He shuts the door.

'I'm going to have to go,' I tell Ellie. 'Sorry. Is there anything else you needed to talk to me about?'

'It can wait,' Ellie says. 'I'll see you on Monday, won't I?'

'Of course you will. Get there early. We'll have time to talk before the jury selection begins.'

I say goodbye to Ellie at Highbury Corner and take the number nineteen bus towards Battersea. As soon as I settle

264

onto the bus, I realise I've left my iPad on my desk. Damn. That means I'll have to go back to the office over the weekend to pick it up. It's little things like this – parking and running up to the office, or running anywhere come to that – that are hard to do with Ben in tow. Hopefully Alex will be over at some point this weekend and won't mind staying in the car with Ben while I run up to my desk.

What am I saying? Of course he won't mind. He never minds. And in actual fact... I pull my phone out of my bag and check the time again. It's now half past two. If there are any delays at the police station – and there often are – I am going to be in big trouble. I wonder if Alex is at work today?

I sit there looking at my phone for a moment, before tapping the little envelope on the front screen and finding his name.

Hi, love, I type into the screen. *You around this pm per chance? On way to cop shop and have horrible feeling I won't get back for Ben.*

There. Done. He won't mind me asking; he might even be pleased. It will show him that I trust him, I tell myself, as I think back with shame to my rather insensitive quizzing of him at the hospital in Oxford, the way I shouted at him on the morning that Ben was sick and didn't turn up at school.

I open my bag to check that I have, if not my iPad, my *Police Operational Handbook*, the forms I need and a notepad and pen. I pull out the notepad and flick through the pages to check there's enough paper left. From the back of the notepad the faxed copies of the statements from Anna flutter to the floor of the bus.

I bend down to pick them up and glance at them again. I flick through the medical report. Is there anything, anything at all, to hold onto, I wonder? I scan through its pages, once again, before turning to the conclusion at the back. *Based on the data available to me, I can't conclude with a sufficient degree of certainty that the injuries were deliberately inflicted. However, this opinion may be subject to modification in the light of any additional information that becomes available.* And well it might, I conclude in turn. Calling this expert to give evidence on Ellie's behalf could easily backfire. If he changes his mind in court and agrees with the prosecution, our position could weaken substantially.

Behind the report is the statement from Jay Barrington-Brown. Here's another one that might potentially help us, but probably won't. Will has already said that we should leave him well alone. I scan through it one more time. Will's right. There's nothing there.

As I get off the bus at Holborn, my phone whistles. I quickly pull it out of my bag. *I can get him. Don't worry. See you at home. X. At home.* The tension melts out of me and I smile to myself as I text back, *You're a lifesaver. Love you. Hopefully back by 7. X*

It is, in fact, nearly seven when I walk out of Holborn police station and head for the Tube. I won't make it back before half past. It really is a very good job that I made the decision to text Alex and arrange for him to collect Ben. I pull my phone out of my bag and switch it back on, then send a quick text to Alex: *All done. On my way. X.*

I walk down Theobald's Road and turn the corner past Red Lion Square, towards the Tube station. I wonder what Alex wants to do about dinner; there's not much in. I click on the icon next to his name and call his number. It rings out, so I leave a message. As I turn into High Holborn I spot the Sainsbury's

Local ahead of me on the other side of the road. I could pick something up here; it'll save me stopping off when I get off the Tube at the other end. I call Alex's number again, and then ring my own landline. No answer. He's probably changing Ben.

I cross the road and head into Sainsbury's, where I walk up and down the cold aisle trying to decide what to buy. I choose a pack of salmon and a tray of Mediterranean vegetables and join the queue at the checkout. I glance at my phone again, but there's still no word from Alex, so I pay for the food and head out of the shop. I join the crowd standing at the pelican crossing, a vague sense of unease tugging at my gut. Why isn't he answering? It doesn't take this long to change Ben.

I cross the road and head into the Tube station. This is the quickest route home, but I also know that I'll have no signal once I head down into the tunnel. It would be good to know before I start my journey that the boys are home, safe and sound, that everything's OK. On a whim, I turn round and leave the station, crossing back over the road the way I've just come. I'll give him another five minutes, I tell myself, and then I'll call again. And if there's still no answer, I'll just go on home; I'm sure I'm worrying for nothing. I'm sure everything is just fine.

I head back into Sainsbury's to escape the cold, but stop just inside the doorway; I don't want to risk losing my phone signal and missing a call. I glance at the magazine rack on the wall to my left and my eyes alight on a copy of *Hello!* magazine. I reach out and take it off the rack. I flick past the pictures of Princess Catherine, who's on a trip abroad somewhere, long-legged and beautiful as always. Victoria Beckham and her glamorous family are next, followed by the inevitable group photo of the latest society wedding – the goddaughter of some duke that I've never heard of who's marrying some wealthy European prince. I'm just about to flick on past it when I suddenly see Eleanor Barrington-Brown smiling out at me from the row at the front near to the bride and groom. She's wearing a huge wide-brimmed white hat with a grey trim, and a matching grey coat-dress with a fur batwing collar. Next to her is a handsome man in his sixties, wearing a pinstriped morning suit: Lord Barrington-Brown.

The instant I see his face, I know I've seen it before. I know that expression; I know those deep-set navy-blue eyes, the way they crinkle at the corners. I know the shape of his nose, the set of his jaw. I stand there and peer at him for a moment in confusion. Suddenly, my gut tightens... it can't be, can it? I quickly scan the rest of the group. There at the very back, head and shoulders only just visible, barely noticeable to anyone who's not looking for him, is Alex.

My blood runs cold. I stare into his face, my heart hammering against my chest, my body numb. Someone bumps into me from behind and I jerk forward like a puppet, the magazine sliding from my fingers onto the floor. I bend down to pick it up, but my legs are so weak that I think they might give way, that I'm going to fall into a heap on the ground. My fingers fumble for the magazine and I manage to stand up and place it back on the shelf, before moving in a mindless daze out of the shop.

And then I'm running. I'm running across the road, without waiting for the lights to change. I'm vaguely aware of a row of cars, all screeching to a halt in front of me, horns blaring, people stopping and looking around in alarm. I run into the Tube station, fumbling in my bag for my Oyster card as I go. I flash it at the card reader, simultaneously slamming my body into the barriers, barely waiting for them to open before I push my way through and run down the escalator, edging my fellow passengers out of my way.

I swear out loud as I round the corner onto the platform and a train pulls away. I stagger backwards on the platform and sink down onto the wooden bench behind me, clutching my bag against my chest and trying to control my breathing. In through the nose, out through the mouth, isn't that what they say? Or is it the other way round?

I pull my bag open and reach inside, my hands now shaking uncontrollably as I pull apart my notepad, and sift through page after page of my handwritten scribble, the notes from the cases I've dealt with this afternoon. *Where are they?* There they are. I pull out the faxed statements from Anna, which are tucked untidily in between a police custody record and a disclosure notice. I flick past the expert report and pull out the statement of Jay Barrington-Brown. The font is small and the faxed print is faint. I squint at the statement of truth and then cast my eyes upwards to read: *Statement of: James Alexander Barrington-Brown. Occupation: Neurologist.*

And in that moment, I know for sure.

I know what's been happening to my little boy.

17

The Tube journey takes less than fifteen minutes but each minute feels like an hour. I stand next to the doors, paralytic with fear, as the train jolts and rattles its way through the blackened tunnels. At every stop – Russell Square, King's Cross, Caledonian Road – I count the seconds, willing the doors to hurry up and close so that the train can start moving again. Finally, at Holloway Road, I leap out and along the platform. I run up the emergency stairs, clutching at the handrail to stop myself falling backwards, my legs numb, rubbery, ready to give way with every step.

As soon as I'm out on the street, my signal returned, I call Amy from the after-school club. My heart sinks in despair as she confirms what I already know to be true: that Alex collected Ben – early, in fact – at around five o'clock. I immediately call 999 and ask the operator for the police. I talk as I walk, then stride, then run the rest of the way back to my flat.

As I suspected, there's no sign of Alex's car outside. I shakily put my key into the lock and let myself in. I pace up and down the hallway from the front room to the kitchen and back again, intermittently stopping to pull back the curtains and peer out into the darkness of the empty street. I try Alex's number again, but it goes straight to voicemail. It's the standard message from the phone provider, telling me that the person I've called is not available. For the first time since I've known him, I realise that I've no evidence that Alex exists: he's never recorded a voicemail message. I've never met a friend or a flatmate. I've never seen an email or a letter addressed to him, no envelope with his name on the front.

An icy chill runs through me. I move over to the mantelpiece and pick up the framed photograph of Ben, a head and shoulders shot that was taken at school at the beginning of term. I start to cry, uncontrollably, as I hold him in my hands, studying every inch of his little face, his mouth, his eyes, the eyes that look up at me so trustingly, giving me the look he always gives me: *I may not know much, but I know that you're my mum. I know that you'll take care of me, that you won't let me come to any harm.*

I sink to my knees on the floor, repeatedly kissing Ben's face in the photo frame. *My baby. My darling boy. Please, God, please don't let this be it. Don't let this be the end.*

I hear the noise of a car engine and leap up off the floor. I run over to the window to see a police car pulling up outside. My heart hammers against my chest at the sight of the vehicle, its fluorescent blue-and-yellow chequered bodywork clearly visible in the dark. Seeing the car parked outside my house, seeing the uniformed officers getting out and walking towards my front door, is like an omen. This is real; this is not just something that's happening in my imagination. The police are here because something serious has happened to Ben.

I move quickly out into the hallway and open the door to let them in. I instantly recognise them – one male, one female – as a response team I've met before, although their names escape me, and as soon as they've said them, I instantly forget them again. Too many thoughts – a zillion thoughts – are already crashing round my fevered brain.

I show the officers into the living room and offer them a cup of tea.

'In a moment, perhaps,' says the female, looking at my tear-streaked face and placing a reassuring hand on my heaving shoulder. She can see that I'm desperate, too desperate to be making tea. She walks ahead of me into the living room, sits down on the sofa and takes out a notebook. The male officer follows and sits down next to her. I fall into the armchair opposite, near the door, ready to leap up the second the phone rings or a car pulls up outside.

'So,' says the female officer. Her eyes spark with recognition. 'It's Sarah, isn't? When did you last see your son, Sarah?'

'This morning,' I tell her. I sit my mobile phone on my lap and spread my fingers out on the armrests of my chair, gripping them tightly. 'When I dropped him off at school.'

'Which school is that?' she asks.

'Samuel Watson. The special school up on Tollington Road. But… he's not there now. They won't know anything. He goes to an after-school club. I've phoned them. They say that Alex… my partner… picked him up early, at five o'clock.'

'And have you spoken to your partner?'

I shake my head. My forehead prickles; I feel faint with terror. Keep breathing, I remind myself. Deep breaths, in and out. 'No. That's the problem, PC…'

'Hindley.'

'PC Hindley,' I repeat. I shake my head again. 'He's not answering. If he picked him up at five, they should have been

273

home by five fifteen at the latest. They should be here *now*. I don't know where they are.'

PC Hindley looks at her watch. 'Well, it's only a quarter past eight. Maybe they went out somewhere? Maybe your partner lost your door key and has taken Ben to his house instead?'

'You don't understand,' I protest, my voice shaking. I put my hands onto my trembling knees and hold them still. 'He's not who he says he is. My partner – he's crazy. He's dangerous... I think he tried to kill his own baby, and now he's got mine.'

She nods, slowly. 'OK. Tell me about his baby,' she says.

'He was in hospital. He got hurt – poisoned – and then he was nearly killed, and... the baby's mother's on trial for his attempted murder, but I don't think it was her... I think it was him.' My words tumble out rapidly, one after the other.

'And why do you think it was him, not her?'

'Because he's not who I thought he was. I saw a photo of him in a magazine on my way home tonight; that's when I realised. He's lied to me about who he is for months. Everything he's told me is a pack of lies.'

PC Hindley nods. 'OK. What's your partner's name?'

'Alex. At least,' I correct myself, 'I thought his name was Alex. That's what he told me. But it's not. His name's Jay. James. James Barrington-Brown.'

'Ballington?' The officer frowns. She stops writing and looks up.

'Barrington,' I correct her, trying to keep my impatience in check. My mouth is dry. I lick my lips. 'B-a-double-r. Barrington-Brown. It's double-barrelled, hyphenated. Look, I know what you're thinking,' I add. 'I asked him to collect Ben, it's only been a couple of hours... he's taken Ben out, his phone's died.

But you have to believe me, it's far worse than that – I know. I know something's wrong. He's done this before.'

'Done what before?' The officer shifts a little in her seat and leans back, frowning.

'He's gone missing with Ben, twice before. He told me Ben was sick… and then there's his son. He made him sick too. He poisoned him.'

This is coming out all wrong. I'm not sure if I'm making any sense.

The male officer stands and picks up the photo frame from where I've left it, lying on the coffee table. 'Is this Ben?'

I nod. 'Yes.'

He lifts his radio. I can hear him giving his call sign, the case reference number, my address while the female officer continues talking to me at the same time, asking me about Ben, his age, his medical history. I explain about Ben's vulnerability, his history of chest problems, his epilepsy. The male officer radios it all through.

'So, your partner.' PC Hindley reads from her notebook. 'James Barrington-Brown. What's his address? And his date of birth?'

'I don't know.' I shake my head, despairingly. 'He told me his name was Alex White and that he lived at a flat in Lewisham, but that's obviously not true; none of it's true. His name's James Alexander Barrington-Brown and he's a doctor, a neurologist. His family are millionaires and he lives in Richmond… or Chelsea. Markham Square. Yes, that's it. He owns a flat in Markham Square. But he spends a lot of time with his parents at the family home in Richmond. He told me his birthday was in August. Nineteen seventy-four, he said, but I don't know if that's true, I don't know if anything he told me was true…'

'What's his phone number?' she asks me. I pick up my phone and find Alex's number at the top of my call log. With shaking fingers, I then hand it to her. She takes down the number, then calls it from her own phone. I wait with bated breath; perhaps it's just me he's ignoring. Maybe he'll answer for someone else.

But the call rings out, as it did for me. I can hear the vibration next to her ear, the pleasant woman from the phone company announcing, yet again, that he's unavailable.

The officer leaves a brief message with her phone number and then ends the call. 'CRO check,' she says to the male officer.

'We want a CRO check on a James Alexander Barrington-Brown,' I hear him say. 'It's a misper. Possibly a domestic.' He pauses. 'Partner's gone to kindergarten to pick up son and hasn't returned on time.' He pauses again. 'Routine,' he says. 'She knows him.'

'No, I don't,' I scream at him. 'I don't know him at all. He's a stranger to me, a complete stranger, and he's got my son!'

The female officer puts a hand on my arm. 'But he's your partner? You did ask him to collect Ben for you?'

'Before I realised!' I protest, tears filling my eyes again. 'Before I found out who he really was!'

'A doctor.' She nods. 'A millionaire doctor.'

'Yes.' This is hopeless. They don't believe me. They think I'm just a neurotic parent who's fallen out with her boyfriend, who's let him go off with her son and now wants him back.

The officer nods slowly, then looks up at her colleague. 'We'll need to do a check on you too,' he says.

'You know who I am. I'm a defence lawyer. You've seen me at the police station.'

'Of course. But it's standard to do background checks. We have to cover all angles. We'll also need to search your home.'

'What for?' I ask, bewildered.

'As I say, it's standard.' PC Hindley smiles. 'You'd be surprised how many missing children turn up in a cupboard or an attic.'

'This isn't a game of hide-and-seek!' I cry out in exasperation. 'My son is severely learning disabled. He wouldn't know how to hide in a cupboard, or what the point would be. I told you, he's with my... he's with Alex. Jay,' I correct myself again, shaking my head. 'They could be anywhere by now. But one thing's for certain, they're not here!'

'All the same. If you don't mind?' The female officer gets up and follows her colleague out to the hallway and into the kitchen. I follow behind them and watch in despair, the minutes ticking away, as they search through each room, opening doors, rooting through cupboards, looking under beds.

'Please,' I beg them, following them back into the hallway, watching as they turn my under-stairs cupboard inside out. 'You have to believe me. You have to circulate this as an abduction – a high priority. I'm begging you. You have to get someone out there now, looking for him. I can give you his vehicle registration. He'll have triggered an ANPR camera somewhere... he can't be too hard to find. And you need to check on his son, too. He might have tried to kill him again.'

'Why do you think he tried to kill his son?'

'Because he's crazy! Please, PC...' I turn to the male officer, who's now standing back up again, his hand on his radio.

'Hood,' he reminds me.

'PC Hood, please run a check and you'll see that I'm telling you the truth. His son is called Finn Stephens and someone tried to kill him on the twenty-fifth of July last year. The case is at the Old Bailey – it's in court next week for trial.'

PC Hindley stands up and shuts the cupboard door. 'But you said the baby's mother has already been charged?'

'Yes. But they've got the wrong person. It's Alex. Jay,' I correct myself for the millionth time, clapping my hand to my head. 'It's Jay who's done this. James Barrington-Brown.'

PC Hindley eyes me suspiciously. She walks back into the living room and I follow her. 'So, what's your involvement with this case?' she asks.

I sink down into a chair and put my head in my hands. I know exactly where this is going. I know how this is going to sound. 'I represent the mother. Ellis Stephens.'

There's silence in the room. PC Hood's radio has gone quiet. I lift my head up and look at them both. PC Hood sits down on the sofa.

PC Hindley is still frowning. 'So, you represent the mother... but you've been having a relationship with the father. Your relationship with the father is now over, and you're now saying that he, not your client, is responsible for attempting to kill their child?'

I nod and lift my hands up, helplessly. 'Yes. Look, I know how that sounds...'

'Isn't that something of a conflict of interest?' asks PC Hood.

I sigh. 'Yes. Of course it is. It's a *huge* conflict of interest. Only I didn't know; that's my point. I didn't know who he was. I found out today – this evening – on my way home.

That's when I realised that Ben was in danger. Like I said, it's happened before. Twice before. He was looking after Ben, both times, and then Ben got ill… sick, and he took him to hospital, and—'

'He took him to hospital,' PC Hindley interrupts me. 'So, what you're telling me is that, both times before, when your partner and your son went "missing"' – she puts air quotes around the word 'missing' – 'what had actually happened was that your son had fallen ill. He'd needed medical attention – and your partner got that for him?'

'Yes, but… now I'm wondering if my son was really ill. I don't know if he was really ill, or if Alex— Jay. I mean, Jay…'

The female officer puts her head to one side.

'I think Jay might have done something to him,' I finish. I take a deep breath in. 'I know it sounds a bit… a bit crazy. But I think he might have made him ill and then…'

'And then taken him to hospital?' PC Hindley has stopped writing down what I'm telling her.

'Yes,' I say, weakly.

'But you told me your son has a long history of medical problems. That he has epilepsy?'

'Yes.' I nod.

'And last time… last time, they'd just gone to A&E?'

'Yes…'

'So… is it possible that your son has fallen ill again?' she asks. 'That your partner has taken him to A&E again?'

'Yes.' I nod. Oh my God. Why didn't I think of this? I've been too busy panicking to think of this. The nearest hospital; that's where they'll be. 'The Whittington,' I say. I leap up. 'We need to go to the Whittington.'

The male officer speaks into his radio. 'Whittington Hospital Accident and Emergency department.' He looks at his colleague and she nods.

'Let's go.'

'm first out of the police car and in through the hospital doors. A strange blend of relief and fear washes over me as I immediately spot Alex, seated in the waiting area. He jumps up to greet me, his face a portrait of anxiety and concern.

'Where is he?' I demand.

'Sarah, he had another seizure. I couldn't wake him up...'

'Where is he?' I repeat, louder this time.

Alex lifts his hand and points towards an open door a few feet away. 'He's in there.'

I turn on my heel.

'I'm sorry,' Alex calls after me. 'I'm sorry if I worried you. I was just about to call you. But Ben was so ill, I couldn't wake him...'

He takes a step to follow me, but I hold up my hand. 'Stay there!' I bark my command, glancing up over his shoulder as the officers walk in through the hospital doors.

I run across the corridor. Behind me, I can hear PC Hindley asking Alex, 'Are you James Barrington-Brown?' and Alex's surprised voice answering, 'What? What's this about?'

I tap on the door to the consultant's room and open it. Ben is in the corner, fast asleep on a hospital bed. His mouth is slightly open and one arm is flung out beside him, his chest rising and falling in a gentle rhythm. I breathe in sharply as I spot the cannula protruding from the back of his hand, but it's empty and there are no drips or wires.

The nurse and consultant are standing in the opposite corner, talking. Both look up as I enter the room.

'I'm his mother,' I say. 'Is he OK? Is he conscious?'

The consultant, a woman, holds out her hand and shakes mine. She smiles. 'Yes. He's doing OK. His breathing is a little irregular and his reflexes are reduced, but that's common after a seizure, as the body recovers. We're minded to simply monitor him overnight and see how he does.'

I ask, 'How long did the seizure last?'

'Well, your partner says—'

'Never mind what *he* says,' I interrupt her. 'What did *you* see? What did you witness for yourself?'

The consultant frowns. 'Well, nothing. He was stable by the time I arrived.'

'What do his notes say? Can I see his notes?'

There's a tap on the door, and PC Hood walks in. The consultant looks from me to the officer and back again, in surprise.

'We've had a report of a missing person,' he says to the consultant. To me, he says, 'Is this Ben?' He points to the bed.

I nod. 'Yes.'

PC Hood lifts up his radio. 'Misper located at Whittington Hospital.' He turns to the consultant. 'How is he?'

'He's stable,' she answers, looking confused. 'We're told by the male who brought him in that he's had more than one seizure this evening.'

'Please… what do his notes say?' I repeat.

The consultant looks from me to the officer again for a

moment and then pulls a clipboard from the back of the bed. She scans the page and looks up. 'He was stable on triage examination. Very drowsy, but not ataxic.'

'Ataxic?'

'There wasn't a complete loss of bodily function. He was much as he is now, it seems. He'll be asleep for some time, I imagine. But his observations are good.'

'Are you sure?' I ask. 'What if... if he'd been given salt? Would you know? Can you test for that?'

The doctor frowns. 'Salt?'

'Sodium. If he'd been fed salt, or... or injected with saline or...'

The doctor looks confused. 'His renal function appears fine. There's no evidence of raised sodium levels. Why do you—'

'I think he might have been given something... something that made him have a seizure...'

'Well, your partner said—'

'I don't care what he said!' I snap at her. 'And he's not my partner!'

Her face falls in alarm.

'I'm sorry,' I apologise. 'I'm just...' I take a deep breath. 'He's not my partner,' I explain. 'He's just someone I've been *stupid* enough to leave my son with.'

I burst into tears as I say the word 'stupid'. The nurse immediately moves over, puts her arm round me and guides me to a seat.

The consultant looks down at Ben's notes again. 'There's no obvious way of telling exactly what has occurred,' she says. 'Not without carrying out further tests. But I'm not minded to go down that route, to be honest. We've run the usual blood tests and they haven't revealed any abnormalities so far. His recent CAT and MRI scans didn't flag up anything either. So,

I think we can safely say that his seizures don't appear to have any underlying cause.'

I wipe my eyes with the backs of my hands. The consultant continues to look vaguely baffled for a moment before she says, 'It's good news, Ms...'

'Kellerman. Sarah,' I say.

'Well, it's good news, Sarah. We'll have to monitor him overnight, of course, but I'd say that he's going to be just fine.'

The nurse smiles at me and puts her arm round my shoulder. 'There,' she says. 'You heard what she said.'

I nod, unable to speak for a moment. 'Thank you,' I say, finally, standing up. 'I really appreciate everything you've done.'

The consultant walks over to the door. 'I'll send someone to take Ben up to the ward,' she tells me. 'And we'll see him again in the morning.' She exits the room, followed by PC Hood. The nurse gives me a sympathetic look and leaves the room too. I sit down next to Ben and stroke his head. A few moments later a porter arrives. I establish the name of the ward that Ben's going to and then lean forward and plant a long kiss on his forehead.

'I am so, so sorry, my darling,' I whisper into his ear. 'I promise – you have my word – I will never, ever let this happen to you again.'

Alex is sitting outside in the waiting area. PCs Hindley and Hood are seated either side of him. Alex jumps up as soon as he sees me and stretches out his arms.

I take a step backwards. 'Don't touch me!' I spit.

'Sarah,' he pleads. 'I can explain.'

The officers stand up. PC Hindley says, 'We'll leave you to talk.'

I turn to face them. 'What? What do you mean, you'll leave us to talk? You mean, you're not going to arrest him?'

PC Hindley shakes her head. 'There are no grounds.' The look on her face is clear: she thinks I'm neurotic. She thinks I've been wasting her time. 'You told me that Ben has a long medical history, a history of seizures, and it seems that Mr Barrington-Brown has behaved entirely appropriately in bringing him here.'

'But he's lied!' I protest. 'He's lied to me about who he is!'

She nods, slowly. 'Well, that's a matter between the two of you. It's clearly not a crime. We'll pass everything on to the Child Protection Team. They may be in touch.'

The officers turn and walk out through the hospital doors. I watch in hopeless silence as they go, before spinning round to face Alex. 'What did you give him?'

'What did I give him?' Alex looks confused. 'Well, nothing. I didn't give him his medication, if that's what you mean? It wasn't due for another hour.'

'I'm not talking about his medication! I'm talking about what you gave him, what you injected him with to make him that sleepy.'

Alex looks at me for a long, hard moment. I recognise the look, instantly. It's one he's given me on many occasions in the past, when I've asked him a question that he doesn't want to answer. *When he's playing for time, more like, trying to think up his next lie.*

'What was it, Alex?' I say again. 'If you don't tell me the truth, I swear...'

Heads are raising and people are watching us. I can tell that Alex finds all of this excruciating, that he is mortified – first by the police presence, and now this public display of emotion on my part.

'What did you give him?' I screech.

Alex takes my arm and guides me away from the waiting area and down the corridor in the opposite direction, towards some empty seats.

'Sit down, Sarah,' he says, meekly. 'Everyone's looking at us.'

'I don't care. And I don't want to sit down.'

'Please.' He sits down anyway and puts his head in his hands.

'Just tell me,' I hiss at him, softly this time. 'If you don't tell me, I'm going to scream.'

Alex looks up. His eyes are bleary and his face is red. 'Diazepam,' he says.

'How much?'

'Ten mils,' he says.

'Alex, he's completely out of it!'

'And then another five. That's all. I swear...'

'Why? Why would you do that?'

'He was fitting. Repeatedly. He had a generalised seizure that lasted for ten minutes. It was a medical emergency. I was trying to save his life, Sarah.'

'No! Ben was fine. It was you. You! You gave him something, something that made him fit. What else did you give him? I want the truth!' I lean forward and grab him by the shoulders and start to shake him. 'Tell me the fucking truth!'

'Sarah, please. Stop it. I swear. I...'

I let go of him, suddenly. 'He didn't have a fit. Did he?'

Alex looks at me for a long moment and then finally shakes his head.

I look at him in astonishment. My tongue is heavy and my mouth dry. I lick my lips. 'So, what happened? You just decided that it would be fun to drug my little boy?'

'It wasn't like that, I swear!'

'So, what was it like, then? Did you do it for attention? What?' I hold out my arms, and shake my head at him.

His eyes take on a faraway look. 'I... I don't know.'

I look at him in silence for a moment, before asking, 'How did you give it to him?'

'What?'

'The diazepam? How did you give it to him?'

He hesitates. 'Rectally.'

I wrinkle up my face in disgust.

'I'm not a paedophile, Sarah,' he hisses at me.

I put my hands on my hips and face him, as he sits in front of me, his face racked with guilt and pain.

'You're a doctor. The fucking irony.' I laugh, an empty, hollow sound that floats off down the corridor. 'Ben couldn't have been in safer hands.'

Alex looks at his feet. 'How did you...'

'How did I find out? I guessed. Eventually. Although, God knows I should have known, right from the start.'

Alex looks at me and says nothing. He lifts his arm and wipes at his brow.

'I saw a photo of you in a magazine,' I tell him. 'Your parents were there too. And then it all made sense: the things you said, at the hospital last time. The medical terminology you used: "partial seizures", "generalised seizures". The words just rolled off your tongue. And then I got a copy of your witness statement, and saw that you're a neurologist – the type of doctor

287

that would know all about seizures. And your name: *James Alexander Barrington-Brown*.' I punctuate his middle name with a contemptuous sneer. 'How could you do this to Ben?' I sob, suddenly. 'How could you do this to me?'

Alex reaches over, and tries to take my hand. I snatch it away. 'Please, Sarah,' he begs me, tears forming in his own eyes. 'Please hear me out. I'm begging you.'

I know that this is the point where I should tell him that he doesn't deserve it, that he doesn't deserve a chance to explain. I should just call Hood and Hindley right back again, tell them what Alex has done to Ben, that he's admitted it this time. That if he's done that to Ben, then surely he could have harmed Finn too?

But what evidence do I have? I know that's what it comes down to. As far as I know, Finn was with Darren or Marie – or one of their friends, God knows who – when Finn was bruised and poisoned; and how am I going to prove that Alex was on the ward that night, that he was the one who pulled out the dialysis line?

I need to know the truth. I need an explanation, an explanation for everything, one that will stop my world from spinning unevenly on its broken axis and set me back on my feet again. I need Alex (or Jay, or James – or whatever he really calls himself when he's not lying to someone) to tell me what I need to know.

Oh, God. Is 'Jay' his client-of-an-escort name? I wonder, suddenly. His *porn name*. I think back to our jokes with disgust. I think of him in bed with Ellie, and then in bed with me.

At the top of the corridor, through the double doors, I can see that it's started to snow, the glare of the streetlights transforming the flakes into a big white sheet. I want to run outside, to disappear into the mist, to throw myself into the elements and let the wind take me away. Instead, I sit down next to Alex and put my head in my hands. I press my fingertips hard against my temples; the pressure feels good, solid, real.

Time stands still for a moment, and then I hear Alex say, 'Sarah, whatever you believe, whatever you think of me right now, there is one thing you have to know, and that is that I love you. I've lied to you mercilessly, I know. But I never meant to hurt you or Ben. I swear. I would never have done that intentionally. I love you. I loved you from the moment I first clapped eyes on you. That part is not a lie.'

I look up at him. I immediately think back to the moment he first clapped eyes on me, in the coffee aisle at Waitrose in Holloway. I think about the moment when he'd rescued me at the checkout and I know now, with a heart that's sinking deeper and deeper by the minute, that my initial instincts had been correct: it was all way too good to be true. This handsome, well-dressed, *well-spoken* stranger, zooming in on a woman like me... I should have known. I *did* know, I reprimand myself, but I ignored it. I cringe, inwardly, as I realise that I'm nothing but a stereotype: a pathetic, lonely, single mother, so desperate for affection, for a father for her son, that I have refused to see what's been right in front of my very eyes, all along. *What kind of a fool have I been?* I open my mouth, but my anger has been replaced with self-loathing and my words now come out in a pitiful gasp. 'How did you... how did you...'

'How did I what?' Alex looks at his knees, penitently.

'How did you come to be in the supermarket that day? The day we met?'

He sighs, deeply, and looks away down the corridor at the snow-white gauze outside the window. 'I followed you.'

'You… you followed me?'

He looks at me, plaintively, his forehead creasing. 'I wanted to talk to you. I was worried about Liss and what she was going to say, in court. I was just planning to talk to you, to be honest with you. I wanted to beg you not to tell anyone about me and Liss… about… about the true nature of our relationship. My parents… they don't know.'

'But…' I break off as I mentally retrace my steps. 'I went to… to the police station that day. At Walworth. And then on the Tube. You followed me all that way? All the way to Ben's nursery?'

He nods and looks down into his lap again, his face flushed.

'How did you know who I was?'

'The Internet. Your photo is on your firm's website.'

Of course. I can feel my own face flushing as I piece it all together, as I realise just how contrived my supposedly romantic rescue in the coffee aisle really was. 'So, you followed me from the nursery to Waitrose… you watched me… and when I dropped the coffee jar, you saw your opportunity… and then you pounced.'

Alex reaches for my hand. I flinch as if he's hit me. 'It wasn't like that, Sarah,' he protests.

But we both know that it was.

'So, at what point did you decide that it would be more fun to lie to me?' I ask him. 'To sleep with me, to spy on me, to manipulate me into giving away the confidential details of my client's case?'

Alex puts his head in his hands and leans forward, his elbows on his knees. 'I was going to tell you the truth. I wanted to.

So many times, I wanted to. I hated lying to you. You have to believe me, Sarah. I love you. I'm still glad we met.'

I look up at him, in disbelief. Does he not realise how sick that sounds? I survey him in silence for a moment. I roll my tongue around my dry mouth and stand up. 'I need a drink of water.'

Alex leaps up. 'I'll get it.'

He walks over to the water cooler and comes back with a plastic cup in each hand.

I lift my cup and take a deep gulp, and then another. 'So, what happens when your parents find out the truth about Finn? About Ellie?'

He turns and looks, searchingly, into my eyes. 'I was rather hoping that they wouldn't.' He continues to look at me with a pained expression on his face and I realise with incredulity that he's actually asking me for a favour. 'If it comes out in court, it will be unthinkable.' He speaks quickly. 'My mother adores Finn. But she's highly respected, socially, as is my father. If she finds out that Finn's mother is a… a… call girl, it will kill her. Her reputation would be in ruins. I mean, it would be a big deal for any mother to accept, but in the circles my mother moves…' He tails off. 'The thing is, Sarah… my father's titled.'

'Anna told me. He's a life peer.'

'No,' Alex says, quietly. 'He's a hereditary peer. As his only son I'll inherit the peerage. It means bugger all to me, to be frank, but it's a big deal to my mother. We're a dying breed, it seems. My mother intends that I marry well, into a family with similar rank and title.'

'And wealth, presumably.'

'And wealth,' he agrees.

I think about this for a moment. 'So, your father's... what? A duke? A viscount?'

'A baron,' he mumbles.

'And when he dies, you'll be a baron too?'

Alex nods.

I heave a sigh, and look away. 'So, what were you doing with me? I mean, beyond your self-preservation, your selfish interest in Ellie's case, that is. You could have had yourself a baroness, a lady – a woman with wealth and style, someone your mother would approve of. Why would you possibly be interested in a commoner like me?'

'Because you're real!' he explodes. 'You're smart, you're funny, you're beautiful and you're real! Have you any idea how it feels to be with someone and to know that your wealth and social status are more important to them than who you are inside? I love you because you're you, Sarah. And because you needed me in a way that I've never been needed before, and for all the right reasons. You made me feel special. You made me feel alive.'

'And Ellie? "*Liss*"? How did *she* make you feel?'

Alex sighs. 'It was never going to be anything more than it was. We both knew where we stood.' He turns to face me, his eyes boring into mine. 'Liss doesn't want it all to come out any more than I do, you know? We both agreed, for Finn's sake, that we'd keep it under wraps.'

'And that's why you carried on seeing me,' I sneer. 'You wanted to find out what her defence was. You wanted to know if she'd changed her mind, if she was going to expose you, to send your dirty secret "out into society" – is that the correct terminology? Make it known that your son – your mother's grandson – is the bastard child of a whore.'

Alex winces visibly. 'I'm sorry,' he says. 'I know that it's unforgivable. But the consequences for my family...'

I feel my anger rising again. 'And what about the consequences for me? Did you even think about me, once, when you were quizzing me about her case? Did you ever consider that if I told you anything, I could be struck off? That my career would be over?'

'I'm sorry. But you didn't tell me anything, did you? Not really.'

'Not for want of you trying!' I yell.

I put my head in my hands again and rewind back through all the conversations we've ever had, trying to recall exactly what I might have said to Alex about Ellie's defence. 'Oh my God.' I look up suddenly. 'The case papers. The ones you helped me scan. The ones you moved into the kitchen cupboard.'

Alex shakes his head. 'I didn't read them, Sarah. I was going to, I admit it, but then you came home and I didn't get a chance.'

I stand up, and move back down the corridor towards the water cooler, my mind fit to burst with disconnected thoughts and tangled-up emotions. There's so much that bothers me about the web of lies Alex has woven that it's hard to unravel it and pick out the individual threads, but something – something beyond hurt and humiliation and anger – is gnawing away at me. Something specific that I can't put my finger on. Something to do with Finn...

I march back down the corridor towards Alex.

'You told me that your parents were dead,' I accuse him. Alex looks up, surprised, no doubt, that I've asked him this. Of all the lies he has told me, this is hardly the worst.

'Well, yes,' he admits. 'I didn't want you to ask questions about them, to find out who they really were.'

'And your brother?'

'That was all true,' Alex insists. 'Every word. I did have a twin. He did drown when we were five.'

'So how did he drown?' I ask. 'What happened?'

Alex gives me a look that tells me he's exasperated, but knows at the same time that he has no right to be. 'Do you really want to...?'

'Yes,' I snap. 'I do.'

'OK.' He sighs. He takes a deep breath. 'He was born with a severe neurological disability. His problems were very similar to Ben's.'

I feel my mouth fall open. 'He was learning disabled?'

'Severely so. Like Ben, he couldn't talk or walk or dress or feed himself with a spoon. But I didn't know the significance, not at the time. I didn't know what it meant until years later. As a five-year-old kid I just accepted it: that's how he was.'

I stare at him. 'Go on,' I say.

'His name was George.' His lips form a smile and his eyes mist over. 'My memories of him are few, but I do remember that I adored him. My family owns a large estate in Esher, Surrey. It's where I grew up. I remember spoon-feeding him his porridge in the morning and pushing him around the grounds in his wheelchair, with the au pair's help, pointing out frogs and butterflies and making daisy-chains for him to put in his hair.' His voice falters and begins to crack. 'One day, I decided that I was going to teach him to walk. I asked the au pair to help me. She told me that we could try. We were down by the lake. We lifted George out of his wheelchair and sat him on a blanket on the grass. But then he suddenly toppled forwards and... he... he fell.'

'Fell... where? Where did he fall?'

Alex looks up at the ceiling. I can see that his eyes are filling with tears, which he tries to blink away. 'Into the lake,' he says. 'He'd had a seizure. And then he drowned. Or at least that's what my parents told me, years later. I don't actually have any memory of it at all. I don't remember anything beyond me and the au pair taking him out of his wheelchair that day and settling him on the grass. The next thing I remember is that the au pair had been sacked and sent home and that my brother wasn't there any more. I must have wiped the whole incident from my memory, because I kept asking my parents where he had gone and when he was coming back. They batted my questions away for a year or so, before telling me that I'd imagined him, that I'd always been an only child. Then, when I found the photograph of him in the attic, they finally told me the truth...'

Alex leans forward suddenly and puts his head in his hands. His shoulders begin to shake, gently, and then to heave up and down, as he begins to sob, loudly, uncontrollably.

'And the truth is, that it's my fault he died,' he says, lifting his head, heavy gasps escaping from his throat.

'What do you mean, it was your fault? You were five years old,' I say, confused. 'How could it have been your fault?'

'But I took him out of his wheelchair. I let him fall. I let him fall into the lake. I should have... I should have done something to save him.'

I say, 'I think that maybe you've been trying to save him ever since.'

He looks up.

'I think you're sick, Alex,' I tell him. 'What you did to Ben... You need to see a doctor. A psychiatrist.'

Alex puts his head back in his hands. I wait while he sobs softly for a moment, the seed of an idea implanting itself in my mind.

'You're a neurologist,' I say.

'Yes.'

'Which hospital do you work at?'

'Nine Elms. South side.' His words are muffled.

Nine Elms. I remember that name. Why do I remember that name? And then it comes to me. I've seen it on the medical report from the hospital in Ellie's case. 'Nine Elms and Southwark St Martin's. They're part of the same trust,' I say.

Alex looks up at me and blinks. 'Yes.'

'So that means that you have a staff lanyard... a key fob? You can get onto any of the wards?'

Alex lifts his arm and wipes his eyes on his shirt sleeve, before turning to me in disbelief. He leaps up from his seat and faces me. 'No, Sarah. No. You're barking up the wrong tree, I swear. Do you seriously think I'd hurt my own son?'

'Well, you hurt mine.'

Alex shakes his head. 'No. No. I sedated him. That's different. I... I never intended to hurt him. I admit that I... I'm messed up. I know that, and I'm sorry. Truly, I am. I sincerely regret what I have put you through, you and Ben. You're right. I'm sick. I know that I have a problem. I know that I have some kind of need for... for attention. For drama... to be needed. In an emergency situation, I... I come alive. It's... it's addictive...' He tails off as he watches my face. 'I'll get help. I promise, I'll get help. I was going to, anyway. I knew that there was something wrong with me... But that does *not* mean I'd try to kill my own son, for Christ's sake. I love him! I love him more than anything in this

296

world! My parents and I, we're all sick with worry that we could lose him back to her... to Liss, that she could walk free from all of this and then hurt him again. My mother doesn't sleep. For her, it's like losing George all over again. She has nightmares about it.' He crouches down, suddenly, and grabs hold of my hands. 'Sarah, I really, truly admire you and I have no doubt whatsoever that you are an excellent lawyer. But you've got this all wrong. It's Liss... Ellie... she's crazy. *She's* the one who needs help. She was right there next to him when it happened. She was there, not me.' He gasps as tears threaten to engulf him again.

I listen to him in silence until he's finished. He's convincing enough, but I don't believe him. He's hurt Ben. He had the opportunity, the means to get onto the ward that night and hurt Finn. And what happened to George... there's more to it than he's telling me, that's for sure. Why would he hold himself responsible for his brother's death if what happened was an accident? Why would a five-year-old carry this much guilt? Did he push George into the water – is that what really happened? And did the au pair witness what he did? Is that why she was sent away?

I watch Alex out of the corner of my eye as he sits back down and puts his head in his hands again, the heels of his palms covering his eyes, his fringe flopping forward and sliding through his fingers.

I reach over and pull my phone out of my bag. Alex lifts his head and watches me for a moment, unsure of me, unsure of what I'm going to do next. I turn to face him and look directly into his eyes. 'I'm going to see Ben now,' I tell him. 'But first, I'm going to call the police. I want you to stay here and wait for them. If you ever loved me, if I ever meant anything to you,

you'll stay here and wait for them – and then you'll tell them the truth.'

Alex looks back at me for a moment. He swallows hard and at first his lips tighten, but then he nods. He stands up and pushes his hands deep into his pockets – a familiar, diffident gesture that I recognise so well. He waits for a moment, watching me. I can see that he doesn't know quite how to say goodbye.

I look back at him for a moment, at the eyes I've gazed into, at the mouth I've kissed, at the hair I've stroked, at the body I've loved. And then I brush past him abruptly and head towards the stairs to the wards, without looking back.

t's late, but Anna's awake, thankfully. I tell her as much as I can and, in her calm, patient way, she listens without interruption, simply telling me not to worry about anything and to get some rest. I toss and turn all night on my camp bed, while Ben sleeps a peaceful, seemingly dreamless sleep beside me. Anna arrives at nine with a copy of the *Guardian* and two Starbucks cappuccinos and settles herself down in the armchair next to Ben's bed, to wait for the consultants to do their rounds.

'I really appreciate this,' I tell her. 'I hope that he's OK for you. But if he's anything like he was the last time, he'll just sleep all day. If there was ever a good day to leave him with anyone, this is the one.'

'We'll be just fine, won't we, Ben? Your mummy doesn't need to worry about us.' She leans over and strokes his head. Ben responds by flipping over onto his tummy and flinging out his arm.

I hand her the key to my flat and kiss Ben goodbye.

'Anna? Don't let him out of your sight, will you?' I ask her. 'Promise me? If they discharge him, or if they don't. You need to be with him at all times. The police can only hold Jay for twenty-four hours without charging him. Even if they have enough evidence to do that, he could be released on bail.'

Anna nods. 'I will. I promise. Tim's on his way, so there will be two of us to stand guard.'

She folds the newspaper and places it on Ben's night-stand. She lifts the lid of her coffee cup and blows at the froth on top. 'Do you think he might have Munchausen's by Proxy?' she asks. 'Jay, I mean. I had a case once. That was the diagnosis.'

'What happened?' I ask.

'Well, similar to you. The child kept getting sick and ending up in hospital, basically. Although it had gone on for much longer. The child was seven and had spent most of her childhood on a hospital ward, poor thing – she even had a number of operations. The mother went to elaborate lengths to convince everybody, including me, that her daughter was seriously unwell, describing all manner of symptoms.'

'So how did they find out that it was her all along?'

'It was just a suspicion at first. Some of the symptoms she described just didn't appear to be borne out. The daughter was removed from her mother and placed into foster care, where she miraculously became well again and began to thrive.'

I think about this for a minute. Finn was removed from Ellie and placed with the Barrington-Browns for nearly two months without anything happening. Also, Jay has had access to him at St Martin's ever since. If he wanted to stage another injury or illness, create his next medical emergency, it would have been really easy for him to do. But, on the other hand, Finn nearly died and Ellie's on trial for attempted murder. All eyes are on Finn. It would be crazy to attempt anything now, especially when Ellie's not around to take the blame, when she might have an alibi.

'I think it's something like that,' I tell Anna. 'Some kind of attention-seeking behaviour. He admitted to me that he thrives on the drama. Something happened to his twin brother when they were children. He says that George fell into a lake, but I think Jay might have pushed him. His brother had a severe neurological condition, like Ben's. He couldn't walk or talk or do anything for himself. Jay says he loved his brother, but I'm wondering if he was jealous of the attention that George was getting because of his disability, or if he somehow got it into his head that George was better off dead, that he needed to commit some kind of mercy killing.'

'Even though he was only five?'

'Maybe.'

'And then he tried to do the same to Ben?'

'Well, yes. Or maybe he didn't intend to kill either of them. Maybe he only wanted to create a life-threatening situation and then be the one to save them. Maybe with Finn, something went wrong.'

'Hmm. Well, it's possible. But that's a lot of "maybes",' Anna says. 'Can you prove any of it?'

I shake my head. 'Not yet.'

Anna frowns. 'The trial starts on Monday, doesn't it?'

I nod. 'I know. I don't have much time. I'll see you later. I'll call you.' I pick up my bag. 'I'm pretty certain Ben's going to be just fine. Whatever Alex's mental state, whatever is wrong with him, I don't think he's done anything serious to Ben. The symptoms didn't worry the consultant last night. But please let me know what they say this morning. I'll keep my phone switched on at all times.'

*

I catch a bus from Archway and go home briefly to wash and change. I put my thick winter boots on, then walk through the snow down to the office. Fortunately, we've woken this morning to just a couple of inches, and the regular Saturday traffic is moving with ease down the Holloway Road. I let myself into the office and run up the stairs to my room.

My iPad is on the desk where I left it yesterday. Here in this room, it's as though time has stood still. I can picture Ellie, sitting in the chair opposite my desk, all bundled up in her fur-lined parka. I can hear Matt's voice as he appears from behind the door to ask me to go to Holborn. It's less than twenty-four hours since I was last sitting at this desk, in this office, clutching my polystyrene cup of deli soup, the heat warming up my cold fingers. But now it feels like a lifetime ago.

I pick up my iPad and place it into my bag before flicking on my computer monitor and opening the web browser. I roll my chair forward and type in 'George Barrington-Brown'. As I suspected, there's nothing – his life pre-dated the days of the internet and was too short to have made him stand out in any way. Next, I type in 'local newspaper Esher Surrey' and select the *Esher News and Mail*. I soon find a number of photos of Lord and Lady Barrington-Brown and even some group ones of the family and of their estate – Grove Park – including some early photos of Jay as a child. But there are none of George and there is no mention of him, either.

Next, I type into the search engine: 'Records of births, marriages and deaths'. There are a number of hits, but one particular website stands out: *genesandarchives.com*. Not long after my mother's death I'd spent some time on this website, researching my family's genealogy and my maternal bloodline in particular. It had felt comforting to know that I was part of something much bigger than myself. In spite of the gaping hole my mother had left in my life, I still had that long line of ancestors to look to; I still belonged somewhere, even though the most important person in my life was gone.

I open up the website and tap in my user name and password. My login is successful and my family tree appears. I blink hard and fight back tears as I see my mother's name sitting there on the screen in front of me inside a little box: Evelyn Louise Kellerman, née Mayfield. Sept 1956–Jan 2012. *I thought you'd been looking out for me*, I reprimand her, silently. *I thought you were guiding me. How could you have let me get it all so very wrong?*

I close down my family tree and start a new one. I type in 'James Alexander Barrington-Brown' and then 'Eleanor Barrington-Brown' and finally 'George Barrington-Brown' into the search engine. A list of names appears and I scroll down until I've found them all, George and Jay appearing one above the other.

George Charles Barrington-Brown, I read, before opening up his entry. The record of birth appears, but that's it. There's no record of death anywhere to be seen. I sit, looking at the screen for a moment, before trying again. Maybe there's more than one George Barrington-Brown and I've picked the wrong one. I scroll back to the entries for both George and Jay and open Jay's. The date of birth is the same as it is for George: *Aug 1976*.

It's definitely the right George. I stare at the screen in bewilderment for a moment. Have I got this all wrong? Could George still be alive? Did his parents in fact put him in a care home somewhere? Has Jay lied to me, yet again? But then I recollect his anguish – the voice racked with pain, the uncontrollable heaving of his shoulders, the guttural sobs that had escaped from his throat when he'd told me that he had been responsible for his brother's death. Why would he tell me George was dead if he wasn't?

I gaze from George's entry to Jay's for a moment, and then I remember that there is a way to search for death by record of birth. I find the page and enter the birth date of August 1976. If Jay was telling the truth – about this part, at least – it would have been 1981 or 1982 when George died. I enter a range from August 1981 through to August 1982 and scroll down, but nothing. There's no entry for a George Barrington-Brown.

I scroll back up through the entries again and look through the names more carefully. There's more than one George in the list, but not the one I'm looking for and the middle names are all wrong. I'm just about to exit the page when one of the names grabs my attention. There's no middle name. It says, simply, *George Kent. Parish: Claygate, Esher.* I stare at it for a moment. How likely is it that two children named George died at the age of five, in the same year, within the same parish?

I open it up and read, *George Kent. Born: Aug 1976. Died May 1982.* Could this be the same George I'm looking for? But these are the only available details. There's nothing more, unless… I glance down. Underneath the index, there are several more hyper-links. I scroll through them until I see what I'm looking for. Here it is: *Order a copy death certificate for above-named entrant.* It costs twenty pounds. Other than the money, I've nothing else to lose. It's worth a go. The certificate will show both the person registering the death and the cause of death. When I see it, I'll know if this is the right one. I click on the link and follow the instructions, updating my PayPal details and choosing the express option, a four-day service with the option of an emailed black-and-white scan of the original certificate before it's dispatched.

I log off the website and switch off my monitor. I pick up my bag and fetch my coat from the hook on the back of the door. Why would George have been given the surname 'Kent' instead of Barrington-Brown, the name he was born with, I wonder? Unless the family really were trying to cover up his death, to hide him away? And why 'Kent'? Where did that name come from?

All of a sudden, it hits me. My heart begins to race. I've come across that surname before, and now I know why.

I sit back down and switch on my monitor, logging onto the website again with trembling fingers. I click on the Barrington-Brown family tree and find Eleanor's entry. I then click on the hyper-link next to it and search through the record of marriages until I find the one I'm looking for: *June 1974. The marriage of Rt. Hon. Lord Anthony George Barrington-Brown.* My heart is hammering against my chest. Before I've even read it, I know what I'm going to see underneath. And there it is, in black-and-white: *Dr Eleanor Anne Kent, daughter of Dr Robert Fitzroy Kent FRCS.*

Dr Kent.

I clap both hands to my mouth and breathe in sharply. For one long moment, I'm immobile with shock. Slowly, I pull my keyboard towards me and tap the name into the Google search engine, Anna's words, when she handed me the case, tumbling simultaneously through my mind: *Father's a life peer and mother's from a family of doctors. Her father's an Old Etonian, a fellow of the Royal College of Surgeons.*

A list of web pages comes up. I click on *images*, and there she is. There's no doubt about it: Eleanor Barrington-Brown and

Dr Eleanor Anne Kent are one and the same person. Eleanor is Dr Kent, the locum doctor who was on Peregrine Ward that night, the one who was recognised by the agency nurse, Stacey Bennett. The police officer and CCTV operators must have either missed her, or dismissed her as irrelevant to the police enquiries, because she either used her medical credentials or a lanyard and fob to legitimately enter the ward – Jay's lanyard and fob, no doubt.

I reach for my phone and then immediately change my mind. It's not enough; I still can't prove any of this. Mary's evidence is gone and my hunch is no more than that – a hunch. I can't prove, beyond all reasonable doubt, that Eleanor Barrington-Brown is *the* Dr Kent, that she was on the ward that night, or even if she was, that she did anything wrong. I have to find evidence this time, hard solid evidence. But there's still one person who knows far more than they're letting on.

*

I take a taxi to Camberwell. I don't dare take the underground, for fear of being out of range when Anna calls. I text her once I'm seated in the cab, heading along Upper Street towards Angel. She texts back: *Ben awake but woozy. Still no sign of doctors, but all fine. Tim says hi.*

I ask the taxi driver to stop at the bottom of the High Street. I cross Eastfield Road and tread carefully through the grey, melting slush that covers the estate, looking around me all the while to see if either Darren or Marie might be around somewhere, watching me from the seat of a car, perhaps, or from the park across the road. As I climb the steps to Cedar Court and walk along the balcony to number 36B, it flashes through my mind how much easier this would be if I were a police officer instead of a defence lawyer – if I could yell, 'Open up. Police!' and have Marie come out with her hands up in the air.

I tap on the glass of her front door and wait. There's no answer. I lean over the balcony to see if anyone might have appeared below, someone who might know where she is. I pull my phone out of my pocket; it's twelve o'clock. The pubs will be open. Maybe I should be brave and venture down to the Camby Arms.

As I turn back round again, I notice that the net curtain in the kitchen window has been pulled up in the flat next to Marie's, the other side to Ellie's, and the same elderly woman's face appears, the one who'd been watching me the last time I came. She screws up her eyes and peers at me intently for a moment, as if she's trying to work out who I am. When she sees me looking at her, she drops the curtain back down.

I give Marie's door a second tap. As I do so, my phone rings. It's Anna. 'All fine,' she says. 'The consultant was happy. Ben's remaining blood tests came back normal; they didn't detect any sign of infection or anything untoward and his observations have been good all night, so they said he can go home.'

I breathe a huge sigh of relief. 'That's great, Anna. Thank you. And – thank God. It could have been so much worse.'

I give her a quick run-through of Ben's favourite *Teletubbies* DVDs, along with a reminder of how to switch the computer on, which web browser to use, and the things that she can give Ben to eat and drink.

The call-interrupt function bleeps in my ear. 'I've got to go,' I tell her. 'I'll ring you later to see how you're getting on.'

The call is from Ellie. 'Where are you?' she demands.

'I'm... well, I'm...'

'Marie's just rung me. She says you're outside her flat.' Ellie's voice is indignant.

'Yes,' I admit. 'I am. Is she at home, then? Can you get her to come out and speak to me?'

'No. She's not happy, Sarah. She says you're stalking her and that she's going to call the police. I think you'd better go.'

'OK,' I tell her, reluctantly.

Ellie's voice softens a little. 'Thanks for trying,' she says. 'But like I said, she's not going to help, Darren or no Darren. She says she's done nothing wrong, and that's that. She wants you to leave her alone.'

'OK.'

'So you'll leave her alone?'

I sigh. 'Yes. I'll leave her alone.'

'OK. I'll see you on Monday.'

'OK,' I agree.

I push my phone back into my pocket. I glance at Marie's kitchen window and then, after a moment's hesitation, I step over and tap on the glass of the flat next door. I hear the sound of movement inside and then the chain rattles and the door edges open.

The woman peers at me, silently, from behind the door. She has white thinning hair and equally pale, papery skin that reveals the veins underneath.

'Hello,' I say. 'I saw you watching me from the window. I'm a solicitor. I wondered if I might have a word with you?'

'What about?'

I lean forward. 'About them next door,' I say, my voice lowered, conspiratorially. I bob my head in the direction of Marie's flat.

'Oh, them. Are you from the council?' she asks.

She has a strong cockney accent, I notice. Her mouth makes involuntary movements as if she's chewing something. A long hair protrudes from her chin.

I hesitate. 'I'm a solicitor,' I say again.

'Well, it's about time. You'd better come inside.'

I step into her narrow hallway, and follow her into the living room. The layout of the flat is the same as Ellie's, but the paint-work is cracking and the wallpaper is peeling. There's a musty, damp smell throughout.

I take a seat in a threadbare tartan wingback armchair with a large white lace doily over the back.

'What's your name?' she asks me.

'I'm Sarah,' I tell her. 'What's yours?'

'Mrs Cooper,' she says. She lowers herself down into the chair opposite me. She doesn't offer me a cup of tea.

'So, what's the problem?' I ask, deciding to let her lead the way. I am aware that I'm misleading her, slightly, as to who I am and the reason I'm here, but I'm hoping the end will justify the means.

'Well, they're so noisy,' she complains. 'It's all the time. If it's not shouting, it's music. And if it's not music, it's children crying.'

'They have children?' I ask, knowing that they don't.

'Well, *they* don't. She looks after other people's children, doesn't she?'

'So, what sorts of noises do you hear?'

'Well, you know. Shouting. Yelling. Her telling the kids to shut up.'

'What about visitors?' I ask. 'Do many people come and go?'

'Well, yes. All the time. Her fella, he smokes drugs and that in there and all sorts come knocking. I can smell it. It comes up through the pipes in my kitchen.'

'Really?'

'Really,' she says. 'And it ain't nice.'

'So, do you know whose children she looks after?'

'I don't know. Just people on the estate. She used to look after the little boy two doors down, before he got taken into care. Poor little lad.'

I lean forward. 'Why do you say that? Poor little lad?'

'Well, he was always crying. They would leave him with that woman and they'd go off down the pub and come home drunk.'

My breath stops in my chest. 'What woman?'

Mrs Cooper blinks at me for a moment and her mouth starts chewing away furiously, her nose twitching up and down. 'Well, that woman with the blue scarf. She don't come round no more, not since the kid got taken away, but whenever I saw her, I always used to think to myself, "Oh my gawd, here we go."'

'What do you mean? Why?'

'Well, like I say, the baby was always howling.'

'While they were gone?'

'Yes. While they were gone.'

'What did it sound like? Was it… sudden, loud crying, or… or grizzling?'

'It was both. And then them two, they'd come home and start arguing.'

'About what?'

'Well, I don't know, do I? But whenever *she* came round, they always came back from the pub in a worse state than usual. And that's when they make the most noise. He smacks her about,' she adds. 'Her fella.'

310

I nod.

She points a bony finger at me. 'I remember you now, you came that time before, didn't you, when they were having an almighty ding-dong.'

'I did,' I agree. 'You've a good memory for faces.'

'Oh, there's nothing wrong with my memory,' she says. 'There's something wrong with my old ticker though and all of this noise and whatnot don't help.'

She makes a ball of her fist and taps at her chest, before heaving herself up out of her chair.

'Just listen to my knees,' she adds as the chair creaks its response.

I smile. 'I think that was the chair that was creaking.'

She frowns at me. 'I'm an old woman,' she says. 'Everything's creaking.'

'I'm sure,' I agree. 'It can't be easy.'

'It's not.'

She walks over to the sideboard, opens a drawer and takes out a packet of boiled sweets. She unwraps one and puts it into her mouth. As an afterthought, she offers me one. I shake my head.

'So what are you going to do about it?' she asks, with her mouth full.

'About what?'

'The noise.'

'Well, I'll be sure to pass on your concerns,' I tell her, truthfully. 'I'll make a report.'

'And what will happen after that? I've been phoning the council for weeks, you know, and nobody ever listens.'

'Well, I think someone will sit up and listen this time,' I tell her. 'Trust me, I'll make sure they do.'

*

As I leave, Marie steps out from the flat next door. I give her what I hope is a fearsome stare and then turn to walk down the balcony towards the steps.

'Wait!' she calls after me.

I turn round.

'What were you doing in there?' she asks. 'What's she said?'

I walk back towards her. 'How much did she pay you, Marie?'

'What?' Marie puts her hands on her hips and faces me indignantly, but she looks frightened.

'How much did she pay you?' I repeat. 'Finn's grandmother. To keep quiet.'

Marie opens and shuts her mouth, then opens it again. 'She didn't. She...'

I look her in the eye. 'Don't give me your bullshit, Marie. I know. I know everything. So how much was it worth to you to keep your mouth shut and let Ellie get locked up for something she hasn't done?'

Marie looks at me for a moment, her mouth falling open again.

'It wasn't like that,' she says.

I shake my head. 'And Finn. That poor little boy! Do you want to think about what you've done to him?'

'Nothing! I ain't done nothing!'

'She nearly killed him!' I yell. 'She nearly killed him, Marie. And then you just stand by and watch while they take him away from Ellie and give him back to *her*!'

Marie stands, helplessly, on the balcony, looking at me. 'What are you going to do?' she asks.

Good question. I don't actually know. I have what the police would term 'intelligence', but I still don't have the hard evidence I need of any wrongdoing on Marie's part. Marie doesn't know that, of course, but I don't think there's much prospect of getting Mrs Cooper and her dodgy ticker onto the witness stand. Even if I could, Carmel would make mincemeat of her. She'd be easily discredited as an unreliable witness who's simply frustrated with 'them next door' and their noise. As for the mystery woman who's been visiting the baby... well, that could be anyone, couldn't it?

No. If Will and I are going to nail this, we need Marie, herself – we need her on the witness stand.

'What do you think I'm going to do?' I bluff. 'If you think I'm going to stand by and let you look after another child, ever again, you are seriously mistaken.'

'It wasn't my fault!' Marie protests, her eyes filling with tears. 'It was her! It was all her! You don't know what she's like!'

She glances round. Mrs Cooper is back in the kitchen, with the net curtain pushed back, watching us both.

Marie steps back and pushes her front door open. 'Please,' she begs me. 'Don't report me. I need that qualification. I need this childminding job. Come in. I'll tell you everything you want to know.'

I glance at Mrs Cooper and give her a nod, before stepping forward and following Marie into her flat. Mrs Cooper nods back at me as she drops the curtain down, satisfied, no doubt, that I've taken her seriously, that I'm now putting my promise into action and investigating her complaint.

Marie's flat smells heavily of cigarette smoke. She walks up the hallway and into the living room, where she flops down onto a voluminous sofa, picks up a pack of Royals from the coffee table, slides one out and lights it.

'Could you open a window?' I suggest.

Marie nods and stands up. She walks over to the door to the Juliet balcony at the rear of the flats and slides it open a little.

'She's a complete cow,' Marie says, shaking her head. 'She's a bitch, that Eleanor. She was blackmailing me.'

'How? How did you get involved with her?'

'Well, she just turned up one day, didn't she? El had gone off to work and put Finn with me. I saw her knocking on El's door and I stuck my head out. El had told me all about Finn's dad and that, that he came from a posh family. I knew straight away who she was. I knew she was Finn's granny.'

'So what happened next?'

'Well, I'd run out of fags,' she says. 'I needed to get some more. Finn was all settled, fast asleep, he was, in the bedroom. I didn't want to wake him. I'd just been trying to decide what to do. First off, I rang Darren to see if he could go and get me a pack, but he weren't answering. I knew he'd be down the Camby Arms, having a good time, and I was riled with him. There was me, working hard, trying to earn money for us, for our future. It felt as though he didn't give a shit about me. I was upset. I needed a fag.'

Marie pauses and takes a puff of her cigarette.

'And then,' she continues, 'just as I was trying to decide how I was going to get myself some smokes, I saw her walk past and knock on El's door, and I thought to myself, "What the hell, he's *her* grandkid. She's obviously here to see him. She ain't gonna mind me asking her to watch him for twenty minutes while I pop out and get a packet of fags." It ain't easy doing stuff like that when you've got a small kid, you know?'

I do. I do, indeed, know.

'So,' Marie continues, 'I go out, and I say to her, are you looking for El? She's gone to work, but your grandkid is in here with me, if you want to see him.'

'And what did she say?'

'Well, she looked a bit surprised, at first. But then she says, "Thank you,"' Marie puts on an upper-class accent, '"that would be very nice," she says. "I don't get to see him quite as often as I'd like."

'So in she comes and out I go. I went down to the Costcutter, but it was shut and so I had to go to the pub. When I got there, Darren was in there with that Tanya Small, drooling over her and dissing me in front of everyone off the estate. We had an almighty bust-up and then I got my fags and went back.

'I'd been quite a bit longer than I said I was going to be, but Eleanor was really nice about it. She said she didn't mind at all, that she'd just been watching Finn sleeping, and how happy it made her. She then told me how hard it was to get to spend time with him, that El wouldn't let her see him very much. I believed her. I knew El didn't have much time for her, but I couldn't see why, to be honest. It felt as though El was being unfair to her. She seemed so nice, and it was her grandkid after all.'

Marie's phone bleeps. She stands up and wrestles it out of her pocket. She looks at it and puts it down on the table.

'She asked me if she could come by and visit Finn again next time I had him,' she continues. 'I knew I was going behind El's back a bit, but I couldn't see the harm. Plus, I was really upset about Darren and Tanya. She asked me what was wrong and so I told her; I had to talk to someone. And then she said, "Look, I'm in no rush to get away. Why don't you go back down the

315

pub and sort it out with him?" She opened her handbag and she gave me a fifty-pound note. She said, "Buy him a drink and talk it through. Take your time. This can be our secret, can't it? You get to make things up with your boyfriend and I get to see my grandson. Everybody's happy, and Ellis need never know."'

She stubs her cigarette out. 'I know now that I should never have done it,' she says, 'I should never have left Finn with her, but I had to get back down the Camby Arms and confront him, Darren. It was eating me up inside.'

'So it became a regular thing, is that what you're saying?'

Marie takes a second cigarette out of the packet and lights it. Without asking her, I stand up and open the sliding window a little wider. A welcome blast of fresh cold air enters. I pointedly take a seat in an armchair nearer to the door.

Marie nods. She takes one large puff of her cigarette and stubs it out.

'And did she pay you each time?' I ask.

'Yeah. I couldn't see any harm in it. We were doing her a favour, and she could afford it, after all. Darren loved the extra money. We sorted things out between us, and he said it was a right result, managing to get paid by El and by her, too. It meant I could go with him when he went out, keep an eye on him, like. I didn't trust him at the end of the day, not with women, not with the aggro he was getting into, the drugs and fights and shit that goes on this estate. I know it was wrong, but it worked, for me. I was getting really good money for the first time in my life. I mean, it wasn't like mega-bucks or anything. But it meant that I could afford to pay my rent and my bills and still have some left over.

'El was earning ten times what she was paying me and I knew she could afford it. And that rich bitch was loaded, so it was no skin off her nose. El kept saying as to how she was saving up and that she was going to get her and Finn off the estate, and I knew when she did that she'd find a proper nanny and that would be it. I knew it weren't going to be a forever thing and I thought I'd take it while I could.'

'So how did it work? She'd just knock on the door every time Ellie went to work?'

'Not every time, just sometimes. We arranged it so that she would call me when she wanted to come and I would tell her if El was working and if Finn was with me.'

'And then?'

'She would come round and give us fifty quid to piss off down the pub for a couple of hours. It was a no-brainer, if I'm honest. Who's gonna say no to that?'

'And when you got home? How was Finn?'

'He was asleep. He always seemed fine. I had no reason to worry about what she got up to. She was his gran, wasn't she? I thought she loved him. I thought she cared.'

'And now? What do you think now?'

Marie says, bitterly, 'I think she's a fucking bitch who has stitched us up, that's what I think.' She sighs heavily and scratches her left shoulder with the opposite hand. 'The first time El got arrested for all the bruises and the burns and that, we weren't sure what had happened. We didn't honestly know if it was El that had done it. I didn't suspect for a minute that it was her – Eleanor. And it certainly weren't me. And then there was Finn. I mean, he climbed on the furniture and stuff all the time, and fell off, and there was one time when I took him on the bus up to the Oval. We were going to Kennington Park. The bus stopped suddenly with a great big jerk, just as we were getting off, and we both went over, Finn and me. I had a massive bruise on my leg and I noticed, a couple of days later, that Finn had one on his arm and one on his knee. But I was shocked when they said he'd been burned. I know I smoke in the house and I shouldn't, but I swear that was nothing to do with me. El said it was impetigo and that the bruises were an accident. That's what she told me her solicitor said. She's a good mate, is El; she never once pointed the finger at me. But then when Finn got really ill and was taken to hospital, that was when I got really scared.'

'So what happened?'

'Well, she was here, wasn't she – Eleanor? El got a last-minute call out to work, so I called Eleanor over and me and Darren went out. I think we went to the Camby Arms first off; I remember it was afternoon when we left, because it was still light. But there was a party on the estate that night, and everyone was going. I called Eleanor and she said that was OK, that she could stay with Finn overnight. It was a bit of a wild party; I woke up on the living-room floor. Darren was gone, I didn't know where. So, I called Eleanor and told her I was coming home. When I got back, Finn was asleep. She said he'd been fine, but within about half an hour of her leaving, he woke up and I could see that he weren't right. He was really pale and floppy, and he was just staring right at me, but it was like he couldn't see me. I called El straight away and she came home.

'Darren was really angry after El got arrested. He'd been up to something dodgy that night, something to do with some shipment of drugs, and so he didn't have an alibi. He called

Eleanor and told her that she'd stitched us up, and that he wasn't going to prison for her.'

'And what did she say?'

'She went mental right back at him. But *really* mental, I mean. She went crazy. He had her on speakerphone and I could hear everything she said.'

'What? What did she say?'

'Well, she just twisted everything and turned it back on us, basically. She started going off on one at Darren, telling him he was nothing but a drug dealer and a loser. She said that if her grandson died, then she would make sure we both went to prison for life. She said we weren't fit to lick her boots, all sorts of stuff like that. Then she said that if either of us mentioned it again, to anyone, she'd call the police and she'd see to it that they locked us both up and threw away the key. She said that, if she was us, she would stay right out of it and walk away while we still could.'

'And that's what you did?'

'Well, yeah.' Marie's face reddens. 'But you have to understand what she's like. It's like… if you are giving her what she wants, like in the beginning, when I let her see Finn, she's as nice as they come. But if you cross her, it's like she's going to destroy you, annihilate you. I was scared, and so was Darren. She said she knew people in high places, judges and doctors and that, people "who could make things happen".'

I think about this for a moment. 'But what about Ellie? She's supposed to be your friend. Did you even stop to think about her?'

'Course I did. For a while, when El was inside, I felt really bad and I didn't know what to do. But then you came along, you and that barrister, and you got her bail, and she seemed more positive after that. She said you were a really good solicitor and that she didn't think she was going to go down for it. Obviously, I should have told her that Finn's gran had been coming round to my house, that she had been paying me to stay with Finn, but I didn't know for sure that Eleanor had done anything to hurt him. All I know is that I didn't touch that kid, I swear. I never laid a finger on him. I wouldn't.'

'What about Darren?'

'Nor him. I know he hasn't got a good track record when it comes to hitting me. But most of the time we'd have a fight, he'd thump me one and storm out, most likely round to that bitch Tanya's house. He never stuck around afterwards, and nine times out of ten, Finn just slept through.'

I fold my arms. 'That's not what your neighbour thinks.'

'You what?'

'Your neighbour, Mrs Cooper, says that Finn was always crying. She says that you and Darren would come home drunk from the pub, that you'd fight. She says when you looked after the children of families on the estate, she heard you telling them to shut up.'

Marie scowls and chews away at her gum for a moment. 'She's such a nosy bitch. She's making it sound worse than it is.'

I look hard at her and purse my lips.

'Look, I'm no angel,' she says. 'I know that. I have my moments, like everyone else. Yeah, I might have yelled at the kids I looked after a few times when they were getting on my nerves. Who doesn't? And yeah, when I was with Darren we used to drink too much together. It was a bad relationship and I'm out of it now, I haven't had a drink for weeks. But she's making it sound like I'm a monster, and I'm not. I'm no different from anyone else on this estate; everyone left school with no qualifications, no one's got any money. Everyone smokes and drinks, because you've got to have something to make you happy, and you ain't got much else to do.

'Most of us are just doing the best we can to get by. People like that Eleanor, they've got no idea what it's like for people like me. She's got everything, I've got nothing. She hasn't even had to graft for it – she's had it handed to her on a silver plate. She don't ever have to lie awake at night, worrying about how she's going to pay the rent, whether she's got enough money for the leccy and if she's going to get cut off. The leccy's what you worry about because you need it to watch TV, and fuck knows there ain't nothing else to do round here. The bailiffs come round, because you haven't paid your leccy; first thing they go for is the TV and then the sofa. What does that leave you at the end of the day?

'That rich bitch, she don't have to worry every time her old man steps out the front door. She don't need to be looking out for the dealers that hang around the estate, worrying if her old man's going to end up a junkie, or even worse, a dealer like them, and whether he's going to get into a fight and end up with a knife in his back.

'The only person I know on this estate that's ever had any money is El, and look what she had to do to get it. I'm not having a go at her, because that's what it's like for people like us. The only way most of the people round here can ever think of getting a foot on the ladder, getting out of this shit hole, getting a head start in life, is to sell their body, sell drugs or nick other people's stuff. There ain't no other way for the likes of us. There's no magic wand that's going to make all our dreams come true.

Working in Costcutter for the minimum wage ain't gonna cut it. And then you see people like her, that Eleanor, who've got everything. Everything. You can't blame people for wanting a bit of what she's got. You can't blame them for getting angry from time to time, for kicking off or shouting at their kids or at each other. You can't blame them for thinking life's unfair.'

I listen to her in silence for a moment. 'I do understand that, Marie. I do understand what it's like. But a child got injured, possibly poisoned, while he was in your care. You admit you were drunk when you were supposed to be looking after him. And Darren, he had people knocking on the door, looking for drugs.'

Marie puts her head in her hands. 'I know. But that's in the past, I swear. I want to make a new start, now, do things properly. Doesn't everyone deserve a second chance?'

I open my bag and take out my notebook. I root around in the bottom for a pen. 'Well, that depends,' I say.

Marie looks up at me. 'On what?'

'On whether they're prepared to help repair the damage they've done. To do the right thing.'

Marie rolls her eyes towards the ceiling and looks out of the window at the sky that's already darkening around us. She gets up off the sofa and walks past me to slide shut the balcony door. She walks across the living room and out of the door. 'I'm going to put the kettle on,' she says.

I get up and follow her into the kitchen. 'I want you to give evidence for Ellie,' I say.

Marie picks up the kettle and walks over to the sink. She turns the tap on and fills the kettle, then continues to make tea, taking cups and teabags out of the cupboard, her back to me all the while.

'The trial starts on Monday,' I say. 'The prosecution have to present their case first, so you probably won't be needed until later in the week. In the meantime, I'll need to take a witness statement from you.'

Marie continues to ignore me for a moment. She places her hands on the worktop, takes a deep breath and sighs heavily.

Eventually she turns round and nods towards the kitchen table.

'You'd better sit down then,' she says.

20

The snow has gone by Monday, but the temperature has fallen to below zero. There's ice on the pavements outside the Old Bailey and, inside, the stone and marble hallway is cold. There are butterflies in my chest as I push open the old wooden door to Court One and peer into the courtroom. At ten o'clock, Judge Collins will take his seat in the huge chair up in front of me, ready to hear last-minute submissions before the jury is sworn in and the prosecutor makes her opening speech. But the biggest item on the agenda for me and Will this morning is how we are going to deal with my relationship with Jay Barrington-Brown.

I find Will in the canteen, where he's seated at a table talking to Carmel Oliver. As soon as I enter, they both turn to look at me, and I can see that Carmel knows. I glance around the room. Does anyone else know? Am I being gossiped about? I can hardly blame them; I know how it looks. I can just imagine what Matt and Lucy are going to be saying when they hear that I've been sleeping with my client's ex-partner, the father of the victim in a major Crown Court trial.

Will ends his conversation with Carmel and walks over. He indicates that I should follow him back along the corridor to Court One and into an adjacent alcove. He sits down at the table and waves me into the seat opposite.

'Are you OK?' he asks. 'You look pale.'

'I'm OK,' I tell him. 'What did Carmel say?'

He presses his lips together. 'Well, as far as you and Jay Barrington-Brown are concerned, she says that it's a matter that's between you and your client and that it's none of her business, and actually she's right. But she did tell me that Jay was released on bail on Saturday...'

I sigh. 'Yes, I know. I spoke to the desk sergeant. He's got a condition not to contact me and Ben.'

Will nods. 'Well, there's been a development since then.'

'What development?'

'He's been sectioned.'

I look at him in shock. '*What?*'

'Jay Barrington-Brown has been detained under section two of the Mental Health Act. It happened last night.'

I immediately feel a combination of relief and bewilderment. At least that's one thing to tick off my list of concerns this morning – I don't have to stop myself from phoning the school every couple of hours to check that Ben's still there. But, on the other hand, I'm surprised.

'He must have gone downhill pretty badly,' I say. 'I mean, I knew from what he did to Ben that there had to be something not right with him, mentally, but if they had to have an urgent assessment, there and then, at the police station—'

'It wasn't the police,' Will interrupts me. 'It was his family. They organised it themselves, apparently, after the police let him go. They must have found two doctors to assess him and certify that he was unwell...'

'Unwell enough to be locked up?'

'It would seem so, yes. But in spite of what happened to Ben,

Carmel says there's no evidence that he harmed Finn. Also, he had an alibi for the twenty-fifth of July, when Finn's dialysis line was removed. He was at the Ivy with his father all evening, until late. The club was full. He was seen by several staff members there, not to mention family friends. As far as the prosecution against Ellie is concerned, it's business as usual, I'm afraid.'

I shake my head. 'But it wasn't him. It was his mother.'

Will frowns and takes his glasses off.

'It was his mother,' I repeat. 'Eleanor Barrington-Brown. She's Dr Kent. *The* Dr Kent. Will, I told you this already. Finn's in danger; big danger. He's being released from hospital tomorrow, to *her*. And if Ellie goes down for this, it will be case closed. They could move away, anything. No one might ever know if anything happens to Finn.'

Will rubs the inner corner of each eye with one finger. 'But how do we know for sure that it was her?' he says. 'And more importantly, how do we prove it?'

'With Marie,' I insist. 'We put her on the stand. Once the jury's sure that Eleanor's the one who injured and poisoned him, everything else will add up.'

Will heaves an enormous sigh. 'And what's her motive? Why would Eleanor want to kill her own grandson?'

'Because she's a nutcase! Because Finn's Ellie's son and – contrary to what she'd have everyone believe – she despises Ellie. Because Ellie and Finn are standing in the way of her plans for her son to marry into the best family they can find.'

Will sighs again.

'Will?' I look him directly in the eye. 'You told Carmel about Marie, right? You told her that we have new evidence that Eleanor was with Finn the first time he almost died?'

Will looks uncomfortable. 'Yes. But she doesn't accept it.' He pauses and his eyes meet mine. 'The thing is, Sarah, Eleanor has been spoken to by the police and she denies that she ever visited Marie. She's made a counter-statement to the police about Ellie. She's going to give evidence against her. Heather Grainger's statement looks positively benign by comparison. She's accusing Ellie of everything under the sun – of being careless with Finn, emotionally detached from him, shouting at him – you name it, it's there. She's told the police that she didn't come forward before out of loyalty to Ellie, but that she now feels morally obliged. Carmel says Marie will have to give her evidence and the jury will have to decide who to believe – Marie or Lady Barrington-Brown. She says Marie's account is devoid of any motive to harm the child on the part of Eleanor Barrington-Brown, and that it's just the kind of story that you'd expect the defendant and her best friend to concoct together out of desperation two days before the trial.' He pauses. 'Carmel's right. The jury just aren't going to believe that she's done this, Sarah.'

I look at him in bewilderment. I try to think who else there is who might back up Marie's story. Mrs Cooper and her dodgy ticker are out. Darren and his friends? No way. There *is* no one else. It was their little secret, after all. Even if there *was* someone else on the estate who witnessed Eleanor's presence there, there's barely any time left to find them – and even less prospect of getting them to give evidence against her if I did.

Will sighs heavily. 'It gets worse, I'm afraid. Eleanor says that Jay is very unwell, that they'd suspected it for some time. She says she was shocked to hear that he'd been in a relationship with Ellie's lawyer, but that she doesn't believe you didn't know who he was.' Will pauses. 'She's blaming you. She's accusing you of professional misconduct. I'm told that… that she's going to report you to the SRA. She says that Jay is very vulnerable and she believes that you… well, she thinks you seduced him.'

My heart skips a beat. 'She… she thinks that I… *what?*'

Will takes a deep breath. 'She thinks that when you met Jay, you knew exactly who he was.'

'But, why? Why would I…?'

'She's saying you were after his money.'

I gaze at Will, open-mouthed for a moment. 'But Jay will confirm that…' I tail off. Jay's just been sectioned. Jay is deluded, mentally unstable. Nobody is going to believe anything he says. I put my head in my hands. 'Oh God.'

I can hear the tannoy sounding outside the courtroom. There's a tinny hum ringing in my ears at the same time, which makes the tannoy sound distant and surreal.

Will gets up. 'Sarah, I'm sorry. I need to go into court. Why don't you stay here for the moment? I'll make our application to the judge for more time and I'll come straight back.'

I look up. 'What are you going to say?'

'I'll be discreet, don't worry.'

I nod. He'll be making his application in open court. There will be reporters there. I hope he doesn't have to tell the judge too much. I hope the press don't get wind of this.

I watch as he gathers his papers and steps out from behind the table and across the hallway.

'Will?'

He turns to face me.

'Do *you* believe me?' I ask. 'That I didn't know that Alex was Jay Barrington-Brown?'

Will looks at me for a moment and then shakes his head. He says, 'Do you really need to ask me that, Sarah? Of course I bloody do.'

I wait in the alcove with my head in my hands, the true weight of what I've just been told sitting like a brick inside my stomach. This has all worked out way too conveniently for Eleanor. Jay's the only person who can verify my story and she's had him taken out of the way, declared mentally unfit. In one fell swoop she has both made it difficult for him to tell anyone the truth of what happened between us, and has also ruined his credibility if he does. I'm not a doctor, but I've dealt with enough mentally ill clients to know the difference between those that need help and those that are so unwell that they need to be locked up and medically treated against their will.

The stark reality of what I'm up against is finally dawning on me. Marie's words ring in my ears: *She just twisted everything and turned it back on us, basically... if you cross her, it's like she's going to destroy you, annihilate you... She said she knew people in high places, judges and doctors and that, people 'who could make things happen'.* No doubt Eleanor knew two doctors who were prepared to help her remove Jay safely out of the way for the duration of Ellie's trial. For the first time, I understand properly what it was that Marie was trying to tell me: that Eleanor Barrington-Brown is a dangerous woman who will stop at nothing to get what she wants.

A shadow looms over me and I jump out of my skin.

It's Ellie. She looks sensational. She's wearing a smart black trouser suit and a crisp white shirt. Her hair is coiled up on top of her head in an elegant French twist. Her lips are painted a

330

delicate baby pink and she has black eyeliner round her eyes, but not too much.

She takes a step back. 'You OK?'

I nod slowly, catching my breath.

'Sorry I'm late,' she says. 'Where's Will?'

'He's in court,' I tell her. 'Trying to buy us some more time. Come and sit down.'

She slides into the seat opposite me. 'I'm really sorry, Sarah. I know you said to be here early. I got held up.'

'That's OK,' I tell her. 'In fact, it's me who should be saying sorry to you. I have something important I need to tell you.'

'I already know.' She opens her handbag and takes out a tube of lip gloss. 'Marie told me everything. And you don't need to say sorry. I'm really glad you did what you did. If it weren't for you, pushing her…' She tails off and shakes her head, sorrowfully.

'You must be pretty angry,' I say. 'That she had evidence all along that could have helped you and she kept it from you.'

Ellie purses her lips and runs the lip gloss over them before screwing the cap back on. 'We spent all day yesterday talking it through. I'm still angry with her, and she knows it. But she was scared of Eleanor, and I don't blame her for that. Look what that bitch has done to me. I often wondered if that had been her plan all along, to take Finn off me, but I never thought for one minute that it was her who tried to kill him and frame me instead. I'm scared now, really scared. What if she hurts him again?'

'She's not that stupid,' I say. 'She won't do anything when she's in the spotlight like this, especially now…' I stop myself. I was going to say, 'especially now that Jay's been arrested for drugging my son' but that's not the best way to start the conversation I need to have with her next. I sigh heavily. 'Ellie, I need to talk to you. There's something more. Something important.'

'What? What is it?'

The door to the courtroom opens and Will walks over. 'Hello, Ellie. Good. We're all here.' He turns to me. 'Fortunately, I didn't have to make my application. There are some exhibits missing from the jury bundles and the prosecutor needs a bit of time to get them brought to court.' I breathe a sigh of relief. At least, for now, my humiliation has remained out of the public arena. 'The judge has given us an hour,' Will says. He turns to me. 'How far have you got?'

'Not far,' I tell him. 'I was just about to explain to Ellie that I may be professionally embarrassed. Not to mention person-ally,' I add.

Ellie frowns. 'You're embarrassed? What about? What does that mean?'

Will turns to her. 'It means that there's a problem that might prevent Sarah – and me, as the barrister instructed by Sarah – from representing you at your trial.'

Ellie's face falls. She looks petrified. 'What? What are you talking about? You can't do this to me! Not now!'

Will holds up his hand. 'Well, it's a matter for you, really, Ellie. The question is, are you going to want us to continue acting for you—'

'Of course I am!'

'—in the light of what Sarah's about to tell you.'

Ellie frowns and looks at me. 'What? What are you about to tell me?'

I glance at Will, who pulls out a chair. He sits down and crosses his arms.

'It's a rather unusual situation,' I begin. 'It's to do with my personal life. I've been having a relationship with a man, since August – in fact, round about the time I took on your case. He told me his name was Alex and that he was a hedge fund manager. I've just found out that he's been lying to me for months. It turns out he's actually Jay Barrington-Brown.'

Ellie's mouth falls open. She sits in stunned silence for a moment before saying, 'You have got to be kidding me.'

I shake my head. 'Unfortunately not. I only wish that I was.'

Ellie looks at Will. He presses his lips together and looks from her to me. His silence tells her that this is no joke.

Ellie's chin juts out and her mouth sets in an angry line. She says, 'How did you meet him?'

'He followed me into a supermarket. My son was having a… well, what most people might think was a tantrum. I dropped a jar of coffee and it broke. I was pretty stressed. He came to my rescue and walked me home.'

Will narrows his eyes and listens intently.

'Did he know who you were? When he followed you into the supermarket?' Ellie says.

I nod. 'Yes. He set the whole thing up.'

I watch Ellie's face as she listens in disbelief to what I'm telling her. Her jaw tightens and her eyes flash with fury.

'Why?'

'He wanted to ask me not to reveal what you do for a living. He wanted to find out about your case.'

Ellie's eyes meet mine. 'And did he?'

'No.' I shake my head, vigorously. 'No, Ellie. He asked me a lot of questions, but I didn't tell him anything. Nothing confidential, anyway. I had my iPad at home, with your case file on it, but it's password protected and I didn't tell him the code.'

Thank God for Apple and their six-digit security code system. 'Talullah' wasn't an option as a password this time.

'He did have access to the prosecution papers at one stage,' I admit, 'which means that he could have read what the other witnesses were saying, what the rest of the evidence was against you. But I never gave anything away about your defence.'

Ellie sits in silence for a moment, her big blue eyes resting on mine. 'How did you find out who he really was?'

'I saw a photo of him in *Hello!* magazine. His parents were in the same shot. He looks just like his dad.'

Ellie nods, slowly.

'Then my son ended up in hospital and it all came to a head.'

'So the relationship is over?' she asks.

I frown. 'God, yes. Of course. It was based on a lie. He hurt my son. He drugged him. I called the police and he was arrested at the hospital.'

'Really?' Ellie looks alarmed. 'He drugged your son?'

'It's a long story,' I say.

Will leans forward. 'Obviously this will raise some questions in your mind about the case against you, about Jay, about his mother. But before we talk about that any further, our question for you is this: in the light of what Sarah has told you about her relationship with Jay, do you feel that you need to instruct a new legal team? It would be completely understandable if you did.'

I add, 'If I'd found out about Jay a few months earlier, I'd have had no option but to withdraw, to send you to a different firm. But I'm not going to do that on the day your trial starts, that wouldn't be fair to you. It's a difficult one for me. You must have a fair trial. If anything goes wrong, for instance, if you're convicted, it might make things difficult for me, professionally. If this comes out during the trial, it won't look great. But, on the other hand, I don't want to abandon you. The trial would have to be vacated. It could be another six months or more before you'd get another date. So I'm leaving the decision with you. If you feel that you want to—'

'I've made it,' Ellie interrupts me. 'I've made my decision. I'm sticking with you and Will. One hundred per cent.'

'Really?'

'Are you sure?' says Will.

Ellie turns to me. 'Jay lied to you and drugged your son and I know your son can't walk and talk and stuff, so you must have been through a really hard time. But you never once stopped caring about me. You've always been on my side. It took me a while to see it, but you made me see that I was someone that mattered, someone who was worth fighting for. And whatever happens at the end of this trial, I'll never forget that about you, Sarah. You're right that I had a crappy childhood and nobody ever gave a flying one about me. Not until you came along, that is. You made me believe in myself. Even when you found out who I was, and what I did for a living, you never once judged me.'

She turns to Will. 'And neither did you. You always talked to me like I was a real person, not some tart who you wanted to poke.'

'Whoa. Steady on,' says Will. Ellie's eyes meet mine and we both exchange a smile.

She says, 'I want this trial to go ahead and I want you both to run it for me.'

'Is that your final answer?' asks Will.

Ellie nods. 'It's my final answer.'

Will rubs his hands together. He turns to me. 'Sarah?'

'I'm in.' I smile.

*

The prosecution case opens in the afternoon, once the jury have been sworn. It's three thirty by the time Carmel has finished, however, and Judge Collins calls it a day. We arrange to meet Ellie first thing in the morning, and then Will and I walk together back to the advocates' room.

Will gives me a sideways glance as he unlocks the security door. 'How are you feeling?' he asks.

'Well, not good,' I say. 'It looks as though I've now got my own reputation to defend as well as Ellie's.'

'It'll be fine,' Will says. 'Don't worry. I'll support you.'

I look up at him. 'You don't have to do that.'

'I know,' Will says, 'but I want to.' We walk into the advocates' room and Will looks around discreetly to make sure it's empty before saying, 'I know you, Sarah. I know how professional you are. I know that you would never, knowingly, get mixed up with someone involved in a case you were working on. I also know that you're not the sort of person that would go out with a man just for his money. At least I hope not.' He gives me a sideways glance as he says this, and I look into his eyes and smile.

'So, do you fancy a drink?' I ask him. 'I'm buying,' I add.

Will laughs. He folds his wig up and places it into its leather case. 'Avoiding the office, perchance?'

I smile, wryly. 'Yes. Wouldn't you?'

We find a small pub on the corner of Newgate Street, not

far from the court building. I buy a lime and soda for myself and a beer for Will, who takes a seat in a quiet corner away from the bar.

'So. I'm looking at tomorrow's batting order,' Will says, as I arrive with the drinks. 'Tomorrow's focus is going to be on Finn's hospital admission on the nineteenth of July. The prosecution are calling Heather Grainger, the social worker, first. Then we have the A&E doctor and the toxicologist.'

'Well,' I say. 'If we believe that Eleanor Barrington-Brown was responsible, we don't dispute that the sodium levels were fatally high.'

Will looks at me for a moment before gathering up the prosecution statements, which he's scribbled all over in red pen. He sorts them into an orderly pile and taps them on the table top, before sliding them into a folder.

He purses his lips and frowns. 'I think we have an issue,' he says, 'as to how we are going to run our defence.'

I give him a half-smile. 'An issue between you and me,' I say.

'Yes. An issue between you and me. Look, Sarah, this idea of pointing the finger at Eleanor Barrington-Brown... I don't think it's going to work. I think we should stick to our original strategy, the one we named in our defence case statement, which is simply to put the Crown to proof that Ellie did it all. We ask the A&E doctor if there are other reasons why Finn might have presented with the symptoms he did on admission; we question the toxicologist as to the potential for Finn to have ingested sodium accidentally; and we cast doubt as to whether Ellie caused the bruising. Yes, by all means, let's get Marie onto the witness stand. Let her tell the court that Ellie left Finn in her care on numerous occasions and, if she wants to, she can

337

blame everything on Eleanor Barrington-Brown. That's fine. It doesn't matter too much what Marie says, or whether she's believed, so long as it muddies the waters as to who was looking after Finn. But I don't think we should actively accuse Eleanor Barrington-Brown of anything. I think it will backfire on us if we do, and besides, if we change our trial strategy at this late stage, we could run into issues with the court. We'd have to ask the judge's permission to run this as a defence.'

'Then let's ask for it,' I say. 'Look, I appreciate that you've been put on the spot at the very last minute, and I'm sorry. But you said it yourself: in the absence of any evidence to the contrary, the presumption of the jury is going to be that Ellie harmed her child. We have to provide that evidence, that evidence that it was someone else, and not her.'

'But how? It's unlikely, in the circumstances, that they'll believe Marie.'

'Well, on its own, maybe not. But we can get Eleanor to admit she's a doctor, that she'd know how to administer a lethal dose of sodium. She'd have known how much a lethal dose was, and she'd have had the wherewithal to get it. It's the simplest explanation for how that much sodium got into Finn's body in such a short space of time. We get Stacey's statement admitted in evidence and then we get Eleanor to tell the court that she's Dr Kent.'

'She might be *a* Dr Kent,' Will says. 'But can we show that she's *the* Dr Kent?'

'Possibly not. But we can ask her about it, can't we? We can ask her if she had access to Jay's hospital lanyard, his fob, if she had a means of getting onto the ward without being buzzed in by the nurses or picked up by the CCTV operators. We can put that to her in cross-examination, can't we?'

338

'Only if we know what she's going to reply.' Will heaves out a sigh. 'The thing is, Sarah, Carmel's right. We have no motive. Even if we can convince the jury that Eleanor had the opportunity and the means to do any of these things to Finn, we also need a reason. Finn's her grandson. Why would she try to kill him? Not liking Ellie, not being happy with the fact that her son has spawned an illegitimate child with her – even if she knows that Ellie's a call girl – it's… well, it's still not enough.'

I lean forward in my chair. 'But what if it goes deeper than that? What if Eleanor Barrington-Brown is one almighty snob, whose family's wealth and title are so important to her that she's prepared to go to any lengths to protect it? Jay's father is a hereditary peer. They're a dying breed; I did some research last night, and there are hardly any new ones being created, unless you're a member of the Royal Family. As his only son, Jay will inherit the peerage. He told me he didn't care about it, but that it was a big deal to his mother. Jay said that she wanted him to marry into a family with a similar rank and title, presumably so that the title can pass on to a worthy successor. Which is totally normal; rank and privilege has to be protected at all cost. Diluting the bloodline with a call girl from a council estate was certainly not going to have been part of Eleanor's plan for Jay, and it wasn't going to do much for his rating in Tatler's Little Black Book of eligible men.'

Will shrugs. 'But Finn is illegitimate. He wouldn't inherit the title anyway, would he?'

'Not at this point in time, no. But there's been considerable debate on the subject in the House of Lords in recent years, and as the wife of a seated peer, Eleanor would know that. What the Lords are saying is that, with the advent of DNA testing, it's now possible for an illegitimate child to prove definitively that he's related to his noble father. So the argument against inheritance by illegitimate children is effectively lost. Since there's no longer any stigma amongst the upper classes to having a child born out of wedlock, there's nothing to stop Finn from launching a legal challenge to the document granting the hereditary title to his family, and it's highly likely that he'd be successful if he did. The upshot is that, all but for the bar of illegitimacy, Finn, as Jay's first-born child, is the Barrington-Browns' next heir apparent. If that bar is removed, Finn inherits the title and any subsequent children that Jay goes on to have will lose out to Finn. That possibility must concern Eleanor immensely – and it may well concern the families of any potential suitor for Jay. Even if Finn didn't inherit the title, he'd have a legal right to a large portion of the estate.'

I pause for breath. 'If Eleanor were to kill Finn and frame Ellie for his murder, it would be the perfect solution. She'd get them both out of her life and leave the way clear for Jay to marry well.'

Will leans forward and takes a sip of his beer. 'You've done your homework,' he says. 'That's an impressive theory.'

I look at him. 'But that's all it is, just a theory? Is that what you're saying?'

Will shrugs. 'I'm sorry, Sarah, but what do I do with that? Without any hard evidence, I can't cross-examine Eleanor Barrington-Brown on that basis, suggest that's the reason for her to kill her grandson. What if she simply denies that it's the case? What do I do then?'

'Then you ask her about George.'

'George? Who's George?'

'Jay's twin,' I tell him. 'He died when Jay was five.'

'Really?' Will leans back in his seat and crosses one leg over the other. 'How?'

'Well, that's the thing. George was born with a severe neurological disability. His problems were very similar to my son Ben's.'

'He was learning disabled?'

'Severely so. Jay says he couldn't talk, or walk. Jay used to push him around the family estate in his wheelchair, in the company of a nanny, an au pair. One day, down by the lake, they'd taken him out of his wheelchair. They were going to teach him to walk, Jay says. But then George had a seizure and fell forwards into the water. He drowned. At least, this is the story Jay's parents told him, years later, after initially trying to pretend to Jay that his brother had never existed.'

'Do you know for sure that he had?'

'Yes. Jay wasn't lying about that. I found George's record of birth and death online. Jay definitely had a twin.'

'Go on.' Will narrows his eyes. I can see that I've now captured his interest.

'OK.' I take a deep breath. 'Well, the thing is, Jay has no recollection at all of George's death. He remembers taking George out of his wheelchair that day, but he doesn't remember anything after that. All he remembers is noticing that George just wasn't there any more and neither was the au pair; she'd been sacked. He kept asking his parents where George had gone and when was he coming back, but they wouldn't tell him. Eventually, after long enough had passed – long enough, presumably, for Jay's memory to fade and for him to begin to question himself – they told him that George was a figment of his imagination, that he'd always been an only child. It wasn't until Jay found a photograph of him in the attic, years later, that they finally told him the truth... or at least, what Jay believes to be the truth: that George drowned and that he and the au pair were responsible. He's been carrying that burden ever since.'

Will purses his lips. 'So, you obviously don't believe that Jay and the au pair *were* responsible for George's death.'

'No.' I shake my head. 'Not any more, I don't. I found out something else on the *genesandarchives* site last night. With twins, the time of birth is recorded on the birth certificate. George was the eldest twin. Not by much, obviously, but he was the first-born of the two. In time, he'd inherit the peerage from his father. I have no idea how Eleanor might have felt about having a child with a severe learning disability. But even if she wasn't so much of a snob to mind that she had an imperfect child, if my theory's right, she's likely to have been extremely concerned about the peerage and what was to become of it.'

I pause for breath. Will waits in silence for me to continue.

'I know that my son, Ben, is never going to get married and have children...' I begin.

Will's face softens and he begins to protest, 'You don't know that. Surely—'

'No, Will.' I interrupt him. 'It's never going to happen. You haven't met him. You'll see, when you do. He's my boy for life.' I smile, to let him know that this is OK – that, on the whole, I have come to terms with this. 'But providing his epilepsy is controlled,' I continue, 'there's nothing to stop that life from being a long and healthy one. If that were true of George, also, then there's every chance that the title would die with him. The only way that Jay could inherit it would be if George died

342

first. And if that didn't happen in any hurry... well, certainly it would reduce Jay's chances of marrying quite so successfully and passing it on to children of his own.

'George seems to have been swept under the carpet,' I continue. 'Hushed up. I don't know where he was buried – probably on the family estate somewhere – but I can't find a single reference to him online. According to the record of death, he died as "George Kent", stripped of the family name and, I imagine, disassociated from the Barrington-Browns in every other way that Eleanor could think of. I think the lie that Jay's parents told him all those years ago was probably wishful thinking on their part; George Barrington-Brown was never supposed to have existed, and Eleanor did whatever she could to wipe him out.'

I stop talking and pick up my drink, indicating that I've finished. I take a sip and peer at Will over the top.

Will lets out a whistle. 'So, let me guess,' he says. 'Eleanor paid the au pair to distract Jay for a moment while she pushed little George into the lake?'

'I don't know,' I tell him. 'But it looks as though I'm going to have to find out.'

Will smiles and narrows his eyes. 'How are you going to do that?'

'I don't know yet. I'm still working on it.'

Will nods, slowly. 'I'll bet you are.'

He looks at me for a long moment and then pulls his file of papers towards him. He slides out the page with the prosecution batting order. He says, 'Well, I estimate that you've got until Thursday. I think that's the day when Lady Barrington-Brown will take the stand. In the meantime, I've got a whole lot of cross-examination to prepare.'

'And I have to go and get Ben.' I stand up. 'So how do we play it in the meantime, in terms of strategy?'

Will smiles. 'I'll just challenge everything,' he says.

21

Tuesday and Wednesday are uneventful, in that the evidence we hear is broadly consistent with the all too familiar statements I've pored over with Ellie and Will for the past six months. We hear from a host of professionals: social workers, nurses, doctors and experts. We see colour exhibits of Finn's burns and bruises and we see him hooked up to life support equipment in the PICU at St Martin's. I watch the faces of the jurors – seven women and five men – as the jury bundles are opened and the evidence of Finn's suffering is sifted through. I try to imagine how they must feel, especially those who are parents. I know that behind their dispassionate faces, Carmel has made sure that emotions are running high.

At each stage, Will does the best he can to raise as many questions as he can in the minds of the jury, but, if I'm honest with myself, little ground has been gained. The toxicologist is especially intransigent, dodging Will's question as to whether it's at all possible that the sodium levels in Finn's body could be accounted for by a badly made up oral rehydration solution, given to him in hospital *after* he'd already become ill, and steadfastly refusing to concede that anything that Finn might have swallowed accidentally could have caused a sodium level this high. Will's cross-examination closes awkwardly, with a resounding declaration from the expert that 'Young children do not spontaneously and voluntarily ingest sufficient quantities of salt to cause significant hypernatraemia. Significant levels such as these are more usually associated with child abuse.'

On Thursday, Ben wakes me at five o'clock and I climb out of bed with a heavy heart, my final late-night online trawl through the archives of the *Esher News and Mail* having failed to provide me with any reference to George Barrington-Brown, either living or dead. I'd spotted several more mentions of his parents and the Grove Park estate through the late seventies and early eighties, and there were even one or two photos of the family, including Jay, but never George. Any hopes I'd had of finding a skeleton in the Barrington-Brown closet have been dashed. Will's 'challenge all' strategy is the only one we've got.

I give Ben his breakfast and then sit at the kitchen table, sipping my tea and checking my emails while Ben sits in his chair opposite me, his finger-food breakfast of bread, egg and chunks of melon spread out in front of him. He swipes up a piece of bread with his fist, pushes as much as he can into his mouth, and plonks the rest down again on the table, his plastic plate having been pushed to one side.

I hear a clunk as my mail drops through the door, and I go out into the hallway to fetch it. It's now been four working days since I ordered the copy death certificate for George and it should have arrived by now. But there's nothing on the mat except for a bank statement and a postcard that is actually an advert from an estate agency. I bend down and pick up Ben's sippy cup from the floor for the tenth time this morning, before sitting back at the table and logging on to *genesandarchives. com*. I look for a phone number, but there is only a contact form, which I half-heartedly complete and submit; I'm never sure if those website forms are going to reach an actual person. But it doesn't matter much, anyway, I tell myself. Even if the death certificate had arrived in time, it would only have confirmed the cause of death, not the circumstances behind it. If Eleanor had, indeed, paid the au pair to push little George into the lake, we'd still be unable to prove a thing.

Once we're both dressed, I drop Ben at school and then take the Tube to court. For once, Ellie is there early and Will ushers us into an alcove, where we run through her instructions again. At five to ten the tannoy sounds and all parties in the case of *Stephens* are called into the courtroom. The usher unlocks the door to the dock and Ellie steps inside and sits down.

As Eleanor Barrington-Brown enters the courtroom, there's a respectful silence. All eyes are on her as she crosses the room. She exudes wealth and style; she's wearing a white cashmere cape over a pair of black trousers. Her hair has been highlighted and is pulled up onto the top of her head in a French twist, almost identical to the one Ellie was wearing on Monday. She's older, of course, but they are similar in height and stature. Watching her from a distance, I can now see how easily Mary's description of Eleanor might have been misinterpreted by the police. She steps into the witness box and turns, elegantly, lowering her head slightly as the usher appears behind her and whispers into her ear. She is then handed a copy of the Bible and is sworn in.

Carmel asks her to identify herself for the court and as she answers the first few questions I'm surprised to detect a hint of nervousness in her voice. As Carmel takes her through her evidence, however, her confidence increases and her answers become more lengthy and profound. She smiles, modestly, as she tells the court of her charitable adoption of Ellie into the family, once she had got over the initial shock of hearing that her son had impregnated a teenage girl that he had only just met. She makes no mention of Ellie's occupation, although she openly admits to having had reservations about the couple's intention to keep and raise the baby between them, whilst living in separate homes. This was not, however, because she had any ill feeling toward Ellie – quite the contrary, she says. She felt sorry for her and wanted to help her. But she could see that Ellie was far too immature and insecure to be a mother.

Eleanor shakes her head sadly as she tells the court that she had known from the outset that Ellie was not ready to have a baby. She had suspected that she was never going to cope, and had mentally prepared herself to be on standby, ready to pick up the slack. She had been unprepared, however, for Ellie's insistence that she was a perfectly adequate parent and had been completely frustrated in her efforts to try and help.

'So what *was* Ellis like as a mother?' Carmel asks.

'Unpredictable. Impatient. And – worst of all – incorrigible,' says Eleanor. 'She thought she knew best and wouldn't be told.'

'Can you give me an example?'

'She would leave Finn lying on the bed, when he was just a few weeks old. I told her that he could roll off and hurt himself, but she wouldn't listen. We had several arguments about that. On another occasion, on my husband's birthday, I noticed that Finn was having trouble breathing. I told her that he needed to see a doctor, and she told me to mind my own business. She took Finn and stormed off out of the house in anger.'

'What else did she do – or not do – that concerned you?' Carmel asks.

'She shouted at him. She lost her temper with him, more than once, in my presence. She didn't seem to understand that he was just a baby, that all babies cry.'

'Well, they usually cry for a reason, don't they?' Carmel says. 'How in tune was Ellis with Finn, do you think?'

'She wasn't at all in tune with him,' Eleanor says. 'She acted as though he was just crying to annoy her. Most of the time, she seemed more interested in her mobile phone than she did in him.'

I can hear movement to my left. I turn round to see Ellie, standing up in the dock, leaning forward and passing a slip of paper down to the usher. I hold out my hand and the usher passes it to me. I open it. It says, in large capital letters, *THIS IS BULLSHIT. NONE OF THIS IS TRUE!*

I turn round and make an 'it's OK' gesture with my hand. Ellie mouths, 'What the fuck?' but she sits back down again.

When I turn back again, Eleanor is being asked about the bruises on Finn's body.

'Of course, if I'd seen them, if I'd known, I would have reported her to the police,' she says, ruefully. 'I *did* feel that she was handling him too roughly. When I tried to suggest that she needed to be more careful with him, she became angry and defensive. That was one of the last times I saw him, before he was admitted to hospital in April; after that argument, she pretty much stopped bringing him round.'

Eleanor's evidence in chief lasts for over an hour. Her shock and horror at Ellie's subsequent ill-treatment of Finn knows no bounds. She looks straight at the jury, dry-eyed and stoic, as she describes the pain she'd felt on finding out that her grandson had been poisoned. But she is unable to hide her distress when she tells them how hard it had been to sit next to his bed in the intensive care ward while 'the poor little mite' battled, a second time, for his life. She sinks down into her seat with her hands over her face, and her shoulders begin to heave. Carmel steps back and waits in a satisfied silence while Eleanor is offered a tissue and a glass of water by the usher. Judge Collins sits there for a moment, too, looking uncomfortable and muttering, 'Take your time, Lady Barrington-Brown.' But when there is still no sign of her sobs subsiding, he gives her fifteen minutes to compose herself. She is released under instruction not to talk to anyone about the case and the jurors are told to take a break.

Will looks at me and winces. This is the atmosphere in which his cross-examination of her is about to begin. I glance across at the jurors as they file solemnly out of the courtroom; while their faces remain expressionless, they can't fail to have been moved by everything they've just heard.

I pull my phone out of my pencil case as Eleanor Barrington-Brown is led out of the courtroom by the usher. I can see that I have missed a call from the school. When Judge Collins rises, I rise too.

'I'll be back in a minute,' I say to Will and indicate the same to Ellie, who remains seated in the dock. I pick up my bag and leave the room, running straight into an alcove opposite and quickly dialling the school office number, without listening to the message that's been left.

The receptionist answers.

'Oh hello, Ms Kellerman. There's nothing to worry about. Ben's fine. But you didn't fill out the consent form for the school trip this afternoon. We just want to know if he can go?'

I breathe a sigh of relief. 'Of course. I'm so sorry,' I say. 'I'll send you an email right away.'

I end the call and swipe my phone screen to the right. The email inbox icon tells me that I have twenty-five new emails. I know this is not the case; my stupid phone seems to keep marking 'read' emails as 'unread'. I open up the inbox and am about to click on the 'Compose' icon when a thought suddenly occurs to me. I go into my settings and into my junk folder, and heave a sigh of annoyance with myself as I see that, sitting there, marked as spam, is a two-day-old email from *mail@genesandarchives. com*. George's death certificate.

I open up the email and click on the attachment, but, frustratingly, it won't open. I put my phone down on the table in front of me and pull my iPad out of my bag. I open my email folder and scroll down to 'Junk', find the email and click on the attachment. This time it works and the death certificate appears.

My eyes scan quickly past the name, date and place of death (Grove House, Esher, Surrey) to the 'Cause of Death' section. But when I read what's written there, in large spidery handwriting, I am completely knocked for six.

I stand there in the alcove for a moment, my heart racing. I then pull myself together and run across the hallway and back into Court One.

'Careful,' smiles the usher, as I collide with her in the doorway. 'You've got another five minutes yet. No need to run.'

Ellie looks up from the dock in bewilderment as I dash past her and slide into the advocates' bench next to Will. He looks up from his papers, his red pen poised above his draft cross-examination of Eleanor Barrington-Brown. He pushes his glasses back onto his nose and looks at me, absently. I can tell his mind is still on the task ahead.

I take a deep breath and put my hand against my chest.

'What's wrong?' he asks, when he notices my face.

Carmel glances over at us. The usher has returned to the courtroom with a fresh jug of water and is also looking in my direction. I can hear rattling and chattering from up above as the public gallery fills up again. There are three reporters sitting directly to my left.

I push my iPad across the desk towards Will and put my mouth to his ear. 'It's George Kent's death certificate,' I whisper. 'Look at the cause of death.'

I watch Will's face as he first checks out George's name, and date and place of death. Then I see his eyes slide across the page and his mouth fall open. Carmel is still watching us from across the bench. She puts her head to one side and sucks on her bottom lip.

Will turns to face me. His eyes widen behind his glasses and seek out mine. We sit there, speechless, just looking at each other for a moment. I pull my lips together to stop a smile spreading across my mouth.

'Right. OK,' Will mutters, finally. He looks from Carmel to the usher and back again and then stands up. 'I need to—' he begins, but before he can say any more we hear a familiar tap on the door and the usher says, 'All rise.'

Judge Collins strides over to his seat and nods to the usher. 'Can the jury be brought in?'

'No!' says Will, abruptly.

The judge narrows his eyes and asks, 'Mr Gaskin? Do you have something to say?'

'I do apologise, My Lord,' says Will, 'but a matter of some importance has arisen. May I address you before the jury returns?'

Judge Collins peers at him for a moment. Carmel seizes the moment and rises to her feet.

'My Lord,' she says. 'I haven't been made aware of any issue by the defence.'

The judge looks from Will to Carmel and then back to Will again. 'Mr Gaskin?'

Will clears his throat. 'My Lord, that's because I have only, in the past few moments, been made aware of it myself. A document has come to my attention, one which sheds a rather different light on the defence case and the way we may wish to present it. With your permission, and of course, after having made my learned friend aware, there are some matters of a rather unexpected nature that I may wish to put to the witness, Lady Barrington-Brown.'

Carmel frowns and shakes her head.

Judge Collins says, 'Well, what is it, then? What is this change of direction?'

'I wish to make a non-defendant bad character application. The defendant believes that Lady Barrington-Brown is lying and is, in fact, the perpetrator of these crimes against her grandson.'

There is an audible gasp from the public gallery. Out of the corner of my eye I can see the reporters, their eyes wide with suppressed shock and delight.

Carmel leaps to her feet. 'I oppose the application!' she shrieks. 'This is preposterous! Lady Barrington-Brown is a witness, not a suspect in this case.'

'So what is this document?' asks the judge.

Carmel makes an exasperated face as I slide my iPad towards Will. He picks it up and moves over to where Carmel is sitting. He passes her the iPad.

'It's a copy death certificate, My Lord. It's the death certificate of Lady Barrington-Brown's first-born child.'

Carmel puts on her glasses and peers disdainfully at the death certificate. 'How do we know that it's genuine?' she splutters, angrily. 'It's an electronic copy. It could have come from anywhere. And the surname's "Kent". How do we even know that this is her child?'

'"Kent" is the maiden name of Lady Barrington-Brown,' says Will. 'She should be able to tell us if it's her child.' He adds, 'She's known professionally as Dr Kent.'

A shadow of recognition crosses Carmel's face as she turns to look at Will, her mouth slightly open. I know that she has made the connection; she's a clever woman, there's no doubt about that. She looks back down at the iPad and studies it carefully before handing it back to Will.

'My Lord, if this *is* Lady Barrington-Brown's child, he would have been just five years old when she lost him,' she says, anxiously. 'She will be distraught. You can't possibly allow the defence to pursue such an insensitive line of questioning.'

Will passes the iPad to the usher who hands it up to the judge. He considers it, gravely, for a moment, his eyes flickering across the screen and alighting on the cause of death. He narrows his eyes and draws his head back as he reads. He then looks up at Will and hands the iPad back to the usher without comment, other than to say, 'Any further observations, Ms Oliver?'

'The defence are required to put the Crown on notice before making a bad character application,' Carmel says, but her voice lacks conviction.

Will rises to his feet. 'As I said, My Lord, this document

was only brought to my attention a matter of minutes ago, just before you came into the courtroom.'

Judge Collins makes a note on his pad and squints pensively at it for a moment before saying, 'I will allow the application. Do you have any proof of origin in relation to the certificate, Mr Gaskin?'

Will glances at me. I nod and pick up my phone. I open the email from *genesandarchives.com* and flash it at Will. Will takes it and reads it out. 'My Lord, it's from a genealogy website, called *genesandarchives.com*. It says, "Dear Ms Kellerman. I have pleasure in enclosing the attached certificate of death as requested. Should you have any queries, please do not hesitate to get in touch."'

'Let me see that,' says the judge. The usher takes my phone and hands it up to him.

'But, My Lord,' Carmel protests. 'It's electronic! It's not signed!'

Judge Collins looks at her over his glasses. 'Everything's electronic these days, Ms Oliver. It's the way of the future, and the right one, in my opinion. The days of costly delays to the court process while we wait for trees to be cut down and bundles of paper to arrive in the post are, hopefully, soon to be a thing of the past.' He peers at the email for a moment and then looks up at Will. 'Do you want to make a hearsay application, Mr Gaskin?'

'Yes please, My Lord,' says Will.

'Then I'll grant that too,' says the judge. 'I will allow cross-examination on the content of the document. Clearly, the jury will be warned that the truth of its content cannot be verified – unless, of course, it comes from the mouth of the witness.'

I'm barely able to suppress a smile as I leap up and move quickly over to the dock. Ellie leans forward. 'What the hell's going on?' she asks.

'You'll see in a minute. Trust me?' I beg.

Ellie nods. 'OK.'

'Do you have your client's full instructions?' the judge asks.

I look at Will and nod my head.

'Yes, My Lord,' Will agrees.

'Then I suggest that we proceed with the cross-examination of the witness,' Judge Collins says. 'May the jury be brought in?'

*

Eleanor Barrington-Brown is angry. Her face is pinched and her lips tight as she enters the courtroom. I can see, instantly, that she is on the defensive when she steps back into the witness box, unhappy, no doubt, at having been kept waiting so long while events unfolded in the courtroom without her, lessening the emotional impact of her evidence. She takes a sip of water and sucks in her cheeks before scanning the courtroom with her eyes, which alight briefly on me. I meet her gaze and attempt to keep mine neutral as I feel her assessing my hair, my clothes, my lack of make-up, no doubt wondering what her son could have seen in someone like me. I am unfazed by her scrutiny, however; I have far more important things on my mind. I am now seated back in the bench behind Will and am so nervous for him that I feel sick. I know that his carefully prepared cross-examination – his handwritten notes, all the red scribble on the edges of Eleanor's prosecution statement – is now redundant. He is about to wing this, and my heart is in my mouth.

Will rises to his feet and says, 'Lady Barrington-Brown.'

She eyes him suspiciously, her jaw tight. 'Yes.'

'James is your only son, is that right?'

She nods. 'Yes, that's right.'

'But you had another son, did you not?'

Eleanor's eyes widen and her mouth gapes. She turns to Carmel, and says, indignantly, 'Are you going to let him ask me that?'

Carmel nods, silently.

Eleanor turns to look at Judge Collins, incredulity etched into her forehead.

'Lady Barrington-Brown,' says Judge Collins. 'Any question that is improper, prosecuting counsel will intervene, or I will, and I do not, and therefore I should like you please to answer the question.'

Eleanor turns back to face Will. 'Yes,' she scowls. 'I had another son.'

Will asks, 'And what happened to your other son?'

Eleanor narrows her eyes and looks from Carmel to the judge and back again, her mouth open. When neither responds, she purses her lips and glares at Will. 'He died,' she says, in a clipped voice. 'He died when he was just five years old. Is that what you wanted to know?'

'Well, it's *part* of what I want to know,' Will agrees, amiably. 'But it's not all of it.'

Eleanor's mouth snaps shut and sets in a hard line.

'So, how did he die?' asks Will.

Eleanor glares at the judge again. 'Are you seriously going to just sit there and let him talk to me like this?' she says, her voice rising in pitch, her eyes flashing.

'Answer the question,' orders Judge Collins, tightly, his eyes flashing back. I note that he doesn't say 'please' this time.

'He drowned!' Eleanor spits. 'He drowned, OK?'

I glance over at the jury. They look as baffled as Eleanor is by this line of questioning, but they, like everyone else in the courtroom, are listening intently.

'How did he drown?' Will asks.

Eleanor's eyes burn into Will's. 'He was… disabled,' she tells him. 'Severely so. He couldn't walk or talk. He had epilepsy. There was an accident. James was pushing him in his wheelchair and he fell into the water.'

'Which water?'

'The lake. There's a lake on the estate where we live.'

'And how did it happen?'

'James took him out of his wheelchair…'

'But James was only five. They were twins, weren't they?'

'Yes.'

'So how did he manage to take him out of his chair?'

'The au pair helped him.'

'The au pair. OK. And what happened next?'

'George fell into the water. We believe he may have had a seizure.'

'But you're not sure?'

'No. I wasn't there.'

'And what was the coroner's ruling? Epilepsy or drowning?'

Eleanor hesitates. 'Drowning,' she says, decisively.

'Death by drowning?'

'Yes,' she agrees.

'No other cause?'

Eleanor hesitates a moment, her eyes fixed firmly on Will's. 'No,' she says, finally.

'Are you sure?'

'Yes.'

Will nods slowly and pauses. The courtroom sits in silence while he picks up a water jug from the desk and fills his paper cup, then takes a sip. Eleanor watches him, scowling. Carmel is leaning back in her seat with her head up, her eyes heavenward, while Judge Collins cocks his head to one side and screws up his face, a look of pure concentration cast across his features.

Will picks up my iPad and walks out from behind the advocates' bench towards Eleanor. 'Why was George given the surname "Kent" on his death certificate?' he asks her, as he gets closer. 'Is it because you wanted to hide him away? Forget about him? Pretend he never existed?'

Carmel leaps up. 'Objection!'

'How dare you speak to me like that?' Eleanor hisses, indignantly. Her eyes, however, look frightened, as she tries to peer at the screen of the iPad that's sitting in Will's hands.

Judge Collins holds up his hands. 'Mr Gaskin, could you please rephrase the question.'

'Yes, My Lord,' says Will. He turns to Eleanor. 'Why was George's surname "Kent" on the death certificate?'

'Because we… because we wanted James to forget about him. We didn't want him to find out that he had had a… a brother.'

'You lied to James about George?'

'After some time had passed, we told him that… we told him that he was an only child.'

'So, you lied to him.'

'He was responsible for his brother's death! We were trying to protect him!'

359

'But he was five,' Will observes. 'How could he have been responsible for anything, at the age of five?'

Eleanor frowns back at him, as if she doesn't understand the question.

'You are a doctor, are you not?' asks Will.

'Yes.'

'So did you sign George's death certificate yourself?'

Eleanor's nostrils flare. 'Of course I didn't!' she snorts.

'Then who did?'

'It was a Dr Michael Phillips. A family friend.'

'But I asked you what the coroner had said and you told me. Are you saying, now, that the matter *wasn't* in fact referred to the coroner?'

'No, it wasn't.'

'Isn't that what you're meant to do when you encounter an accidental death?'

'It wasn't an accident,' Eleanor says, quickly.

'I thought you just said it was.'

'He had a seizure,' she says. 'It was a pre-existing condition.'

'But you just said that—'

'I know what I said!'

'You said that George drowned. I asked you if the cause of death was "death by drowning". I asked you if you were sure, and you said "yes".'

I quickly scan back over my notes. Will is correct. This is exactly what was said.

Eleanor explodes. 'This is outrageous!' she splutters. 'How dare you question me in this manner?'

'Well, that's my job,' says Will.

'Then do it properly!' she roars.

'All right,' says Will. He pushes his glasses back on his nose with one finger, lifts up the iPad and peers at it. Eleanor's eyes move from him to the iPad and flicker with fear.

'"Cause of death: Hypernatraemia,"' reads Will. '"Accidental ingestion of salt by child with mental retardation." You're a doctor. Can you explain to the court, please: what does that mean?'

Eleanor licks her lips. 'What? What are you talking about?'

'It's the cause of death cited on a copy of George's death certificate that has come into my possession. It's only a copy, of course, and I can't say with certainty that it's a true copy of the original. But it *is* signed by a Dr Michael Phillips. And your friend Dr Michael Phillips says that George died of hypernatraemia. A lethal overdose of salt. Accidental, of course. Your good friend Dr Michael Phillips does not, for one minute, suggest otherwise.'

Eleanor's face freezes. Her eyes scan the courtroom and seek out the three reporters sitting at the front of the bench to my left. She has that same look on her face that I'd seen on Jay's face so many times: she's searching, desperately, for her next lie.

'What this death certificate seems to suggest,' Will elaborates, 'is that your son, owing to his intellectual difficulties, accidentally picked up and ate something containing a highly concentrated form of salt.'

He pauses again for a moment and cocks his head to one side.

When Eleanor doesn't respond, he walks back to the bench in front of me, puts down the iPad and scratches his head. 'I'm puzzled,' he says. 'I'm wondering why you've told the court that George drowned? Well... that he had a fit, and *then* drowned,' he corrects himself.

Eleanor continues to stare blankly at him for a moment and then, suddenly, her mouth drops open. 'I... I had forgotten all about that!' She gazes at Will in bewilderment, as though he has done something amazing. She claps her hand to her forehead. 'I must have... I must have buried the memory, or confused it with a different one. I... that's correct. Yes.' The tone of her voice has changed completely. 'It's all coming back to me, now,' she says. 'He did eat some... some...'

'Some what?'

'Baking soda,' Eleanor says. 'I think it was baking soda.'

I immediately lean forward and thump Will on the back as hard as I can.

He turns round to look at me. I hold up my hand. I scribble 'How?' on a piece of paper and hand it to him.

Will looks at it and reads out, 'How? How did he eat the baking soda?'

Eleanor looks confused for a moment. 'He got hold of the tub,' she says.

I tap Will on the back again. 'Where was the tub?' I scribble. I hand the piece of paper to him. He reads out my question.

'In the kitchen,' she says.

'Where in the kitchen?'

'On the worktop.'

I already have the next question ready. I tap Will on the back and hand it to him.

'How did he get the lid off?'

Eleanor frowns. 'What do you mean, how did he get the lid off? He unscrewed it. Pulled it off. Whatever you do with a tub of baking soda.' Her tone is less friendly, now.

I tap Will again. 'How?' I mouth at him.

Will says, 'How?'

Eleanor's face suddenly turns red. 'Are you going to let her keep doing that?' she screeches at Will.

'Doing what?'

'Feeding you questions!'

'Yes,' says Will.

Eleanor looks at the judge, her mouth open, the rest of her face screwed up into a dubious sneer.

'Lady Barrington-Brown, Ms Kellerman is Mr Gaskin's instructing solicitor. She's there to assist him. Now, answer the question,' says the judge.

'With his hands. How else?'

'How exactly?' asks Will, who has now worked out where we are going with this.

'What?'

'How did he get the baking powder out of the tub?'

Eleanor shakes her head in a sudden rapid, gesture, one that would make your ears ring. 'With a spoon,' she sneers. 'What do you think?'

I'm used to writing quickly. You have to keep up, both in court and in police interviews, but when I hand Will the next sheet of paper, I've written so fast that I am worried that he might not be able to read it.

Will peers at the paper. He turns round and points to a word.

'What does that say?' he mouths to me.

I mouth back, '"Neurological".'

Will continues to look at the piece of paper and then stands up straight. 'Your son had a severe neurological disorder,' he says. 'Isn't that right? He couldn't walk or talk. And yet he was able to get up out of his wheelchair, take the tub of baking powder from the worktop, prise off the lid with his fingers, pick up a spoon and spoon a sufficient quantity into his mouth to kill him.'

He turns back round to me, his hand out ready. I duly hand him the last piece of paper.

'His fine motor skills must have been pretty good,' says Will.

Eleanor stares at him for a moment before she erupts. 'How dare you? How do you know what he was or wasn't capable of?'

'Not to mention the fact,' adds Will, 'that this court has heard from a toxicologist, an expert, during the course of these proceedings, and he told us that...'

Will stops and flicks through his papers. I beat him to it. I rip the appropriate page out of my notebook and tap Will on the back. 'Ah, here we are.' Will takes the piece of notepaper from me. '"Young children do not spontaneously and voluntarily ingest sufficient quantities of salt to cause significant hypernatraemia",' he reads. '"Significant levels such as these are more usually associated with child abuse."'

Will steps back, picks up a pen and gives a single tap on the table top.

Eleanor glares at him, open-mouthed.

Will asks, 'Lady Barrington-Brown, did you kill George? Your eldest son?'

Eleanor continues to glare at Will for a moment and then turns her head towards me. Her eyes flash with hatred and her lip curls. 'Who the hell do you think you are?' she snarls at me. 'You think you're something special? You think just because you were clever enough to go to law school, that you would ever be good enough for someone like my son? *You* – with *James*? Don't make me laugh! Do you realise who we are? We're royalty. Royalty! James can trace his ancestry back to King Charles the second. And you, what are you? You're nothing. You're common. You sit there, scribbling on your cheap paper, in your cheap suit with your cheap haircut—'

'Did you kill George?' Will persists.

'You were nothing to him. Nothing!' Eleanor continues to snarl at me, ignoring Will's question. 'You *are* nothing! James used you, that's all! Just like he used that piece of cheap trash behind you.' Her finger points at Ellie. 'Whore!' she hisses at her.

'Lady Barrington-Brown—' Judge Collins begins.

'Slut! Harlot! Gold-digger! Do you think you can become a member of the aristocracy by batting your fake eyelashes at my son? Do you think that's all it takes?'

'Lady Barrington-Brown... I'm going to ask you one more time,' says Will. 'Did you kill your son, George?'

'Lady Barrington-Brown, will you please answer the question,' says the judge.

'I did what I had to do!' she rasps, turning to Will, small globules of saliva escaping from the corners of her mouth. 'He wasn't fit to inherit. Our bloodline is strong – it goes back centuries. One has to preserve one's heritage! But I don't expect someone like *you* to understand that.'

Will says, 'Did you, on the nineteenth of July last year, at Cedar Court in Camberwell, inject your grandson with a near fatal dose of saline?'

Eleanor leans forward in the witness box, her hands gripping the rail in front of her, a loose strand of hair falling across her cheek. Her jaw is clenched so tightly that the tendons on her neck are visible. 'My *grandson*?' she spits. 'That child is not my *grandson*. He's just the bastard of a filthy whore!'

Will continues, 'Did you on the twenty-fifth of July last year use your son's Nine Elms and St Martin's Foundation Trust lanyard and door swipe key to enter Peregrine Ward at Southwark St Martin's Hospital, and did you detach Finn Stephens' dialysis line with the intention that he bleed to death?'

Eleanor turns to Ellie again. 'Did you seriously think I was going to let someone like *you* infiltrate a family like mine? Did you really think I was going to stand by and watch while that half-breed of yours came along and took everything? *You*, a piece of trash from a council estate, mixing up your family's blood with mine... it's like cows mating with horses. It's disgusting!' she spits.

Will comments, 'You sound more like a member of the Third Reich than a member of the aristocracy. I thought we'd evolved beyond that.'

'Then, how little you understand, Mr Gaskin,' she shoots back at him. 'How little you understand about the historical significance of the class system, about the importance of rank and title. How little you understand about the sickness and disease that's spreading across this land, about the plague of low-lifes that are infesting this country.' She points at Ellie again. 'It's whores like her – uneducated, filthy, low-life scum, like her, that are bringing this country to its knees. And you, you stand there, defending it – defending the scum that's eating away at the very foundation of civilisation, eating at the core of the civilised way of life!' Eleanor's rant is so venomous and so unexpected that I'm too overwhelmed by it to see or hear anything much else besides the torrent of abuse that has descended on us. I vaguely hear Judge Collins saying, 'Silence in court,' and then, 'That's enough! Get her out of here.' In my peripheral vision, I'm aware of the usher picking up the phone.

Eleanor turns to the jury and then sweeps her gaze around the courtroom. 'Look at you, you… bunch of commoners, you dare to sit there judging me? Who are *you* to judge *me*? You're not fit to lick my boots!' Her voice rises to a scream.

The courtroom doors burst open and two security guards run in. They stride over to the witness box and grab hold of Eleanor's arms. She flaps them violently and slaps the face of one of the guards. 'Get your filthy hands off me, you low-life scum. Do you realise who I am?'

With that, she is dragged out of the door, screaming a torrent of abuse at the security men.

A stunned silence descends over the courtroom. We can still hear Eleanor outside in the grand hallway, her rants and screams echoing round the marble walls and up into the domes above. We continue to sit in silence as her voice becomes more and more muffled, as more security staff arrive and she is dragged away. After a moment, Judge Collins regains his composure and announces that if anyone wishes to leave the courtroom, now is the moment to do so. Nobody moves a muscle.

A second later, the door to the courtroom opens and a member of court staff announces to the judge that the police are on their way. Carmel confers with Will for a moment and then speaks to the judge and I hear the staff member being given instructions that a local police escort and Social Services will need to be contacted as a matter of urgency to go to the Barrington-Browns' house in Richmond and ensure that Finn is safe.

Judge Collins clears his throat and takes off his spectacles. He turns to Carmel and says, 'Your position, Ms Oliver?'

Carmel stands. 'I offer no evidence, My Lord.'

'Good. Well, in that case, members of the jury, it falls to me to make a formal direction to you.' He explains to the members of the jury that, since the Crown no longer wish to proceed with the case against Ellie, they must find her not guilty. The foreman is asked to stand and the court clerk reads out the charges.

To each one, the foreman says, 'We find the defendant not guilty.'

Judge Collins thanks the jury and dismisses them. He then thanks Will and Carmel for their assistance and gives me a nod. The usher unlocks the door and lets Ellie out of the dock. Within moments, the courtroom is surreally empty, all except for Will, Ellie and me.

I don't know if Ellie feels anything like the way that I do, but my heart is still thumping gently against my chest and my legs feel as though they are lead weights, glued to my seat.

'Are you OK?' Will asks both of us.

I look at Ellie, and shake my head in disbelief.

Ellie shakes hers back at me. 'Crazy bitch,' she says.

I suddenly remember something. I glance up at the clock on the wall. It's five to one. Am I too late?

I stand up on my jelly legs and grab my phone. 'Excuse me a minute,' I tell Will and Ellie and run out of the courtroom. I can see a big commotion halfway down the staircase as Eleanor, surrounded by court staff, security staff and police, is put into handcuffs. I dial the number for the school and move through the double doors into the corridor, where it's quieter.

The receptionist answers. 'Oh, hello, Ms Kellerman. I'm glad you called. We never got your email. I've been trying to call you.'

'Am I too late?' I say, quickly. 'Is it too late for Ben to go to Farmer Fred's?'

'No, you should just make it. They're just getting on the bus. But you'll have to send it in the next two minutes.'

'I'm sending it now!' I end the call, go into my emails, tap out a quick note of consent and press the send button.

When I step back through the doors, Ellie is out in the hallway, on the phone. As she spots me, she says, 'I've got to go' and ends the call.

She says, 'I need to know Finn's OK. Who can we ask?'

I touch her arm. 'I'm sure he'll be fine. The police will be there by now.'

Will walks out of the courtroom.

'Can we find Carmel?' I ask him. 'Find out if Finn's safe?'

'Of course. I'll go and speak to her now.'

I phone Anna and give her the news and then walk down the corridor and sit with Ellie on the concourse outside the advocates' room. Before long, Will comes back out and reassures Ellie that Finn's just fine, but that he's being taken to Kingston Hospital to be checked over.

As I watch the relief flood Ellie's face, a film of tears appearing over her eyes, I know for sure that my instincts about her had been right all along: she loves her little boy. Her brusqueness, her defensiveness, were simply threads in the cloak she'd wrapped around herself as protection from the system, the system that was meant to take care of her, that was meant to give her the same opportunities, the same chance to have as fulfilling a life as the next person, whatever her background, wherever she was from.

She pulls her sleeves down over her hands and wipes at her eyes. 'Can I see him?' she asks.

'Anna will make some calls,' I tell her. 'She says you can go down to her office now, if you like, and she'll see what she can do.'

She leaps up out of her seat. 'And will I get him back?'

I stand up. 'I would think so. Possibly not immediately, but Anna said she'd get straight on to Social Services and get things rolling.'

'So that's it?' she says. 'It's really over?'

'It's over.' I smile.

'I don't know what to say.' She turns and looks from Will to me and back again. '"Thank you" doesn't really cut it, does it? You probably saved my little boy's life – and you got mine back for me, too.'

She hugs both Will and me and then heads off down the stairs.

We watch her go.

'So, do you fancy some lunch and a lime and soda at the pub?' Will asks me. 'I've got a strangely empty diary this afternoon.'

'Me too. Sounds great,' I agree.

We go back to the advocates' room where Will de-robes and we fetch our bags and coats, before walking out onto the chilly street and heading down Ludgate Hill to the Cheshire Cheese. Our table by the fire is empty and after glancing through the menu, I take a seat, slip off my shoes and warm my frozen toes while Will orders the food and gets the drinks. When I lean back against the old oak-panelled wall behind me and close my eyes, I can still see the orange flames dancing against the backs of my eyelids. As the warmth of the fire spreads up my body and onto my face, I think back to the heat of that August day – the day I got the call from Anna, the call that had first brought Ellie into my life, followed closely by Alex. Little had I known at the time that it was a call that would rock my world.

'I'd offer you a penny for those thoughts of yours,' says Will, sitting down beside me. 'But I suspect they're worth *way* more than that.'

I smile and open my eyes. 'I was just thinking what a crazy few months this has been. And what a day, today. No wonder Jay was so messed up, with a mother like that.'

'Hmm.' Will sits down and takes a sip of his drink. 'What I don't get is why she waited until George was five before she killed him. Why not do it sooner, as soon as she realised he was disabled?'

I sit up. 'Maybe it took a few years for her to realise quite how disabled he was; that he'd never be in a position to inherit the title, or – more importantly – to pass it on. It wasn't immediately obvious to us – Ben's dad and me.'

'Wasn't it?'

I shake my head. 'Ben was nine months old before we really knew there was anything wrong with him, and even then … well, the doctors couldn't tell us what his prognosis was, what the future would bring. We kind of jumped on that, gave it a positive spin. They'd said he was "delayed" but a delay implies that you'll get there in the end, doesn't it? You could say we were in denial, but having that hope was what made each day bearable. It's what got us through the first few months, the first few years, even. When we were on our own, in our own little bubble, we could tell ourselves the story that Ben would catch up, that everything would be OK.'

'But…'

'But, out there in the real world, we were confronted with other children of the same age; friends' children, children from our antenatal group, the kid who lived across the road who was born in the same month, who'd go toddling past our window, then running, then riding a scooter, while Ben still couldn't stand or crawl. There was always another child around, one who was doing all the normal things that Ben wasn't, who was developing at a rapid rate and clearly leaving him way behind. Every time that kid went running past our window, our hopes were dashed a little more. Slowly, over time, the bubble burst and we were forced to confront the truth.'

'That must have been extremely painful.'

I nod. 'It was excruciating.'

'But you seem to have come to terms with it, now? The way you talk...'

'Yes. Over time, it became unavoidable. Ben's father bailed out, but for me there was never any other choice but to deal with it.'

Will's eyes seek out mine. 'I wish I'd been there for you,' he says.

I smile. 'You didn't know me then. Well, actually, you did. But not like...'

'Like this?'

'Yeah. Like this.'

'Well, I wish I had.'

I look back into his eyes. 'Me too,' I say.

'So, can I meet him?'

'Ben?'

'Yeah. Of course Ben.'

'You really want to?'

His eyes sparkle. 'Yeah, I really want to.'

I pull my phone across the table towards me. 'Well, I have to pick him up at five thirty today. You could come to Farmer Fred's with me if you like?'

'Farmer Fred's?'

'He's gone on a school trip this afternoon.'

Will nods slowly. 'Great. I'd love to come.'

'OK.' I take a sip of my drink and peer at him over the top.

'OK.' He nods back, and grins.

My phone rings.

'It's Anna.' I jump up and head out of the bar, pulling open the door and stepping out onto the pavement. I walk up the alley a little towards Gunpowder Square and stand on the other side of the empty mews underneath the overhang of the building opposite, facing back towards the black wood façade and antique lead windows of the pub in front of me.

'I thought you'd want to know, I've spoken to my contact at the local authority,' says Anna.

'And?'

'Finn's absolutely fine. Ellie's gone to the hospital. They've allowed her to see him, although any contact will be supervised for the time being and Finn will have to be placed into foster care until we can get the matter into court and make our application to have the interim care order revoked. Ultimately, though, I can't see the local authority opposing it.'

'That's great.'

'So, your instincts about Ellie were right,' she says.

'Hmm. But I was wrong about so much. I was wrong about Alex.'

'Well, you're not the only one. He seemed so nice.'

'I think he's probably a good person, deep down,' I say. 'He's as much a victim of his mother as Ellie was. But he did some good things as well as some bad things. He taught Ben to walk and to use a computer. That's opened up so much for Ben.'

'Well, exactly,' Anna agrees. 'There's always another side to the story.'

The door to the pub opens and Will pops his head out. 'Food's here,' he says with a smile.

I give him a thumbs up, say goodbye to Anna and walk back down the alleyway. As I go, my eye is drawn towards the chalkboard that's propped up on the pavement in front of me. *Hot Food Served All Day. Lasagne. Fish and Chips*, it says. Something makes me walk round to see what's written on the reverse. I smile to myself as I read, scrawled across the blackboard in big pink letters, *See the other side*.

I open the door to the pub, where Will is waiting for me beside the fire.

ACKNOWLEDGEMENTS

Oh dear. This is going to be long! So many people have helped me to write this novel and I consider myself incredibly fortunate to have had such a fantastic network of support.

Firstly, I want to thank my dear friend Tracey Ann Wood – mainly for always being there, but also for taking so much time out from reading her own scripts to make and send me (by text!) her meticulous early edits to mine.

A very big thank you to Jemima Forrester of David Higham Associates for her considerable help with the plot and structure. My thanks also to Anne Williams of Kate Hornden Literary Agency for her interest and observations on the opening chapters.

A huge thank you to everyone at Head of Zeus for your dedication to finding new authors and for all your hard work in bringing this story to life. A special thank you to my editor Sophie Robinson for believing in it and for inspiring others to believe in it too.

I am truly grateful to my gorgeous sister-in-law Karen Draisey and to my lovely niece Shannon Draisey, who both took time out of their busy lives to give me some detailed and hugely helpful feedback and encouragement. My thanks also to my friend Ian Astbury for his interest in the story and for brainstorming ideas with me, some of which developed into crucial aspects of the plot.

The following friends were a fantastic help in reading early drafts and responding with their thoughts, giving me ideas for improvement as I worked on rewrites: Catherine Scammell, Christine Lawson, Amy Eastham, Penny Lillie, Helen Ellis Astbury, Sharon Organ and Lindsay Jopling. A big kiss goes to Helena Eastham, whose texts of encouragement perked me up more than once when I'd been writing through the night. Huge thanks also to Marcia Lecky for stepping in and being my fresh pair of eyes when I made some changes at the eleventh hour.

Thanks to Becca Stern and Patricia Marquis for their hugely helpful insights into hospitals and nursing and to Shemina and Justin Kirby for answering my questions regarding toxicology. Thanks also to Paul Organ for his valuable advice on police practice and procedure.

Massive thanks to my lovely friend and colleague, Kirsty Craghill of Craghill at Tuckers Solicitors in Brighton for reading the book in five hours straight and for the second opinion on the legal aspects of the story. Thanks also to the other fabulous people at Tuckers in London and Brighton who were willing to read and feed back to me: Kelly Thomas, Fiona Dunkley and Cath Diffey. As women and as lawyers, you inspire me! Huge thanks also to my lawyer friends in Oxford, Catherine Scammell and Simon Graham-Harrison, and to Howard Wilson for reading and giving me his thoughts on the final Crown Court scene.

Thanks also to the Royal College of Paediatrics and Child Health (RCPCH) for kindly allowing me to reproduce part of the following sentence: 'The existing evidence suggests that young but otherwise healthy children in the UK do not spontaneously and voluntarily ingest sufficient salt to cause significant hypernatraemia', which appears in the following article:

RCPCH 2009. *The Differential Diagnosis of Hypernatraemia in Children, with Particular Reference to Salt Poisoning. An evidence-based guideline. Summary of guidance: Page 5* and *Causes of Hypernatraemia: Page 51.*

On a practical note, my thanks go to Matthew Pitt of Matthew Pitt Photography in Oxford for his friendly professionalism in taking photos for the cover shot and to Victoria Pitt for the Frizz-Ease – and for putting me at ease (as well as for being an approachable custody sergeant!)

I also want to give my huge and sincere thanks to the following people, without whose help this book would never have been written: Dawn Blaine, Kerry Day, Sue Simmonds, Sue James, Anna Shelton, Tracey Mutch, Tracey Carnegie, Holly Jones, Alex Wilson and Karen Fourie. Thanks also to Tom Guy, Alice Bent, Amy Appleton, Kayleigh Gamblin, and Jenny Eyles, everyone at Core Assets Children's Services – and to all the other amazing people across the country who have chosen to spend their lives working with our special children and vulnerable adults. I dream of a day when the true value of the work you do is properly recognised in our society.

Finally, my thanks go to my husband, Mark, for listening to me while I talked about this book (a lot), for putting up with all the time I spent in the writing cave over Christmas 2016 – and, most of all, for never bailing out.